I0738433

DEEP CUTS
FROM THE
EDGE OF NEVER

ZOMBIE CIVIL RIGHTS SAGA
BOOK 2

DEEP CUTS FROM THE EDGE OF NEVER

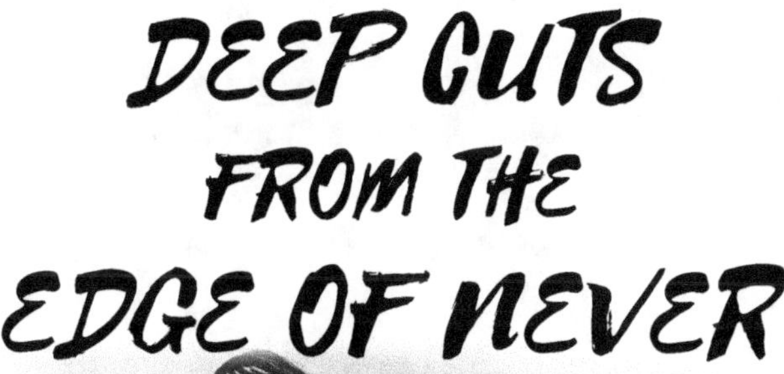

STEVEN MIX

Edited by Red Adept
Cover illustration by Bookfly Design
Internal Ashley illustration by Zia Daugherty
Book internal design by Auryn Creative
Author photograph by P.I.C. Photo

ISBN 978-0-692-97237-3
eBook ISBN 978-0-692-97239-7

stevenmix.com

ACKNOWLEDGEMENTS

I NEED TO THANK my beta readers: Bejahn Malekzadeh, Ryan Goddard, Adam Wilson-Selby, Sara Jane Yoders, Cody Parcell, Jessica We, Kayla Ringo, Jadine Buckman, Jennifer Moreno, Cheri Cartwright, Justin Powell, Devin Marra, Damon Marra, Stephen Shumaker, Nicholas Ramirez, Mary Dixon and, especially Sheryl R. Hayes. I sure did appreciate all your support. I also need to thank my loving wife Megan for putting up with my insanity, and my writing coach Lauren Sapala, who is amazing! I must thank my editors at Red Adept, and my cover art from Bookfly Design. I should also thank Setsu Uzume, Elanor Finster, Susie Rodriguez, Carrie Sessarego, David Holladay, M. Todd Gallowglas, the Parcells, the Daughertys and the Morenos for being excellent friends. I have to thank all of BayCon for your love and support in the Sci-fi/Fantasy scene. My brothers and sisters, the few I know I love, even though we lost out on 30 years of life. I wish we hadn't. I'm sure I'm leaving someone else out, and I'm so sorry for it. I need to thank Mom and Pops. Mom, thank you for making me strong-willed and sometimes wise. Pops thank you for making me charismatic and respectful. I hated to see you go Pops, and I sure miss you. Lastly, I need to thank my kids. Nyla, I love you, and you always make us proud. Mason, I can't stop smiling whenever I see you. You're the best book I ever wrote.

-STEVEN

FOREWORD

I accept it. After staring at the manuscript for book two, I accept it, and I'm taking responsibility for it. My zombie stories are not filled with typical zombies. They're monstrous strange things that crept out of my nightmares. They are a metaphor for terrorism. With terrorism you can either fight it and risk becoming a monster yourself, hide from it or dance on through. In this life, I've done all three.

I also accept it. My main characters aren't the sort of folks you might rally to in an apocalypse. In a real-world scenario, you'd want to rally around the soldier. Here my characters represent art, science, music, and magic because that's the sort of things I'd hope would fight monstrous things crafted out of fever dreams.

Deep Cuts from the Edge of Never is not your typical zombie story. It's filled with comedy, adventure, magic, pop culture and some wicked twists and turns. It's not chasing cans of beans while you bitch about the world. It's accepting the world for what it is and running with friends along the edge of what is left while laughing most of the time.

For Pops.

*Dance, O goddess, choose steady, surefooted steps
and let the beat echo through us as the night
rages on.*

You lost yourself, you silly thing.

Where do you go when you daydream?

Is it bright exciting landscapes where heroes tread,

or worlds crawling with dark things better left unsaid?

Wake up! Wake up!
Life lives or death knocks, may we never be caught
in between.

1.

San Jose
Zombie Civil Rights Group
Present Day

A DARK-HAIRED Asian girl climbed over some of the rubble littering the back entrance of the mansion, an aluminum baseball bat strapped across her back. Its hilt perched just over her left shoulder. In her left hand, she held a rifle by its lower receiver, not bothering to carry it at the ready.

"What exactly is it again, Donathan?" she asked.

In the days before, the mansion had been a tourist attraction in San Jose, California. The mansion was a maze of insanity, with secret passages and strange architecture. The woman who built it was heir to the Winchester fortune—the rifle that had won the West. She believed she had to build an insane house to trick and hide from the spirits that had been killed by her family's creation. After years of neglect, the front side of the house had fallen in, the roof caving down and blocking entry on that side. She had noted that the front door still stood, separated from the rest of the dilapidated building, its stained-glass panels and dark wood still untouched and unopened as if it was just ignoring the undead world around it.

"Well, Ashley, the man who clued Nyla into the job seemed to think it was a Whip, but they aren't exactly known for holing up in one spot very long." Donathan scrambled over the same rubble Ashley had just passed over.

As he stepped over the upended chunks of concrete, his long black leather duster parted. Two holsters clung to his hips, each with a nickel-plated pistol tucked inside. Ashley had rarely seen him clean them, but they always seemed to shine too bright for this dusty world.

A younger man sighed, glancing up at the midday sun. He reached up to check that his hockey mask was resting in the up position just above his face. The paint was still drying on his new creation. He grunted while lifting the heavy M240 Bravo machine gun up into his arms and stepping tall across the concrete. The gun's weight, along with his Interceptor body armor, painted with red camo, made it difficult for him to move as easily as his friends.

"Either way, it's just one zombie, right?" he asked. "No surprises?"

"Right, Mason, because there're never any surprises?" Ashley replied.

Once they were all inside and staring up a dark hallway, Donathan began the process of draping a mic cord over his neck. When he finished, the square box of an ancient radio mic hung down from one of his shoulders.

Donathan cued up his mic with a chirp. "Nyla, can you hear us?"

After a flash of static and a slight chirp, Nyla replied in her usual spacey tone, "Roger! We haven't seen anything out here."

They'd met up with Nyla and Princess Jae in Half Moon Bay. Most of Half Moon Bay had been destroyed when they fled it the month before, wrecking a vehicle in the process. After a couple days of searching, the group managed to find a replacement truck but was low on coin. Collectively, they decided that the best plan was to double back to San Jose to see if any hunter jobs were available. Jae was older than the rest of them and better at driving, so she opted to stay with the vehicle. Nyla stayed with her to act as operator and overwatch, surveying the mansion from afar. Together, they would be the mobile command center for the mission. Most hunter operations would have them using stealth and sign language, but Ashley argued for a few minutes with the group, saying that when dealing with a creature as aggressive as a Whip, having comms up was more important than stealth in case something went wrong. They expected only one creature, but Nyla warned them that Whips were difficult to kill, and if the trio of friends became lost inside the house, they might need to call for backup, so the radio had been the best plan.

Ashley, Mason, and Donathan dragged off their packs and rummaged through them to find red-lensed, L-shaped military flashlights. Donathan clipped his light to the front fold of his duster. Ashley tucked hers onto her waistband at her right hip. Mason attached his light to one of the front pouches on his IBA. Afterward, he dragged out another belt of ammunition and draped it across his shoulders.

Donathan cued up the mic, adding, "We're ready."

The microphone chirped back, and Nyla replied, "Okay, so, hang on..." A shuffling of paper could be heard.

"No, here, I'll hold the mic. You handle the map." Princess Jae's voice sounded a ways off from the handset.

"Okay." The sound of paper shifting died down as Nyla committed to her job. "You're going to walk up a long hallway and then make a right, but don't use the door at the far end of the next hallway because it opens up to a two-story drop."

Ashley cued up the mic, unsure she'd heard correctly. "What?"

"Yeah, two-story drop," Nyla confirmed. "Don't open that door."

Leaving their bags by the front door, the group fumbled their way down the dark hallway. Making a right, they traipsed up another corridor, past a stairway leading up to the ceiling. Eventually, they wound up in a round room that looked as though it had several cupboard doors and no other exits.

"Some of those large cupboard doors will open up to walls. One should lead out of the room. Seen anything yet?" Nyla asked excitedly across the radio.

Even in the dim, red-lit room, Ashley rolled her eyes over Nyla's elation at the hunt. Nyla's lack of fear and passion for studying the science of the undead often annoyed Ashley. Nyla seemed to be observing the world instead of being a part of it. Princess Jae never seemed to mind, but she had known Nyla much longer than Ashley.

"Nothing ye—"

Donathan was interrupted by a loud hiss erupting from behind him.

The three spun on their heels. Ashley shouldered the rifle at the high ready. Donathan had already drawn both of his pistols and was staring down the sights. Mason fell over in a loud clatter of gear and gunmetal. Somehow, he managed to keep his mask on.

An uncomfortable minute ticked by. Mason remained lying on the floor and dragged his machine gun into position in front of himself.

Ashley whispered, "Did you...?"

Donathan shushed her.

Another minute passed. Nothing.

Lowering his pistols, Donathan holstered one and looked in Ashley's direction. Shrugging, he whispered, "I don't think we—"

A sinister growl erupted close behind the trio. They spun around again just in time to see a sharp-fanged mouth framed by a warped, leathery face in the red light. The face let loose an ear-piercing scream.

Donathan raised a pistol at the same time he was cueing up the microphone and yelling, "Not a Whip!"

He fired a round, and the zombie's face and body shattered into black smoky smudges that exploded out from its form across the room. All three friends stood in the quiet dust-filled room, blinking and wondering what had happened.

Confusion sprinted across their faces as each looked from left to right at one another. A second later, Ashley stepped back from the other two, turning to walk away. Mason matched her movement, spinning in the opposite direction. Donathan did the same. A half step later, their clothes changed. A complete step later, the world changed.

———

Finally, Friday had come. Mason felt as though he'd waited a lifetime, and today was the day! He hoped they would arrive on time so he could relax and enjoy this weekend. If they didn't show up…Well, he didn't want to consider that option.

Mason sighed, staring at the numbers on his LCD computer screen with frustration as if they were drilling holes through his eye sockets. The desktop music player was churning out heavy saxophone-filled experimental jazz. Looking up past the cuffs of his white button-up shirt, he drank in the excitement of Friday in the office. The accounting department desks were all lined up on the far wall of the office, facing his direction, giving the place a crowded feeling. The actual office was behind the doors and glass windows on the other side of the large room. Corporate had seen fit to move them out there so that the workmen could get a head start on painting their walls before the weekend. Across from Mason's desk, facing him directly, was Jenson's desk. No matter where Mason moved the keyboard, turned the monitor, or shifted in his chair, he was always forced to stare at Doug Jenson. The man never loosened his tie. The man never unbuttoned his top button. The man loved numbers more than his wife. His fingers never slowed, and he was always overflowing with tired old office clichés—every manager's wet dream.

Mason was the polar opposite of Doug Jenson. He dreaded trudging into work every morning. He was always thinking about the weekend, and for the life of him, he could never keep his mind on his task.

Mason said aloud, "Three full paint cans of whipped-cream white paint. That paint has just enough tint that it looks more pleasing than plain white under fluorescent lighting." He eyeballed the workmen, their paintbrushes, and the cans of paint in the next room. He couldn't hear anything through the glass, but they all had weary expressions on their faces and plenty of paint splattered all over their smocks. None of them looked too enthusiastic about their job.

Jenson didn't even look up from his screen, and his fingers were blurs. "What's that now, buddy? I don't want to throw you under the bus to management...but I am giving a hundred and ten percent today."

Mason wrinkled his nose and looked back down at his screen. He moved his mouse pointer in the direction of the music player. A double-click later, bass-filled hip-hop belted a familiar song out of the desk speakers. He made sure to turn it up before looking at Doug Jenson's face.

Doug still hadn't peered up from his work but announced, "This sort of music isn't going to help you push the envelope, friend. You need high-end production tunes."

The lack of reaction and continued clacking of Doug's keyboard caused Mason to clench his teeth. He let his eyes drift about the room until they rested at a desk littered with office supplies. Behind the desk sat a woman with long flowing red hair and large green eyes that matched her fashionable green top and skirt. She smiled from behind her desk and flashed long eyelashes in Mason's direction.

"We should try to be more proactive in our work here, buddy," Jenson added, his eyes still lost on his computer screen.

Mason smiled toward the woman then looked up and away. After a moment, he let his eyes drift back toward the woman's desk.

Jenson managed to take his eyes off his computer screen long enough to look back over his shoulder and see where Mason was staring. After a few seconds, he turned back and asked, "So is today the big day? Are you finally going to make a play at her?"

Enough was enough. Mason stood up and stretched for a minute before heading toward the red-haired woman's desk. She smiled slyly as if having expected him long before. The smile unnerved him, and he froze in place for a moment, shifting with nervous energy. Then, reaching down slowly, he scooped several black permanent-ink markers off of her desk.

Shocked, she protested, "Hey, those are mine!"

Mason didn't notice or care about anything she said as he sprinted toward the room full of maintenance men.

He didn't have to coax the workers at all. He just stuck his head into the room and announced, "Break time!"

One of them even threw down his brush before they all walked past Mason and out of the room. Mason picked up the brush, took a can of the white paint, and found a large static spot of the old blue wall. His hand sprang to life, draping paint from the can to the wall until he had a large oval patch of white paint.

For some reason, he knew one light coat of paint on another acrylic could dry in approximately seven minutes. Mason then uncapped the pens, lined them up on the carpet in front of him, and chose which pens to use. As he grasped them, he turned to face the wall. His breath grew ragged. His skin tingled. The pens danced across the freshly dried paint, their ink flowing smoothly until, finally, an image appeared. Mason stepped back to admire his work.

"Hockey mask?" Doug Jenson had torn himself away from his data entry long enough to walk into the room and pass judgment. "And who the hell is the woman with the headset drawn on top of the hockey mask?"

"It's not a drawing. It's a plain hockey mask," Mason replied. "She's a painting on top of it." Sighing, Mason stared at the woman with long flowing hair that he knew to be blond. He couldn't take his eyes off his work. "I know her somehow."

Doug Jenson stomped his feet and, in a frustrated tone, added, "I don't know what's going on here, but I'm going to go get upper management." He took two steps toward the door before looking over his shoulder and adding, "You are destroying this department's synergy!"

Mason didn't move from his spot, still staring at the woman, trying to make sense of his sudden burst of artistic expression. Doug Jenson came back in, leading a few bald men from management.

The men swarmed around him, shouting jibes like "What is it you think you're doing here?" and "You're supposed to be data entry, not maintenance."

A woman in a sharp business suit came in shortly after that. Her focused voice informed Mason that "This sort of behavior is highly inappropriate. It is destroying company property." Another older fellow with a brown business suit and graying hair sauntered in and informed Mason he was fired. The only time Mason looked up was when Doug Jenson complained to the others that Mason's work was "not even art!"

A bike messenger opened the glass doors, loped into the room through the chaos, and stuck an envelope into Mason's hand. All of management was shouting at that point. One man was waving his fist, demanding that Mason "clean out his desk and hit the bricks." Oblivious to them, Mason signed the messenger's slip. After ripping open the package, he pulled out two bookmark-shaped badges with lanyards hanging off them.

Mason read aloud the large bold print across the first glossy badge. "Anthrocon, the World's Largest Furry Convention. Admit One: Mason Meeks."

A scream erupted from Mason as he threw the ticket down. Falling back, he kicked his feet against the ground, struggling with his sudden loss of balance, trying to scramble away from the paper. "No! It can't be!" Mason clutched at his face. "I can't be!" His hands brushed a hockey mask that hadn't been there before. He pulled it down to hide behind it, revealing the image of a smaller version of Mason looking up from the middle of a chess board. The painting of Mason was surrounded by chess pieces, each with sharp edges and blurry lines.

"Noooooooo!" The world warped around him as his sharpened scream ripped through reality.

———

"It sucked. I sucked!" Ashley shouted at her friend, throwing her surfboard onto the sand in frustration.

Jennifer's jaw dropped. She raised both her hands wide, lowering her shoulders, "What are you talking about? That was an amazing run!"

"The hell it was!" Ashley's fists clenched. She raised one angry arm towards the ocean, "The waves are garbage today! Not an A-framed wave in sight, and it was bullshit that they told me to take off when I did!"

"You stand a good chance at winning!" Jennifer's tone was full of frustration.

Ashley countered, "No! You stand a good chance of winning!" She left her board on the sand as she stormed away.

"What are you even saying?" Jennifer's tone had become whiny as it faded off into the distance.

Ashley crossed the hot sand, passed the competition dividers displaying signs from various sponsors, and picked her path through the crowd of onlookers. Ashley looked up long enough to see a blond girl with long hair and a white tank top, wearing a headset. The girl mouthed Ashley's name as Ashley strutted past. There is no time for this nonsense, Ashley thought.

A tanned, dark-haired boy with long khaki shorts and no shoes was standing between Ashley and the sandy parking lot. His face had a five o'clock shadow. His abs looked chiseled out of stone by Michelangelo himself. Ashley froze and stood wide eyed for a moment, her breath held as she realized his eyes were drifting down and back up across her body. A familiar hip-hop song coasted in off the wind from someone's car radio in the parking lot. Ashley became aware of how long she had been standing in place and continued on her path toward the guy.

"Great set today!" The boy chimed in with the seasoned, long-toned voice of a valley guy. Ashley stopped again just a few feet away then blushed and brushed her hair back behind one of her ears, looking down at the sand.

She managed to take a step forward and sheepishly answered, "Thanks," as her shoulder coasted past the guy.

From behind her, the boy flirtatiously added, "You looked good out there. Seriously."

Ashley halted midstep, feeling blood rushing through her cheeks. Her hands were warm, and she couldn't tell if that roar was coming from the ocean or just echoing through her red, sunburned ears.

In an instant, she spun around and swung a wide punch at the face of Mr. Chiseled Abs. When her knuckles connected, he squawked a swear word in protest.

Stumbling back and holding his gushing nose, the guy managed to groan, "Psycho!" before turning to run back toward the beach and away from Ash.

She grinned, watching the sand kicked up from his trail as he sprinted off before looking down at her knuckles. Studying them, she murmured, "This doesn't feel—"

"It's my turn at bat!" A girl's voice cried out in frustration.

Ashley stood on her tiptoes, peering back and forth across the parking lot, trying to see the source of the commotion. She spotted a girl and a boy playing with a bat and ball near the open space in the front entrance of the parking lot. She crossed the lot as they settled their squabble and exchanged a pitch and a swing.

"Can I just...?" Ashley motioned for the bat from the girl.

The girl looked up at Ashley with a confused look on her face and hefted up the bat. Ashley took the baseball bat by the barrel, flipping it up out of her hand. She let it spin a full rotation before reaching forward and snatching it out of the air, gripping the bat by the handle.

The boy remarked, "Coooooooool!"

It was cool. It is cool.

"This..." Ashley loosened and flexed her hand, causing the baseball bat's mass to lower and rise. "This is real."

"What's that?" the girl asked, pointing at the street beyond the parking lot.

Ashley looked up and stared in the direction the girl was pointing. The road was clear and barren. Only the wind seemed to cross it, yet something was there. Her eyes couldn't focus on it, but it was there. Part of the street shifted and warped as something lunged at her.

Ping! Clank! The sounds of the aluminum bat connecting twice with a mass of flesh rang out across the parking lot. Something stumbled back and away from Ashley as her eyes narrowed and a smile crossed her lips. The world shook around her.

———

The summer sun was angling in through a set of arched windows and laying bright beams of light over the blanket and sheets. Bouncing out of bed, Donathan stood in front of his windows in his striped pajamas, staring out at the early morning. No work. No responsibilities. Just a gorgeous day ahead.

After brushing his teeth and showering, Donathan chose a fresh suit from his closet—dark Italian silk that coasted and drifted across its length, a starched white shirt with an open collar, and not a necktie in sight.

Donathan took a moment to eyeball his reflection in the mirror, fixed his hair, and remarked, "This suit feels sharp. Powerful."

When he'd decided his hair was just right, he let his eyeline lower until it came to rest on a stack of mail on his bedside table. He shifted it aside, sifting through it. An envelope fell from the stack and landed face up on the floor. The letter addressed to him looked formal. The return address was listed as "Gun Enthusiast Quarterly." What a strange piece of mail. Donathan had never held a gun.

He found his wallet and keys and made his way to his black Jaguar. Inside, the leather interior smelled fresh and inviting. The engine revved to life as he angled the vehicle toward 101 South.

He managed to find a parking garage with an open space right up front so he didn't have to hunt. The first restaurant Donathan passed turned out to have an artichoke theme. He doubled back toward it, and after he climbed to the top of the stairs, the host seated Donathan with a gorgeous view overlooking Cannery Row. The meal was immaculate: fresh artichoke fashioned into a burger, grilled to perfection. The waiter only breezed by the table once to check how everything was. The restaurant was empty and silent.

Back on the street, Donathan became conscious of how sober he was, and a few minutes and a hill later, he found himself inside a dark Irish-themed pub. The large man behind the counter was happy to set down his rag and search the mass of bottles behind him. After a minute, he poured a double scotch into a wide glass with three ice cubes.

As Donathan raised the scotch to his lips, a girl cleared her throat off to his left. Sighing, Donathan set down the glass and turned in the direction of the woman. Long blond hair drifted down her shoulders, and bright eyes lit up her face. For some reason, she wore a radio headset on her head.

She smiled and said, "Dona—"

Donathan cleared his throat to signal his lack of concern for any interruption. Ignoring the woman, he turned back to his scotch, raising the glass high and admiring the amber-colored liquid as it shifted about the ice cubes. The smell was mellow and didn't bite at the nose. The liquid did bite at his throat, though. He felt as if the wind had been kicked out of him on his first mouthful.

After a second double scotch, his head felt light and breezy. Outside, the day was warmer and more comfortable. Half an hour later, he was sitting on a rock, staring down at Whaler's Cove, watching the waves drift in across the sand. Cypress trees were growing sparsely out of the beach rocks surrounding the inlet.

Donathan sighed and let his gaze rise until he was staring at the ocean's horizon, clean air filling his lungs and good whiskey filling his head.

His hand snapped down and up, holding a nickel-plated pistol forward as he squeezed off a round into the peaceful scene in front of him. Everything jolted and crumbled around him until he was standing back in a room lit by the dim red hues of military-grade flashlights.

Nearby, Mason and Ashley groaned, clutching their heads.

Donathan heard a rush of footsteps and drew his second

pistol to aim at the doorway while his friends struggled to get their bearings. A head with blond hair and a headset perched on top of it appeared in the room. She held a shotgun at the low ready as she stepped inside.

"Oh!" Nyla sounded surprised and announced into the headset, "Jae I found them! They're fine."

Donathan's headset echoed Nyla's voice into the darkened room. He took the cue to tuck his pistols away and fished through his chest pockets for his Zippo lighter and a lone cigarette.

"We're not fine." Ashley motioned toward the corpse with a fresh bullet hole, a splatter of necrotic flesh having scattered out from it across the floor. "The hell was that?"

At the quick sound of metal flicking, the room lit up for a moment as Donathan ignited his cigarette. For a fraction of a second, an amber glow flashed across his vision, meshing with the darkness.

Nyla studied the corpse for a moment and then added with surprise, "A Maelstrom!" Her voice was enthusiastic as always. "I've never...I mean, I've only heard of what they can do." She sounded relieved and added, "You're lucky to be alive!"

Through clenched teeth and lips still gripping a cigarette, Donathan asked, "Aren't we always?"

2.

New York
Todd
Twenty Years Earlier

PAVAROTTI. Pavarotti is the only real way I can explain it right now. That isn't much of an explanation. It isn't much of anything.

I'm standing here, smelling copper and biting flesh, tasting the song of life gushing forth into my being. I feel Luciano Pavarotti, holding a long bassy note, its tone echoing off the walls of every opera house in the world before depositing that energetic burst right here in my being.

I'm in an alleyway, devouring the face of a transient, but somehow, I'm hearing Luciano Pavarotti echoing into the world. The music I'm feasting on becomes weak and then tastes acrid. Death and infection are taking hold. It no longer tastes like the song of flesh and blood. Letting go, throwing aside a spasming man, I step back to watch him struggle violently with his fate. The dark shadows of the alley grow, and I'm surrounded by the fading sunlight of the world. I don't know how long I've stared. I just know the man is standing before me, swaying slightly, parts of his cheek and neck ripped away. I can't take my eyes off the large gashes and bloodstained clothes. The streetlights kick on, and I need to be somewhere else. Turning away, I step out of the alley. The newly dead man follows. A few steps later, I spin around to face him under a streetlight. The man sways a bit and looks back at me with hollow eyes. Another step away, and the man steps forward again.

This is new! Two of us. Car tires squeal, and Pavarotti's note echoes past. I follow the scent of it down the street. None of this makes sense to me. The note grows louder as something dances in my lungs. The man behind me lumbers along, audibly sniffing the air. He's found the note too. Clearly, something is here. We trample an old flowerbed, sprinting across a parking lot until we finally find the source of the night's music. Bright floodlights angle down, piercing the darkness. Shades of deep green and earthy browns fill my vision from somewhere. Is this applause? What is this?

A softball game?

Middle-aged men sprint around the bases. From the stands, someone shouts in frustration. After a minute of running, a person slides into a base, and the flexing movement of the crowds cheering and jeering settles down as we approach a chain-link fence on the darkened side of the field.

People are passing around hot dogs, some tugging at shared blankets and digging sweaters out of backpacks. Others argue over stats and teams as they watch the players face challenges on the field below the bleacher seats. The song is coming off the crowd. I can feel it. I can smell it. I can taste it. It is life and technology breaking through the darkness. Somehow, these things are finding beauty and excitement—a moment of safety, which the universe rarely knows. It is all so beautiful, and hey...

Where the fuck is he going?

The newly turned undead has climbed the chain-link and is sprinting across the field toward the game. Doesn't this asshole realize I found them first? This is my song, not his.

Spitting and hissing, I climb up the chain-link. Scaling a fence is difficult while I'm no longer fully conscious of how my legs feel.

I chase after my newly turned friend, and we find ourselves running into the lights of the field. We shuffle toward the shocked players. The crowd laughs at first. I suppose we look amusing, two strange individuals with obvious muscle-control issues.

The smell of the song engulfs us both, and our steps become more sure footed as our engines gather steam. The right fielder approaches us, asking if we need help, inviting me to leap first, sinking my teeth into the man's face. Drinking deep of the song, I glance up to see the crowd screaming and scattering off the benches. Some hold their places behind cell-phone cameras while others throw objects in our direction. My friend leaps at the player swinging a bat in his direction. Amateur hour in the land of the dead. The newbie takes a bat to the side of his face, finding himself on the ground. He dusts himself off and pounces again, finding his proper place on top of the batter's struggling form.

I suddenly realize I have left the field and am running toward the people rushing out of the bleachers. After vaulting over the dugout chain-link and clacking my teeth, I find myself between two people, a teenage girl and an overweight, middle-aged man. First-world undead problems. Both have their arms up defensively, frozen in fear. Their eyes are pleading for safety. Hey, that fat guy has a beard and looks like Pavarotti. I leap and find, in fact, he tastes like Pavarotti should!

Police and fire sirens ring out. Smoke wafts past as I chase neon lights. The song carries me up one street and down another. The feeling intensifies. Sometimes, I snap a chunk of flesh from the masses. Other moments, I clack my teeth and hiss a warning, culling the crowd, shoving it away from me and into some newly minted friends. Their forms screech delight while rending flesh.

I remember standing next to a fresh-faced muscle-bound undead man as he roared rage and destruction. He was probably still slightly pumped from steroids and protein shakes. A second later, he was cut down by a hail of gunfire.

I bet he misses the gym.

Old ladies don't seem so old when the song finds them. I observe one wearing a blue wig screaming, gnashing her teeth, and climbing a streetlight to leap through a second-floor window.

Suddenly, I am up on a roof, watching a mass of undead tumble down a chimney like Santa Claus chasing the holiday spirit. Such a clatter.

A flash shuffles past, and I'm sprinting up a wide street, leaping up and onto a windshield. My fists are hammering down, trying to unleash the music hiding inside the parked car. The glass flexes, resembling the white pattern of a spider's web, before shattering. The screams surrounding me are pulsing with excitement.

I can hear the beat of chopper blades long before I feel the whiz of bullets. By this time, though, our mass is pulsing into and through buildings, smashing windows and splintering wood wherever we find it. Sometimes, we are beaten back...but the band plays on. The night belts out hit tunes, and as it turns out, I love to dance.

Electricity surges somewhere. I'm screaming at the moon while struggling to hold a man beneath my knuckles. My brothers and sisters latch on and proceed to rip him apart. I have never felt so powerful. The world has never felt so right. Confidence is trampling through, enlightening the masses. Liberating a beat.

I might be dead, but I have never felt so alive. Another blink, and I'm standing in the seats of Yankee Stadium, just up from the third baseline, gnashing my teeth into a man wearing a security jumper.

Hey, look at me! I'm in Yankee Stadium! I made it to the big show!

3.

Los Gatos
Dean
Present Day

"HELLO? IS SOMEONE THERE? I could use some help... please..." Panic had long left Dean's voice, but he was still quite conscious of the thick walls surrounding him.

Discerning night or day was hard since they'd locked him in there. How many hours have passed? Was it hours? Or minutes? Not much sunlight was there to begin with in that place. Old supermarkets were devoid of windows, making them either excellent places to hide out when night fell or a far worse place to be trapped inside.

He had been foraging for food, but the darkness made it difficult to search, so he mostly just ran into things. Occasionally, Dean would bump into aisle endcaps, and he'd hear things clatter to the ground, ancient boxes of scouring pads or sometimes packs of batteries that had long since gone bad. At first, he had tried to gather the things up into a neater pile so he wouldn't trip over them later, but after a while, he quit doing that altogether. Too much time had passed, and nothing was worth the effort. The place was too big, too dark, and too full of items for him to avoid stepping on things. At one point, he had tripped and fallen face-first into what he later realized was an old waist-high industrial freezer that had once been overflowing with TV dinners and various freshly butchered and wrapped meats. Dean knew it hadn't stored those items for years, maybe decades.

Who had done this? He remembered waking up one evening to the sound of laughter and the footfalls of people running outside the supermarket. He was excited at first. Dean had been anticipating the thrill of human contact. A lot of time had passed since someone came to trade, and he was weak with hunger. His supplies had been low for a while. The generator bucked and snorted to life as he pulled back on the metal lever. Gasoline churned inside its engine, and the cogs and machinery spun to life, transforming combustion to electricity powering the lights of the supermarket and lighting the parking lot so that survivors would know the place was safe and they could find supplies there.

Then he tried the door, though. Lord, did he try the door.

It just seemed chained at first. Dean thought he could feel it give ever so slightly as he shouldered into it. He spent hours kicking at it, throwing his full body weight at the metal door. Pushing it open should have been simple. Perhaps if he could've gotten it to open half an inch, he could've wedged something else in it to pry it open. It never gave, though—not even a millimeter.

God Himself seemed to have placed a mountain behind the door. The generator's engine seized up a short time after that. Dean had no idea whether lack of oil or gasoline had finally stopped the engine, not that it mattered. Not a gas or oil can was anywhere inside the store. The lights died with the generator, of course.

Dean had spent hours crawling up and down the walls. At one point, he even made it to the top-down steel slide curtains that had been pulled down and secured along the front of the store. The whole time, he was trying to find an opening, a tiny gap of space, something he could heft and pull or just yank open to see a fraction of the outside world, some small opening that could give him solace that the end to his temporary incarceration was close. Dean knew those slide curtains had initially been drawn so people could open the store and line the front entrance with fresh foods and vegetables, produce that would bring happiness and full bellies to the masses. Then his supplies ran low. Sure, he was still overstocked on coffee mugs, brooms, and ancient celebrity magazines of a long-forgotten empire, but food and water had run out long before.

Long? How long have I been locked up inside here? Dean was suddenly very conscious of the darkness engulfing him and the silence within himself.

Then he heard something, a beat. It faded in from a distance. The beat had a rhythm, various tones, singing, and the squealing of tires.

Wait, what? The squealing of tires? A large crack rang out through the supermarket as shards of metal splintered and light fanned out through an opening in the roll-up steel security windows. Smoke rose from the hood of an old 1980s brown Datsun that had become stuck in the storefront. Its form had slowed from the impact of the steel curtain windows and then collided with the checkout counters farther inside.

Dust drifted into the beams of light flooding the large market. Dean had never been so thankful. As three figures stepped into the light, he rushed out of the darkness to meet them and then halted midstep just as the fluorescent glow flooded his eyes. Something about that woman's face jabbed at him with an electrified needle in his mind.

———

Ashley observed the man walking out of the darkness. Her friends had their weapons drawn, but she left hers holstered. She stared at the man, whose face was corpselike and shriveled, folds blending into other folds, his complexion pale and malnourished. His eyes were almost entirely white and much of his hair gone.

"Dean?" Ashley asked. "Is that... Are you Dean?"

Dean nodded. His voice strained and cracked. "Dean, yes...I...supplies?"

"No." Her voice was strong, unquestioning. "We do not need supplies."

A look of recognition crossed Dean's face. He drew in a breath that jilted in spurts as it rushed in.

"One of my—no...not you. No." Dean stepped back in panic.

Donathan angled both pistols in his direction at the same time. Mason reached up, lowering his hockey mask onto his face to reveal a painted stop sign as he raised his machine gun.

Dean weakly raised his hands then slowly limped two steps forward. "I don't—"

Donathan's pistol cocked, and Ashley drew her bat out of the holster on her back.

Dean continued, "I mean, I didn't... It wasn't exactly my idea."

All the faces staring at Dean had sharp eyebrows and glares that could burn down the sun.

Dean sighed and continued to limp, pacing back and forth in front of the three friends. "Look I'm...not who I was. I've...I'm so weak. Why even bother?"

"I—" Ashley fumbled for words for a moment before whispering, "You know why."

Dean stopped as if calculating what she'd said. He looked up and to the left, as if trying to shake away some fog. After a moment, he seemed to understand the wisdom in her words and nodded slowly, weakly. Then he asked in a hushed tone, "Did you know we age?"

Ashley looked at him curiously. Dean leaped forward with lightning reflexes. He sprinted at her and fell back to the ground, sliding between her legs. Ashley stumbled as she tried in vain to hold onto her bat. Dean's inertia and the sudden shock of energy caused her to lose footing at the same time she lost her grip on her weapon.

Dean flexed and then was standing and throwing the aluminum bat at Donathan's form. The metal collided with his pistols just as one fired up toward the ceiling. Dean had already taken three more steps and raised a boot to the side of Mason's face, sending him flying like a rag doll. Mason's mask flew off his head, clattering against something in the darkness. Then Dean ran forward toward the light, toward the exit of the hastily breached hole in the shredded metal and directly into Nyla, who held a black combat shotgun.

The appearance of the small woman wearing a white T-shirt, pink pants, a pink beanie, and glasses caused all of Dean's forward momentum to grind to a halt. Her tiny form blocked his only exit. Giving the woman a flabbergasted look, he raised his arms.

Nyla cleared her throat and said, "I think it's..." She fumbled with the front stock of the shotgun. "I really should know this, but honestly, I've never used this model. I-is it...?" The shotgun tilted a bit to the right as Nyla tugged on it but succeeded only in causing the metal to click slightly.

Lost in the moment, Dean added, "I think you need to—" He pointed at the forestock and the action bar.

"That's right," Nyla added and then giggled for a second. "Like every other shotgun. Wait, no..."

Dean chuckled a bit too and said, "No, I think you do this part"—he pointed again at the middle of the gun—"and then sharply pull it back toward you."

"I think it's called 'racking,'" Nyla added as she racked back the forestock, angling the weapon up slightly, then the shotgun went off in an explosion at point-blank range into Dean's face, sending him crumpling backward in a mass of dead flesh. The force of the gun going off knocked Nyla back into a sitting position, still facing the torn metal opening of the store.

Donathan's head peeked through the shredded entryway with a look of hesitation. He let his eyes trail from Nyla back down to Dean's lifeless form.

"Goodness!" Donathan exclaimed before smiling at Nyla and helping her to her feet.

"You kids find all the closure you needed in there?" Princess Jae asked from the driver's seat of the black pickup as the four friends edged their way toward the vehicle in the midday sun. She smiled in their direction, her cloche hat perched atop her cheery face as if she was anticipating good news.

"Not quite," Ashley replied.

"Well." Jae sighed. "There's a lot of road ahead of us today and plenty of time to think things over."

4.

North of Morgan Hill
Zombie Civil Rights Group
Present Day

"WHAT EXACTLY are we doing here?" Ashley asked.

Donathan replied, "Jae dropped us here while she scouts the road south. She seemed to think there might be a problem up ahead. We'll shift to town and signal her with a flare tomorrow."

Ashley shook her head. "No, I know that. I mean what are we doing on this golf course?"

"Well, I had to give up tagging the different hordes because we don't have the anti-necrotic-flesh security-fence system here," Nyla whispered. "I had already mapped most of the various hordes' territories and movements...but also sticking migratory tags in zombies to track horde movement without anywhere safe can blow up in your face." She spoke in a breezy tone, nodding absentmindedly.

Ashley raised her top lip in shock and upturned her palms while shrugging in Donathan's direction. He just smiled and shook his head back toward Ash.

Avoiding the argument, Ashley asked again, "So what is this?"

"Oh, it's a simple experiment." Nyla pointed over the dune in the direction of a television set up on the lush green of the long-abandoned golf course. An orange cord trailed off toward an aged clubhouse that had power, which Nyla had determined at sundown. "Mason is always talking about how he made that zombie laugh once, so we figured we'd try and test to see if there was any emotional resonance of their former life."

Donathan pointed back at the television. "So...you're showing them old recordings of TV shows."

"Sort of." Nyla stood a bit taller before stating, "We made a zombie soap opera."

Donathan's smile faded away, and Ashley's jaw dropped.

Somehow, Ashley managed to force out the syllables, "Meaning...a...?"

Nyla answered, "A soap opera starring Mason and me dressed as zombies, mimicking guttural noises, shuffling around, and making dramatic pauses. To see if it triggers something and holds their interest."

"This is what you did last night on your guard shift?" Donathan asked.

Ashley said in a snide tone, "These two shouldn't be grouped up on guard anym—"

Nyla shushed everyone then whispered, "Look! He's strayed from his horde."

One lone member of the undead shuffled past the light of the television set and back into the darkness.

"It's a warm night," Mason whispered in Donathan's direction, a bit too loudly. "I'm going to take off my IBA vest." Donathan shot a frustrated look at Mason and nodded as Mason began the long process of setting down his M240 Bravo, removing his red-and-black-camo ballistic vest, strapping it so that its mass hung off the side of his backpack, and redonning his gear.

The zombie had come back into the light and shuffled a bit closer toward the television. They could hear dramatic piano music and slight groans echoing through the television and VCR's playback system. The zombie groaned back then chuckled a bit.

"Son of a bitch," Ashley groaned.

Nyla nodded in her direction, whispering in elation, "I know! There might be some truth to what Mason is saying! Some remnants of consciousness seem to remain."

Ashley's tone was overflowing with frustration, "No...I..." She took a deep breath before asking, "Mason, are you wearing a glow-in-the-dark shirt?"

"Yeah!" Mason answered proudly without whispering.

Ashley's response was something between a whisper and a gasp, "You're fucking wearing a glow-in-the-dark T-shirt?"

"Yeah!" Mason replied again.

"In a zombie apocalypse?" Ashley asked.

Mason nodded. "Yeah, I got it at the flea market."

Donathan cleared his throat, "Mason, there hasn't been a flea market in California in like..." In the moonlight, Donathan's eyes rolled as he thought the answer through. "Best guess, ten years."

"Yeah, I know," Mason added nonchalantly.

"Ff-ff-ff-ff-ff-ff-ffffff," Ashley hissed then bit her lip, her eyes sharp and narrow.

"You guys." Nyla motioned toward the television impatiently.

The zombie was no longer standing there.

Donathan's eyebrows furrowed. "Where—"

The zombie lunged over the dune directly at Nyla as she fell back, trying to get out of the way. A shout and a flash later, Donathan was standing over Nyla, holding a smoking pistol and extending a hand to help her up. Nyla took hold, and after standing, she let herself rest a moment while gathering her bearings.

"Everyone okay?" Ashley asked.

Mason nodded.

Donathan said, "Fuck, I think I've got blood coming from me." He flicked his arm and held a hand up to the moonlight. "I don't think I..." His eyes grew wider, and he added, "It's not my blood."

"Oh dear." Nyla held up a dripping hand. "He nicked me."

Ashley took a deep breath. Mason rummaged through his pack, pulled out an old gray medical bandage, and gingerly handed it to Nyla.

Nyla unwrapped the bandage and tended to the wound.

Donathan took in a deep breath, cleared his throat, and whispered, "Nyla, I'm—"

Nyla interrupted in a spacey tone, "It's good now!" She held her hand back up under Donathan's gaze, the full moon framed behind him staring down at the bandaged appendage. "Let's go back to camp." Nyla strolled off ahead of the group.

Ashley had her head cocked in Nyla's direction and asked, "All this time she's been tagging zombies and studying science." Locking her gaze with Donathan's, she continued, "She doesn't know how the infection spreads?"

Donathan started to answer, but Mason stepped closer and said, "It isn't possible."

Donathan fumbled around, patting pockets before pulling out a cigarette and an old Zippo lighter. He placed the cigarette between his lips and raised the Zippo before dropping it on the grass and swearing loudly. "I can't even." He sighed and looked nervously between his friends then raised his eyes skyward. After a few seconds, he wiped a hand across his face and sniffed. "Mason's right. She knows. She's too into science to not know." He sighed. "This is denial. We have to—"

"We can't!" Ashley stomped a foot and rounded on her two friends. "It's Ny, you assholes!" Ashley shoved Donathan with enough force that he had to steady himself, drawing backward a foot and squaring his shoulders. "And fuck you, Mason! She's pretty innocent."

"Not that innocent," Donathan replied. "We live in a world surrounded by the various forms of the undead. She documents them, tracks their movements, classifies them..." Donathan's voice faded off again before he reached down to search the grass for the lighter. "She knows."

Light and flame burst forth from the metal, and the glow of an ember on the tip of the cigarette lit up the night as Donathan took a deep drag.

"Real tactical," Ashley added out of frustration.

Donathan took another drag and replied, "Honestly, Ash, I kind of need it tonight." After another drag, he said, "I'll take the first guard shift. You all go to sleep and halfway through the shift, I'll—"

"I'll do it," Mason interrupted in a dark tone.

"What?" Ashley and Donathan both asked in unison.

Mason reached down and dragged the M240 Bravo into his arms, clutching it tightly while angling it up toward the night sky. His unusually strong voice echoed back to his friends. "I... She's my close friend. It's my job to do this."

No one argued with Mason after that. No one really wanted to argue about it. He'd agreed to do something no one else could. Somehow, Mason had become the clinical doctor of a bleak prognosis. They gathered up their gear. Mason dragged his IBA vest back on, and with heavy footsteps, they followed Nyla's path under the dark sky, back toward camp.

5.

Gilroy
Fine Line Protectorate
Present Day

"AN ICE-CREAM TRUCK?" Goblin asked. "This was the chariot of choice."

Crooks's bald head peeked out from the back window, smiling and nodding in excitement.

Nym said, "Well, I'm sure it's cozy on the inside."

Crooks looked inside the truck and stuck his head back out, nodding again, before leaning out farther to look at the various faded stickers of popsicles, ice cream, and rocket pops.

"I wouldn't bet on any of those still being in there, Crooksy. They would be two decades old." Nym wrinkled up her nose. "You would probably still try them, huh?"

"You ate a man's face last night. Don't judge him," Goblin teased while poking around the back wall of the parking garage.

Chipped yellow paint covered a cement wall with two large block letters reading D3. A door painted the same color yellow, including the doorknob, was centered in the middle of the wall next to the alphanumerical combination. Goblin examined it.

"I wasn't judging him!" Nym exclaimed before walking to the open edge of the parking garage and peering over the waist-high wall, down a three-story drop. "She kind of picked a nice spot for this, didn't she? Seated in a city infested with hordes, the one building most people wouldn't scavenge through for supplies. Plus, it's still connected to the power lines leading up the trail to Falling Sands. Did we thank the runner from the Protectorate that gave us this info?"

Knocking noises could be heard from inside the ice-cream truck as Crooks made himself at home.

Goblin was still staring at the door and added, "Yes, well, no...I mean, we ate him three nights back."

Nym looked back curiously at Goblin then strolled over to the door he was facing. "He was a runner from the Protectorate?"

"Yeah. You couldn't tell? He was screaming, 'Help, help! Don't eat my face. I'm a runner from the Protectorate.'" Goblin waved his arms around a bit for emphasis.

"Oh pfft. They all say that." Nym sighed and laughed before observing, "This symbol right here..." She pointed at a purple dab of paint that had been originally sprayed through a stencil of some kind. "Is that a Mardi Gras mask?"

Goblin studied it and added, "There's a tiny moon between the eyes of the mask. That's a Knight's Moon mask."

"Oh well," Nym's voice gushed with elation, "I believe we've found a secret, dahlings."

With that, she reared back and smashed a foot into the door, just under the knob. Chunks of the metal door careened into the back of a darkened room. Stale air filtered out as Goblin reached in, fishing for a light switch. Finally, his hand caught something, and the room lit up with a pulsing green neon light.

Goblin stared at the light a moment then turned back to Nym. "What in the—"

Without letting him finish, Nym brushed him aside with a metal-gauntlet-clad hand, then she pushed to the back of the room. She paused in front of a table holding an oversized metal orb with flattened discs cascading out from under it. Each disc was wider than the last until the base disc, lying on the table, three feet across, held up the rest of a silver metal contraption. The entire monstrosity pulsed on and off with a blinding green neon light. Tendrils of emerald green would occasionally pop and hiss off of it. Nym held her hand out in front of it and froze, staring wide eyed at its electric reaction. After a minute, she reached down to the table next to the item, picked up an old brown leather notebook, and thumbed it open.

"Experiments... Grand ones!" Nym spun around to hand Goblin the book and jab a finger down on the page.

"If this is real—" Goblin said.

"Oh, it's real," Nym said.

"Then Christmas has come early." Goblin smiled vindictively.

Crooks appeared in the doorway, holding a large, unfurled sheet of paper with big, worn grid squares stretched across it.

"Oh, what did you find?" Nym asked as she took the sheet from Crooks's fur-covered hands. "This is   Wow." Nym smiled. "I think Crooks might have found something much more fun."

Crooks waved his hand out of the room, and Nym and Goblin followed. Goblin flicked off the switch as he stepped through the doorway. An old red wagon sat there with a three-foot-wide plank of wood stretching ten feet in length, a smaller plank of wood about five feet in length and one foot wide, and a red sheet draped partially over Crooks's furry mascot head perched in the wagon. All the items were set up near the wall of the parking garage.

"Where the hell did you find something like that?" Nym asked before glaring back at Goblin, who was shrugging with an innocent look on his face.

Crooks held a hand out in front of his face, cocked his fingers forward at a forty-five-degree angle and made whooshing noises while he stared at Nym with questioning eyes.

"No," Nym answered. "Absolutely not! You know why."

A look of frustration crossed Crooks's face, and he continued making whooshing noises while waving his arm more intensely up at an angle.

Nym moaned, "Look, this never turns out different."

"Aw, come on," Goblin's voice was deep into his faux British mode, the syllables drawn long as he continued, "Let's just see... He might actually get it right this time."

Nym sighed before asking, "Will it make you happy, Crooksy?"

Crooks nodded with ferocity.

Nym shrugged, "Go ahead."

————

Five minutes later, Goblin stood behind Crooks, who was seated in the red wagon with the black handle pulled up and back into his lap. Duct tape and wooden boards were laced under the wagon so that it hung out to the sides as a set of makeshift wings. Crooks had fashioned a cape from the red sheet and tied it around his neck, letting its mass drift down into the wagon behind him. He reached over the side of the wagon for his mascot head and raised it up onto his shoulders before reaching up again near the furry ears and lowering a pair of pilot's aviator goggles over the furry's cartoonish eyes.

"All set?" Goblin asked.

Crooks stared forward at a large plank, mounted up onto the edge of the parking-garage wall and forming a ramp. Crooks glanced back over his shoulder and nodded slowly to Goblin with determination.

Goblin quoted Peter Pan: "The moment you doubt whether you can fly, you cease forever to be able to do it." With that, he sprinted forward, pushing the wagon as he went.

"Steady!" Nym shouted from somewhere behind them, "Steady! You've almost made it!"

At the last moment, Goblin steered around the ramp, shoving the wagon with skidding tires and pushing Crooks straight into the cement safety wall. Then he stood back up and added in an unsurprised voice, "Oh, whoops."

Two minutes later, they were lined up for the ramp again. Crooks looked back and glared at Goblin. Even behind the canvas and fur, Goblin could feel the look of frustration.

"What?" Goblin asked in a shocked tone. "You were steering!"

"Okay." Resigning himself to the moment, Goblin recited his speech again. "The moment you doubt whether you can fly, some motherfucker might push you into the wall." He was running at that point, shoving the wagon forward. The front wheels of the wagon jolted as they dashed up the makeshift ramp. The ramp flexed, and the wood strained when the back wheels connected. Suddenly, Crooks was over the wall and in the air.

————

The world rushed forward. The blue sky framing the buildings around Crooks blended into a cyan dome. The white clouds hung still in the afternoon sky. The air felt crisp. The sound of the wheels still spinning below the wagon could be heard, but it hung in the air eerily, not reverberating off any ground. The wagon banked slightly to the right. Crooks could hear Goblin and Nym cheering behind him. The cape flowing after him extended in the wind, and he could feel it taut as he hung in the heavens. The wagon banked deeper to the right and started to nosedive.

Crooks looked ahead at the ground, seeing it as a freeway wall rushing up to meet his out-of-control vehicle.

Above him, Goblin shouted, "Bet you're thinking, Oh shit, now!"

Crooks collided with the ground and collapsed into it, scattering broken bits of wood and warping the bouncing steel cart. It toppled a few feet up the street before coming to rest in the gutter.

———

"It's like watching a hippopotamus compete in diving at the Summer Olympics," Goblin said in an amused tone.

Nym looked down at the pile of unconscious fur on the sidewalk and said, "Can you please go scrape him off the pavement now?"

Goblin stared off, looking vacant for a moment, then added, "I had an idea...just now."

Still staring down at Crooks on the sidewalk, Nym asked, "Yeah, what's that?"

Still glassy eyed, Goblin replied, "A sane asylum."

A shocked look crept across Nym's face before she glanced in Goblin's direction. "Like the opposite of an insane asylum?"

"Yep," Goblin smiled.

"I love it," Nym said in a calm voice. "Let's do it."

6.

North of Morgan Hill
Zombie Civil Rights Group
Present Day

"I STILL DON'T THINK we should do it," Ashley whispered in Donathan's direction.

He was already shaking his head. "You think she would want to add to the zombie population? Would you?"

They had arrived back at base camp, a gutted-out swim center with a long-empty indoor swimming pool. They had already explored it when Jae first dropped them off. It was empty, and someone had reinforced most of it with thick wooden planks that seemed able to survive most tornadoes. Once inside, they determined they could block the main doors with a little effort, using some old columns of wall lockers wedged between a door and a hallway wall. The pool was deep, so they didn't need to exercise light discipline and even pondered lighting a fire before they realized how smoky the place might become. Up until the recent turn of events, the night had seemed pretty fortuitous.

As everyone approached, they slowed their steps, as if creeping up carefully on a bomb that could go off at any minute. Down in the pool, Nyla had already lit up an old gas lantern she toted around in her bag and rarely got to use. She was currently rummaging through her pack and had her sleeping bag all unfolded. A few heavy steps on the tile had alerted her that they were near.

She looked up and coughed loudly before sniffing and adding, "I think I'm getting sick."

Wide eyed, Donathan glanced at Mason, and Mason just nodded back with a gaze that seemed unfazed. Ashley felt her rage growing as her eyes narrowed. She glared back and forth between Mason and Donathan.

"Listen, I..." Donathan's voice seemed weak. "This place is pretty well protected. We don't need two people up on guard tonight." He stepped in front of Mason and jumped down into the pool with a loud whump. "Let's let Mason take the first watch by himself. Nyla, you can get some rest."

"Really?" Nyla sounded shocked. "We never do one person on watch." When she was done talking, Nyla cleared her throat forcefully.

Ashley's heartbeat grew faint, and her realization of the situation finally took hold. "Yeah, just..." She lowered her eyes, unable to look in her friend's direction before finishing with, "Nyla, just...get some rest, hon."

Nyla sounded relieved. "Thank goodness because my throat is on fire!" She climbed into her sleeping bag and rolled in the direction of the dark corner of the pool.

Ashley mouthed, "How can she not know?" toward her friends. Donathan shrugged back, but Mason just reached down and brought his machine gun back into his arms, holding it tightly.

Donathan and Ashley shook their heads then hugged each other. After that, both of them huddled around Mason to mumble a thank-you before sneaking off to unfurl their sleeping bags. Ashley whispered for Mason to scream if things went sour. Mason just nodded.

As Ashley tiptoed past Nyla's sleeping body, she held up a hand signing, "I love you." She then noticed both Donathan and Mason were signing the same thing.

A few moments and a few tears later, Ashley was tucked into her sleeping bag, hoping she'd be fully asleep before the shots of Mason's machine gun rang out.

———

Ashley yawned and sat up slightly. She felt rested. Why do I feel so rested? That wasn't an everyday thing.

She lunged upward and tried to take in her surroundings, tripping slightly on the sleeping bag wrapped around her legs. After tumbling to the ground once, she whispered forcefully for Donathan to wake.

A moment later, Donathan was standing with both pistols drawn while murmuring something about a bridge.

"The fuck is wrong with you?" Ashley whispered. "And why didn't we get woken up?"

Donathan glanced around and noticed Nyla still wrapped in her sleeping bag in the same corner they'd left her.

"Wait." Panic had set into Donathan's voice. "Where's Mason?"

Mason groaned, "Up here."

Donathan dropped to his knees and unconsciously aimed a pistol up out of the pool.

Up on the edge of the cement hole, looking down into the pool at them, with dark circles under his eyes and frazzled blond hair, stood Mason, still clutching his machine gun tightly to his chest. "I couldn't, I just..." After several moments, he shrugged and whispered, "We can't kill her! I don't care if she's infected!" He motioned toward Nyla's sleeping bag and added, "It's Nyla!"

Ashley's frustration got the best of her, and she sneered at

Donathan through clenched teeth. "I said the same thing!"

Donathan held up both of his hands, still gripping the pistols, and whispered, "Well, she's probably about to turn... Let's just pack up and leave her here. If she was infected last night, then—"

"I'm not infected," Nyla announced in a loud and determined voice from her sleeping bag. "I can't be infected."

Ashley gasped as surprise trampled across the faces of Donathan and Mason.

Nyla sat up in her sleeping bag, an annoyed look on her face. "I can't be infected because I was inoculated against it."

Ashley's jaw dropped.

Nyla's tone seemed unchanged. "And so were the rest of you."

———

"Do you remember the Knight's Moon festival, when we first met?" Nyla asked while scrambling up the side of a partially collapsed bowling alley just south of town. She stood on Donathan's shoulders as he boosted her up to stretch their height against the wall. They'd taken most of the day to navigate around the town.

"You mean the giant rave where we were surrounded by a glowing blue electrified fence that destroyed undead flesh, and we partied most of the night, only to have it crashed by Mary Helen and the Protectorate Army? Then it ended with Barbie riding on a giant pink spider and us escaping in convoy?" Donathan asked plain faced, still leaning up against the wall.

Nyla replied, "That's the one."

Donathan's face remained unchanged as he looked from Mason to Ashley. "No. I don't remember it."

"Okay, well..." Sounds of scraping erupted from the roof before Nyla said, "Goodness!"

"You okay?" Ashley asked.

"I'm good," Nyla answered as her head peered back over the roof, looking down at her friends. "I just realized I only have two star-cluster flares left. We need to resupply."

Mason was peeling dried paint off a wall of the building in the warm morning sun.

As Ashley eyeballed him, Nyla disappeared but continued talking. "Do you remember how you entered the compound at the rave?"

"Through the gate?" Confusion had found its way into Ashley's voice. "Wait...after they had blood tested us for the infection."

Mason paused in his process of peeling the paint away in sheets, causing a long gray strip of cement to take shape. "Wait! I remember that."

He leaned back as the whiz of a flare shot overhead and a ruby-red star cluster of flares slowly drifted back down toward earth.

Mason's head tracked the color and light as he leaned back, his jaw lowering before he said, "Wow, are those bright in the day."

"Yeah, my creation..." Nyla sounded as though she was admiring her work for a second before adding, "I'm terrible at basic chemistry, though. I didn't know many chemists. I wish there was a brighter reaction."

Ashley looked dumbstruck. "Nyla, those are as bright as the sun!"

"Oh, ha ha." Nyla sounded a bit offended for once. "The sun is ten to the twenty-sixth power in watts."

Ashley just shrugged at Mason as he stepped forward, pulling more paint off the wall before continuing, "That night, we weren't supposed to look at the test in the med tent, but I looked anyways. They never took blood. They just tried to distract me with someone else and poked me three times with a needle, quick like."

"Right, they do that to everyone." Nyla sounded amused. "The test is just a cover story in case the Protectorate Army ever shows up. The Protectorate's bread-and-butter income comes from the trade of undead to the science enclaves." Nyla sounded a bit sad as she added, "They don't want this world to change because they're all living in luxury behind strong walls."

Nyla climbed back over the wall and dangled down until Donathan stepped up, standing tall and letting her feet perch on his shoulders. Ashley rushed forward to help keep Nyla's balance as they shifted back toward the ground. Mason just went back to peeling paint.

When Nyla was finally on steady ground, she picked the conversation back up. "We aren't testing for infection, though. We're inoculating against it."

"How, though?" Donathan asked.

Nyla replied, "With long inoculation needles."

Donathan shook his head with force. "No, how are you inoculating against it? Who came up with the medicine?"

"Well, the Half Moon Bay Science Enclave that my dad used to run had developed part of it a few years ago." Nyla shoulders slumped a bit. "It's probably why the Judge turned his attention towards us and why the enclave was run into the ground by Falling Sands."

"Those motherf—" Donathan caught himself but was still almost snarling. "Are you telling me that, all this time, they've known there is a cure?"

"Well," Nyla replied matter-of-factly, "it's not technically a cure. Zombies still exist. They won't be getting better anytime soon. They still eat people." Nyla held up her wounded arm. "But if they bite you, you can't get infected."

"So that's why!" Ashley exclaimed. "That's why you are always working up close with zombies and doing strange things like tagging them to track their movements." Ashley motioned in Nyla's direction. "You're immune!"

"No, no, that's not it," Nyla replied. "I just find them interesting."

Ashley shrugged in frustration.

"So why didn't Falling Sands destroy the specimen so that no one could ever use it," Donathan asked.

Mason answered before Nyla could respond. "Secret lab. We've been there, remember?"

Nyla grinned widely, looking pleased. "Mason is paying attention these days!"

"Sort of," Ashley added, pointing at the dragon etched from removed paint, which had cropped up on the wall during the conversation.

"Lovely," Nyla remarked.

Without even looking back, Mason just shook his head and added, "No." He turned a nose up toward it. "Too ordinary." He sighed. "I need a real project."

Ashley stepped up next to Mason, eyeballing the dragon and studying its webbed wings with ornate patterns and its tiny curled claws arching forward. Its form perched on the edge of two mighty legs, the front ones curled forward as if on the verge of striking. The dragon's great head tilted upward to give the illusion of roaring. As Ashley leaned forward, she noticed the dragon had tiny battle scenes of men fighting across its head, giving the illusion of scales.

Ashley looked over her shoulders and mouthed the words "The fuck?" while motioning at the artwork.

Donathan's smile picked up as he just nodded with his usual smirk.

A squeal of tires signaled Princess Jae had noticed the flare and was well on her way to their rendezvous.

"Anyways." Nyla motioned toward a dust cloud on the horizon, moving quickly toward their position. "So, Dad's samples work, and I've been happily replicating them in that lab for some time. The Knight's Moon, which happens to be comprised mostly of what's left of Half Moon Bay, has been secretly inoculating people up and down the Shytown Trail under the guise of all-night rave parties as an entertainment enclave.

"I can't take credit for it, though," Nyla continued. "Old members of the Knight's Moon came up with the plan years ago. I just synthesized Dad's inoculation, developed the security fence, tapping its energy off Falling Sands Power grid, and—Ahh!"

Donathan had stepped up and lifted Nyla off her feet in a huge bear hug. He was still hugging her when Princess Jae arrived a few minutes later.

As he set Nyla down, Princess Jae said, "Sorry I missed the party..." She motioned toward the sand cloud behind her. "We've got the worst kind of company."

7.

Southwest of Morgan Hill
Zombie Civil Rights Group
Present Day

"GOOD GOD. It has a mountain of legs," Donathan said as the truck bounced along. He handed the binoculars to Ashley and then stuck his head in the cab window to ask, "So what happened?"

"Well," Princess Jae shouted over her shoulder as Nyla rolled down the window to peer out the passenger side back toward the trailing creature. "You know I left, trying to scout. When I got out to refuel at lunch, I fell in some webby sinkhole."

"Did it explode into spores?" Nyla asked.

Princess Jae nodded in the bouncing vehicle. "I guess so."

"Were they mostly brown or gray?" Nyla didn't sound very excited for once.

Princess Jae answered, "Well, it was dark when I was climbing out, but I think gray."

Nyla shrugged and said, "Exocites. They bind to protein strains in the body. In this form, they bind to you and let it hunt you down wherever you go." Nyla peered through the window at Donathan. "We are going to need a massive explosion or a lot of fire. The queen won't stop chasing until she's either killed or converted Jae."

"And we just found out she can't do the second," Donathan remarked.

Nyla nodded.

"Just found out?" Princess Jae wondered aloud.

Nyla nodded to her. "They didn't know we had been inoculated. They almost killed me."

"What?" The tires screeched as Jae almost lost control of the truck.

———

"Go, go! Rig them up quick!" Princess Jae shouted as everyone sprinted off the vehicle.

Halfway down the road, they had spotted the markings for a Knight's Moon refueling station. Refueling stations appeared as abandoned vehicles with a purple mask spray-painted nearby, signaling either that a full tank of gas and a tube were nearby for siphoning, or that something holding fuel was stashed somewhere in the vehicle. In that case, it turned out to be a plastic gas can of fuel hidden behind one of the abandoned car's tires. As Ashley and Nyla dragged it into the vehicle, Donathan yelled for Mason to sprint back up the road and paint over the marking of the mask so that they knew to refill it. Mason was all too happy to oblige.

"Just slather paint on it!" Donathan shouted. "We haven't got time for much else!" Donathan turned and trotted back toward the truck, muttering, "God help us if we don't kill this thing by nightfall."

A moment later, Mason returned, smiling from his quick paint job. "So, what does this thing look like?"

Donathan handed the binoculars to Mason as they climbed into the back of the truck.

Peering through them, Mason asked, "It's like a giant armored centipede?"

Donathan nodded.

"Not really," Nyla shouted back through the window as the truck fired off and jolted forward. "Centipedes have legs. The reason it slinks from side to side and sends up all that dust as it moves is it doesn't have legs." She climbed out the window until she was sitting on the frame of the door, then pointed back toward the hulking mass a mile back. "That thing has twenty arms."

"Weird," Mason remarked, still peering through the binoculars.

Nyla nodded. "They're nasty, unpredictable things. Real powerful. Some days, when their spores get into things, they will hold their prey with their twenty arms and just relish in their screams as they devour the victim slowly. Other days, these queens will wrap people up in their arms and turn them into walking zombie spore sacks that sort of lumber around slowly until they explode." For a moment, Nyla grinned mischievously, enjoying the reactions her friends were giving her. "On their worst days, they'll just violently beat things to death."

The truck bounced a bit to one side, and almost everyone grew wide eyed, steadying themselves. Nyla looked comfortable as ever and just shifted her weight across the top of the cab.

"I have an idea," Donathan said before leaning forward and sticking his head through the window to ask Jae, "How partial are you to this truck?"

———

Prey. Victim. Feast. Flesh. Rage. Those were the only truths in the world. This was her time. She fed. She infected. She killed. Hssthynyss knew of nothing else. Her elongated jaw flexed and dripped with saliva as her arms stretched out and grasped to flex and pull her forward.

She had been gaining on the victim. She saw its vehicle traveling, watched its form grow. Her arms, working in unison, let her flow forward, shifting down dusty streets and grassy, overgrown fields and past thick, ancient trees. Once or twice, she had to crawl over the ruins of fallen buildings, often destroying them in the process. It didn't matter. She knew she could climb over any obstacle, run down any prey, kill anything. She was a queen of the food chain, with bloodlust her king. Her muscles started to ache, but the hunger screamed through her. She would soon be upon it. She would rend flesh, rip it from its bones, watch as the light vanished from its eyes.

Hssthynyss had run too far and chased too long that day. There would be no quick and easy death for that one. She was going to relish in its screams.

The four-lane road drifted down to two lanes as she entered a small town. Slithering between the buildings, she could feel it—her prey was close. Hssthynyss moved up the narrow street between a movie theater and an old record shop, then past a strip mall to a three-way intersection with a crooked stop sign. The pole of the sign looked as though it had been smashed long before. An abandoned, burnt-out husk of a sedan lay nearby. The vehicle partially blocked the road she was on.

It was there.

The flesh was there.

Scanning back and forth, she couldn't see the prey, but the presence was intoxicating. She could feel its life force right there—every heartbeat, every pulse of a vein, every breath. It was right there somewhere. In a flash of movement, she slithered forward. Her body lifted her torso up, the arms padding over and picking through the abandoned frame of the vehicle. Nothing. She flexed her back arms, and her torso carried itself higher as Hssthynyss spun her large mass and peered about her surroundings. Nothing. Perhaps dinner was behind the brick wall lining the long road to the intersection. A second later, she scrambled up it and peered over. Nothing.

She could feel it, though, smell it—wanted to devour it. Where can it be?

Light flickered across the ground, and Hssthynyss lurched forward, hissing and spitting. Fear made victims easier to kill. She flexed all her arms and stretched them wide then elongated her spine and swung in a wide, loping circle around the activity emanating from a manhole in the street. Her size widened and stretched as she readied to strike, issuing forth a tremendous roar.

Something shifted and moved in the darkness of the manhole.

Enough of this. Hssthynyss slid forward and managed to get her front two arms into the manhole. Her head followed next. Unearthly rage flowed through her from the effort the prey was causing. A guttural growl erupted from her chest and carried forward into the tunnel. Just beyond her reach, she could see the victim standing there, wearing a cloche hat, waving and cocking a rifle. It was no bother. A moment later, a shot plinked harmlessly off Hssthynyss's carapace-covered head. More unbridled rage bubbled, and she struggled, forcing another arm and her shoulders farther down into the hole. She could feel the concrete around it start to give.

She heard a tire skid just up the street. An engine revved as it drew close. The jolt of steel and kinetic force buckled her body as she was forcefully ripped up and away from the tunnel. A second later, Hssthynyss had a momentary bird's-eye view of the manhole as she struggled to right herself. Chunks of cement, steel, and bricks flew around her as her body smashed through the brick wall lining the road.

———

The queen was screaming in agony wherever it had come to rest. Jae had two arms looped under Donathan's armpits and was trying to drag him out of the truck when Mason and Ashley ran up. Even though half of his torso was still in the truck and a gash was bleeding above his left eye, Donathan was somehow still trying to light up a cigarette with his Zippo. Once on his feet, he took two long drags off the cigarette as Ashley offered Jae the gas can. Without saying a word, Jae took hold of the can, lowered her gaze, and walked toward the unearthly screams of rage and pain. Donathan let the cigarette perch between his lips and stepped up alongside her, unholstering a nickel-plated pistol and replacing a magazine.

Ashley drew her bat over her shoulder and flexed her wrist, letting the weight and shape of the aluminum drift forward, up, and around in an arc before coming to rest comfortably out in front of her. She gripped it loosely, the bat dipping up and down slightly with every step.

Mason dragged his backpack off one shoulder and fumbled through it for a moment until he dredged out a long strip of belt-linked rounds. A moment later, he stepped up alongside Ashley and reseated the weight of the machine gun, letting it dangle off the shoulder strap before popping open the cover assembly, laying the long belt of ammunition across the feed tray, then slapping it shut. A step later, he lowered his mask, replacing his face with the image of a pixelated skull smirking a fleshless grin.

Nyla stepped up alongside her friends, casually brushing the dust off her tank top and pausing to adjust her glasses before placing both hands on her shotgun and racking it. The undead were always a passion of hers, but that didn't seem to stop a slow smile from spreading across her lips as her friends closed the gap to the monstrous queen.

When they got within a few meters of the creature, they could see the carapace on its face had almost completely ripped free. Pulsing gray muscles and torn tendons surged underneath what was left of it. The queen was struggling to right itself, but its torso was twisted at a strange angle, and several of its arms seemed broken or shattered. The creature screamed, thundered, and thrashed but never succeeded at doing more than spin at odd angles in the dirt.

Jae's eyes looked glazed over, shoulders hanging forward as she stared at the thrashing creature. Donathan reholstered his pistol, reached over, and dragged the gas can out of her hand. She looked up, shocked for a second, and he just nodded back at her. Colors blurred with motion as he surged forward and around the scene, and the smell and sound of splashing liquid seemed to echo around. Donathan's surge of speed came to an end with him facing his friends, still holding the gas can in his right hand. He set it down gingerly in the dirt, turned back around to face the thrashing creature, and took one more drag off his cigarette.

He turned back toward his friends and asked, "Does anyone have any paper or something we can light to throw at it?"

Ashley cleared her throat and asked in a slow, pained tone, "Why not something...like a cigarette?"

Donathan dragged the cigarette away from his lips and sighed before saying, "Seems a shitty way to waste a smoke." He tensed his fingers then flicked the smoldering cig in the direction of the beast.

The creature's eyes widened. Its motions intensified as it watched the trail of the tiny burning ember fall toward its gas-covered mass.

With a loud whoop, fire erupted, burning the twisting mass of necrotic flesh. Its screams grew high-pitched and panicked. A scent like burning tires and pork drifted about, causing Mason to reach up under his mask to cover his nose.

Princess Jae just whispered, "Dead things should stay dead."

8.

Los Banos
Ashley
Eight Years Earlier

"I'M EXHAUSTED," Ashley groaned.

They had been scavenging for days, lengthy days when the sun seemed to hang in the air for far too long. Although the nights were shorter than normal, they never seemed to be absent of distant screams and terror. The group could hear stalking too close to wherever they decided to bunk down for the night. Mom's exhaustion showed in dark circles under her eyes, and her motions looked almost as weathered as her hands. They simply hadn't pulled in enough of a haul, and supplies were dwindling. Ashley knew it but had kept that fact to herself. They wouldn't venture that far from an enclave unless they were desperate.

After the fifth industrial building of the day had held no copper piping, having been picked bare, Mom decided to take the initiative to improve morale. "How about a break?"

They settled inside one of the barren warehouses attached to the main office building. Thick beams of light drifted in through the windows, the flicker of dust fluttering through them. The steel rebar rod threaded under the straps of Ashley's pack, along with the chains inside it, clanged as she dropped her gear onto the cold, hard cement. Mom began the process of handing out peaches and bread for lunch.

"Strange right, Mom?" Ashley asked, looking around the building. "Everything is so empty these days."

Ethel replied, "I don't think it is strange at all, considering how much coin Merced's enclave has been giving for anything scavenged." She sighed. "They've just picked the world dry around here."

Ashley shrugged. "I'm sure we'll find something."

Ethel's frown confirmed that she wasn't as positive as her daughter.

After they finished their meal, Ashley asked if they could play Challenge Baseball.

Ethel agreed. "That seems like a good idea. We'll wander back toward Merced in an hour or just find a sturdy door to chain and rebar until the night is over."

The chain and rebar always held through the evening in industrial complexes. Meeting vast hordes of the undead around Los Banos was pretty rare. People could usually just hide behind thick doors until morning.

Challenge Baseball was a game Ashley and her mom had made up to pass the time. They used to play regular stickball with a dowel rod and tennis ball, but on the fifth day or so of playing, it became apparent to Ethel that Ashley was too good at connecting with the ball. They would often have to find a new ball or quit the game and hide because Ash's swing would send the ball out into the world with such force that it would attract the undead. That was the same reason they stopped running pretend bases. Zombies were drawn to the sound of feet sprinting across concrete. The new game involved almost no running and usually was just one of them pitching the ball and the other swinging at it then repeating. The only catch was the batter had to swing the rebar one-handed. Extra points were awarded if the batter could flourish across the batter's box or if they swung at the ball with their non-dominant hand. Ashley still cleaned up doing that, and Ethel would win pretty rarely. Still, the game was a fun way to keep their spirits up.

Ethel threw the ball overhand, and in an instant, Ashley stepped across the batter's box, spun, and let the rebar extend down and away, in one quick motion. The soft thump signaled that she'd connected with the tennis ball, and it bounced with a thunk off the concrete and into a wall.

"You think maybe we should try Clovis?" Ashley asked.

Ethel was already fast walking toward the tennis ball and shook her head before answering, "No." Hesitation crept through her voice. "Last time in town, I heard whispers that they were having serious problems keeping out the dead."

"Meh." Ashley felt repulsed. "I thought their enclave had huge walls and plenty of firepower."

"Me too," Ethel replied before turning to lob the ball back in Ash's direction.

Ashley reached out with one hand and caught the ball deftly before setting the rebar down quietly on the cement. "You think they're having problems with the undead or the Protectorate?"

Ethel just shrugged at her daughter before picking up the rebar and turning. Ashley's pitch dashed toward Ethel. She stepped across the imaginary batter's box and swung side-armed at the ball, whiffing as she did so.

On the second pitch, Ethel managed to connect and squealed excitedly before stepping forward to hand off the rebar to Ashley then fast walk to find the tennis ball. Ethel usually fetched the ball. She was good like that.

Ashley stepped up to the pretend plate, tapping the rebar on the heels of her shoes to knock pretend dust off them. She drew her shoulders in tight then brought the well-gripped rebar up until it almost matched the height of her eyes. Ashley hunched forward and gazed with determination at her mom, awaiting the pitch.

Ethel smiled and threw overhand. The pitch went wild, and the tennis ball made a thuk thuk sound off the concrete ground as it rolled away.

The ground trembled.

Ashley's eyes grew wide, and she locked gazes with her mom while whispering, "What was that?"

A moment of fright spread across Ethel's face as the ground shook again.

Both ladies fell back as the rear wall erupted into a cloud of debris, showering the room in metal and fractured concrete. Ashley was already back on her feet and inching away in the direction of her mom when a tall, thin zombie with hollow eyes stepped into the room. Its rotten skin was gray and green in patches. Its upper torso's limbs looked folded up, resembling a straitjacket.

As Ashley helped her mom to her feet, Ethel looked up with a doomed stare and whispered, "Whip. Run!"

They managed to snatch up their packs, Ashley trying to run and tuck the rebar behind her. In a dead heat, they sprinted toward the exit. The creature loped forward with lightning re-flexes. It quickly closed the gap between itself and the ladies, dashing around them and blocking their exit. The Whip's head tilted on its axis, bouncing back and forth in strange directions. It let forth a shrill scream that trailed off to a chirping tone. The ethereal speed and sudden proximity of the creature had fro-zen both ladies in their tracks. The undead's chirping drifted into sounds and beats until the noise sounded rhythmic, almost hypnotic. The creature was even bobbing its body to the left and right, letting its form rise and fall off balance before re-center-ing just after its head drifted in those directions.

All at once, the beat stopped, and Ashley felt something slam into her. She realized Ethel had tackled her to the ground just as the room exploded around them. Overhead, through the dust and rubble, two elongated limbs folded in on themselves until they were wrapped once again around the Whip's form.

Coughing and sputtering, Ethel dragged Ashley back to standing while screaming, "Run!"

Crossing through the gaping hole where a wall and door had once stood, they noticed half the room had fallen in on itself, blocking their only exit. Behind them, Ashley could hear the beat of the Whip winding up again.

"This way!" Ethel shouted, grabbing Ashley by the hand and dragging her toward a door marked Stairwell.

The door behind them slammed shut, and they were suddenly in darkness. Ashley cracked a green glow stick. Long shadows and emerald light draped around the room, bobbing in motion as they sprinted up the stairs.

A moment later, they were clutching the handrail for support as another thunderous crack rang out below. After wrenching open another substantial steel door, they found themselves standing in a large, gutted office bullpen on the third floor. The wind whistled past the jagged, toothlike broken glass rounding the length of two large bay windows. A three-foot-tall ribbon of a wall dividing the windows trailed into the middle of the room. The once-pristine carpet was dusty and gray. The floor was slanted and angled down a foot. The smell of dust and mildew was overpowering.

Ethel tore her pack off her back and fished through it. The beat of the Whip chimed from the stairwell.

When the room exploded, the Whip found himself itself standing and staring at an empty office building—no occupants. A small ribbon of wall rose between the two broken bay windows with a frayed tan rope tied around it.

Settling his arms back into position, he edged forward slightly until he could pitch his head down to see the two women dangling precariously from a rope below, their eyes wild as they shouted, trying to scramble farther down the line toward the ground.

Dinner was escaping. The time for the end of the hunt had come.

The world faded from color back into gray as his head tilted left and right. Air filled his lungs, and his mouth opened as sounds fell out of the air around him and into existence. The world blurred, but one thing remained in focus. Dead center in the spinning axis of view, his eyes focused on the half-size wall that the rope was looped around.

Stepping back, he let the beat become a tirade of sound escaping from his lungs. Spots drifted across his vision. The corners of his sight rounded out. He stepped forward and, in one quick motion, snapped his arms forward, feeling the rush of destruction.

———

Ashley looked up from the flat of her back as dust settled overhead. Concrete chunks were littered around her in her new resting place after the fall.

Ethel sat up gasping and said, "We need to get a longer rope."

Ashley was surveying the damage. She knew why the third-floor office had been angled downward. The warehouse had almost caved in. The walls had collapsed at an angle, leaving a concave form as the rest of the building rested precariously on a load-bearing wall that had just about given way. The sharp way the wall drifted wide and up seemed to hint that it might give way at any moment.

"Run! Run!" Ethel dragged herself back to her feet and pushed Ashley out of the way as another slam and more flying dust signaled that the Whip had opted to leap out the window after them.

With eyes on the horizon, they both sprinted away from the building.

Each step grew heavy. The world seemed to be echoing. The

smell of dust took on a sharpness, stinging Ashley's lungs. She could feel every grain of sand shift under her feet as she ran. Her sprint slowed then stopped altogether. A strange purple haze flashed across her vision as she unslung her pack, dropped it, and then drew the rebar from it.

Realizing her daughter was no longer next to her, Ethel turned around and shouted at Ashley. Ashley could feel the words echoing through the air. She could hear the long, drawn-out tones, but they seemed distant and detached from the world. She spun on her heels.

The zombie's beat had begun issuing forth, its gaunt cheeks expanding and contracting.

A bass note hung in the air as Ashley's stride widened to match the beat. She flexed her arms and let her wrist roll forward. Her fingers ran loose as the rebar drifted until Ashley found a decent pivot point where the bar seemed to arc comfortably. Her fingers tightened and let the metal carry itself down, around, and back up as her next step loomed forward.

Another beat belted forth from the creature, and it drew a foot backward, preparing to strike.

Ashley let the rotation of the rebar spin back around, extending her arm with it. She let go. The whirling piece of metal sailed in the direction of the Whip. The creature snarled then sidestepped out from its stance to dodge. Ashley fell backward, her forward leg stretching ahead. Her body fell back onto itself, sliding in the dirt between the legs of the creature. The iron rebar pinged off the building ahead of her.

In an instant, she sprang back to her feet and doubled back, running again at the Whip as it scrambled to turn around and face its victim. Without thinking, Ashley extended one foot and stepped up off the creature's knee. The other foot planted on his chest while she leaned her momentum up and forward, vaulting her body over the creature as it let its arms snap forward.

Ashley's feet connected with the ground, and she sprinted at full speed toward Ethel, whose eyes grew wide. She turned and raced in the same direction, away from the building and the creature. A massive blast behind both women threw them both to the ground.

Coughing and sputtering, Ethel dragged her daughter back to her feet and then hugged her tightly for a full minute before they both turned and admired the scene. The entire office building had collapsed forward, triggered by the Whip's long arms snapping into what had been left of the load-bearing wall.

"The world's been pretty dry on miracles for a while." Ethel drew a deep breath before continuing, "But I'm pretty sure we witnessed one today."

9.

North of Gilroy
Zombie Civil Rights Group
Present Day

THEY HAD TAKEN SHELTER for the night. Jae called the building the Phoenix, having named it after a similar theater also known as the Phoenix, located in Petaluma. It had thick cement walls, many of which were already painted with cartoony scenes from Alice in Wonderland. Mason had gushed about half an hour over the paintings as they secured the place. The area was littered with piles of things to fish through. They even found a disheveled skateboard ramp in the main theater area.

Though Donathan cautioned that the place could be a death trap, Nyla said, "The only hordes that ever come through North Gilroy are light roams, often numbering in only one or five creatures. Usually easy to counter. Plus, if things get hairy, you can go up to the rooftop of the second floor and jump to one of the other buildings next door and climb down."

Nyla set up lanterns strategically around the room. Most everyone else spent an hour piling rubble up against the main door until a mountain leaned against it. Instead of helping, Mason sat down and rested his M240 Bravo at the base of the stairs before unpacking his paint and becoming lost in redecorating his mask. That seemed to suit the rest of the group just fine. When they all finished working, Mason stood up, stretched, and perched his mask back atop his head before stepping down the stairs into the rubble piles. He sifted through them, trying to find hidden treasures, which to him, usually came in the form of art supplies.

Jae disappeared from the room. Donathan found a resting spot higher up on the stairs and sprawled out. After a few minutes passed and Ashley was sure no one would notice, she pulled a small block of wood and a needle from her pack, stabbing the needle into the top of the wood before setting it down on one of the stairs. Then she sat cross-legged, retrieving a thread from one of her other pack pockets.

Ashley sat staring at the block of wood with the tiny needle poking out of it.

"What are you doing?" Nyla asked.

Startled, Ashley looked behind her then sighed. "Something Waterfalz said... I'm trying to throw this thread through the needle."

Nyla asked, "From how far out?"

Ashley scrambled to her feet, blushing a bit. "From anywhere, really." She paused to look at the thread before holding it up and offering it to Nyla. "It's not working from ten feet out... or two inches."

Nyla took the thread and smiled sheepishly at Ashley before plopping down to face the needle mounted on the wooden block. Nyla's eyes focused on the eye of the needle, and she drew a deep breath.

Ashley stood up taller as she watched Nyla concentrating. Thoughts of dread filled her head as Ashley considered the fact that Nyla tended to accomplish most things she tried.

Nyla raised her right hand, holding the thread, until it was just under her nose. Not taking her eyes off the eye of the needle, she finally flicked her hand forward. The thread tapered through the air slowly and floated off to one side, falling a foot short of its intended target.

Nyla stood up and said in a determined voice, "Not possible. Not without changing some details. Perhaps you misheard her."

Ashley shrugged. "I don't..." Then she looked up, thinking about it. "Maybe."

From afar, the sound of shuffling items was followed by Mason gasping. More clutter fell as Mason scrambled over a pile of junk that he was salvaging in the back of the theater.

"Look!" Mason thrust out an arm in the dim lantern light, holding a card toward the rest of the room.

From halfway up the stairs where he was resting, Donathan lifted his head and peered over his right shoulder to his friends down below. "New art project?"

"No, it's a Garbage Pail Kid!" Mason gushed as he pulled it back, cupping it in his hands and staring at it. "A first edition, no less! Black borders and one of the best cards, Wendy Witch!"

In an instant, Ashley sprinted toward Mason. She leaped up the wall, ran two steps down its length and springboarded off it, over a pile of rubble. After plucking the card from Mason's grasp, she stuck her back toward him and hunched forward, staring at the card.

Mason protested and tried to reach around Ashley to grab the card, but she just gave him a sharp nudge backward and curled her shoulders in more to shield the card from his view.

Frustration and protests flooded out of Mason until he finally reached forward and dragged Ashley's bat out of its holster on her back. Ashley turned around to face him just as Mason choked up on the bat and swung in her direction. Ashley stepped back and out of the way, causing Mason's swings to whiff.

"Give it back, damn it!" Mason shouted sharply. He drew the

bat back farther, rage screaming from his eyes.

Suddenly sensing how furious he was, Ashley stepped back and, in a disgusted tone, said, "Ew! No."

Mason rushed forward, swinging the bat in an amateur overhead swipe while almost losing his footing. She stepped aside, but that time, she snapped a foot up and into Mason's backside as he passed her. His mask fell backward, clattering onto the floor as he stumbled onto a pile.

"We just going to let this happen?" Jae returned and was halfway up the stairs next to Donathan, shoveling microwave popcorn into her mouth.

The scent of freshly popped salted kernels filled the air.

Confused, Donathan looked from the bag up to Jae, studying her graying hair under her cloche for a moment before asking, "How did—"

"Found a microwave rigged up in the back of the main theater. I've been carrying this bag around for the last six months, waiting for an opportunity." She smiled widely. "I don't know how old they are. Safe money is on, well, over twenty years. Still taste okay, though." She cocked her head sideways, eyes wide as she grinned, holding the bag out toward Donathan.

Donathan hungrily grabbed a handful then turned his attention back to the fight. Through mouth-watering crunches, he managed to answer Jae's question from earlier. "Better to..." Crunch. "Not get involved." Crunch. "They'll drag you into it." Crunch. "Let them wind themselves down." Crunch. "Plus, more for us." He motioned to the popcorn bag and helped himself to another handful when Jae nodded approval.

Ashley picked up Mason's mask and perched it atop her head before dodging two more of his limp-wristed swings. He climbed on top of the rubble nearest the front door and was holding the bat straight up over his head, glaring down at Ashley with a look that was a mix of anger and fear.

"Well all right, now you're committed to this attack." Ashley reached up to lower the mask in front of her face, revealing a pixelated version of a firebird symbol. She turned to face Nyla's direction and said in a mocking impersonation, "Look ath me. Ah'm Mason. Ah have a machine gun Ah never fi-re." Ashley looked back and up just in time to see Mason lunging down at her with the bat. She easily slid under it then away and across the room until she was standing near the front door with her back facing the pile of rubble blocking their main exit.

"How do you see through this thing?" she asked, cocking her head from side to side. "And why does it smell like pork and diesel?"

Nyla held up a hand. "Wait!"

Everyone froze.

"I smell it too," Nyla whispered.

Mason stopped midstep, trying to keep still, balanced on one foot, the bat hefted up over his shoulder. A second of silence passed before he fell backward, sending the bat clattering across the room. Everyone else shushed him in frustration.

Nyla reached down to gather her belongings while keeping her eyes locked on the front door. Everyone else followed suit, and they made their way up the stairs to the second floor then up a ladder to a rooftop hatch. The light of a full moon cast down on the roof. The group crept over to the edge and peered down.

Nyla immediately sat back and signed, "It's a Match. It hasn't taken full notice of us yet."

After a moment, Nyla mouthed the word "Match" to Jae, who nodded. They'd learned a few days back that Princess Jae didn't know sign language. Mason spent an afternoon trying to teach her until she had finally managed to sign, "Go paint your face," to get him to leave her alone.

Jae sneaked up to the edge of the roof and balanced her rifle on the tiny hub wall, angling it downward.

Mason signed, "What is she doing? You said it hadn't noticed us."

Nyla nodded in the moonlight. "It won't take full notice of us right away. They're mostly blind. They don't smell too well, probably because they constantly smell of burnt flesh. If you alert it, then it flames to life."

"So why not just leave it alone?" Ashley signed while wrinkling her nose.

Nyla signed, "Normal breeds, yes, but a Match travels alone, and if it slightly senses people, it will follow them and stand in place for days, facing wherever it was disturbed, until something finally makes too much noise and it is certain someone is there, then..." Nyla signed the last word, "fire," with both hands. She took a deep breath then continued, "The Match is standing still like that, which means it took an interest when we went inside. It's going to wait there for us. We try to leave, and it hears even the slightest noise, it'll follow. We set it off in the open, we're finished. Either we try to kill it, or it tries to kill us."

Nyla continued, "I wish we could stay and study it. It looks like such an incredible specimen!" Her hand motions were quick and sharp, and a smile spread across her face.

Ashley always felt concerned when Nyla said things like that.

Ashley leaned up against the wall next to Jae, who was peering over it then back down to adjust her rifle. Ashley decided to edge up and peer over just for a second. A shadowy figure was standing on the other side of the street. It wore a pair of scorched blue jeans, no shoes, and no shirt. Its body seemed malnourished, and its hands and head were completely black. Ashley peered closer, trying to see features. Suddenly, a loud squeal erupted from behind her. Her vision blurred as she spun around, scrunching her nose, facing Donathan's narrowed eyes.

Donathan whispered, "What the fuck?"

Princess Jae shrugged forward off the wall and onto her knees. Her jaw hung low, her eyes wide as shock tattooed itself across her face. Mason was standing with nervous eyes, holding a deflating balloon in his right hand. He looked down sheepishly and, with a few more squeals of elastic and escaping air, managed to tie a knot around the balloon.

Ashley glanced over the wall at the creature, which seemed unfazed by the sounds and just continued holding its place. Annoyed, Ashley stood, stepping away from the roof's forward wall to jab Mason in the ribs while making a shushing sound. Taking the hint, Mason lowered his head in shame, letting the balloon drift out of his hand toward the ground.

A loud pop exploded in the night, and a chill of fear stomped through the group. The whole world seemed frozen in place for a moment. Ashley glanced around, taking stock of what had just transpired. Nyla had ducked down. Donathan had already drawn a pistol. Ashley found her hand raised as she'd subconsciously reached up over her shoulder for her bat. Princess Jae, for the second time, shot a dumbfounded look and directed it toward Mason.

After a moment, he whispered with forced tones while signing at the same time with sharp hand gestures, "Fine, fine! I'm sorry! Fine!"

Princess Jae slouched back down and stuck a shoulder up against the wall. After a moment, she slowly crept to the small ledge until she could see in the creature's direction. Ashley scrambled forward and let her head edge up until her nose was level with the top of the tiny wall.

The Match still stood in place, seemingly unaware of all the commotion. Ashley shot a confused look at Princess Jae, who seemed just as bewildered by the events. Jae shrugged.

White-hot lightning exploded through Ash's brain as a sudden sharp jolt of ripping paper burst through the dim night behind her. Everyone spun around with pointed stares of rage to find Mason hunched over, eyes angled up and tense, both of his hands holding recently torn halves of an ancient newspaper.

Exasperation hemorrhaged across Ashley's face as her arms and hands blurred into sign language so forceful it resembled kung fu. "Stop! Finished! No more!"

Everyone seemed to hold their breath, letting the night devour another minute. Finally, Ashley let her head rotate around to peer back over the wall at the zombie. It was still standing, frozen in time.

Ashley sniffed quietly.

The creature hunched forward and retched a stream of fire in Ashley's direction. The fiery blast dripped out of the air and down to the street below.

Ashley snapped, "Son of a bitch!"

Flames lit up the hollow cavities that had once housed the creature's eyes before it was undead. The orange fire fanned out to the rest of its face. The fire in its ocular cavities focused and shrank down to tiny red eyeballs. The creature stepped forward, flexing its skinny arms as flames spread down them, before screaming and running toward the building. Down below, the sounds of popping and hissing echoed as the theater started going up in flames.

Jae gasped out a lungful of frustration.

Nyla said, "I guess the truck is out because it's right next to the building."

Jae shrugged while taking a second to tug at her cloche. "It's just as well. I can't believe that thing still ran after the accident."

Orange flames were appearing on the wall nearest them. The group jogged to the edge of the rooftop that overlooked the roof of another building.

"All right, it's six hours until daylight," Donathan said. "How about we scamper out of here and try to find another building in town to hide out."

"No," Jae said. "That fire will become a beacon for everything within five miles. Even when daylight comes, they'll all try to hide out in the buildings around here to avoid it, and then we're twice as fucked." She sighed, still fussing with her hat's brim. "Let's just get down on the backside of this building and see if we can't head up that creek that we saw, coming into town, out of line of sight. With any luck, we'll find shelter or a vehicle a few miles up."

"Well, whatever we're going to do, we need to do it now," Nyla said as the roof started to creak from the flames beneath. With that, they jumped across to the next roof.

10.

Los Gatos
Ashley
Seven Years Earlier

"THERE ARE A FEW CARS here, Mom," Ashley observed as they crossed the parking lot in the dimming light.

"Maybe we can borrow one of them," Clarence added in a gruff voice. His bushy white eyebrows rose as he lifted the rifle in his right hand. After another step, he chuckled dryly. "Or just rent them their blood and flesh in exchange for our supplies and a vehicle." Clarence's face was grizzled and sharp with wrinkles and angles, as if he were a raisin fashioned into existence with a dull razor blade.

Ethel looked at the old man, studying his liver spots, untrimmed white beard, red flannel, and jeans. "I'm all for helping people out, but... Clarence, that's a little creepy to say in front of the children."

As if reassuring herself, Ethel looked down at the pistol in her right hand. However, she and Ashley knew they hadn't been able to afford ammunition for quite some time. They'd never told their companions.

The other woman traveling with them, named Angela, looked about forty-five. The weathering in her face and dark circles under her eyes could be deceiving. It gave her a gaunt, unhealthy appearance and made her seem otherworldly. When Ethel had asked Angela her age, she had told them twenty-four. She was most likely lying. Plenty of people did on the road. Trust wasn't doled out freely, even for the little things. Her weapon of choice was an old rusty shotgun that no one in the group was banking on ever being functional.

Clarence looked over at the two children, one young and the other only a foot shorter than the rest of them, then back at Ethel and said, "World's not fair, is it?" in a callous tone.

"Sup-piles? Mom, the sign pointing to the store says 'sup-piles.'" Ashley pointed at a large wooden sign propped up against the side of an old 1980s sedan in the parking lot. At the top of the sign was a large, black arrow pointing toward the grocery store.

"I think they mean 'supplies,'" Ethel replied.

"I think they mean 'trap,'" Clarence added.

Ethel stopped midstep and shot him a frustrated look.

"Whot?" Clarence's voice croaked. "This is Butcher country, after all."

"They're wives' tales." Angela's tone was cold and defensive. "High-functioning zombies that look and act like us. Hide amongst travelers to trick, trap, torture them before killing and eating them in grand, murderous ways? Complete bullshit." As Angela finished the tirade of words, she rolled her eyes.

Clarence laughed maniacally at the end of her speech.

Jennifer, a small blond girl with short-cropped hair and an oversized Batman T-shirt that seemed to be swimming on her little frame, had stopped walking and looked up at Angela with fearful eyes.

Ashley and Ethel had both taken notice of the strange rants. Mother and daughter locked eyes in concern. They had only just met those travelers one city over and agreed to head to Wanestown, a new makeshift shantytown that had just cropped up in Big Basin State Park. Beyond a night or two of brisk conversation in some tightly crammed spaces to avoid the darkness, they knew nothing about their new companions. The young girl had lost her parents and was just trying to find her uncle in Wanestown. The other two sort of overheard their conversation in the town square and offered coin for traveling companions. Ashley didn't want to go with anyone, but they offered enough money to fund a few meals and plenty of water for the road.

Both Ashley and Ethel had been struggling with hunger pains for days. They didn't exactly have a trade other than scavenging what they could. Ashley had heard some people could make big money scavenging, but they could probably afford tools to do so, maybe even vehicles. The two of them had to make do with their bare hands and aching backs. Once, they had carted an entire metal sink into a town, figuring they would get hundreds for it. Instead, the shopkeeper pissed and moaned that he'd just have to strip the piping from it and melt it down to be able to do anything with it. He offered them only a few bucks for their day-and-a-half trek with the giant sink. They were too tired to reject the offer and, for once, too tired to complain afterward. Those had been a long couple of days.

The sun was down far enough that the sky was orange and rising to blend with deep purples. Off in the distance, a screech broke the dusk sky.

"Won't be long now." Clarence chortled. "Best to take shelter inside the trap."

Ashley hated the man's sense of humor. She also hated the fact that he was probably right, but they didn't have many other options. Braving the trap was probably less dangerous than dealing with the undead outside, rending flesh from bone with their teeth. With any luck, they'd have enough money at least to secure their safety until sun up. With lots of luck, the place would be a legitimate supply depot with illiterate people running it.

Ashley couldn't tell if she wanted to laugh or cry at the frustration of knowing they were never that lucky.

Parking-lot lights hummed to life and lit up the subset.

"Lights?" Ashley's eyes were wide as she pointed, her head angled toward curve-topped lights with clam-shaped sconces covering their upper sides.

The beams of light that illuminated large circles of the parking lot were already attracting moths and mosquitos around their warm bulbs. Dust seemed to hang in place under the lights in the stale summer air.

"So a trap." Clarence chuckled.

"For Christ's sake!" Ethel stamped her feet during those last syllables. "It's okay, kids. They probably just have a generator to let travelers know there is shelter."

The grocery store had large rolltop security doors. The rest of the store seemed to be made of gray concrete that matched the paint job of a heavy metal door with a sharp, oversized pull handle on the front. Ethel approached the door apprehensively and, after a moment, summoned enough courage to knock. Clarence lowered his gun. A frustrated Ethel motioned for him to raise it again. He fumbled for words, claiming a senior moment, before reseating the buttstock in his shoulder and hefting the muzzle back up. The metal door creaked open after a moment, and a man with wavy dark-brown hair and nervous eyes peered back out. The muzzle of his rifle was wedged up and out the door, less to take aim and more to show the travelers that he was armed. Angela sidestepped out from behind Ethel and flashed her shotgun as a warning. Ethel stood, arms lowered and shoulders unsquared, trying to appear as nonthreatening as possible.

"Night falling. I suppose you want gas or shelter?" the man asked quietly.

"Just shelter," Ethel said. "We have coin."

"We're low on food supplies," the man warned.

"So are we," Ethel lied.

"Well now...hang on." The man backed away from the door, which slammed shut.

Aside from the buzz of crickets and the low hum of the parking-lot lights, no sound could be heard, not even the restless dead roaming the land at night.

Another minute passed, and Clarence cleared his throat violently. Angela shot an annoyed glance at him. Clarence just looked back at her and shrugged, letting his heavy eyebrows drift down in amusement.

Finally, the door creaked open. Ethel waved the children through and then went ahead of Clarence and Angela. When they were finally all the way through, the man with the wavy brown hair let go of the metal push bar on the door, allowing it to slam behind them. All the travelers spun on their heels to face him, staring uneasily. Clarence still hadn't remembered to reraise his rifle during the whole exchange. The man matched their gazes with an equal amount of apprehension. A loud buzz was originating from a black construction-sized generator chugging away in a dark, long-abandoned deli section off to their left. Not many lights were over there, and Ashley wondered how they ran it inside without much sound outside and without the fumes affecting them all.

"I'm Dean," the man said. "Those friends over there"—he nodded in the direction of one of the fluorescent-lit grocery aisles where two worn women, one blonde and one brunette, and a large, thick-muscled man with a white head and tank top stood—"are my only companions." The brunette woman held a rifle one-handed with the muzzle angled down. The blonde held a long pistol. The muscular man held just a two-by-four and nodded in their direction.

Dean cleared his throat once for effect. "As long as you don't try any funny business, we'll offer what trade we have here, let you stay the night, and you'll be on your way in the morning... If you try anything, though"—Dean nodded again in the direction of his friends—"we will take everything you've got and leave you out in the parking-lot lights for whatever undead roams through."

Ashley stepped close to her mom. Ethel lowered her arm holding the pistol and wrapped it around Ashley. Ashley in turn wrapped her arms around the tiny Jennifer.

Ethel said, "I don't think you'll have that problem with us. Just show us where we can sleep, and we'll be out of your hair."

"Fair enough," Dean replied.

He nodded past the clearing they were standing in, next to the maroon checkout counters with magazine racks and pillaged shelves. Some of the contents, dusty and ancient, had toppled out of their baskets and were shoved into piles on the floor. Cobwebs hung off some of the cash registers. As if taking a cue, the brunette woman walked over and motioned them to follow. She led the group past fully stocked shelves of groceries, drinks, candies, and batteries. The entire store passed. Some of the aisles seemed clean, stocked, and unaffected by the rampaging apocalypse outside its doors.

"They lied to us about the food," Ashley whispered to her mom.

Ethel whispered back, "We lied too," motioning to the large pack on her back.

Finally, the brunette woman passed an empty aisle, which was stripped bare, and walked them up the middle of another aisle that was just as barren of all items.

"Certainly aren't taking any chances of us stealing anything," Clarence commented and shrugged a shoulder in the direction of the empty shelving.

The brunette woman finally halted and turned around to face the group. "You'll sleep here. We'll go lights out in a half hour to conserve generator power and clean the air in here. At that time, we'll light a few lanterns and leave them around the store." The woman's tone seemed cold and rehearsed. "If you wish to buy or trade anything, my friends will be by just before lights out. We'll also drop off bathroom buckets, and our folks can take a list of what you need, and we'll have it prepared for when you leave in the morning." Her voice became forceful. "Do not leave this aisle. If we see you try to steal anything or come after one of us, we will shoot you. Do not leave this aisle." Then she seemed to prepare herself and added, "We're going to need your weapons."

"What?" Clarence groaned, his eyes wide and mouth hanging open.

"We're not going to be gunned down in the middle of the night. You want to rest, then pony up the weapons." Her forceful reply was aimed at Clarence.

Ethel asked, "What's to stop you from doing the same to us?"

The women turned to face Ethel and asked, "What's to stop you from heading back out into the night?"

All at once, the adults of the group looked defeated. Eventually, it was Angela who stepped up first and handed over her gun, followed by the rest of the group.

The woman accepted the weapons and paused to straighten the newly formed pile of equipment in her arms. "Now"—she regained some composure—"do you all have blankets?"

Ethel nodded as Ashley dug in her pack to find her blanket and set a large, green binder onto the tan linoleum next to her bag.

Jennifer stared at the binder before pointing at it and asking, "What's that?"

Ashley waited until the other woman trotted off then slowly flipped open the cover to reveal plastic pages filled with different collectible cards. "Mostly baseball cards, football cards, and various other strangeness we find on the road." Ashley looked up at Ethel then back at Jennifer's excited face. "My father and I used to collect them. He said, before the dead came, people would trade and sell them..."

"Are they worth anything now?" Jennifer asked.

Ashley pulled the binder closer to herself. "I don't know... I wouldn't sell them. They're..." She looked up to meet Ethel's gaze.

Ethel finished the sentence for her. "They remind her of her dad."

"Can I see them?" Jennifer asked with enthusiasm. After receiving a nod from Ethel, Ashley slowly pushed them in Jennifer's direction. Jen flipped through the pack, studying the images and comments on each card.

After a minute of observing the smaller girl, Ashley sighed and tugged her thick down sleeping bag from the bottom of her pack to spread it across the cold linoleum floor.

11.

Just outside Watsonville
Fine Line Protectorate
Present Day

TWO DAYS HAD PASSED—two long days without food, only water from a bucket with a ladle that they all had to share. The cement walls had to be a foot thick, and although a large bay window was there, the panes were reinforced with barely visible wire mesh throughout their length. An ancient television with rabbit ears was sitting in the corner of the room nearest the window. It was constantly on, and static blared throughout the night. Anytime they tried to shut it off, a blond orderly would appear from behind the desk-filled office area and shout, "It's television time!" Her hair was tied back in one long ponytail, a small paper nurse's cap perched on top of her head, and her blue scrubs had a name tag that read Bob. No one had bothered calling her Bob after the first day.

On their first night in captivity, the functioning electric lights had dimmed in the sterile, oversized room. Shadows lurked ominously in the corners as if waiting for the "patients" to lower their guard long enough to leap out from them. A large tanned man raged that night, throwing a wooden coffee table against a wall and demanding to be let out. The nurse walked in with a fur-suited individual whose bat face had a doctor's orthoscope above his left eye. The woman explained that they had just the treatment for him and that he'd never be worried again. The man protested and tried to fight the two individuals, only to be punched by the blond woman and sent careening into one of the concrete walls. She then spat on him and had her furry friend drag him out of the room. The tan-skinned man returned a few hours later with a bloody gash sewn up on the top of his head. The nurse propped him up against the far wall next to a thick, heavy wooden door where he stood, peering at the other occupants of the Asylum, for the next thirty-six hours. Not once did he sit down to rest, nor did he even respond when someone offered him a ladleful of water. He had, however, groaned and screamed at random intervals throughout the first night.

Janice could shut her eyes and still hear his voice and the random guttural syllables he was producing in the darkened room. Although six other patients were there, two of whom were rather large men, no one bothered to speak out or tried to overpower their captors after that display of force.

They had been told they were being evaluated for sanity and they would eventually meet with a doctor and be released. Every few hours, the blond nurse, Bob, would appear, call out a name repeatedly for several minutes, and after getting no response, return to the back, shaking her head. They only saw her when she was calling names or serving them another jug of water. That was maddening, but whenever they asked how long they'd be there, the nurse would say in a matter-of-fact tone that they "had to go in order of the file names" and that they would "get to them eventually." She always seemed very put off at having to repeat the line.

The only chairs in the main room were frustrating, torturous creations. The backs came up at too sharp of an angle to sit comfortably, unless you were completely straight-backed, which made slouching or lounging give you sharp lower-back pains eventually. The sides of the chairs were large flattened wooden planks that had been smoothed and lacquered. The chairs themselves were like three-walled boxes. Once or twice, Janice had pushed two chairs together to create a makeshift bed. However, if they were spaced too far apart, her back would sag painfully out of it, and if they were pushed too close together, she could get only her upper torso in it and had to let her legs and arms dangle up and out of it. The limbs would eventually go numb, and she'd give up on the technique for a few hours.

She had no blankets or pillows through the cold nights.

In the daytime, for some reason, they would turn the lights on to a blindingly mind-numbing level of fluorescent, and either the doctor with his exaggerated hand gestures or the nurse and her barking frustrations would order everyone to sit up, even refusing to let the few who wanted to sleep on the cold, hard linoleum to sprawl out.

"Meal time!" Nurse Bob was pushing out a meal cart. "Scrumptious and utter dee-delicious, dahlings."

The six "patients" rushed out to line up near the cart, all starving after their two days of incarceration. A red-haired woman made it in line ahead of Janice. Nurse Bob opened the cart, placed a plate into the woman's hands, then shoved her aside. Suddenly, a bowl was thrust into Janice's hand, and she was forcefully pushed away as well.

Janice reached for the spoon then realized what the mass in the center of her bowl was. "I've had it! It's bad enough we're living with no end in sight, not knowing what we did or why we're here, but now this?" She motioned down at her bowl, her hand a sharp knife edge of frustration.

"What? Something wrong with the food?" the woman asked in a shocked voice while adjusting her Bob name tag.

Janice stomped a foot and announced, "Yes, of course something is wrong with the food!"

As she finished talking, one of the men, balding and appearing to be in his late forties, stepped up next to her, nodding.

"Are you making demands of us, patient?" Nurse Bob glared at Janice while flaring her nostrils.

Janice furiously replied, "I'm not a patient... My name is Janice!"

The woman studied Janice for a moment before shouting, "Chef Gobbles! Che-e-efff Gobbllles!"

All of the patients winced and tried to cover one of their ears with their free hands as her voice became a shriek on the last two words.

Back behind the office area, a door slammed. The fur-suited doctor came first, followed in tow by a pudgy man wearing a white, stained T-shirt and a big floppy chef's hat. The furry doctor came to a halt next to Nym, placing his hands on his bat-costumed face in shock as Chef Gobbles came to a stop on the other side of Nym.

"Yesss, Nym?" Goblin asked.

Nym sniffed. "This...Janice over here says something is wrong with the food." As she spoke, she extended an accusing finger, pointing directly at Janice.

"What's wrong with the food?" Goblin's mouth hung open as he glanced from the bowl back to Nym.

"For starters..." Janice lowered her free hand into the bowl and, with her thumb and forefinger, carefully lifted a severed foot out of her bowl. "You're trying to feed us flesh! You're trying to turn us into the undead!"

Goblin cleared his throat before squaring his shoulders and replying, "That's soup...straight from the can."

"You don't even give us anywhere to sleep? I mean, we're sort of safe from the darkness outside," Janice reasoned, "but the least you could have done is give us a place to sleep." Her eyes pleaded with them for a morsel of sanity.

"There are beds in the back room!" Nym answered in shock as the furry doctor nodded to her in support.

Janice drew a forced breath before whispering painfully, "Can we at least push the three-foot-high piles of living worms that are covering the beds, onto the floor?"

Goblin looked quizzically at Janice. "But uhhh..." He held the last syllable to emphasize his confusion. "Where would the worms sleep?"

Janice threw both the soup and the foot to the ground. The bowl clattered off toward the darkened window before she clenched her fists and tensed up, angling her face towards the roof to scream, "Why are you doing this?"

Nym raised an eyebrow toward Goblin, who just shrugged back. She squared her shoulders before turning back to Janice to answer, "Well, I mean, Mercury is in retrograde after all."

Goblin burst out laughing at that point, repeating, "Mercury in...fucking retrograde!" He had to force the words through loud guffaws.

The furry doctor leaned forward at that point, placing his hands on his knees, his fur-suited head bobbing up and down though no laughter issued forth.

Goblin had tears in his eyes and pointed at the furry doctor. "Even fucking Crooks is laughing!"

Janice had finally had it. She sprinted at Nym with clenched fists. In an instant, Nym grabbed one of her outstretched arms, spun on a heel, and slammed the screaming Janice into the cold ground. Janice screamed gibberish through sheets of pain.

Nym stood the woman back up and told her, "I think you need an hour or two in solitary!"

Crooks, Goblin, and Nym surrounded the woman and heaved her struggling form toward the thick wooden door that the vacant-eyed man stood near. Crooks rushed ahead of the group and patted down the waist of his suit before producing a key from some unknown pocket and unlocking the door. He placed his back to the door, facing the group forcing the woman along, then twisted the knob, leaning out slowly.

Green and white, pale, sickly hands pawed their way through the opening. A zombie's face with a sharp nose hissed through the crack in the door. Some of the patients watching the scene gasped as Janice screamed, her appendages and torso forced through the small opening between the door and its frame. Arterial blood sprayed through, covering the three orderlies as they worked to shut the door, eventually leaving one of Janice's severed legs behind, still twitching.

Nym took hold of the severed leg and stood up, wiping the blood from her face before adding, "Any more complaints about the food?"

No one spoke up.

"Well then," Nym continued. "Tomorrow, we'll be serving Janice!"

12.

Just outside Mountain View
Razorwrist
Present Day

"MARSHLANDS," Razorwrist chirped. "That'll do just fine."

He nodded his bald head with a mishmash of scars stretching in random places across his flesh before turning to admire his undead followers. Tall ones, skinny ones, fat ones, any that were within a five-mile radius were stalking around with him. They'd grown and changed since he'd last walked with them. Their numbers had indeed increased, but so too had their special abilities. Some were, of course, defiant. Some would have to be tamed, and some might have to die off. Twice in the previous night, he had run across a few who had to be forced to follow his lead, and he could only control those for so long. Eventually, he edged too far from them or just lost his train of thought, and they would all bolt away into the night.

Queens had always been a source of frustration for him. Yes, something certainly would have to be done.

The hordes there were good, though. The skinny ones that hunted well together, screeching and leaping into things, certainly had their uses. He'd found Dredges that could latch onto a person and hold them down while they sprayed a toxin both in gas and liquid forms that would paralyze some of the living. That was useful. Some with oversized teeth resembled sharks more than humans. Others could even control base elements like fire or lightning. Some hunted in numbers and had staked out territory that he was passing through while others seemed to roam alone. So many different breeds now. Such a fun world...

"Some are old, and some are new. Some are red, and some are blue." Razorwrist cackled after reciting the bastardized lines from a childhood book, words that seemed to fade in from the wind and get caught in the branches of his mind.

Death twisted below him, catching somewhere underneath him. Its icy tendrils were taking hold of whatever life was being purged somewhere in the mud and salt water. It all mixed below Razorwrist's feet, forming the marsh. The smell there was overwhelming. He could feel the darkness dancing with him where he stood, slowly sinking into the murky mud below. Death wanted to drag everything down except his creatures. Only his creatures and the reeds seemed to lurk here. He nodded at the closest monster, who turned and hissed to the others. They began to fan out, to hunt. Some of the solo creatures were adjusting to the larger group under his leadership. Many of his underlings would return, and some would even bring live tribute. Razorwrist thought back to the first night that a large fat man was brought into his kingdom of undeath. Once the man figured out Razorwrist could reason with him, the man would not stop screaming and pleading for his life. Razorwrist would have considered turning him into one of his own if the man hadn't been so pathetic about it. Eventually, the man succumbed, and

Razorwrist's belly filled.

He felt some of the darkness slink off, away from his control, trying to find their quarry. That was all right. Plenty of darkness existed in the world, with not enough food to go around. The fewer, the better, for now. His power would grow the longer he walked among them. Eventually, the whole world would kowtow to his will.

"No. Not you. Skinny thing. I'll call you Tom." Razorwrist motioned to one of the nearby creatures clacking its teeth and trying to slink off, its arms pulled in tightly like two tiny claws waiting to strike out. The monster hunched forward, and it would often cock its head from one direction to another, chirping unholy noises until it made eye contact with its prey. Razorwrist had seen those divine creatures function the first night. One would screech, and the others would descend upon their prey. Such teamwork, such glory. He decided one of those should remain close to him at all times—his royal guard, so to speak.

"Tom." Razorwrist paused as the creature skulked in close, angling its head sharply to one side, its eyes staring off into the sky. "Have you ever heard Mary Shelley's fairy tale, Frankenstein?"

Tom clacked his teeth, and Razorwrist knew he'd never have a decent conversation with the fellow.

He continued anyway. "The tale is a great one. You see, there's a mad scientist creating life in a cold, dark, gloomy"—Razorwrist looked around at the dark sky and the brightly lit moon—"part of the world." He crouched his skinny form and thrust one of his hands into the marsh below him and drew up a handful of mud and soot, bringing it close to his face and smelling it before letting out a childish giggle. "Not so different from this place." He nodded in Tom's direction as if he were receiving a response from the quite undead fellow. "Fair enough. I've never been in a castle. At least, I don't believe I have." Razor's stare was far off for a moment as his mind drifted into the abyss. He felt even more of his minions slip away under their own guidance again. Ah well.

Razorwrist dropped both of his hands and thrust them deep into the mud. He felt it blossom off himself, the darkness of the infinite black spilled forth from his chest, down his arms, and erupted cold into the mud and soil. It drifted down and it spread out, but as it expanded, it only grew in strength.

"Such a holy place." Razorwrist's darkness bled out and down.

He felt the last gasp of living things. He felt their final cries, their secrets spilled forth, their sights, smells, and ultimate feelings of accepting eternity into their cold lungs as their hearts pumped their last beats. He felt their flesh rot and slip off their forms. Darker creatures were pulsing through them, feeding on their death, growing life from them and finally succumbing to more death. He felt sulfur gases pulsing up through the muck. Eventually, his power waned, and he could feel life in the reeds, growing its sickly, sweet energy from his power. His breath grew ragged, and he felt life clawing at the gray matter of his mind. He pulled back, gasping.

Razorwrist reached deeply again, calling for calcium. Pockets of white and gray emerged in bubbly masses, twisting and warping. Bones and teeth rose through the mud. Their masses breached the surface, glazed bright white as the murky water drained off them. Clumping together, the whiteness of long-dead skeletal structures pulsed and glowed as Razorwrist willed the matter to crumble. Eventually, the hill-shaped mass of white and gray filled a twenty-five-foot-square space in front of him. He flexed and pulled his power from the ground below until it completely encompassed the base of the remains before him. Razorwrist screamed, letting pain jolt through him. The ground shook, echoing as he chose a form, and the skeletal remains stretched into being. He paused a moment to admire his work.

"Tom," Razorwrist said to the creature that the rest of the world called a Raven. "Mary Shelley's tale describes a mad scientist who creates life from a mass of dead things. She seemed pretty in tune with how things work—bone and flesh sewed together to bring things to a simpler form of life.”

Razorwrist's hands twisted in the muck, and he closed them until he formed fists filled with the bacteria-laden salt-and-fresh-water compound. Then he pulled them both out of the mud and held them aloft.

“We need flesh!” Razorwrist flexed his back and smashed both of his fists forward, sending water splashing ahead of him.

As the wave spread out, instead of dying down, it rose in a mass, bringing rotting carcasses to the surface and spilling their mass forward. The smell of various states of decomposition was acrid and overwhelming. Even some of the undead backed away. The sound of ethereal screams echoed as a pile of death flowed like water over the skeletal carcass, stitching and binding itself to the mass until a giant, lizard-like creature lay with water and mud washing up against its cold gray skin in the marshlands. Its broad muzzlelike head and high-browed arch with multicolored patches of flesh lay angled and lifeless as the Raven stalked forward, sniffing the air from afar and studying its mass.

“You see, Tom, Dr. Frankenstein creates a monster. But by the end of the story, after the monster comes to life, the power dynamics change. He turns on his creator, and he is the one holding power.” Razorwrist dusted off one shoulder and grinned at Tom before quoting Dr. Frankenstein, “If the multitude of mankind knew of my existence, they would do as you do and arm themselves for my destruction. Shall I not then hate them who abhor me?”

Razorwrist sighed, admiring the oversized monstrosity he'd created before turning back to Tom and adding, “The real monster in this world...is man.”

As if he had understood Razorwrist's point, Tom the Raven spun around and chirped.

Razorwrist stepped up to the giant flesh-golem dragon and placed a hand upon its beaklike nose. “The reason I'm here is to rebalance the system. I'm here to hunt the hunter. I'm here to prove there is always something more monstrous than man." He lunged back, holding his hands before him as if presenting something while grinning widely in Tom's direction.

The wind picked up and drifted through the reeds, creating a rustling noise as their masses shifted and leaned in the muddy land.

After a moment, Razorwrist turned and shot a confused look at the dead dragon formed from the myriad of undead flesh. "I'm missing something." He paced back and forth in front of the dead creature. "Flesh, bone, sinew, fangs...I'm missing something." He paused to apologize to Tom as he strode past. "It's been so long since I've fashioned something so large... It's... Aha!" Razor exclaimed while spinning around to face the creature. "In Frankenstein"—he edged forward another step, raising a fist before opening his palm and pointing a lone finger at the creature—"when the scientist creates life"—kneeling down, he let one knee lower into the mud before whispering—"it was a dark and stormy night."

A crack of thunder shattered the clear evening. A blinding azure streak jolted up around Razorwrist. Bending its form in an instant into crisscrossing forked snake tongues, a single large blue bolt leaped into Razorwrist's frame and jumped from his pointing finger into the oversized creature's twitching mass.

The Raven screeched at the sky as the oversized lizard opened its hollow eye sockets. The dragon fumbled slowly to its feet until it was finally standing on all four legs, stretching while emitting a low, guttural noise. The sound grew in bassy tones until it leaned back its elongated head and roared toward the sky. In a sudden flourish, its wings twitched to life and rose alongside the creature. The bones laid throughout them and the ethereally stitched flesh formed a spider-web pattern across their length.

"Yes! Yes! It's alive!" Razorwrist screamed and violently shook his arms toward the creature as Tom cried out alongside the undead dragon. "Rise! Dagron! Rise, O mighty Dagron the

Dragon!" Razorwrist exclaimed in an excited, high-pitched voice, pleased with his bastardization of language and of life.

Dagron flexed downward then leaped up into the sky, his great fleshy wings making whump-whump sounds as they generated huge gusts of wind, forcing reeds into the mud and causing Razorwrist to shield his eyes with one hand from the suddenly blustery night as he watched his dragon ascend.

"Now," Razorwrist shouted, "we are going to show the living what a real monster is!" He watched Dagron the Dragon's form grow smaller as the creature faded off into the night.

Razorwrist felt the creature's presence wane as it flew farther and farther away.

The night fell silent. Even Tom the Raven was quiet.

"Dagron?" Razorwrist called out. "The Dragon...? Did you...?"

Finally, staring at the horizon and accepting defeat, Razorwrist murmured, "Well, fuck."

13.

Six Miles outside Gilroy
Zombie Civil Rights Group
Present Day

"ARE WE FAR ENOUGH AHEAD?" Ashley whispered. "It's not like we've heard any noise in a while."

"Yeah, I think so," Jae whispered.

Donathan sized up the giant sycamores above, their trunks extending into the night sky, partially blocking out the moon. "At least there's plenty of big trees. We might be hidden from sight."

Ashley glanced over at Mason, who had just finished painting his mask. He had been working on it the whole way, crafting some pattern that was difficult for her to see in the dark. Mason smiled and raised the mask onto his head until it was seated comfortably, its hidden image facing skyward.

Donathan stretched, then in a flash, he was gone and standing up above them on the edge of the creek, looking back down. He smiled and waved at the rest of them.

"Show off," Jae muttered.

"Not one more fucking inch." A shotgun racked as a man spoke behind Donathan.

Donathan sighed, raised his hands, and turned slowly to face the man. The man's dark form lurched forward, smashing Donathan in the face with the buttstock and sending him careening back down into the creek. Ashley gasped. Two more shadows of men appeared at the edge of the creek, looking down at the group, rifles in hand and their muzzles all aimed in Donathan's direction.

"He's the one they warned us about." Someone holding another flashlight appeared, and the light felt sharp and bright in Donathan's eyes. "We'll have to deal with him now." The voice had all the warmth of a black-masked executioner.

Mason lowered one of his raised hands slightly until he tapped the top of his classic-style hockey mask, dropping its plastic expanse over his face to reveal a picture of a painted blue beartrap on a forest floor. Its teeth were silver, and two had white points painted on their tips so that they looked sharp and dangerous.

Ashley looked up long enough from Donathan to mouth a quiet question in Mason's direction, "How do you do this?"

"Whoa whoa whoa whoa!" Princess Jae announced, stepping in front of Donathan as one of the rifles cocked. "Guys, I don't know what you think you know, but we are on official Protectorate business on our way to Falling Sands as a personal favor for the Judge." Her hands slowly lowered toward a pistol tucked in her belt.

With a crack of gunfire, scattershot rounds impacted the dirt near Princess Jae's feet.

A dim green light bloomed up the tree trunks and canopy behind their attackers. None of the men with drawn weapons seemed to notice it.

The man facing Donathan said, "I recognize your face too.

You're hung up near every field office around Falling Sands and practically every major enclave down the Shytown trial." The man sighed a moment as if admiring his work. "You all will ensure we're never hungry again. They might even let us live in their enclave land that branches across Stockton for turning you five in!" As the man's friends all perked up at the mention of Stockton, the man paused as if re-evaluating the situation. "Well, the four prisoners and one corpse." With that, his rifle swung back in Donathan's direction.

The light had become a glowing lime green behind the men. It was bright enough that even though its source was behind the men, Donathan could make out their grizzled facial features, short beards, leather hats, and jackets. Their weapons didn't look the least bit rusted or worn—bounty hunters for sure, but not exactly pros—probably been watching long enough to see the Match go off, maybe even shadowing their movements on the side of the creek.

A young girl's laugh erupted from the tree line.

One of the men spun around and shouted, "What the fuck is that?"

The shock of their comrade's sudden exclamation caused the rest to turn on their heels to face the source of the green light. Sensing their moment, Ashley and Jae tried to sprint up the creek's steep bank while Mason and Nyla stood there staring upward for a moment until they realized what everyone else was doing and followed suit.

Donathan stumbled to his feet and surged up the bank until he was standing on the edge of the creek. In an instant, he tore the shotgun out of the hands of one of the men and then turned, smashing it into the face of his friend. With another step, he jolted into his power and crashed an upraised foot into another man's back, sending him flying forward toward a glowing green girl. The world warped and chugged back into motion around Donathan as he froze, trying to figure out what he was seeing.

The bright-green girl giggled, her feet floating a few inches above the ground. Her outline was the source of the glow. It would brighten and dim every other second, casting its light off the tree trunks and leafy foliage above it. Her hair was tied back in pigtails and slightly lighter than the rest of her form. Her eyes glowed bright yellow, never seeming to illuminate or dim with the rest of her form. Patches of energy drifted lazily across her skin.

She giggled again, that time jumping up slightly and forward until she landed with her knees bent and her head forward, slapping both hands down on her knees in a playful manner. She was facing the man who had previously held a shotgun toward Donathan and was now scrambling to get to his feet.

"Play!" The girl laughed maniacally, her form brightening to an almost blinding intensity.

Ashley and Jae rushed over the edge of the bank and stood next to Donathan, watching the scene unfold.

"Don't you want to?" the otherworldly girl questioned, her voice seeming to drift from an unknown source echoing around them.

The man still trying to get to his feet looked back in Donathan's direction, eyes screaming with fear, his trimmed white goatee tinged by the jade light. The wrinkles on his face were slight but still showed he had seen the world long before it fell. He looked to be about Princess Jae's age.

"Please, God, help!" the man cried out in their direction.

Mason and Nyla ran up to Donathan, who glanced over at Nyla. She backed away, taking the cue, as Donathan raised both arms, angling the shotgun between his friends and the phosphorescent girl.

The older man managed to stand up and lean forward, taking one sprinting step away from the specter.

"I said play!" The girl's form still seemed to glow green, but her eyes flashed from yellow to red as she lunged toward the fleeing man and disappeared into him.

The man spasmed violently as he floated forward and then upward a foot until he was hanging in the air, bobbing slightly. The surprise at seeing the girl vanish and the man float stopped the group midstep. The hovering fellow looked as if he was trying to scream and gasp at the same time. He tried to sprint but was still suspended in place. His skin appeared to be smoldering green in splotches across his cheeks. The man raised his hands to study them, watching the skin peel back and melt away in spots. The sleeves of his leather jacket were also dissipating in smoke and bright-green embers. A red cloud drifted out of the pockets of glowing green flesh and engulfed the man and his clothing. Three seconds later, all that was left was a dark crimson cloud, and the glow changed from green to red until, all at once, the cloud pulsed and the crimson drained away, revealing a glowing green version of the man standing in front of them, with a pale lime goatee and brightly lit yellow eyes.

The man smiled, his gruff voice issuing forth as the yellow eyes became red, and he shouted, "Play!" He leaped forward, his body diving into Donathan's and vanishing as Donathan felt his feet leave the ground.

For Donathan, a moment of confusion was followed by a sudden realization that he had no oxygen. He convulsed and kicked his feet, spinning in the air to face his friends. The texture on his skin felt cold and slick. He felt as if he was moving slowly as gelatin enveloped him. He could feel it stretching across his skin, pulling at his flesh, and creeping up his nasal passages. Bubbles drifted past his face as they shifted through the translucent mass.

Donathan tried to surge and felt the jelly shift around him violently. He reached a stiff membrane that repeatedly bounced his seizure-like shift back. The jelly clouded with bubbles around him until, after a second, it subsided as his strength felt overpowered. The mass of gelatin felt thicker, stronger, its entire form stiff and impeding his movements. Donathan thought to reach for his pistols but couldn't even move his wrists at that point. His cheeks, arms, and parts of his legs were burning. A sort of gelatinous gray smoke seemed to drift slightly up and past his eyes, which were rapidly glazing over. Donathan tried to blink the mess of slime out of his eyes.

Outside his gooey cocoon, all four of his friends were looking up at him. Nyla shrugged with a concerned look on her face toward Mason, whose mask was raised again, and then back at Ashley. Mason reached down, secured his machine gun, and fired a burst of rounds into the creature's form, creating a loud braaap that echoed through its mass. It jolted and bubbled as it had a few seconds before, but none of its form gave way. When the bubbles thinned, Donathan could see Ashley's face raging. She drew her bat from its holster and smashed it violently toward Donathan. Each time it connected with the barely visible membrane, a thuk could be heard echoing through the creature. His whole body felt sharp, and his mind was screaming with pain.

Princess Jae stepped forward, grabbed Ashley by one of her shoulders, and threw her back and away with force. She drew a pistol and pressed it up against the membrane of the creature and pulled the trigger. A heavy object suddenly smashed into Donathan. An abrupt flash and rush of sound exploded into the night as Donathan fell backward onto the sandy soil, covered with a thick layer of green slime. Hands reached forth out of the evening, raising him up into a standing position as two people rushed up under his shoulders and arms to hold him up. The world turned from gray to black as Donathan drifted into unconsciousness.

———

When they had finally found a road with an old wooden bridge extended across the creek, they decided they'd had enough of the night. The group opted to stay under the bridge to wait out the last few hours of darkness in hopes that no other creature would choose to take shelter from the light there as the sun came up.

"What the fuck was it?" Ashley asked.

Nyla answered in a matter-of-fact tone, "I don't actually know what anyone calls it. I've only seen them two times. They're rare to encounter. I call them ghosts."

"That was a ghost?" Mason's eyes went wide, and his mouth hung open.

"Not really, no," Nyla answered. "It's some kind of undead. It certainly dies to my antiundead system of electricity, so I can only assume it's some zombie, but it's... It actually reminds me of a jellyfish..." She brushed and shrugged off the observation before straining under one of Donathan's slime-covered shoulders as they lumbered toward a comfortable spot in the creek bed under the bridge. "For obvious reasons."

Nyla and Ashley leaned forward, lowering Donathan onto the ground as Princess Jae stepped out a few feet, aiming her rifle into the darkness, providing security as the rest of them waited for the night to end. Mason unstrapped his machine gun and walked to the other side of the group, laying it down on the rocks and dirt and taking up a sector of fire in the opposite direction of everyone else.

"I've never seen anything like that," he whispered as he got comfortable.

"I have," Princess Jae grunted from the other side of the hasty camp. "Only a nightmare level of flame and heat can usually destroy those things. I had no idea if that would work or not."

With a confused look, Ashley asked, "What exactly happened there?"

Princess Jae cleared her throat and said, "I'll explain whenever Donathan wakes up. No sense in going over this twice. How's he look?"

"He'll live," Ashley said in a relieved tone as Nyla fumbled through her pack for medicinal supplies.

"With the headache he is going to wake up with, I bet he'll wish he hadn't," Princess Jae whispered as she settled in, eyes scanning the darkness as she waited for the night to end.

14.

Los Gatos
Ashley
Seven Years Earlier

ASHLEY SAT UP suddenly, wondering what noise was piercing her eardrums. Her eyes took a few seconds to focus on the scene in front of her. A large puddle of blood had spread across the linoleum floor, its length edging closer toward Ashley's blanket-clad feet. The lights were bright. The generator was buzzing across the supermarket. Angela was screaming and clutching a bloody stump where her right hand once was, jamming what looked like handfuls of napkins against it.

How long has this all been going on? The contents of her bag lay spilled in the crimson puddle. Streams of words fell out of Ethel where she stood next to Angela, trying to calm her down and trying to get a hand past Angela's panicked, flailing arms to help staunch the flow of blood.

Clarence stood on the far side of the aisle, staring blank faced at Angela. The only thing that seemed to galvanize him into action was Ethel screaming at him, "For fuck's sake, Clarence, help!"

A moment later, Dean and a blond woman showed up, surprised and panicked. Dean was holding a shotgun. The blond woman was cradling a long-muzzled pistol in one of her hands. Both were demanding to know what had happened.

Ethel spun to face the duo as Clarence took over trying to help Angela. "Like you don't fucking know?" she said in an accusatory tone.

"No," Dean said, stepping back and raising the iron sights of his shotgun. "We don't know. We've been watching the doors and alternating guard and rest shifts." Then to demonstrate that he wasn't afraid of the woman, Dean sniffed before adding, "We haven't been within fifty feet of the rest of you."

Angela collapsed into a mumbling, weeping bloody mess on the floor.

Ethel's face lit up with fury. "Well, she certainly didn't chop off her own hand in her sleep."

"She could have," Clarence added drily. "I mean, anything is possible in this world these days."

"Isn't she your friend?" little Jennifer whispered to Clarence.

Clarence shook his head. "I had met her only a day before I met the rest of you."

"She didn't cut off her own hand, Clarence!" Ethel's frustration was boiling over as she stomped her feet and almost slipped in the puddle of blood.

Dean lowered his rifle, appearing as confused as the rest of the group.

His blond companion asked incredulously, "How would someone not see the person cutting off her hand?"

Through loud sobs, Angela explained that she couldn't feel pain from what was left of her wrist. Whoever had chopped off her hand had numbed it somehow. She hadn't felt a thing until she woke up bleeding everywhere.

"Are you certain there's no undead in this building?" Ethel asked Dean and the woman.

Dean responded forcefully, "Are you?" Then, pointing his barrel in a nasty form of accusation, he let his shotgun muzzle dance its aim among the heads of the newcomers while he said, "Any one of you could be one of those Butchers."

A moment of uncomfortable silence passed.

Suddenly recognizing the gravity of the situation, Ethel said in a calm voice, "Give us our weapons...and we will be on our way."

"Fine with us," Dean told her, "but you're going to have to ask Miller for your weapons."

Ethel nodded with wide eyes to the rest of the group, who hastily shoveled their bloodied items and blankets into their packs. Ethel managed to get Angela's pack on over her own before helping the trembling Angela to her feet.

A minute later, Dean and the blond woman were leading them back up the empty aisle and toward the front of the store. The group passed the checkout lines and walked into the darkened deli section past the gas-guzzling, fume-spewing generator and toward a shadowed corner. A set of purple velvet steps led up to a curtained plateau roughly five feet above the group. The curtains were thick, crushed red velvet and hung from a bar mounted on the edge of one aisle toward the back corner of the store. Dean reached into one of the aisle shelves, and a pop from a power strip could be heard. Each of the steps was illuminated by small spotlights aimed from various angles up above the aisle. After another second, white Christmas lights wrapped around the curtain rod hanging above lit up. Their white glow created strange shadows at the top of the red velvet curtains. Dean's other companions, the brunette woman holding up a rifle and the burly man brandishing a two-by-four walked up behind the group.

"Da hell is this?" Clarence asked with a quaking voice.

Dean looked shocked at Clarence and hefted the muzzle of

his shotgun up to his shoulder, letting the weapon point up lazily toward the ceiling. "I told you," he said snidely, pointing up toward the top of the curtain-covered stairs. "You have to ask Miller for your weapons."

Clarence and Ethel exchanged frightened glances over the top of Angela's head as Ethel tugged her close. Jennifer stepped up close to Ashley, burying her face in Ash's shirt, trying to hide the scene from her eyes.

Silence drifted through the store as the four denizens just stared at the newcomers until Clarence finally stepped forward facing the stairs, cleared his throat, and asked weakly, "Uh...can we...have our weapons?"

"Not like that," Dean corrected the man. "You have to pay respect first." Then lowering his gun and aiming it at Clarence, he said with force, "On your knees."

Clarence was wide eyed but slowly let his knees buckle until he was kneeling toward the stairs and fumbling over his words. "Mr. uhh... Miller...sir, please give us our weapons back."

"Screw this," Ethel whispered and nudged Angela into Ashley and Jennifer.

Everyone got the clue and backed away, leaving Clarence on his knees begging the hidden Miller. After two steps, the large man with the two-by-four forcefully nudged Ethel and Angela forward. Angela fell screaming onto the linoleum, clutching at her wounded arm.

"Everyone!" The brunette woman exclaimed fanatically. "Pay homage to Miller! Our king!"

Dean began chanting, "All hail Miller. All hail our leader," nodding repetitively as the words fell out of his mouth.

His comrades, picking up the cue, repeated the litany aloud. Clarence also matched his words. Dean dropped to his knees, facing the steps and waving his shotgun in the air. He increased the speed of his chant. The blond woman, aiming her gun at Ethel, stepped forward and kicked the back of Ethel's knees. She fell forward. The brunette woman was screaming the chant behind them. The children slunk down to their knees.

"I said homage!" the brunette woman screamed and waved her gun in the direction of the children.

Everyone chanted, "All hail Miller. All hail our leader."

Minutes seemed to become hours. Ashley was crouched down at a strange angle, looking up the stairs towards the curtain trying to make sense of everything. Finally, the burly man stepped up toward the stairs, reached forward to take hold of the crushed velvet curtains, and in one quick movement, flicked them back to reveal a metal folding chair at the top of the stairs. Perched on the seat of the chair was a lone, empty Miller High Life bottle. The chanting came to a sudden halt as the residents of the store all burst out laughing.

Dean turned to the blond woman and shouted, "I fucking told you we could get them to worship a beer bottle!"

"I mean, it's not really a fair bet," Blondie protested. "After all, they didn't know what they were worshipping."

The burly man with the two-by-four stepped past the stairs toward Dean and, through fits of laughter, added, "Also, we had to do it at gunpoint. Still an amazing feat."

"A bet's a bet," Brunette replied. "Dean and I win."

The visitors scrambled to their feet and tried to help gather up Angela. Dean stepped forward and kicked Angela out of their grasp. Ethel fell back, still trying to keep hold of her.

Blondie rushed forward to step on Angela's stump, pinning her, struggling and screaming, to the ground by her injured wrist. "Dibs!"

"No way, bitch! Dean and I called first pick." Brunette stepped forward, stamping a foot and pointing. "And I choose her!"

With the last word fading, Brunette fell upon Angela, sinking her teeth into the woman's face. Blood spurted up and out as Blondie hissed and lunged at Clarence, dragging him off his feet.

Ethel kicked at the burly man's legs and succeeded in causing him to slip in the growing puddle of blood. Dean lunged at Ashley and Jennifer. Ashley instinctively shoved Jennifer behind her while kicking the man in the groin. He hunched forward with a wheezing sound. Ethel ran toward the kids and pushed Dean hard in the back, knocking him off his feet.

"Run!" Ethel screamed at the children.

15.

Gilroy
Zombie Civil Rights Group
Present Day

"SAGE POWERS are a bit different from Champions'," Princess Jae said as they strolled up the ramp of a parking garage.

The midday sun was shining over the open safety walls and across the faded and chipped painted lanes.

Donathan glanced in her direction and asked, "Different how?"

"Well, for starters, we all began as Champions." Her face scrunched up a bit as she looked upward momentarily before adding, "I think... Waterfalz might be a whole other story."

Mason had lolled behind the group, fumbling with the solar charger on his backpack. Donathan and Ashley both had official-looking manufactured solar chargers mounted on the center of their packs. Each folded out with petal-like arms, causing the solar panels to resemble a flower. Mason's solar power came from a makeshift charger fashioned from a piece of a solar panel with the shape of a flower painted across it. Jae remembered Donathan telling her once that Mason's charger was finicky and unlike the rest of the group's gear. He always had to fuss with its cable to get power to trickle in.

Jae glanced back in his direction before striding forward and continuing with her story. "I don't know what causes the change, but some Champions become Sages. The change is different for everyone. I had weird visions of a seaside battle from ancient times."

Princess Jae continued, "So each of the Sage's new powers will manifest...well, it is different for everyone...or at least all I've seen. But I've only seen a handful."

Donathan had his head cocked in Jae's direction and made a loud huh before asking, "So does the Protectorate know?"

"Well, they know something about the powers wielded, but I don't think anyone's explained the rules. Waterfalz is impossible to capture, and my capabilities make me difficult to hold." Jae squared her shoulders and stood taller for a moment.

Donathan cleared his throat before politely asking, "So what exactly happened back there when that thing grabbed me?"

"One of my simpler abilities is I can manipulate things when fire is involved...but it's volatile."

"Meaning you can't control it?" Donathan asked.

"No, I can use it whenever I want, so long as there's a flame or explosion. Just...the results come out strange and different every time." Jae looked up into the air a moment and rubbed her chin. "Nyla, help me out."

"She glitches stuff affected by combustion to change reality, changing form into random things. It does not matter whether the thing is propelled from combustion or just burning by itself. It's tremendously neat to witness. Sometimes, there is even data hanging in the air. Which sort of makes sense. I mean, when they finished matching the human genome, the strands of data were all on and off switches, primarily binary. If that's true for us, then it is possibly true for how matter is manipulated in reality itself. If this, not this—if this, perform this. Reality could be just natural forms of machine code." Nyla smiled serenely before adding, "Princess Jae can force that code to bug out and throw something different in its place where there is fire or an explosion."

Mason had stopped fussing with his charger and whispered, "You're kind of blowing my mind, here."

Princess Jae nodded as the group reached the halfway mark up the ramp. "Bullets from guns, hand grenades..." Jae lowered her voice a bit and added, "Shit, I can even glitch pistons in a vehicle or rocks kicked up from a blast."

"So what exactly happens?" Confusion crept into Ashley's voice as she stopped suddenly in front of Mason, causing him to fall backward on the ramp, before she turned to continue upward.

Jae pretended she didn't notice the exchange and said, "Randomness. I have zero control over it. When I use it, I can feel a sharp jolt of energy shotgunning out of me, and for a split second, it seems like I've become whatever the object is." Jae's eyes glazed over. She looked up and away, staring off in the distance and letting the feeling wash over her. "Just a moment, then all at once, the form changes. It can become a table, a knife, a vacuum cleaner, a hippopotamus, literally anything."

Donathan nodded. "So what did the bullet become when you shot it into that undead to save me?"

"A ship anchor." Jae grinned widely. "I'm so excited when it turns out well. Occasionally, it does not. I once changed a bullet being fired in my direction, on impulse, and it became a mass of knives. Then I really had to move. Another bad day." Jae sighed and then rambled on, "There's more of course. Sages also—"

"Who would do this?" Nyla interrupted.

The group was standing before a yellow-painted room with a darkened doorway and splintered wood and metal thrown out across the garage.

Donathan looked across at the broken door and replied, "Are you asking who would loot something? I mean, it's pretty standard on and off the Shytown Trail." Aside from some scabbing on his face and hands, he had recovered pretty well from the night before.

Princess Jae looked at him and shook her head slightly.

"It's just... I chose a barren parking garage because it's open," Nyla said. "It is hard to hide here, so people wouldn't explore this place, and it is pretty empty, so looters wouldn't be attracted to it. The only thing I had worried about was nesting undead." For once, she sounded disappointed.

Mason removed his mask and set it on the ground and crawled low, sniffing toward Ashley's knees.

"What uhh...?" Princess Jae reached up and adjusted her hat while studying Mason's actions.

"Who the hell knows." Ashley lowered her gaze in Mason's direction before shrugging as she walked up to the door to peer inside the tiny yellow-framed room. "What did they take?"

"Experiments, mostly." Nyla had resumed her usual spacey tone. "Also my spare truck. An ice-cream truck with the security system mounted along the top side."

Ashley stepped up, eyeballing the skid marks out of one of the parking spaces and angled sharply down the ramp below. "I'm more curious about how they got it to peel out."

Mason's constant sniffing and crawling across the ground was the only sound heard for a moment, his head still at knee height. He began sniffing back in Ashley's direction, following some hidden path.

Ashley finally snapped. "Mason what the f—"

"There's something here. Some smelly thing," Mason said.

Nyla crouched and sniffed next to him. "I smell it too," she said before turning to Donathan. "May I have your lighter?"

Donathan reached into one of his pockets and produced his old Zippo. He tossed it gingerly to Nyla. At that point, Mason was lying on the ground. Nyla leaned down until she was facing Mason, just inches from his face. She brought the lighter close between them and flicked the lighter. A jet of green flame bolted up from the concrete between their faces. Mason yelped and shuffled back a little as the fire's direction trailed out and around where he was lying. Everyone who was still standing stepped back as the flame flowed along a path. When it was all ignited, it formed bold calligraphic letters that read "F L P."

Mason was still lying down, framed inside the letter F where it connected with the top of the L, and asking, "Guys? What uhh... Guys?"

"FLP?" Ashley asked.

Donathan shrugged. "Looters just having fun? What makes this flame green, Ny?"

Nyla shrugged, her face blank. "I recognize the chemical." She motioned toward the broken door. "I had a gas can full of it in the back of that room. I made it during my chemistry days. Didn't have a name for it." Nyla sighed and let her shoulders hunch forward. "I have never met any chemists, so I'm not terribly good at basic chemistry."

Jae stepped up and patted Nyla on the back to reassure her.

Mason chirped, "Seriously, can I get up now?"

16.

Deep Cuts from the Edge of Never
Hunter S. Thompson
Twenty Years Ago

THIS WHOLE UNDEAD APOCALYPSE was the best thing to ever happen to me. It was shocking at first. The dead roaming in packs through the town. Children eating the faces of their parents. Most gun ammunition was expended or stashed. No Jeopardy on channel seven at 6:00 p.m. Serious, dire things had transitioned into existence, and the whole world was suffering because of it.

But there was always the flip side. I never had to wait in line at the grocery store. No cops were around to bitch at me for driving on the sidewalk, and my personal favorite: Gas prices were down, way down. Free, in fact. Well, not entirely free. I mean, you could siphon it from other vehicles. If you had drunk too much the night before, or the day after, or even while you were trying to siphon gas, it was pretty easy to screw up. Then you'd have the taste of the inner guts of a Chrysler LeBaron stuck in your mouth for the next two days. There were always gas stations, though. You had to scout out and see if the pump still worked then find a clear path to that particular station, but it wasn't terribly difficult. Drive a vehicle with plenty of girth that was built in the late sixties to early seventies, and you would hardly notice the myriad of unlife you were smashing through on your way to the pump. Try to avoid bashing them when you can, though. Hell, unlife is life too. If you see a living lawyer, you could run him down. The zombies are more alive than those bastards have ever been.

One day, a few hours before nightfall, I wound up at the local Pump 'n' Go, trying to take their name in the literal sense, when around the corner sprinted a man running for his life from the undead. Classic mistake in the new world. You didn't run from the undead and let them know that you were a healthy target. I had figured out six months back that if you tossed enough booze and illicit substances into your bloodstream, kept your heart rate low when you needed to blend in, or kept your blood pumping at breakneck speed when you needed to react, the undead weren't even a problem. It was the living that pissed me off.

"You've got to help me!" the man screamed, his brown overcoat hung tattered. Somewhere in the chase, he had lost a shoe.

The wails of necrofied life sounded not far behind the man.

"Why would you piss them off in the daylight?" Rage filled my voice as I raised a golf club and waved it violently in his direction.

That amateur was bringing hell down on my doorstep. Well, gas station anyway.

The man gasped and sputtered, hunching over to hold his hands on his knees and let his breath wheeze and strain as he recklessly tried to catch it.

"Jesus Christ, man," I cautioned, the gas trap overflowing and spilling gasoline down the side of the Cadillac before clicking with force to a halt. Glancing down at the spilled gasoline, I fished around in my pocket a moment before producing a cigarette, raising it to my lips and lighting it with a Zippo lighter from the opposite hand. "How the hell have you lived this long?" I questioned, taking a long drag from the cigarette before removing it from my mouth with my right hand. Using the same hand still grasping the cig between two fingers, I hoisted the gas siphon out of the car and hung it back on the pump. I raised a foot to kick shut the flap on the gas tank without pausing to put the gas cap on the trap because I'd lost that gas cap about a month back.

"I just... It's just... Fuck!" the man said, gasping.

"Yes, I'm sure it's a story for the ages. But I'm not taking any hitchhikers unless you've got something to offer."

The balding, middle-aged man with a brown overcoat and an old white stale button-up business shirt fished through his gray slacks until he produced a small cellophane bag with a round white ball, a knot of plastic holding it in place as it trembled in his outstretched hand.

Son of a bitch, the man had a bag of cocaine.

All in one breath, I added, "Well for fuck's sake, man, what are you doing over there? It's dangerous, get the fuck in the car—"

One of the undead lunged out from behind the wall of the gas station mini-mart, latching onto the screaming man's back and plunging its teeth into the back of his head. I scrambled for the sawed-off shotgun in my backseat, raising it in a split second. I aimed it at the screaming man pleading for help. He was still holding the bag of Columbian gold in his right hand.

"Hold fucking still, I can't..."

The barrel swayed from one side to another as the screaming undead chowed down on the back of the man's head. Blood sprayed up and backward. Finally, an explosion boomed forth from the shotgun, sending scattershot into the zombie, folding it backward into a pile of necrotic flesh behind the injured man.

When he reached both hands back to cover his wound, I screamed at him, "Not that hand!"

Having a second to adjust from the sharp pain and letting the dull ache of infinity and infection creep through himself, he eyeballed my shotgun, assuming I was threatening him. It took me a full two seconds to realize he was afraid of me before I lowered the barrel, apologizing profusely.

"I just meant... it seems a shame to let good coke get more bloody than it already has." Somehow, calm and reason had become my mantra at the moment.

The man's life force dripped out of the gash in his head, spilling down his back, gathering into a puddle at his feet. He seemed to understand what I meant and knew the gravity of his situation, the infection that was going to overtake him. He raised his hand again to offer the cocaine when another undead suddenly leaped out from behind the building and latched itself onto his back.

"Son of a bitch!" I screamed at this game of Columbian cock tease as I scrambled for another shotgun shell in the backseat of my white Cadillac.

What had become of this world, where a man had to shoot zombies off another man's back just to get a toot of nose candy?

The click and folding down of the barrel, the racking of the gun and the blast that spewed forth into the second undead all seemed to rush by in a surge of adrenaline.

I could taste the drip that was going to coat the back of my throat. I had earned this sauce. The man before me, drenched in blood, had a look of ferocious pain on his face. Still, he didn't grasp with his right hand at the torrent of blood gushing down his head and face.

I lowered the shotgun again, attempting to look as nonthreatening as possible before throwing out some reason. "Look, man, I could have lit you both up with the gun, but I was decent enough to raise the shot high." Realizing how callous I sounded, I changed my tone. "I'm sorry, man." Shrugging, I let sympathy fill my voice. "Maybe you'll become their leader, you know, promote for your cause?" I tried to quietly make light of the situation by raising a lone fist and whispering, "Equal brains for all."

Something seemed to click in the twitching, blood-drenched fellow wracked with pain. He giggled slightly. Blood rained down from his wound. Then he burst out laughing. The bag of coke trembled in his right hand as he rested it on one of his plasma-covered sides and cocked his head back, laughing hysterically at what I had said. I laughed too. After a good minute of laughing, he sighed, wiping a tear from his eye with his left hand and offering up the coke with his right, walking comfortably toward me.

Two more undead leaped out from behind the building and latched onto the man's back. He screamed and struggled to remain on his feet, dropping the coke onto the pavement. I almost ran to the coke then stepped back, studying the situation. The blood-soaked wrinkles on the man's face. The screaming, guttural noises issuing forth from the undead as their teeth snapped across the man's shredding flesh. The wet, sloppy sound of sinew and flesh ripping free.

Finally, a synapse jolted across from one neuron to another, and I completely realized the gravity of my situation. I leaped into the Cadillac's driver seat, revved the engine once, and threw the cigarette out across the station. Dropping the emergency brake, I jammed the gas pedal down towards the center of the earth, letting the squeal of tires and burning rubber issue forth as I smashed into and over the screaming man and two undead.

I didn't run him over because he was being eaten. I didn't run him over because he was going to turn into one of them. I didn't run him over because, during the exchange, that son of a bitch had finally dropped the eight ball of cocaine into a puddle of blood, although that was a serious consideration.

The reason I ran him over, hopefully smashing the life out of him, was because, at the end of the whole debacle, I finally realized, as he screamed and struggled, letting death devour his flesh, that before the whole fall of society, that son of a bitch had been a congressman.

Who hasn't wanted to do that?

17.

West of Gilroy
Zombie Civil Rights Group
Present Day

"WHY ARE WE SPLITTING UP?" Ashley asked through clenched teeth.

Princess Jae shrugged in the morning sun and revved the engine of an old dirt bike Nyla had jury-rigged an hour before. "We need to inform the Knight's Moon about Nyla's stolen tech. There's a good chance it's in the hands of the Protectorate now. I'll catch up to the rest of you at Pier 39 in SF." She revved the engine a second time before joking, "Plus, there's no room on the dirt bike for you."

Donathan asked, "Yes, but what if we encounter something like that jelly creature again?"

Jae dropped the clutch, and the dirt bike exploded into motion and sound, kicking up dust in her wake. Over her shoulder, she shouted, "You're their leader, not me! You'll do fine, I'm sure!"

Seconds later, she was out of earshot, leaving behind the fading sound of a nasal old bike engine.

After the bike engine drifted into oblivion, a quiet creaking noise could be heard.

Donathan raised an eyebrow and let his head drift up slowly. "What's that sound?"

A look of disdain crossed Ashley's face. "More importantly, where are Nyla and Mason?"

After a few minutes of searching, Donathan and Ashley found the other two in a dilapidated barn just behind the dirt lot where they'd left Jae. Ashley's jaw dropped when she and Donathan stumbled upon the scene before them.

Three zombies were struggling in rope snares while hanging from what appeared to be a wagon wheel secured just under a large brown wooden beam running across the top half of the barn. The back part of the barn had fallen in, leaving wood and debris strewn across the floor. Sunlight beamed in, bathing everything in an amber glow. Nyla and Mason held a rope leading up to the wagon wheel.

"The heck is this?" Donathan asked after a moment, patting his chest pockets, looking for a half pack of smokes he'd managed to secure in an abandoned Gilroy house the night before.

"It's okay, really," Nyla said. "They're only Shufflers. They don't move fast. Don't have many tricks. They're mostly dead from starvation."

Nyla was right. The zombies were graying and skinny. One was missing most of the flesh from his face. Their skin was pockmarked with black spots that looked like rot. Two of the zombies groaned and struggled. One of them hung upside down, limp and seeming pretty dead—sorry specimens, for sure. Ashley became quite aware of an awful stench drifting off them.

Ashley clamped a hand over her nose. "Mo' impo'tantly, how di' you catch them?"

Nyla tilted her head in Mason's direction. "Last night, on guard, we came here and set this up. Since I'm no longer tagging them, it seemed like a fun experiment to see if we could ensnare something wicked. Instead, we got three tame things."

The metallic clank of a Zippo lighter signaled that Donathan had found his quarry in a fresh cigarette. "No more guard shifts with you two together." Donathan's tone was dry. "You're clearly not doing guard, and you definitely shouldn't be sneaking off without telling the rest of us."

Nyla replied, "I understand. It's just... We needed something to do."

When the group had first met Nyla, she was traveling around the state in a Winnebago, tagging zombies to track their movements. She had grown a little stir crazy since they had lost her vehicle.

The upside-down zombie jolted to life and struggled in his bonds. Its sudden motion caused Mason to jump. After settling back on two feet, Mason reached up and pulled down his mask, revealing a painting of an empty cliff overlooking some water.

Behind the mask, Mason added, "Just watch!"

Nyla and Mason, still clutching the thick rope tightly in both of their hands, began the process of sprinting along the far edges of the barn's wall, occasionally struggling to hop over piles of broken wood and trash. A loud creaking echoed through the barn as the horizontally situated wagon wheel spun beneath the beam. The three zombies struggled more as the ropes tangled and then untangled, fanning them out via inertia and spreading them apart in a circular spin near the center of the barn. Instinctively, both Ashley and Donathan stepped back from everything near the barn's door. The zombies groaned in frustration. The spinning sped up as Nyla and Mason made it back around to their original spot and halted to view everything. The zombies kept spinning as the two dropped their end of the rope.

The zombies' forms blurred. Suddenly, three zombies became five, then they seemed to be all one zombie held in five separate places, each displaying one moment of animation. The two right-side-up zombies were spinning on their heels. Suddenly, they flipped over to stand on their head, hands dangling loosely from their forms and then back to whirl on their heels. Even more remarkable was how the scene seemed to flow from left to right as the undead spun in circles inside the barn.

Mason raised his mask and let his eyes stray just long enough from the scene to turn, look over his shoulders at the others, and add, "It's like the dance isn't as important so much as the act of dancing."

Donathan's cigarette dropped from his mouth into the dirt. Ashley gasped audibly and let her hand drift from her nose to her chest. Her hand open, fingers spread wide. Her fingertips pressed against the cloth of her shirt, her knuckles slightly whitened.

When the creaking subsided, Donathan cleared his throat, sniffed, and said with audible respect, "Fuck... Mason, you kind of...outdid yourself this time."

When the zombies finally stopped spinning, Ashley pointed back at the dragging rope and said, "Do that again."

18.

Abandoned Shack
on the Outskirts of the Shytown Trail
Fine Line Protectorate
Present Day

ASHLEY SPRINTED UP the hallway. "This has gotten out of hand too quick."

Behind her, a large golden Shat smashed up the hallway. Its long, spindly legs tore through the walls, sending stucco and paint everywhere. Ashley dashed out of the hallway and slid loosely across the linoleum floor until she finally found her footing. She sprinted past Mason, who reached above his head and pulled down his mask to reveal a picture of a Tyrannosaurus rex eating a sandwich. Mason held a shotgun in his arms. When the golden Shat finally broke free of the collapsing hallway, rubble rained down around it as part of the roof collapsed. Three shots rang out from Mason's shotgun. The Shat jilted backward, the light from the day beaming in and glinting off the bright sheen of its carapace. The creature leaned back on its hind legs and flexed its mass. It unfolded its bulbous body until a large narrow head with toothy fangs appeared and a large set of eyes perched on its body rolled forward and opened. Its voice was hoarse and unearthly as it roared and then shifted its tone into a high-pitched scream.

Mason raised his mask and ran after Ashley, who had already made her way out the front door. Once outside, they met up with Donathan, who was smoking a cigarette, already perched behind a large machine gun. The front door of the building exploded in a flurry of wood and stone as Donathan squeezed the trigger and let a burst of ten rounds issue forth. Bra-ta-ta-ta-tat. Braaaaaa-ta-ta-ta-tat went the belt-fed weapon system as round after round impacted the Shat, shoving its dense body mass backward with force.

Eventually, when the creature had been smashed back enough into the rubble, Donathan looked in Mason's direction and said, "The itsy-bitsy spider," while he flicked his cigarette in the direction of the golden Shat.

Kaboom! The building and the Shat exploded all at once in a fiery ball of flame. Ashley ran into Donathan's arms, laughing. After their giggling subsided, they both simultaneously edged back from their hug, staring wide eyed with apprehension and shock. Their eyes fell into each other. Donathan leaned in first, and Ashley pushed in the rest of the way until their lips locked and the world faded around them. Lost in they'reiere mo—

———

"They'reiere?" Goblin asked.

Crooks's furry head was off and strapped to his back. The fur suit's head bounced somewhat as he nodded.

"They'reiere..." Goblin stared up and away as the slow syllables drifted out of him. "Okay, I see what you did there." His faux British accent kicked into overdrive as he added, "Nicely handled."

Crooks nodded excitedly, rubbing his two fur-covered hands together and smiling over his accomplishment.

"I think you mixed up they'reiere weapons, though," Goblin said while pointing at one of the pages he held in his left hand.

A loud screech of metal tore through the room. Goblin dropped the papers, and both he and Crooks winced, pressing their hands against their ears to try to block out the noise.

Nym stood by the door of the ancient shack, her metal gauntlet pressed against the corrugated siding that lined the building's walls. She was half smiling, showing off her teeth. "Did I disturb you?"

"Fuck's sake, woman, there are better ways to get our attention," Goblin groaned while Crooks nodded in agreement.

Nym cleared her throat, stepped away from the wall, and used her gauntlet to knock some of the dust from her clothes. "The bad news is, no bodies."

Crooks shrugged.

Goblin remained unfazed, then he realized what Nym's left hand held. "Is that a fucking Betamax tape?"

Nym smiled smugly and nodded.

"Fuck yes." Goblin sprinted to the other side of the room and dragged out an old cathode-ray television set mounted to a rolling frame. Directly under the TV was a shelf housing an ancient Betamax VCR.

After a few minutes of juggling stuff around, plugging in the TV, dragging in chairs and firing up a generator, their shack had been converted into a makeshift theater. Crooks had disappeared during the setup process but returned, holding a bag in his right hand and stuffing his face with his left.

Goblin glanced up from the generator with a look of shock. "Where the fuck did you get popcorn?"

A struggle ensued over the bag, eventually sending kernels flying around the room until Nym started the tape in the VCR and shushed them. The three members of the Fine Line Protectorate found their three seats in front of the television just as the staticky image warped and dimmed into view.

"Eh... Black and white?" Goblin complained.

Crooks set his furry costume head on the floor then propped up his feet up and continued munching away on the remaining contents of the popcorn bag. Goblin picked up a few kernels off the floor and threw them in Crooks's direction before finally letting his eyes focus on the action on screen.

On the television, the back wall of a cement room was lined with a red curtain. Mason came sliding into frame, his machine gun bounced across the cement uncomfortably, and his mask fell off and slid in the other direction. Ashley charged in after him, brandishing her bat.

"Are they fighting?" Nym asked.

———

"Walked us right into it, didn't you?" Ashley raged.

With a burst of speed, Donathan was standing in front of Ashley, his hands raised defensively toward her bat.

Donathan's tone took on that of a parent trying to soothe a child, "What's done is done. Let's just get out of here." To emphasize the situation, he motioned around the dark room with one lone reinforced window casting light on their left side.

"Why aren't you mad?" Ashley questioned, pointing the bat at Donathan's face accusingly. "This is the most obvious trap ever, set for us! Look at this fucking place! A hospital or something, and he sprints in here because there was a painted sign on a sheet strapped to the wall outside that read 'Art Museum.'" Ashley stood on her tiptoes, trying to raise the bat over Donathan's shoulder and point it at Mason before attempting to charge through Donathan. Nyla tiptoed up behind Ashley, doing her best to look neutral and not add to the chaos.

Mason said defensively, "I didn't think—"

"You never think!" Anger was dripping sickly off Ashley's tongue as the words fell out. "This is always your problem! Art art art! Just once, you should worry about us before your obsess—"

Sharp feedback echoed through the room as everyone jerked downward for a moment, trying to cover their ears. A bright strobe light came to life, pulsing through the darkened room. Instinctively, Donathan held up a hand and signed the number eight. The rest of the group followed suit, donning headphones and pawing at their mp3 players until the song was cued up. When the beat sprang to life through the headphones, they all clutched their weapons at the ready and fanned out and away from each other.

Another crash of feedback was followed by loud, long bassy music that seemed to flood the room. The beat was heavy and interspersed with an occasional screaming voice and another sudden drop of heavy tones. The sound overpowered the group's music.

Ashley lowered her headphones, mouthing, "Fucking dubstep?"

Donathan tried to shout over the music but succeeded only in moving his lips through a string of curse words.

Mason signed, "Just use sign."

Nyla pointed two fingers up to her eyes then away at the door across the room.

Four gruesome creatures stalked into the room. The members of the ZCR all stepped backward. The first monster had dark-purple skin, a broad, toothy grin, and what looked like wiggling worms hanging down over its eyes. Large, floppy horns bounced as it moved. Stopping midstride, the creature let out an unearthly roar.

———

"The hell is that?" Goblin was up and standing next to the TV. His eyes narrowed as he peered as closely as he could at the monitor without blocking anyone's view. "The living worms hanging out of its flesh over the eyes is a good touch, but…" Goblin looked away from the monitor and shot Crooks a stunned look. "Did you sew fabric horns onto that one after we turned him?"

Crooks jumped up, spilling his popcorn, bouncing from foot to foot while nodding.

Nym protested, "Down in front!"

Crooks settled back into the chair as Goblin studied the view with more detail.

Goblin asked, "That one you hung the worms out of its ears and gave him fabric spikes?"

Crooks chirped agreeably.

Goblin continued, pointing at a different figure on screen. "That one you made long fake fabric fangs mixed with dangling worms."

Crooks folded his hands behind his head and leaned back in the chair, beaming with pride.

"And that one is…" Goblin drew in a deep breath before bursting out laughing. "Did you just sew a shoe to her face?"

On the screen, a red-haired woman stalked up next to the other three monstrosities, her arms curled forward like sharp claws. A side-mounted shoe was sewn across her face, covering one of her eyes.

Nym echoed Goblin's laughter and fell out of her chair. Crooks was smiling from ear to ear.

Hyperventilating with laughter, Goblin finally managed to groan, "That's fucked up."

Nym stopped laughing to add, "What's really fucked up is Crooks and I turned three of them. She's still human!" More laughter echoed forth from Nym as she climbed back in her chair. "We just broke her mind!"

On the screen, the excitement had begun. No sounds could be heard, but Donathan had fired two shots off the screen, most likely to try and silence the speakers blaring music. The blasts, of course, galvanized the undead. One of the large zombies lunged forward, and Ashley slid under it and away as Donathan ran across the room, dragging Nyla away from another of the undead. Mason lay down on the ground at the edge of the screen and opened fire with his machine gun, shredding two of them. Ashley's bat knocked the last one back, and Donathan shot it cleanly in the head with his pistols. The final woman just stood there trembling.

"Damn," Goblin said, looking back at Nym. "Did they figure out she wasn't undead?"

Nym gasped, curled up a lip, and shrugged. Another minute passed, and the broken woman seemed to be talking to the rest of the group. Donathan helped her cut the shoe off her face. Ashley dug a small pistol out of a pack and handed it to the woman, who even on the black-and-white screen, looked thankful before she sprinted down and away from the security camera.

Crooks threw popcorn at the screen.

"I agree. Just shut it off, already!" Goblin croaked.

"No no!" Nym said. "There's phase two."

On screen, Ashley, Mason, and Donathan had finally noticed the red curtain. Donathan peeked behind it and pulled it forward to reveal a square urinal with a signature in the corner. Mason jumped. The other two studied him for a moment, then everyone backed away.

Nym's jaw dropped before she said aloud toward the television set, "Not a fan of Dada, huh?"

———

"Huge fan of Dada," Mason said.

Donathan located the side door to the building. After a few minutes of prep, they mounted a bit of explosive and detonated it, freeing themselves from the building. The red-haired woman immediately sprinted away to freedom. She'd clearly had enough of that place. Mason exited afterward.

Nyla was the first to follow and lightly asked, "What's Dada again?"

Ashley stepped through before Donathan emerged and let the door slam behind him. He paused a moment in the hot sun before fishing in his pockets for a cigarette. Then he trotted over to the sheet sign reading Museum and ripped the fabric down.

"Dada, the art movement," Mason said. "That piece was mimicking one by Marcel Duchamp called The Fountain."

"A urinal?" Donathan asked.

Mason set his mask down on the ground next to his pack and rummaged through it for paint. "Yeah. The artist wanted to take items that were aesthetically neutral and turn them into a work of art. It didn't matter that it could be artistic or symmetrical." Mason looked up and smiled, holding a bottle of blue paint in his right hand. "Although it is symmetrical and quite pleasing on the eyes once you notice it. It just mattered that it was something you wouldn't normally care about." Grinning from ear to ear, Mason set a second bottle, black paint, next to the blue on the broken concrete ground. He then produced a paintbrush from the bag. "The Fountain changed art entirely. It proved that anything could be art. The urinal piece helped to shape modern art into what it is today."

"That actually seems like something you would want to rub on your face." Ashley's tone was dry and judging. She looked down at her squatting companion, who was currently dabbing paint across his mask.

Mason looked up and wrinkled his nose. "Not really, no. You can respect the piece and even understand how influential the art movement is but still not trigger a trap." Mason sighed. "Remember? I'm not stupid."

Donathan asked, "Yeah, but a urinal? That's art?"

Mason nodded. "Duchamp would love that sort of reaction."

———

Crooks tried to add another chair to the pile he had been stacking up in the corner of the shack for the last fifteen minutes.

"So, what now?" Goblin asked Nym even though he was staring at Crook's busywork.

"Well, there's this." Nym held up a tiny gold ring between the fingers of her gauntlet-clad hand.

Goblin looked up for a moment then dropped his intense gaze back to Crooks as the furry managed to wedge another chair back atop the pile. "The ring the Judge asked us to put on General Mary Helen's finger?" He sighed, observing that Crooks's collection was still standing.

The Protectorate Army General had recently lost a fight with the ZCR in Half Moon Bay. General Mary Helen was stabbed through the back of the head by a green Shat. The oversized spider-like creature currently had her body, mind, and nervous system under its control. The Judge had sent the Fine Line Protectorate after her with the promise of placing the ring on her finger. "The trap is in place. We've set it not far from where she and the creature were roaming. The real question is how do we get that on Mary Helen's finger once we catch the green Shat?"

Nym gave the shorter man a determined look from across the room. "I'm not worried. Our traps always work out, Gobbles."

Crooks was on his tiptoes, trying to stack another chair

precariously onto the pile. Goblin kicked out the bottom chair, sending them all skittering across the floor in a loud clatter of plastic and metal.

Smiling mischievously in Crooks's direction, Goblin said, "They do, don't they?"

19.

East of Watsonville
Zombie Civil Rights Group
Present Day

"DAMN IT." Ashley's voice was overflowing with frustration.

Late in the morning, they still hadn't broken camp. They'd spent the night in a run-down roller rink not far from the Asylum. The roof had partially collapsed, giving them a view of the sky, but the walls were semi-reinforced with no windows, so it seemed secure. Nyla and Donathan ransacked a back room and found some items they could barricade the doors with, and finally, when they were certain the place was safe enough, they lit a fire inside, just under the hole in the roof.

The night seemed almost peaceful. Early in the evening, they would hear a roar or a scream a ways off, but nothing appeared to take notice of them. The stars overhead twinkled in the night sky. The moon coasted past. Light and shadows drifted back and forth as the fire crackled. Occasionally, Donathan could be heard getting up to break down a piece of derelict furniture to fuel the fire. Mason spent half the night rummaging through the piles of wreckage in the corners of the room then painted his mask for a bit before curling up next to the fire. As Mason struggled to keep his eyes open, Nyla remarked on how the walls were blank and maybe they'd all wake up to Mason spreading paint across them.

Mason sleepily whispered, "Can't... Low on paint."

Shortly after that, the world drifted apart around Ashley, and she fell asleep.

In the morning, the fire was burnt out, and all that remained were a few hissing ash-covered logs and the smell of hickory hanging in the air. Everyone else was resigned to a late start, so Ashley dragged herself out from under her blanket, wadded it up, and shoved it into her bag. Then she fished out some crackers and cheese for a morning breakfast. Afterward, she was tucking the surplus food back into her bag when she wound up poking herself with a needle. That damned needle.

In a few minutes, she had unearthed an unburnt piece of wood, half covered in ash from the fire, and stood it on an old, broken, warped metal lawn chair across the room. She jammed the needle deep into the wood until only half of it could be seen. Eyeballing the eye of the needle, she backed up five feet and tried to throw a piece of thread in its direction.

Each toss darted the thread forward, then it would flutter away to the ground. Once, Ashley managed a straight shot for almost three feet until the tiny cord of fabric fell away. Cursing, she continued her attempts for two full hours.

"I still think it's an impossible task," Nyla remarked.

Ashley gasped and spun around. Nyla was always too quiet in her approach.

"You know?" Nyla added. "Like it isn't something you're meant to do but some message you're supposed to get from it?"

Ashley brushed it off. "I don't think Waterfalz is like that." Her tone became softer as she said, "Well... I mean she's definitely all wise-sagey, but she just doesn't seem like someone to give a bullshit task."

"You're right on that one," someone replied.

Both girls spun around in surprise to find a dark-skinned woman wearing a silver jacket with a mandarin collar. Her tiered dress extended downward with the same smoky gray color. Her alluring eyes drank in the abandoned rink while Mason and Donathan scrambled to their feet. A smile drifted across Waterfalz's face as she rubbed her ring-covered hands together.

After a moment, she tugged at the string of herbs woven in and around her waistband before clearing her throat and adding, "I did not give you an impossible task."

Donathan shook the sleep off and set his smile into overdrive as he asked, "How did you get in here?"

Waterfalz locked her gaze on Donathan and then asked, "Nyla, what do I say to people who ask those sorts of questions?"

In her spacey voice, Nyla said, "Shut up...child?"

Dropping the serious look, Waterfalz changed her voice to warm and humorous. "Exactly."

Ashley waved a frustrated hand for attention before motioning at the needle and thread and asking, "If this is possible, then why can't I do it?"

Waterfalz let her eyes drift slowly from the eye of the needle to the thread in Ashley's hand before adding, "Perhaps you're using the wrong thread."

Ashley didn't get a chance to protest as Donathan motioned for them to pack up quickly. Then Waterfalz ushered them away from the smoldering campfire and toward the back of the large rink. Rubble had been moved around by Mason during the night, so the Sage didn't have to climb over anything too large.

As they slowly approached the back wall, Waterfalz told them, "When the world births Champions such as yourselves, heroes and villains in mass numbers, there's often a reason—an artifact that is acting as a focal point, throwing the balance of life and death off." Her face looked a bit grim in the room, dimly lit from the morning sun coming through an opening in the roof. "The last time this happened was when Hitler found the Spear of Destiny."

Donathan half chuckled and said, "The spear that pierced Jesus' side? You don't take us for religious, do you?"

"It isn't necessarily about religion." Waterfalz stopped mid-step and turned to face Donathan directly. "Jesus had powers too. Did you ever wonder if the Spear of Destiny became what it is because it pierced Jesus' side, or did the fact that it was an artifact with its own unique power enable it to pierce his side?"

Donathan raised both eyebrows and with wide eyes looked at Ashley, who returned his gaze, her jaw hanging open.

Ashley's voice was high pitched and confused. "So that spear had power before that happened?"

Waterfalz nodded. "Most religions figure out which objects have power. It isn't hard to notice them when you're in proximity. Even less difficult when you're a Sage and can sense their use."

She pantomimed inhaling a cigarette toward Donathan, who patted down his chest in search of a pocket that held his lighter and pack of smokes. After a few seconds of uncomfortable silence, he held out a cig, then after a flash of metal and flame, Waterfalz was taking a long drag off the thing.

She blew out smoke, coughed a moment, and continued, "Religion just sort of latches onto the legends of these items. Sometimes a Sage or a Champion will find their way alongside it. The people are amazed by the abilities of both Sages and the artifacts. If someone sinister is involved, they might trample across Europe, bringing genocide with them, or kill someone far stronger than they are."

"So, religion is wrong?" Donathan asked.

Waterfalz took another drag off the cigarette before replying, "I didn't say that, did I?" She smiled and looked from left to right at the members of the Zombie Civil Rights Group.

"Religions usually have some piece of the pie, a slice here and a slice there. The truth is a bit stranger than you might imagine."

"Which is?" Ashley asked with frustration.

Waterfalz glanced at Ashley then waved her hand with the cigarette while calling out, "Nyla?"

Nyla answered from behind the group, "Shut up, child!"

Smiling, Waterfalz again stepped toward the back of the room as everyone else followed suit. She continued as she strolled past the heaps of junk, "The artifact that just reappeared is a ring. We need it. Just try not to wear it."

Mason asked, "Is it going to turn us into a strange half creature that creeps around hunched over and begging for his Precious?"

Waterfalz laughed and shook her head. "No, nothing like that." She paused, glanced down at Mason, and gave him a long look while shifting dust around on the floor with one foot before adding, "It just has...side effects. Our team needs to get it back."

Donathan looked unfazed and shrugged.

Nyla stepped ahead of them, gazing up at a blinking neon sign just over a large hole that looked as though it had been torn into the wall. The surrounding edges had sharp, jagged chunks creating an archway overhead. The hole was slim for about a foot upward before it stretched out wide. Its entire doorway was filled with darkness. The sign was bright pink neon with a blue square fringe around it. The word was "Echoes."

"Where did this come from?" Mason asked.

Before Waterfalz had a chance to look up from her cigarette, Nyla once again echoed, "Shut up, child."

Amusement crept into Waterfalz voice as she said, "I need you to see something, though, just to make sure you stick to the path when it gets rocky."

"You already explained last time how some people are born Champions and other societies' Champions can be your villains." Donathan's smile grew a bit. "We pay attention sometimes."

Waterfalz sniffed in his direction before throwing down the cigarette and stamping it out. Her voice suddenly became dry and sad. "You know, you still have no idea who you are, but I'm glad you've made it this far."

Donathan gave her a wide-eyed look for a moment and then just shook his head.

Motioning to the hole in the wall, Waterfalz said, "Go."

"But what's in there?" Mason asked hesitantly.

"Shut up, child," Nyla, Donathan, and Ashley announced in unison.

Ashley was already stepping up and through the hole and fumbling about in the darkness, trying to find her L-shaped red light. Nyla and Donathan dug theirs out before they stepped through.

"Oh, and before I forget," Waterfalz shouted, "when the time comes, throw shiny copper!"

Donathan shouted back through the hole, "Is that a euphemism?"

"No idea," Waterfalz replied. "It's just something I have to tell you."

Mason paused at the doorway and turned back to Waterfalz to ask, "Can you say, 'Only what you take with you?'"

Waterfalz chuckled and then croaked in a high-pitched, slightly gritty voice, "Only what you take with you."

Mason clapped excitedly and stepped through the hole into darkness on the other side, tracing his way up the hallway toward his friends' red lights.

———

The building was overflowing with life. It looked as though it had been an expensive hotel. Broken couches with regal but ripped patterns were scattered in random parts of the room. A grand staircase in the center of the room flowed up and then across to a balcony. None of the carpet could be seen. Ivy was growing knee deep over it all and snaking up the staircase, even winding itself through the balusters and stretching up the handrail. A chorus of birds above echoed down through the large open room. Beams of golden light were cascading in from the missing roof above and spreading their warmth through the ancient hotel lobby.

"I..." Mason's mouth gaped, but he was at a loss for words. He resigned to using up the last of his paint and set his mask on the ground in front of him. After fishing through his bag to produce a few mostly empty bottles of acrylic, he took hold of his paintbrush and let it dance across the surface of the mask.

Ashley kicked aside some rubble and perched on the edge of a ruined couch, staring at the stairs of ivy leading up while mumbling, "It's like the world is alive again."

In the back of the room, Donathan shoved some trash aside and cheered. Seconds later, he cursed loudly, and a bottle smashed against the back wall.

"Gin?" Ashley asked out loud.

Donathan sighed and replied, "I thought we'd found heaven for a second."

Nyla asked, "Doesn't he like alcohol? He doesn't like gin?"

Mason looked up from his painting to shake his head and mouth the word no.

Ashley looked away from the ivy long enough to clear her throat and add, "Yeah, he's not...himself on gin."

Donathan sniffed in frustration and leaped over the side of the tattered couch, causing the sofa cushions to bounce down the line, jolting Ashley a bit. His smile widened a bit as he looked in Ashley's direction. "This place sure is gorgeous, though I wonder why she showed us this—"

The wind gusted, tiptoeing in from above as the sky darkened. Clouds drifted overhead, dimming the light slightly. Fluttering sounds echoed through the room as the ivy stirred and waved with the gust. The room flashed, which was followed by a loud crack of thunder.

Donathan jumped up from the couch, wearing a look of apprehension. For once, his smile had almost vanished. Ashley opted to stand and face the ivy, looking at the opening in the roof above them. Mason reached up and placed his mask on his face, revealing a painting of a black background with a red scribble of paint trailing up and widening at the top to form the shape of a tornado.

The sound seemed distant, but it quickly spread until a loud humming reverberated off the walls of the room. It intensified, causing some of the rubble near the walls to fall over. Nyla covered her ears and crouched down while Donathan drew both his pistols.

The ivy trailing up the stairway fell away, and below it, stars were twinkling through space, stars unlike any seen by a naked eye from earth. Yellow, red, and blue all seemed to traipse across the mass of their light. The space between the stars was intense royal blue. All at once, the glimpse of the cosmos blurred, spun into a whirlwind of light and sound, and blinked out of existence. The room was pitch black. The group collectively toggled their flashlights back on. The room filled up with subdued red light.

"Everyone okay?" Nyla asked cautiously.

Ashley's voice sounded tattered and strained. "I'm all right."

"Did you see all that color?" Mason asked frantically.

Ashley couldn't see him, but she could hear him tripping over rubble as he scrambled to get over to his friends.

Donathan let the light drift around the room toward the stairs where the universe had previously shone through to them. "How could we miss—" He surged backward two feet as the light flashed. In one quick breath, he asked, "The hell did I just see?"

Slowly, he raised the flashlight back toward the center of the room, and a strange yet familiar face, giant and dimly lit around the edges, could be seen in place of the stairs.

Nyla, Ashley, and Mason rushed up to Donathan until all four were huddled around the red-light source and staring up at the large face. Its eyes blinked, and its form stepped back.

"That's..." Mason said.

"It's you!" Nyla's voice overflowed with wonder.

A larger version of Mason was standing before them, his form filling up the warped viewing space, extending wide and all the way up the now-missing stairs. He wore the same outfit but looked rested and clean. The background was hard to make out. He seemed to be looking down at them.

The Mason from this world took a step toward the image and raised his mask nervously, squaring his shoulders and angling up toward the doppelganger. The vision of Mason looked down and clapped his hands. No sound echoed through the room.

Mason's double stepped back, growing a bit smaller in form until standing next to him were matching versions of Donathan and Ashley. The other Ashley also looked rested and clean. Ashley pointed up at her double's image and turned back to the others, her mouth hanging open.

"I wouldn't be caught dead in that outfit," Donathan motioned up at the version of himself standing above. Both were wearing the same black duster with the same hair. They looked like twins.

Ashley just shot him a confused look as Nyla asked, "Well, where am I?"

"Is that really us?" Ashley brought a hand up to her mouth, curling her fingers in front of her lips and mumbling through them, "Seriously?"

The other versions of Mason, Ashley, and Donathan looked as though they were giggling. Other Ashley suddenly made a sour face toward other Mason and mouthed a long string of words which no one on this side could hear. The calmness drained from other Mason's face as he snapped a reply, then all three huddled together, arguing for a moment.

"Oh yeah, that's us," Donathan answered. He stepped forward toward the image and used sign language. "Can we sign? Do you know sign?"

Other Donathan and Ashley laughed.

Other Mason nodded and signed with a dipping fist, "Yes."

"Where are you?" Donathan signed curiously.

The other version of Mason signed, "That doesn't matter. We don't have long to talk."

More looks of confusion as Donathan shrugged up to the image. The other versions of themselves whispered and shook their heads.

After other Mason looked around, Donathan signed up to the doppelgangers, "Do you know Waterfalz?"

Everyone nodded back at him.

Donathan asked, "Do you trust her?"

A look of confusion sprinted through the group before the other Ashley stepped up and signed, "Yes!"

From the back of the room, Nyla gasped and asked, "You don't trust her?"

Donathan looked back and shrugged, "We don't know her like you do."

Other Mason said something then finger spelled R-A-Z-O-R-W-R-I-S-T, followed by, "When you encounter him, just run."

Other Donathan said something to his Mason, and their version of Ashley just shook her head.

Mason signed again, "I mean you should run, but you probably won't at first because we are all stubborn." All the other versions of themselves in the vision laughed at that.

Donathan's doppelganger looked sober for a moment and signed, "Trust Mason. Believe him when he's sure of something."

A bright flash lit up the room. Donathan, Mason, and Ashley all winced and shielded their faces.

Ashley asked aloud, "So what's a Razorwrist?"

Another bright flash lit up the room, then the ivy-covered stairway returned.

"So do we chase the artifact, or do we chase Razorwrist?" Donathan asked.

Mason added sheepishly, "I don't want to chase anything named Razorwrist."

Donathan looked back and said, "Fuck...the tunnel we came through is gone." Glancing about the room he announced, "I think there's a hole in the wall over here that we can crawl through." He strolled over to the wall then crouched and scrambled through a jagged hole near the ground.

"So how"—Ashley shot a look of judgment toward Nyla—"Do we know we can trust Waterfalz?"

"Nyla says we do!" Donathan shouted back through the hole. "Also, apparently we say we do too."

Defensive, Ashley asked, "But how do you know we can trust them?"

"Hell if I know. I'm just as confused as you are!" Donathan shouted back.

The three friends trailed after Donathan, their sounds echoing away until the room hung still and the dust settled.

20.

Abandoned Shack on the Outskirts of the
Shytown Trail
Fine Line Protectorate
Present Day

"TAPE TIME, TAPE TIME!" Nym was wearing a fake flat
policeman's cap and shrieking into a bullhorn.

Goblin, covered in blood, poked his head out from behind
a wall while muttering, "Oh goodie. We were getting bored."

Shocked, Nym gasped. "You're eating?"

Crooks walked out without his fur-suit head and nodded
intensely with a huge smile across his face.

Goblin feigned surprise. "What? You didn't hear him
come in?" Shrugging and glancing up slowly toward the sky,
he added, "The Protectorate sent a runner asking for news
again."

"Fuck the Protectorate and their news." Nym couldn't

hide her frustration. "I was so hungry."

More fake surprise from Goblin. "Were you?"

Nym's lips drew in tight as she shot an icy glare in Goblin's direction before waving an annoyed hand and pointing to the tape in her other hand.

"More Betamax!" Goblin squealed with excitement as Crooks began the process of wheeling the cart and VCR up from the corner of the room.

Crooks inserted the video and cued it up on an empty room. "I didn't get a chance to find the spot yet." Fuzzy lines of offset video jolted across the screen as Nym fast-forwarded the tape.

The loud screech of metal on concrete echoed through the shack as both Crooks and Goblin dragged up chairs.

Nym continued watching the screen as the tape wound ahead. About a minute passed by, and she added, "I'm sorry—"

Goblin said, "No, it's fine, really—"

"It's just I thought I had already..." Her voice trailed off as they watched the screen flicker.

Another uncomfortable minute passed before Nym asked, "So the runner was from the Protectorate?"

"Yeah," said Goblin.

"He uh..." Nym glanced away from the screen as if searching for something to say. "He have anything to say?"

Goblin nodded. "The usual of 'Blah blah the Judge wants a report' and 'Uh uhhh.'" His eyes went wide as he held up two hands and clasped them together before he added in a high-pitched voice, "'What are you doing? Don't eat me!'"

Next to Goblin, Crooks was nodding and smiling widely.

Another uncomfortable minute passed as Nym let out an audible sigh of frustration.

"I think we saved you a little," Goblin added.

"Here!" Nym pressed Play then sprinted across the room to drag over a chair. Right before sitting on it, she eyeballed the red stains on Crooks's fur suit before giving him a long stare of frustration.

Crooks shrugged, pretending to lick his paw before cow tailing it over the back of his skull, petting down his hair like a cat cleaning its head.

Nym pointed at the television. In the center of the screen was a bucket with a few scattered bits of trash and an aerosol-paint spray can.

"I missed it. Did we leave a big lure on the building this time?" Goblin asked.

"Well, sort of..." Nym sounded proud of their design. "While you set this up, we made the outside look like it was inhabited."

"That's the real trick of it all," Goblin said. "Pretend waypoint on a dark, desolate highway."

A look of judgment tiptoed across Nym's face as her lip curled up. "Did you just throw out an Eagles song reference?"

On screen, Mason sprinted toward the aerosol can with Ashley was trailing after him, her arms out, obviously suspecting something suspicious. Mason didn't stop and ran up to grab the empty paint can before disappearing down out of sight as the floor gave way. The untacked carpet fell into the hole, and on screen, Ashley spun around, trying to outrun the drop before her eyes grew wide and she was dragged back into the pit. Donathan, who had been just off screen, appeared, just standing on the carpet, steady footed. He turned to run but had already slid forward enough and vanished into the hole. Wide-eyed, Nyla was clutching the carpet as it dragged her down into the darkness a moment later. The entire scene took only a couple of seconds.

Goblin, Crooks, and Nym were all laughing.

Nym was hugging her sides and in too much pain to stand up. "Please!" She gasped. "For goodness sake..." More gasps. "Rewind that shit!"

"No no no no no no no!" Goblin chirped. "This will be the best part!" He was pointing a waggling finger at the screen and choking back laughter.

Most of the carpet had wedged down in the hole, save for a corner that had still seemed tacked down off screen. After a moment, a tiny hand reappeared on the edge of the chasm, and Mason, apparently propped up by his friends, was struggling to pull himself out of the hole. The final corner of carpet began to slip, and even through the black-and-white closed-circuit Betamax tape, his face appeared white and fearful. The last of the carpet slid farther into the hole, along with his form. A rope attached to the corner flexed off screen. Then back on screen, its length went vertical before it fell, along with a large oversized anvil, which dropped into the hole from directly overhead.

"How very Acme of you!" Nym giggled.

Goblin's voice was overflowing with elation. "I couldn't help myself!"

The trio rewound the tape and let it replay while laughing through more tears. After the second playthrough, Nym finally stepped up and pressed the Stop button before announcing, "I think we need to make an appearance next time. "Next time, we need to make an appearance."

———

Nym sounded almost pleased. "It took a while, but we finally caught her!"

"This is, by far, the stupidest thing we have ever done..." Goblin glared at Nym, his upper lip quivering a bit before turning and staring down at the green Shat trapped between two buildings. It had been speared in place by long, thick wooden dowels launched through windows on opposite sides, across from each other, triggered as the undead spider-like creature trampled up the alleyway. The trap had gone off perfectly, and a phalanx of wooden poles suddenly blasted at both sides of the monster, overwhelming it and tangling it in place. Its entire mass was shifted down, forcing it to remain stuck in place but still with some freedom of movement. Its carapace was emerald, but for a Shat, its form seemed streamlined and thinner in mass than usual. It had given up trying to raise its long swordlike appendage, which was also forced down by the trap.

"Those things are still fucking dangerous to us," Goblin added.

Wide-eyed, Crooks nodded as he took his furry bat-costume head off his back and raised it up over his face. Large cartoonish eyes continued to nod up and down long after the furry's head had settled over his skull.

A loose-limbed person snapped free from part of the trap and lunged forward, its form dangling like a rag doll from the center part of the Shat's carapace. The body was that of a young girl with matted, raven-colored hair, cut short. The face contorted, hissed, and spat as it lurched forward and back again. Both Crooks and Goblin jumped back.

Nym stood her ground in front of the two other men as the body formerly known as Mary Helen, General of the Protectorate Army let out an ear-piercing screech, her mouth lolling open and jaws snapping, teeth clicking in Nym's direction. Nym crossed her arms in determination and shot back a wicked look like a queen staring down her nose from a throne. She stood eyeballing the woman merged with the monster, and for a moment, both ladies seemed to be sizing each other up. Nym broke the silence with a sniff of amusement and said out loud, "It doesn't matter. We have to get it on her finger. Judge's orders."

"Can't we just tape it to her forehead?" Goblin asked.

Crooks made a whimpering noise then pointed forcefully at Mary Helen and the Shat before shrugging in shock.

Goblin had been watching Crooks's gestures and replied in a quiet tone drenched with sarcasm, "Yeah... I don't like roller coasters either."

Crooks shook his fur-covered arms in the direction of the creature in a frustrated manner.

Goblin reassured him, saying, "Okay! Okay! I get it... You wish you were a farmer?"

Crooks lifted his furry head and shot Goblin a nasty look.

Goblin finally got serious and said, "Nym, Crooks wants to know how we do this."

Nym finally glanced back from the creature toward her two friends and held up a ring in her left hand. "Just...run...at her?"

Goblin couldn't mask his horror. "Again, this is the stupidest plan we've ever had."

21.

Los Gatos
Ashley
Seven Years Earlier

IN THEIR FULL-SPEED sprint, they had tried the front door but, in their panic, had been unable to figure out how to unlatch it. Ashley and Ethel both lost sight of Jennifer during the chaos. Angela's screams were shrill and sharp. The ladies managed to find a door leading to a lit-up office that had once been a manager's workspace. An old metal desk was there, along with a chair, a cabinet, and even a piece of corporate art that showed a duck on water and was captioned, "Success! You can be the only duck in the pond."

If not for the sheer terror, Ashley would have sat and wondered about how awful that motivational poster was. They only stayed in that room for a second, though, giving it up as a death trap. They sprinted around the corner, following the wall until they found another door leading to an empty stockroom with white paint slathered over the brick and mortar walls. A tiny light bulb on the end of an orange extension cord was hanging in one corner of the room. The shadows were long, and the light was too dim. Angela's screams had died down, but a new slew of jeering comments designed to bring them out of hiding had begun.

Dean himself kept screaming for the "little girlll" to "come out and playyy…"

Ashley was assuming he meant Jennifer and hoped she'd found a good hiding spot.

"Mom, what do we do?" Ashley asked fearfully.

Ethel sprinted up the hallway, muttering in frustration, "That damned voice told me we shouldn't have stopped, but I didn't listen."

Ashley sighed nervously and said, "Mom, we… What do we do?"

"Here! Now!" Ethel found another door in the darkened room and waved a hand quickly.

After a cold rush of air and mist, both women found themselves standing behind a chain-link fence with a wide metal gate and a thick piece of chain wrapped around that. The roof of the building extended an awning to the top of the chain-link fence housing an old garbage dumpster on wheels. A ramp led down to the fenced area, which had once been a shipping dock. Ashley pushed on the fence to see if they could climb under it. It was held tight by a thick metal cord that ran through the bottom and recinched to each pole. The concrete was littered with some scraps of clothes, and even with the moonlight shining at an angle from under the awning, brown stains could be seen stretching across the ground's surface.

Ashley couldn't hide the hope fading from her voice as she said, "This is a cage." Her voice became a low whisper of shock. "We walked into a cage for holding victims."

"Those assholes can't build decent cages, then." Ethel was already rushing behind the dumpster. "Give me a hand."

Ashley raced up next to Ethel, and with a creak of metal and rust, they managed to get some decent momentum behind the dumpster and smashed it, with a great clash of sound, into the fence. Ethel dashed back around it, and Ashley followed suit until they rolled it back again and then smashed it once more into the chained door on the fence. Again, they backed up the dumpster and slammed it forward. Then they ran back around to view their work. The space between the door and the frame seemed to stretch as the pole holding it warped a bit.

Ashley pressed her face up against the fence. Part of the chain-link had torn in the collision, and a wire was angling out, digging into her cheek. She tried to back up and reposition herself but found Ethel standing behind her, shoving her through with force. Ashley protested as the metal tore into her cheek, but after a moment, pain gave way to freedom as she managed to drag her torso and head through.

Ashley held a palm against the gushing wound on her cheek and turned around, whispering, "Come on, Mom!"

Ethel just stared a moment as the night closed in around the two women.

Ashley whispered again with force, "Come on, Mom!"

Ethel just sighed. "Baby, I can't fit through that."

Tears flooded Ashley's eyes. "Just... You..."

Ethel seemed calm. "We both know I'll never fit through that." Tears ran down Ethel's cheeks. "And we've made too much noise."

Ashley couldn't find words. She just sobbed.

Sagely, Ethel said, "I wish you'd known your father longer. He was a good man."

Shouting echoed closer from inside the grocery store.

Ethel continued, "There's so much darkness in this world. I don't know how we made it this far."

Footsteps were clapping on the pavement from inside the building.

"Ash, be strong." Ethel took a deep breath and added, "I've seen you do it." She nodded toward Ashley. "I've seen you face down darkness and win." Ethel sniffed loudly and said, "But it has to be on your terms and never its own."

Ashley jumped back when the door swung open and Dean and the large man grabbed Ethel from behind. Too focused on Ethel, they didn't seem to care that Ashley had made it outside the fence. She fought back at first, pressing herself against the chain-link and then kicking for leverage off the dumpster, trying to knock them off balance.

During the struggle, Ethel managed to scream, "Just run and remember I love you!" as she she gasped between kicks.

After Ethel was dragged into the other room, Dean shouted, "I love you too!" in a taunting voice.

Crying, Ashley stumbled backward into the darkness. She tripped and fell hard onto one knee. Pain flooded into her, alongside sadness and regret. The mist hung thick under the lights of the parking lot.

After a minute, Ashley gathered her thoughts. They'd be searching for her outside the place soon. She would also have to worry about other denizens of the night who could have heard the crashes and shouts. Wherever she was going to hide, it would have to be close.

Ashley ran back around the building until she was standing in the darkness just outside the parking lot's tall lamps. She eyeballed the mass of vehicles until she ran around the farthest one, a busted-up black BMW. She tried its doors first—all locked. She tried a Volkswagen van next—locked. She checked under the vehicle for hidden keys or weapons. She tried a blue four-door Nissan Sentra next and came to the sinking conclusion that she was quickly running out of vehicles. On her final attempt, an old gray Saturn, she found the back passenger door unlocked.

As she cracked the door open slightly, a very aggressive creak issued forth from its hinges. Ashley slowly slithered through the opening and into the passenger seat then over the stick shift and centerpiece housing the emergency brake, into the driver's seat. Reaching back across, she tried the glove compartment and found nothing. She searched under the seat and lowered the shade, praying she might find a key, a working engine, and a tiny bit of fuel. Her night was dry on miracles, though, and she had no such luck.

She spied movement beyond the sign, derelict vehicles, and lit-up doorway. Ashley's heart skipped a beat. She held her breath, thinking first it was the monsters from the store, and then monsters from elsewhere. However, a man, woman, and child slowly and nervously stepped up to the door in the middle of the night and knocked. A minute passed, and they knocked again. Another minute passed, and they began walking away. Then the front door of the grocery store edged open, and a clean-faced Dean stepped out, waving his arms back into the store. The family rushed forward and into the trap.

Ashley couldn't believe what she was seeing. Halfway through the scene, she started to roll down the window to try to shout something, but her voice was too hoarse, and all she could muster was a squeaky whisper. When the realization of what had just happened took its toll on her, Ashley started to cry again. The tears and sadness became rage as she gripped the wheel of the car tightly and threw her shoulders forward, cursing. Her clenched fists pounded on the dashboard, then all at once, she threw herself back into the seat, letting the rage fade from the car until her hands lay down at her sides. She took in deep breaths of frustration. Her right hand brushed something, and she realized it must be the emergency brake. She took hold of it, yanking it up to engage it out of frustration. Its mass flung upward with her arm. Sniffling through tears and shock, she let air rush deep into her lungs as she tried to figure out what she was seeing.

Ashley was holding the pommel of an upside-down bat, which someone had laid across the length of the emergency brake. Crawling in, she hadn't noticed it because most of its length was stretched out into the backseat.

Shaking her head in disbelief, she took hold of it with two hands and awkwardly turned it around in the small car until she was holding it in front of her. Her eyes drifted from the handle, up across the shiny aluminum barrel glistening in the moonlight, to its end cap. The handle had been wrapped in worn black grip tape and felt soft to the touch. Ashley's thoughts drifted back to Ethel's shouts and final words. She thought of all the terrible times they'd pressed through and all the close calls.

Rage and fear rushed over her again, and she whispered, "Get control," to herself. "Focus."

She almost began crying again but then drew a deep breath, let her eyes drift back down to the bat, and said with confidence, "Focus."

A moment later, she looked up from the bat and let her eyes settle across the parking lot on that brightly lit door leading back into the grocery store.

22.

Deep Cuts from the Edge of Never
Hunter S. Thompson
Twenty Years Ago

"FOR CHRIST'S SAKE, get off the damn golf course."

This was a real problem with these damn binoculars—they had great magnification. Great magnification means a giant pair of lenses. The big expensive kind you'd expect to see on an African safari, hunting rhino. What no one tells you is that when you use these mammoth sets, you've got to find a place to set your fucking beer down or you'll wind up dropping the damn binoculars or worse, spilling your beer.

"Either go find some fuckhead to chew on at a goddamned Chevron or get the fuck off the ninth hole."

Suppose you've made a decent living and retired to southern California. You spend a few years partying, fucking, and trying to live alongside Hollywood, but you're still trying to avoid being jack-off ordinary. So you buy a nice little condo, decorate it with artsy shit and glass tables that suit your habits. You try to avoid it for as long as possible, but eventually you meet your neighbors and learn their names are Frank and Sandra.

They seem like nice people until, one day, you wake up, and Sandra has eaten Frank. All of society has collapsed around you, and you're left scrambling for some semblance of that life you previously referred to as jack-off ordinary.

The cliché answer is "you do a massive amount of drugs," but the truth is you would do that shit anyway. Now, it's just nice and legal because the fire brigade ate the cops in town.

But eventually, you might need to take an overdose level of quaaludes, steal a seafaring plane with pontoon skids, pretend you remembered those few lessons you mostly slept through just so you could brag you had a pilot's license, and then pilot that shit...

Well, sail it really—because you never quite got it up out of the water—to an island named Catalina.

Catalina is this glorious beach resort of an island not terribly far from the mainland but with just enough ocean and tide that you don't have to worry about too many undead washing up on shore.

So now you've got museums, surf, golf courses, grand weather, and a small slice of heaven. This was a perfect place to live out the apocalypse. Truth be told, on some other timeline, I'd have probably offed myself by now.

I mean, the zombies are still here—they are fucking everywhere these days—but a smaller population means smaller occupation. So you just avoid them.

When you hear that knocking outside your beachfront house late one night during a summer storm, don't be that idiot that rushes out to latch his gate. Let that shit bang. It's probably the tiny island's population of undead.

Treat them like a tribe of people that deserve respect and space, and they will do the same. You enjoy your coconut shrimp and golfing.

They will enjoy whoever is left.

Best of both worlds, in my opinion, and the golf-course greens are usually empty because of it.

Which brings us back to the present. I was spilling my fucking beer because I refused to let go of it and set down these oversized binoculars I'd pilfered, but even worse was that one of the island's endangered species, me, was having his golf game interrupted by a member of the roaming undead.

Unfortunately, I had run out of ammo a day before, and I didn't think the golf cart could take another hit. So it was the waiting game.

A screech erupted next to the golf cart.

"Fuck!" I exclaimed, leaping out and away. I dropped my binoculars and twisted to grab a golf club and place it between myself and the roar. This was just perfect. I'd spilled my fucking beer. "Are you out of your goddamned mind?" I roared back at the undead twitching just across from me in the middle of the street.

A moment later, he sprinted towards me, so I ducked around the fence and dipped inside the open door of a house. Two bolts later, I was racing frantically through the house, making sure the rest of the rooms and windows were already secured tightly. A few were boarded up, and I had to admire their cliché craftsmanship of "just slap a couple of boards across it and pray for the best."

A few minutes later, I untucked a flashlight from my belt and had the refrigerator door open, peering past a mountain of rotten food that had gone sour whenever the island had lost power.

"These fucking people." I drew a painful breath before continuing my tirade. "These uppity, rich white assholes." Then I paused a moment to pull out a cigarette and stack it on my extender before sparking it up and taking in a deep breath of life-giving nicotine.

"These fucking people ran the goddamned world into the ground."

Digging deeper into the fridge, I threw things over my shoulder, letting them smash into the wooden floor of the kitchen. A few things managed to crash into the waist-high island stove with six burners and a metal rack overhanging it.

"They fucking tell us every day that," I paused before lowering the pitch of my voice and belting out a half-hearted Southern accent, "we are fine! It's just the flu! It's just people using the drug bath salts!" My accent dropped, and I spun back out of the fridge, holding a bottle in my left hand. "There's no zombie apocalypse... Pfft." I twisted off the top of the drink and took a large swig out of it before holding the bottle up to eyeball the label. "Is this fucking Boones?" I belched with force before adding, "I fucking hate Boones. Weak pisswater. Last time I drank it, I was like, well, I'm really full." I sighed. "No buzz. Just damn full." I threw the bottle across the room, shattering it, and tried to drag the refrigerator forward to dump it over. After a few hernia-inducing minutes, I gave up on this task and decided instead to explore the house.

Kicking aside old stuffed animals, broken glass, and flowers from a long smashed vase, I marveled at the undamaged seventy-inch plasma TV mounted on the back wall of the living room.

"Fucking grand screen." I sighed. "No power here."

The hallway led up to a large master bedroom. A king-size four-poster bed sat in the middle of the room with a partially torn pillow-top mattress and no sheets. The damn thing looked inviting for a few good seconds until I noticed a large brown stain splashed across the far side of the bed. The stain was too light to be shit and too dark to be water. Something grim had happened in this room, with no remains to be found. When nothing but a stain was left, you knew the dead dined well here.

A chill ran up my spine as I passed another room with light-blue walls and yellow trim. I poked my head in long enough to see a toppled child's bed and confirm nothing dark was living in one of the corners, then I shut the door tight.

Such a giant lack of humanity in this world. I would feel so much better if my remaining traipse of it would die off. Maybe it was time to throw in the towel. There was fun to be had, but it was all insanity without the shock of regular people around. I just felt a bit hollow these days. I couldn't even get a decent golf game in. Was this the kind of world I wanted to live in?

During this whole thought process, I'd meandered down a smaller hallway, to a stairwell that rotated tightly down into a cellar. Here, red-carpeted walls flowed down onto burgundy carpeted floors. A moment later, I flicked on my flashlight and let the beam drift around a room filled with whips, chains, various pieces of black leather furniture, and—

"Hang on a minute. What the fuck is this?"

This was a bondage room. A bondage club of sorts. Owned by some tight-knit, button-down, oxford-cloth Ivy Leaguer who was probably an environmental attorney. I bet he'd retired to Catalina to spend his days on a yacht, fishing and raising kids with his family, but he was secretly a bondage king.

Stumbling through the various accessories of pain and pleasure, I wound up staring eye to eye with the person who owned the room. She was in a tiny picture mounted dead center in the far wall. Blond hair pulled back in a bow, a wicked smile on her face that screamed mayhem, and a cut-out bra showing a tight little rack as she led around a man behind her, on all fours wearing a chain and collar.

"My God," I mumbled. "A bondage queen?" My stomach churned with Boones a little as I sat up taller and added, "Why not? It's the twenty-first century."

Chains rattled from across the room. I nearly jumped out of my skin while yelping with fear. The sound I'd made was an octave higher than I'd rather admit. My muscles froze in place. I should have been sprinting up their stairs, out the door, and into another house—preferably without subpar booze in it—but something rang in my head, and a morbid curiosity took hold. This just had to be explored. Besides, just five minutes ago, I was thinking of cashing in my chips. Why not run another edge? I forced myself to turn and take two strenuous steps back into the room.

Chains. I had clearly heard chains. Trembling, I slowly let the beam of light drift across the room until it settled on a huddled form. A dog's metal choke chain was dangling around its neck. A thicker chain stretched off of that, mounted to the wall behind it. Shirtless, the corpse struggled when the light shone on it, and it hissed and darted forward suddenly. My scream was a bit deeper and peppered with a tirade of curse words as I jumped back onto the stairs.

This time, I froze halfway up the stairs and let the flashlight drift back down the stairwell, just waiting to see if the bondage zombie gave chase. The chains were clearly shifting about, but nothing was shambling up after me. I stalked my way back down the stairwell and edged forward back into the room. When my light fell back on the chained corpse, it started groaning and threw itself full force at me. This time, I kept the flashlight trained on him and watched his legs and torso extend forward violently as his head snapped back at the strength of the chain. The zombie himself collapsed, frozen on the ground for a minute. Then he groaned and shifted, climbing back to his feet as chain clinked around him.

All at once I realized this could be fun! I'd first need to mark his limit. I stepped forward again, shining my light ahead of me and murmuring to the corpse, "Hey? Hey, buddy? You and the missus had some fun, huh?"

The zombie lurched forward and was jolted violently back onto the ground. This time, I grabbed a strange piece of furniture that looked like the frame of a wooden crate with occasional parts of it wrapped in padded cloth. I have no idea how a person sits on this thing. Shoving the heavy thing, I maneuvered it across the carpet until the far end of it was lined up against the balls of the zombie's feet. Limit set. We would, of course, have to test it.

The creature managed to gather itself up after a few more seconds, and keeping myself still a few feet shy of the bondage box, I stepped left and right with my two arms in front of myself, mimicking a cliché zombie walk.

I was baiting a reaction by singing off key, "Cause this is thrillerrr..."

The zombie crouched down and lunged forward, and his torso and legs sprawled out from under him. The balls of his feet came to rest just shy of the strange padded box. Perfect. I'd flagged the end of his limit. After powering off the flashlight, I waited until I heard chains shifting again. Then flicking the light back on, I angled it up under my face while asking, "Can I interest you in a new long-distance service?"

A clank of chains followed by the loud thump of a body collapsing on the carpet was the response. I almost died laughing. Forcing myself to calm down, I powered off the flashlight and waited again.

When I heard the metal shifting, I flicked on the light, strolling to my right, holding a pantomimed protest sign with my free hand before exclaiming, "Unlife is life too!"

Clank, snap, thump.

Flick. "I wanted a Bud Light!"

Clank, snap, thump.

Flick. "You're the worst party clown I've ever seen."

Clank, snap, thump.

Flick. "Run! A taxidermist!"

Clank, snap, thump.

Flick. "Seriously, I am a fucked-up individual now."

Clank, snap, thump.

This time would be one for the record books. I edged up so I was perched right behind the torture chair, hunkering down behind it. In the total darkness, I heard the familiar sounds of chains dragging. Flicking on the light, I angled it at the creature while shouting, "A g-g-g-g-ghost!" followed by my sadistic cackling at the situation.

Instead of leaping, the zombie stood up, screaming an ear-piercing cry. I felt the world around me shifting even before the form of the zombie exploded into black puffs of smoke that darted around the room. I turned to run away, and my clothes changed. A step later, the world around me changed.

———

The depression that stomped in on Tuesday afternoon when working in a call center could be measured on the Richter scale. Each thunderous beat of hopelessness could be physically seen on the faces of my co-workers as they braced for the fact that there were still three more days until the weekend. Three more mindless days of droning on with one-liners like "Well, ma'am, let's try rebooting the system" or "Sir, you should try calling the web browser's tech-support line" and my personal favorite, "I know we did not cause all those pop-ups to appear."

The worst part about this call center was we didn't even have cubicles. I had three tiny walls mounted on the corner of a large communal desk and ultimately shared this pretend working space with five other people. All of us in our faux cubicle hell.

I was about three frustratingly slow lines of instruction in on explaining to an elderly woman how she could reboot her system. Phil Dunhill, who is only a low-level tech in this company—but as far as I'm concerned is CEO of Smug Butthole and Associates—poked his head around the blue woven-fabric walls of my workstation and said, "Hey, Thompson!" Finally remembering to cup his hand over his microphone but not bothering to whisper, Phil said, "I just e-mailed you the funniest fucking e-mail! Check it!"

I managed to grunt a reply and wave a hand, feigning interest in my call. Phil doesn't have a personality or a sense of humor that extends beyond the office. Whatever he's e-mailed me will probably involve a cat fact or a Chuck Norris joke of some kind.

A moment later, I was caught looking too relaxed in the other direction and was promptly glared at by my boss Peter. Peter was never happy. I wanted to believe that Peter had a hard life. I wanted to find justification for why he always had some reason to complain about my being late or my being on time or my being ten minutes early instead of fifteen minutes early. I once even daydreamed that Peter had lost his parents when he was young and grew up in an orphanage and only owned a single crayon as a child, but the truth was, Peter was just an asshole. He knew he was an asshole. He even had "Asshole" on his coffee mug, which he would often show off as he drifted past the line of fake cubicles toward his actual desk in the corner of the room.

I was still yammering on with the old lady, trying to figure out what she meant by her computer having a foot pedal, when Phil re-emerged from his hole just long enough to say, "Thompson! Burgers for lunch? Tuesday right? No brainer!"

My stomach churned, and for a moment, I felt violently ill. Who the fuck talks like this? This place seemed like a combination of being lit on fire and drowning. Everything was so ordinary and painful. They even had an old-style clock mounted on the wall at the far end of the room, with a long red hand ticking down seconds as the day dredged on. The clicks between seconds were so long I could feel time stretch out in front of me, could see whole civilizations rise to power and then in sudden, shocking moments, fall as everyday people scrambled to the corners of the earth to dodge the devastation. Another second finally ticked by, and the world seemed to warp out of existence. I could feel celestial bodies spinning on their axes. Comets, meteors, planets, and suns spread out amongst the vastness of space, and my being stretched out with them. Everything that existed was a part of me, and I was a part of everything. I knew all the secrets of the universe, which in fact, weren't secrets at all. Just plain things, everyday things that physics, particles, and mass knew by default but mankind had somehow thought was just some spectacular, thrilling wonder. So we'd built an empire of questions to hide the fact that we were minuscule things functioning in the cosmos. Another second drifted by, and I was back out of infinity and back into eternity. The woman on the end of the phone line was still droning on. I let my fingers press down on the mouse, which gave an audible sharp click in response.

"Motherfucker!" I said aloud, jaw dropping while I faced the computer screen. Without realizing it, I had half leaped up out of my seat. I let the generic desk chair on wheels slide back and away from myself. I was still hunched forward a bit, the headset stretched taut as it tried to remain on my skull. Shock drifted across my face in the bright blue fuzzy glow of the computer monitor.

The woman gasped loudly. "I'm sorry, what did you say?"

"Ma'am," I drew in a deep breath, "I said M-O-T-H-E-R-F-U-C-K-E-R."

Looking around, I was suddenly aware of the silence in a normally loud call center. Every drone's judgmental eyes were focusing on me.

"Motherfucker!" Without hesitation, I slammed down the headset, stood up tall, and took long strides toward the door. "I have too much dignity to continue on with these shenanigans."

Peter was standing up but frozen in a corner of the room. He was still holding his coffee mug, but from this angle, all I could read was "hole."

I collided with the front door, and warm summer air washed over me. A moment later, I was sitting behind the wheel of my Cadillac El Dorado, hands flexing and wondering what happens now.

Another second later, I was pulling a long-barreled pistol from my caddy's wide glove compartment then dashing back inside.

The whispers of the room turned into screams as people jumped up and sprinted past me out the door. Phil looked relieved when I let him scramble past. Peter still stood frozen in the back of the room, holding his coffee mug but trembling intensely.

I waited a moment, holding the gun skyward and striking a strong, square-shouldered stance.

He still stood in place, trembling.

I watched a second tick by on the clock face of oppression before raising an eyebrow and shouting, "What the fuck are you still doing here?"

All at once, Peter dropped his mug and sprinted like a chee-tah out the door.

Finally, in this perfect moment, I raised the barrel at the computer screen. I could still hear the old lady droning on about her problems with her machine.

In a moment of realization, I shouted down toward the headset, "Computers don't have foot pedals! That's a mouse!" before slapping the disconnect button with my free hand. I let a leg drift back behind me, adopting a strong executioner's stance. Every tendon tensed as I slowly squeezed the trigger while star-ing down the iron sights at a paused video of Rick Astley. "Fuck you, Phil," I whispered right before the crack of the bullet exited the barrel. A shower of sparks followed.

Breathing a deep sigh of relief, I let my shoulders sag for-ward then drifted across the room toward Peter's desk. Setting the gun down on the brown tabletop, I fished open a comically deep drawer.

"Jackpot," I muttered as I dragged out a bottle of amber-colored liquor and ripped off its lid, angling the bottle up and appreciating the sudden sensation of fluid dripping down my parched throat.

After a minute, something felt downright strange. I loos-ened my grip slightly on the neck of the bottle and brought my arm down slowly, studying the label.

"Is this fucking Boones?"

A face leaped out at me from the label, and I screamed and threw the bottle across the room. The bottle was gone, replaced by a clatter and bone-jarring tumble of light and shadow as I flung myself backward. The flashlight collided with the zombie's face. Halfway through my fall, something connected with the backs of my legs, and I felt my stomach drop. My legs went up higher than my torso, knocking over the padded chair thing. The wind left my lungs as my back smashed to the ground. A second thump rang out from the room. I couldn't tell if the ringing in my ears was caused by the impact or the sudden shift in realities.

Still struggling to gasp, I crawled up to all fours then shakily stood on my feet. The flashlight was on its side next to the far wall of the room, and I could see the silhouette of a zombie sprawled out on its back just a few feet away from me. Fuck the flashlight. I scrambled for the stairwell and took my chances fumbling up and out of the darkness, away from the chains, corpses, and fake office environments. I didn't know what the hell had just happened. Either I would find another flashlight or just struggle against the darkness somewhere else.

23.

Watsonville
Zombie Civil Rights Group
Present Day

"WHAT'S IT LOOK LIKE?" Ashley asked.

Donathan just shrugged and handed over the binoculars.

Scanning through them, she observed a fenced enclave, small in size for most enclaves on the Shytown Trail. Surrounding it were wire-mesh Hesco baskets filled with sand, their tops covered with razor wire. On top of the compound was a square, sandbagged overlook for watching who or what might approach the place on all sides.

"The front door is wide open," Ashley said. "And there's no movement up in that tower."

The time was midafternoon, and they needed to find a place to bunk down for the night. That place looked the most promising.

However, Nyla asked in her usual tone, "Trap?"

Ashley and Donathan both echoed at the same time, "Trap."

Mason was crouched down, dragging a paintbrush across his mask. He'd been abnormally quiet lately.

After a second, Nyla pointed out, "He's not actually painting."

Donathan cleared his throat and whispered, "We've seen this before." Nudging a shoulder toward Mason, he continued, "He's out of paint."

Ashley didn't bother whispering and added, "More useless than usual."

"So what do you think?" Donathan asked. "Go in with headphones on, expecting a fight?"

Ashley got a wicked smile on her face as she reached down to her shoulders, grasping the earbuds and looping them up into her ears. "It's been too long."

Donathan nodded, and both Nyla and he followed suit. Mason was still pretend painting. Donathan reached an arm down and shook Mason by his shoulder until weary eyes looked up.

"Headphones on," Donathan said in a gentle, warm voice.

Mason just nodded and tucked the paintbrush into one of the pockets on his IBA vest before donning the earbuds. After a moment, Donathan flashed the hand sign for song number fourteen. Ashley echoed his movements, as did Nyla and Mason, then all at once, they pressed Play on their mp3 players.

They began the assault. Ashley grasped the rifle she had pilfered a few days before and sprinted toward the compound for a few seconds before throwing herself down into a ditch. Nyla leaped up to her feet and did the same, going for the far side of the compound. Donathan jumped up a few seconds later, aiming toward the center. Their movements matched the beat. After a minute, they realized that something wasn't quite right.

The song blasted into Mason's ears, lyrics about a failed relationship accompanied by an acoustic melody. Mason felt confused by the choice of music but sprinted full speed toward the compound. He sprinted past Ashley in a ditch, nodding in her direction, and just kept running toward the door.

Seeing Mason sprint past, Ashley ripped out the earbuds, yelling, "What the fuck?"

The song continued on about two folks hating each other and ruining what was left of their relationship. Mason was trotting across the great wide-open expanse. He was nearing the razor-wired Hesco baskets, and he tugged at his machine gun, gripping it by the carrying handle and trying to reseat the strap more comfortably on his shoulder.

"Oh for fuck's sake," Donathan muttered as he motioned for Nyla to take out her earbuds. Then he shouted in her direction, "He's got the wrong song! He has a slow song. He thinks this is a close ambush!"

A few seconds later, Mason made it between the sand-filled Hesco baskets and was rounding up to the vast compound doors. The building looked as though it had once been an office building of some kind. The lyrics sang into his ears, droning on about wishing everyone would die.

Mason edged up on the door and counted to five before rushing around the corner into the building while whispering, "Why is this even on our mp3 players?"

———

"Mason?" Ashley's voice was tiptoeing somewhere between a whisper and irritation. "Mason, are you in here?" The room was a scattered sea of broken old desk furniture and toppled cubicles. She raised the volume of her voice again whispering, "Mason?"

A hand grabbed her and dragged her down behind an ancient desk as she yelped in surprise. Donathan, Nyla, and Mason were all crouched down behind the desk.

Donathan whispered, "Found Mason."

"So why the fuck are we still here?" Ashley asked.

"They let us walk in." Nyla motioned toward the open door.

Donathan nodded. "Might not be safe to walk ou—"

A loud squawk of feedback snapped sharply across an old PA system. A man's voice rang out in a smooth-talking flood of a late-show-host impression. "You've been up and down the Shytown Trail. You've been to the Knight's Moon festival, but you've never seen a show like this! Presenting, for one night only, live on stage, the members of the Fine Line Protectorate! Crooks, the no-nonsense furry with a rebel streak a mile wide."

Mason's face went white at the word furry, and he peeked out from behind the desk.

The man with the mic gasped for one second, drawing in some air before he continued his high-speed monologue, "The one, the only mistress of fang and fun, Nym!" Shuffling could be heard in the distance before the man continued, "and I am your humble host, Goblin the pristine yet unclean."

A loud, uncomfortable throat-clearing sound echoed through the room.

"No?" Goblin had dropped the late-night-announcer accent and drifted to a fake British one.

At that point, Nyla, Ashley, and Donathan were all peering out across the room. A tiny stage was there with black curtains, and a giant spotlight lit up most of it. No forms could be seen standing in the giant spotlight.

Goblin sighed into the mic and picked up the announcer impression again. "The troll with a sensitive soul."

A cough echoed through the room.

Goblin went back to British and sounded unamused. "Are you fucking with me? This is getting old!"

The announcer's voice chimed back in. "These are the vampires, devourer of blood and flesh, fangs and feasting, the ultimate in Protectorate defense! The ones, the only, the Fine Line Protectorate!" He dragged out the last syllable for almost a minute until another cough signaled he should stop.

Loud feedback echoed through the chamber, and far off, Goblin could be heard saying, "You know what... You take over."

"Hello, dahlings." Nym giggled. "My furry friend Crooks is bringing out your first consolation prize."

A bat furry with large cartoon eyes and ripped-off wings stepped out of the darkness into the spotlight, setting down a stool from one hand and—

"Three cans of paint!" Nym shouted descriptively.

Ashley, Nyla, and Donathan all lunged at Mason and piled on top of him, holding him down. A mix of pain, protestation, and growling erupted from Mason as his friends worked excessively hard to keep him in place.

"No? Nothing?" Nym asked quizzically. "Shame... Well, we will dump that shit out." The sounds of splashing filled the room, and Mason's frustration fled from him for a moment. As his friends cautiously sat back up off him, Nym continued, "Well, all right. Next prize, Crooksy, if you will?"

The furry stepped back into the spotlight and set a bottle of alcohol down on the stool.

"This lovely, crystal-clear, delicious bottle of ninety-four-proof..."

Donathan's smile hadn't edged up or down.

"Gin!"

"Ha!" Ashley chortled loudly then covered her mouth in shock.

Donathan allowed a wider smile and nodded in her direction before consciously flipping the bird from behind the desk in the direction of the stage.

"I...huh?" Nym shouted something strange away from the mic. "Still nothing, huh? All right, dump it, Crooksy."

A loud shatter drifted from wall to wall as Nym continued, "Well, lastly we have a limited-edition Barry Bonds baseball card from the San Francisco Giants that we're going to burn."

In confusion, Donathan mouthed, "What?"

While Mason and Nyla shrugged back at him, Ashley sprinted out from behind the desk, shouting, "Hold the fuck on!"

"Ooo-ooo-ooh!" Nym's squeal was bursting with elation. "I told you we could get them to walk up freely."

Donathan, Mason, and Nyla had all stepped out alongside their friend, weapons drawn, as the spotlight powered off with a clang and the main lights of the room flicked on.

The back of the room behind the stage displayed a painted green logo of a mouth flashing fangs, marred by plenty of drips and smears. The shorter man, Goblin, stood across the room holding a fire axe. Bowing his head and flashing a smile, he stepped out from the back part of the stage to the front edge. Crooks followed suit, wearing his full furry costume but with a flat gray military-grade cap perched on top. He held an old Thompson machine gun strapped and dangling free under his right arm.

Nym smiled wickedly and stepped forward, bringing the mic to her lips and announcing, "The ZCR. I'm so happy to see you in the flesh." With a slight giggle on the last word, she flourished one of her lace-covered arms right before she reached the edge of the stage. One of her hands was wearing a steel gauntlet from an old suit of armor. "We are the Fine Line Protectorate." Nym curtseyed as Crooks bowed and Goblin dipped his head slightly while dramatically extending both arms. "The Judge sends his regards." Nym stood taller, smiling widely before adding, "But the traps... Those were all us."

"Who are you, again?" Nyla shouted across the room in a calm voice.

Nym cleared her throat then raised an eyebrow before handing the microphone to Crooks.

Crooks waited for Goblin to set the axe down at his feet before taking the mic and replying, "I'm sorry?"

Nyla kept her usual tone and repeated, "Who are you, again?"

Goblin replied in a high-pitched tone, "Uhh... The Fine Line Protectorate, sent by the Judge of the Protectorate Army."

Donathan, Ashley, and Mason all turned back to look at Nyla as she cupped one hand up to her mouth and shouted calmly, "What were you, again?"

Goblin cocked his head to one side before glancing toward Nym and Crooks and saying, "We're vampires...?" As the last syllable left his lips, he turned back in Nyla's direction.

"I've never seen a vampire before." Nyla cupped her hands again and shouted, "Are you sure?"

Nym's jaw dropped, and her top lip curled up into a sneer. She took the mic back, saying, "I can assure you, little one, we are the real deal."

Donathan stepped up in front of Nyla, waving a hand and pointing a pistol at the stage. "Enough of this."

Crooks took a half step forward and raised the Thompson.

"If it's a fight you want," Donathan shouted. "We'll give you one!"

A moment passed, and nothing happened. Donathan stepped back and shouted, "Do your thing, Ash!"

"She left," Mason whispered.

"I—what?" Donathan spun around in shock, surveying the room.

Nyla whispered, "She left while you were shouting at them."

Donathan turned back forward to face Goblin, Nym, and Crooks. Crooks was still staring down the iron sights at the rest of them. An uncomfortable moment spread throughout the room. The microphone on stage picked up the sound of someone sniffing impatiently.

"Doesn't matter!" Donathan shouted. "It's still a fair fight!"

Nyla whispered, "Mason left too."

"The fuck is going on here?" Donathan whispered back over his shoulder.

"We should leave," Nyla said in a hushed tone.

Donathan could hear her feet trot across and around the rubble and back out the exit.

"Well?" Nym announced into the mic. "This is awkward."

Crooks opened fire, and in a burst of motion, Donathan surged out of the room. The gunfire clattered and halted as dust resettled.

"Did you see how fast he can move?" Goblin asked in surprise.

Nym drew a long breath before telling her friends, "We need to nerf that motherfucker."

24.

Los Gatos
Ashley
Seven Years Earlier

SHE HAD LET IT ALL GO. In this world, someone could hold onto their fears or die screaming encouragement for their child. Ashley was through with fears. They had no purpose to them. Clutching the bat in her left hand, and with no plan whatsoever, Ashley crossed the parking lot, no longer caring that she was bathing in the buzzing beams of overhead lights. Each step felt heavier than the last. Off in the distance, something growled, and Ashley felt some internal demon screaming to shake itself free from her skull. Another step later, the scenery seemed to quake suddenly. She could run. Run and hide. That was usually the best option, but that was what people did when they had something to lose. Ashley thought, *If I have to go down, the least I can do is break someone else's teeth on the downward spiral.*

The sound of her knuckles rapping on the metal door sounded strangely hollow. Ashley stepped back several feet from the door, loosened her wrist, and let the hand spin the bat once in place as she drew a deep breath. Oxygen danced within her lungs. A heartbeat later, it flowed through her veins. Half a pulse later, it began a sudden flood of endorphins into her brain. She'd never appreciated something as simple as drawing a breath before that moment.

The door opened partially at first as Dean peered out. Another second went by as he laughed and flung it open, pointing in Ashley's direction and jeering that she had come back to be turned.

Ashley lowered her gaze, flexed the hand holding her bat, and sprinted toward the door. After she got one step inside, the world seemed to pulse violet, and her heart felt as though it would burst. Dean's eyebrows rose, and his face flooded with confusion. Another step later, her pulse returned, but the light itself took on a purple haze and held it. Ashley flexed her legs into a long stride. Dean stepped back out of surprise and defensively tried to close the door. A second passed, and Ashley saw a flash of indigo light. She flexed her shoulder muscles and let her wrist trail behind her then, with a sharp twitch, let the motion carry forward, her arm tracing across the light. Her wrist tracked the movement with a sharp snap ahead of her. Before she knew what had happened, Dean was crumpled on the concrete ahead of her, and she was inside the building, the door slamming shut behind her. A flood of sound and activity rushed through her. All the world swung back into focus, quickly and violently. The large man and the skinny lady were both aiming barrels at her from near the aisle end caps.

The family from earlier were standing clutching each other tightly, between the two gunmen. Dean was gasping and struggling to climb up on one foot.

He managed to limp a few feet away, clutching his chest and gasping, "Just kill the bitch."

Bright violet light shone to her right, and she chased it. A pop and a snap flickered past her as all the heaviness faded from Ashley's form. The violet light pulsed and faded, creating a tendon-stretching effect across her vision. As Ashley leaped up and over a cashier's kiosk, she felt a bullet whistle past. She turned and sprinted down an aisle of fully stocked greeting cards. When she was halfway down the aisle, the purple light pulsed, and Ashley let her momentum focus on preparing for the turn left. Her rubber-soled sneakers squeaked as she sprinted across the cement down the back aisle of the supermarket. All at once, the indigo light snaked diagonally from her lower right to her top left, and Ashley followed the movement. The bat connected with a ping, and the skinny woman that had just jumped out of an aisle was thrown backward. At another strange pattern of light, Ashley let herself spin on her heel, swinging the bat back down, and the lighter aluminum of a rifle magazine crumpled against the heavier aluminum of the bat. The light flickered again, and Ashley turned to sprint down another aisle.

"What the fuck just happened?" Dean shouted.

A woman shrieked back, "She's... My fucking hand." Frustrated, she added, "She broke my magazine!"

"With a bat?" Dean's voice rose with anger as he motioned in the direction of the big man with the shotgun. "Fucking kill her already, Carl!"

The large guy turned to run down one of the aisles when Ashley sprinted out of it, snapping her arm swiftly forward with the grace of an eagle swooping down for its prey. Her underhanded swing connected and then arced backward with quick momentum as she rolled her shoulder farther forward, letting her front knee bend as the bat pivoted around and back down on the large man's head. In an instant, his skull, flesh, and gray matter splattered out, and the twitching mass of dying tissue collapsed.

"What the fuck is wrong with your...?" Dean's words tapered off as Ashley focused on him.

The light didn't seem to follow him, so she let him sprint back off toward the office area that they had sneaked through earlier. The family that had been held captive sensed their moment and rushed past Ashley, thanking her as they found their way out of the unsecured door and into the late night. She knew she should follow them. The violet light snaked violently to the left, and Ashley felt that it wasn't something she should chase, but she trailed after it anyway. She followed it back past the checkout counters again, down the far aisle of the store, in front of the pharmacy counter, where Ashley found the corpse of her mother, lying empty eyed and staring at the grocery-store roof in a pool of her blood. The hunched-over form of Jennifer was gnawing, teeth gnashing through the flesh of Ethel's neck. Suddenly, Jennifer lunged to her feet and screamed a long guttural tone, her tiny form standing full of defiance, with closed, tense fists and arms flexing at her side.

The violet light had become forked tongues of lightning that flashed and faded from Ashley's vision. She dropped her bat with a clank and fell forward onto her hands and knees, gasping for air.

Behind Ashley, Dean croaked, "What's really going to piss you off is...numbing that bitch's arm and chopping off her hand while she slept was Jennifer's idea."

The memories raced through Ashley's head, and she struggled to catch her breath.

Amusement had returned to Dean's voice. "Setting up the trap, leading you here... It was all her plan."

Ashley could hear Ethel's voice echoing through her head from when they'd agreed to take Jennifer to Wanestown in search of her uncle.

Still screaming, Jennifer flexed her arms with tense motions and rubbed the blood from her hands and face across the oversized Batman T-shirt.

Her voice from before drifted through Ashley's thoughts: "Isn't she your friend?" Jennifer had asked Clarence of Angela, knowing full well she herself was the monster. She'd planned the ambush, baiting them to the death trap with tears over her deceased parents and pleas for someone to take her to meet up with her uncle. Who would let a small child travel in the darkness of this world?

Jennifer's voice grew shrill, and her neck stooped forward, her eyes narrowing in Ashley's direction as the blond woman walked up behind the child, holding her rifle with the broken magazine in her left hand. Her right hand was curled up from having been shattered.

The world drifted around Ashley, turning gray as she panted in shallow breaths, trying to pull her thoughts together, trying to find the courage to spin and at least dive at her bat before Dean pounced. She wished the purple light would strike through her vision again and direct her where to go or at least comfort her before those teeth and claws sank in.

The two butchers in front of Ashley cackled evilly as both took a step forward. A form leaped out from over the pharmacy counter, kicking Jennifer aside and bringing the metal husk of a desk-mounted blood-pressure machine down onto the skinny woman's skull. Clarence stood taller than normal. Jennifer picked herself up off the ground and tried to sprint toward Ashley as Clarence stepped to intercept, grabbing the small girl from behind and hugging her struggling and raging form.

His shoulders lurched, his pale face and bushy eyebrows finally revealing a current of concern as his gruff voice snapped Ashley back into the moment. "Run, damn it!"

Grabbing the bat, Ashley jolted to a standing position and spun on her heel. Near the end of the aisle, Dean was grinning and holding an oversized fire axe with a red triangular blade. Ashley sprinted toward him as he let one arm drop and drew the fire axe up and back, his feet spreading as he brought the axe over his head and to the right. After another step, Ashley dropped back onto her left leg and let her right leg arch ahead, laying her form back. A whiff of air rolled past as Dean's swing went down and across, behind Ashley. She let her momentum and the slick floor slide herself between Dean's open legs.

Her head trailed back behind her, and she observed the look of shock on Dean's face. He spun around and hefted the fire axe back onto his shoulder. Behind him, Clarence was losing the fight to hold onto Jennifer, his arms flexing and stretching against her form. Ashley leaped to her feet, turned away from the scene, and sprinted toward the exit. Her breath sounded ragged, and each step seemed to shake her vision violently. The world skewed in one direction and then the other as the frame of the unsecured door grew bigger, closer and then flew open as Ashley sprinted out of the supermarket and into the sunrise of a new day.

25.

South of Watsonville, Just off the Shytown Trail
Zombie Civil Rights Group
Present Day

NYLA HAD NEVER SEEN her friends that upset. They hadn't spoken all day.

Eventually, they made their way to an old gas station and mechanic garage that had been gutted but still had a working rolltop security door on the bay entrance. Silently, they secured the place for nightfall. Once satisfied with their preparations, they dragged out their sleeping bags and prepared for the evening ahead. Since the place was pretty safe, they would only need one guard up. Mason sat with his machine gun in his lap, facing the garage entrance, accepting the first shift. A small lantern next to him gave off a dim glow.

Donathan hadn't smiled since the exchange with the Fine Line Protectorate. His face seemed almost sour.

When Nyla settled back into her sleeping bag, she heard something, a trickle at first but then a flood of tears and sobs.

Donathan peeked up from his sleeping bag, staring in Nyla's direction at first, then shock settled in. Ashley, huddled up on her bag, was hugging her knees and sobbing audibly.

Donathan and Nyla scrambled out of their bags, and Ashley squawked protests, facing away from the rest of them and toward a dark corner of the building. Mason's machine gun clattered to the ground as everyone stood around Ashley, trying to figure out what to say or do.

Nyla had never seen her cry before. She'd seen Mason cry on a few occasions, but Ashley seemed too strong to weep, sometimes just too angry to weep, as though the world had weathered it out of her years before. From the looks on everyone else's faces, no one else had seen it before either.

Finally, sniffing and wiping away tears, Ashley muttered, "You don't understand... It was years ago."

Mason was the first to crouch and try to make soothing noises toward Ashley's darkened form. Soft-hearted Mason, who saw only in color, form, and light, whispered calming notes, trying to slow down her sobs.

She continued, "I didn't mean to bail on you all. I just..." Ashley's voice trailed off with tortured notes.

Nyla followed Mason's lead and crouched down, patting Ashley on the back, trying to walk her away from her anguish.

"She killed my mom!" Ashley confessed to her friends. "She looked younger, but that was her."

The room pulsed, and in an instant, Donathan had his arms around Ashley's form, hugging her close, whispering promises of safety.

Up until that moment, Nyla had been comfortable following the others' lead and watching actions like that play out—studying her friends and their enemies, letting those moments occur as she stared at the reactions and waited for the next time she could tinker with science and odds.

That night, she silently promised herself that she was done observing these things from afar and doing only what was necessary. Her friends had already proven themselves enough. The undead, the Judge, the Fine Line Protectorate... No one was going to corner her friends like that again.

26.

Falling Sands
The Judge
Present Day

SLICK, SHINED FLOORS with sharp-edged patterns seemed to mimic the image of a large square carpet in the center of the chamber.

"Coadjutant! Co-ad-ju-tant!" The Judge's voice groaned through a mouthful of turkey.

Several ornate glass chandeliers dripped with crystal, the electric lights on top pulsing. The light cast from them reflected on grand square columns with white sheets wrapped around them.

A bald head wearing round-framed glasses angled into the room just beyond a door frame. "Yes, Your Honor?"

Twenty circular tables were set up with a mix of blue and white tablecloths, napkins folded and fanned alongside place settings as if prepped for a large wedding. The center of each table was filled with large culinary delights ranging from Peking duck to fresh salmon. The dishes were cooked, glazed, fried, or sautéed, but even with place settings for a hundred missing guests, the only seat in the house was taken by the large, bulbous form of a fat man. He was squeezed into a tight three-piece suit with his tiny flop of hair parted dramatically to one side. He lolled left and right, his monstrous hands stuffing turkey flesh from one table into his face.

The Judge sat back in his chair, floundering a bit with his massive form. "Oh good." He sounded unamused. "I thought you'd forgotten me."

The bald man stepped into the room and surveyed everything.

Through a fresh mouthful of turkey, he groaned, "Still haven't noticed it yet?"

The Coadjutant shrugged then ventured a guess. "You have all this food and want some company?" His tone went up at the end as if he would welcome an invite to the feast.

The Judge sat up, enraged. "No gravy!"

Silence filled the ballroom as the Coadjutant just stood his ground, basking in the smell of hundreds of plates, trying not to show surprise before finally adding, "I'll go tell the cooks to—"

"Wait, wait!" The Judge motioned a hand over the table.

"Yes?" the bald man answered with a wide grin.

"Any news?" the Judge questioned.

"Oh." The bald man sighed, his shoulders slouching forward. He paused for a moment to readjust his glasses. "Well...we had an uprising in one of the slave pens."

The Judge glared down at his food before looking back up at the Coadjutant. "The mining or the refining operation?"

"Refining, Judge." The Coadjutant cleared his throat. "Your Honor, we haven't had a real uprising in the mining slaves in years."

The Judge nodded. "Heavy chains saw to that."

The Coadjutant looked uneasy and nodded. "Also, a scavenger brought news from General Mary Helen."

The clatter of plates echoed through the room as the Judge shoved his tabletop aside. "Yes! And? Why is this the first I've heard of it?"

The Coadjutant sniffed nervously. "I learned of it this morning, and...well..." The bald man's shoulders looked a bit tortured as he stared wide eyed around the banquet room, hoping the Judge would pick up the hint. After an uncomfortable silence, he added, "We've been busy with—"

"Don't test me, boy! I'll breed you with the undead stock and sell you off to a science enclave!" the Judge shouted, waving a turkey leg he had just fished off the floor.

The lean, bald man shifted his weight nervously. "General Mary Helen is in fine health and thanks you for the assistance of the ring, but she states that your dogs are off their leash."

The Judge looked confused and turned the phrase over aloud. "My dogs are off their leash?"

The Coadjutant added, "I believe she means the Fine Line Protectorate. They have been eating most of the runners we send and torturing a lot of enclaves as they chase the Zombie Civil Rights Group up and down the Shytown Trail." He had had enough and reached toward the nearest table with a large bucket of steamed oysters.

"Ah ah ah ah ah! Coadjutant!" the Judge cautioned.

The bald man jumped up a bit and settled back down with a hesitant smile spreading across his lips.

The Judge waved an arm. "Drag that table over here. I could go for some oysters."

Loud scrapes erupted as the lean bald man heaved the metal table across the shiny finished floor as napkins fell over and utensils clattered to the marble floor. Eventually, that table supplanted the previous one, and the Judge began the process of shucking oysters only after shoveling a handful of fresh couscous between his fat lips.

"So, the Fine Line Protectorate... They are...?" The Judge waved an oyster knife in circles while bobbing his head up and down.

"Eating people from the tiny enclaves and towns, smashing things, and staging traps," the Coadjutant answered.

The Judge harrumphed and sat back, dropping the flesh of an oyster to the ground with a loud schlick. "They are—I mean—is it affecting trade?"

The bald man sighed. "No, thankfully?" he said, testing the waters until the Judge gave him an approving nod. "They seem to be leaving the large enclaves who create all the decent trade and just destroying the smaller, mostly family-sized townships."

The Judge wasn't even looking up at that point. His large hands were wiggling the tiny fork into an oyster.

The bald man sighed and added, "Also, a strange group of undead is gathering around Mountain View."

"What?" the Judge asked with shock. "That close?"

The Coadjutant nodded.

"It's probably nothing." The Judge shrugged and turned back to his food. "Send some troops to South Bay to investigate."

The Coadjutant nodded and slouching in defeat, backing out of the room.

The Judge sighed audibly and said, "Oh, and...?"

"Yes, Judge!" The bald man's voice was high pitched.

"You also forgot mustard," the Judge added with a voice of disgust.

Nodding, the Coadjutant disappeared out of the room and back up the hallway while the Judge muttered about having been unable to find a decent meal in twenty years.

27.

North of Hollister
Zombie Civil Rights Group
Present Day

"SHOULD WE GO INTO Town or scavenge?" Ashley's voice was a bit hoarse.

The hot daytime sun beat down on them as they looked down from a hill, peering at either a small enclave or a ghost town. Seven days had passed since their last encounter with the Fine Line Protectorate. Ashley was glad for that. They'd had a particularly bad night with a horde Nyla referred to as Curmudgeons, stubborn, sinister creatures, adept at smashing headfirst through most walls. They spent nearly the entire night running and, at one point, had to bait the monsters among themselves at a great distance just to keep them charging back and forth until the daylight came. After that, they'd put as many miles as they could between them and Curmudgeon territory.

Nyla kept wondering out loud how they'd even wound up over there. She was continually studying her map and a small notebook labeled Migration Data.

"It still doesn't make sense," she moaned. "They were so far out of their usual haunt. That horde should be much further south!"

Ashley couldn't remember ever having seen Nyla pout before.

"It's not a big deal," Donathan added. "Everybody makes mistakes."

"It was not a mistake." Nyla's tone turned defensive. She slapped dust off her jeans then began the process of tucking her map and notebook back into her backpack.

"Can we not go into town?" Mason asked.

Ashley shrugged. "What if they have paint?"

"Can we please go into town?" His voice suddenly warped into a strange pleading.

"Please stop fucking with him, Ash," Donathan said. "He's already strange enough without paint."

Nyla pointed down then hoisted her backpack over her shoulder. "I believe it is a functioning enclave. The map claimed they're capable of food and supplies, but I had a star placed for caution." She turned her palms up and shrugged slightly. "I didn't log whether they have a problem with Knight's Moon members or just travelers in general."

Donathan grinned a little more widely. "I thought you didn't make mistakes."

Nyla muttered something about "oversights maybe." She seemed rattled too. She hadn't been herself since their last encounter with the FLP. Ashley thought Nyla seemed more aware but also a bit more stressed. Seeing Nyla stressed and not spacey or carefree was strange.

By contrast, though, Mason had just been weird of late. They would find him some mornings just standing, facing the sun and tracing patterns in the air with two fingers. His arm held steady while his wrist flicked. He looked as focused as any master artist except that he was losing his mind. They weren't sure when the last time he ate was, he hadn't been sleeping much, and one day before, he'd quietly tucked his mask away in his bag. He hadn't pulled it down in a while anyway because no new paint was on it, but he used to keep it in the upright position over his head because it was his favorite thing in the world. Lately, he just tucked it away as though it didn't matter.

Even Ashley had to agree that life was much better when Mason was artistically insane and not insane insane. She was starting to see that, in Mason's case, art healed the soul as much as it infected.

Eventually, they picked their path down the hill and made their way toward town. Nyla had been quick to caution them that the hordes living near that borough weren't always nocturnal, so they needed to be careful. The sun felt too damn hot for that late in the year. They were low on food, and everyone was sweaty, dusty, and hot tempered. No one complained, though, because they knew what they were doing, sprinting between towns and taking their chances at finding shelter each night.

The world could end at any moment for us, Ashley thought, so it's just best to live each moment like it's our last. Mason knows this. Nyla knows this. Donathan honestly doesn't give a shit about how bad everything is. I'm the only one that gets angry about it. Maybe it's time to let go and be happy with the family I've found.

A moment later, they all were standing before the town gates and a giant dirt berm mounted around the outside. Everything was broken down, including the front entrance.

"Goodness, something terrible happened here." Nyla's last syllable fell off.

"Well." Donathan sighed. "Let's just scavenge and see what we can find."

Ashley reached over her shoulder and drew the bat off her back, which usually worked as a makeshift crowbar when they encountered ghost towns. "Start with the big building in the back?"

Everyone nodded and walked past the berms down the desolate street. Something squeaked off in the distance as wind gusted past the group, carrying dust and decay along with it. Sagebrush had grown between some of the buildings. Patches of dark paved road were showing through the last couple of years of dust storms and disrepair. Ashley paused to reflect on how the new West had reverted to the old West when the apocalypse arrived. Go figure.

They passed a run-down Walgreens on the left. That would probably be the next target for scavenging. Even if they didn't need medical supplies, those traded well. Some actual houses cropped up as they edged closer to that large building in the distance.

"What is it?" Ashley asked, hesitation tiptoeing into her voice.

Donathan shrugged. "It looks like it used to be a history museum."

They strolled up the curb and onto the sidewalk then angled toward the building. Their path weaved past big statues lining the walkway and up to two wooden metal doors, one toppled in and hanging awkwardly as one hinge had given way. Donathan went first. Nyla followed him, and Ashley stuck her arm carrying the bat into the darkness as she stepped inside.

Something wasn't sitting right with Mason. He had seen something a building back. They'd walked past something next to that Walgreens. It tugged at him like a splinter in his brain. He looked at the entrance with broken doors, one smashed inward, and just couldn't shake the nagging feeling that had washed over him.

He knew he had already made his decision, but that didn't stop him from at least trying to go through the motions of common sense.

He spun around and sprinted down the dusty street toward the Walgreens. A minute later, he was passing the store, angling right off the walkway toward the far side. He ran past an alley and then stood before it, marveling.

"Art Supplies," read the sign above the door. Mason's lungs ached—not because he'd just run but because he'd forgotten to breathe. The sun seemed to be peeking down from the clouds, leaving golden beams of light basking on the whole scene. Mason picked up half a brick sitting out front of the store. Somewhere in the back of his head, he felt the moment's need for music. He dragged the earbuds off his shoulder and cued his mp3 player to Brother Ali's "Palm the Joker." Stepping to the front of the store, Mason let the brick fly forward to smash the long glass panel in the front, and he climbed inside.

———

"Again?" Ashley couldn't believe their bad luck. "Another trap? Do these assholes have our playbook or a tracking device?"

Nyla racked the shotgun in her hands, and Ashley drew the bat off her shoulder as Donathan cocked his pistols.

"Something isn't right here," Nyla cautioned, shouting a bit over the sound of rushing water.

A tarp was mounted over the trio on a construction scaffolding. The four metal legs of the scaffolding stood around the group at strange angles. Water dripped and trickled down where they were standing, cascading down the front, sides, and back of their position in thick, gushing sheets. The sound of rushing water was almost overpowering. Just beyond their reach, standing against a back wall of the building, were Nym, Goblin, and Crooks, all unarmed and waving. "I can't figure out what they're trying to do here," Nyla remarked.

"Make a wet room so we can't use our mp3 players?" Ashley spun around before asking, "Wait, where's Mason?"

———

The song washed over Mason with uplifting tones and a beat that could have trickled out of heaven. With each step, he felt somehow more alive. He passed the cash registers, old signs of last-minute sales frozen forever in their ancient kiosks. Mason paused to upright an old grocery cart that had been toppled long before. Even over the loud music, he could still hear the squeak of its front wheel as he traipsed slowly up the first aisle. Fountain pens. Mass-produced throwaway Bic pens, fancy-looking Stipulas, the exalted and highly sought-after Pilot pens with their dark, flowing ink. From quill pens to markers, everything was there, from Sharpies to glorious hundred-dollar Letraset packs designed to attract the graffiti market. Mason let an arm drift out and just began slapping things off the shelves into the cart. When items flew forward on one side, he'd swat his arms in the other direction, just trying to pull as much as he could into the cart. At the end of the aisle, he turned right and followed the signs. Woodworking, fake floral designs, Styrofoam, arts-and-crafts kits, acrylic paints! The cart steered awkwardly as Mason sprinted forward and turned, skidding into the wall of the aisle.

Bottles of acrylic paints organized by brand, with several thousand shades of color, lined the floor up to just below the ceiling. Aside from a few toppled packs, the aisle looked mostly untouched by the outside world. Mason stepped forward, head raised high, studying the top shelves. Unshouldering his machine gun, he set it down and dragged his backpack off, opening it.

All at once, Mason began laughing and crying.

———

"He's not here," Nyla said. "Do you think he's stuck outside?" Her eyes trailed back to the scene until she noticed a strange object emitting jade light next to Nym's feet. Nyla focused on a break in the sheet of falling water and a coil.

"Doesn't matter. These assholes are done." Donathan flexed his hand on his pistol and took a firm stride forward.

"No! Don't—" Nyla shouted as Donathan surged forward, pulsing into a blur for two steps before his head connected with a drop of falling water. The kinetic force of the water droplet suddenly shifted from light to heavy as it continued its descent. A loud crack shook the room, sending Donathan flying backward and ping-ponging against the sheet of water behind them before sliding to rest at Ashley's feet.

"The fuck?" Ashley looked up from Donathan to Nyla with wide eyes.

"It's a kinetic redistribution factor caused by the green light." Nyla pointed in Nym's direction. "They were the ones who stole my creations. It swapped the force of Donathan's super-speed sprint with the force of a falling waterdrop. If you try to move into the water with any fast motion or shoot through it, it'll knock you around, hard!"

"So what the fuck do we do now?" Ashley asked in frustration, staring across at the forms of Nym, Crooks, and Goblin, all laughing at their misfortune.

No sound was heard, but Nym had placed an arm on Crooks's furry head to keep from falling over. Goblin hadn't bothered and was rolling on the ground, his face red and his eyes wet with tears of laughter. At least they couldn't hear the FLP's jibes over the river of water passing between them.

Nyla elevated her shotgun and aimed it at the FLP trio. Their laughter stopped, and their heads all rose excitedly as if waiting for what was about to happen next. Nyla then hoisted the shotgun and looked down its sights before tilting it on its side and continuing to stare in the direction of Goblin, Nym, and Crooks.

After a few seconds, Ashley said, "Look, Ny, I'm all for 'hold that thing sideways because that's how it came in the box,' but I don't think it's possible with a shotgun—"

Nyla shushed her and stepped toward the front-right scaffolding leg, holding the shotgun out ahead of her until the buttstock was propped up against the leg and the muzzle was facing the sheet of water. Nyla pulled an arm back and strained to hold the gun up with one hand as she looped the nail of her thumb over the edge of the trigger and slowly squeezed. The round fired, and in a second, the kinetic force transferred into the shotgun, ripping it from Nyla's grasp and sending it through the scaffolding leg. The scaffold and the tarp toppled forward. Crooks pressed up against the wall. Nym and Goblin both went wide eyed, scrambling to get out of the way. A torrent of heavy water smashed down on them. Kinetic, shifting liquid ripped a hole in the ground and the wall behind them. A bright flare of emerald light flickered when the mass of water flooded over the coiled machinery.

Nyla had been waiting for that, and she took a step forward. Mimicking Donathan's power, she surged to life. The falling water slowed its descent. Ashley's face froze with her jaw hanging open. She was still watching the water tumble forward. Part of the roof was collapsing from the damage the structure had sustained.

Nyla grabbed Ashley and slung her form over her shoulder. After two more steps, Nyla reached down, grabbing Donathan's waist with unearthly strength, and tucked him up under an arm. With Donathan dangling off the side of her waist, she sprinted out the way they'd come. Not pausing to open doors, she just kicked forward with force. The sudden burst of speed and power caused them to splinter outward. She stood in place for what seemed like an eternity but only amounted to a second, letting the chunks of wood explode ahead of them. Then she belted into motion again. She spied Mason a block down, frozen midstep, grinning while sprinting behind a shopping cart full of art supplies.

Nyla thought, Sorry, friend, as she flexed a foot forward and made a beeline for him.

Mason had been skipping along for the last five minutes behind a shopping cart full of paint and markers. His backpack was almost full to bursting. He'd had to tie twine between two zippers to make sure the pack didn't unzip itself from the sheer pressure of paint tucked inside. He was feeling like his old self, the creative self, the one who could pull ideas for projects out of anything. As the sound of shopping-cart metal exploded across the pavement ahead of him, he imagined what he would create with each piece of rubble and garbage that he strode past. Paper airplanes and wind. He had to do something with paper airplanes and wind. He had a fresh pad of yellow paper from the tiny office-supply section in that art store, and he wo—

The cart wrenched away and the world warped around him. An explosive gust of air echoed as sun and earth shotgunned him away from his treasure of supplies. He could feel himself screaming through the maddening pulse of light and sound until he found himself lurching forward all at once onto the dusty ground of an open road, collapsing into two other people.

Looking down at his empty hands, Mason whispered, "No."

He tried to stand before another gasping body yanked him off his feet while she was also trying to get up.

"What the hell, Nyla?" Ashley coughed and sputtered through dust-filled air. "I didn't even know you could fucking do that!"

Nyla said, "Sorry, I... This looked like the softest part of the ground."

Mason, still staring at his hands, whispered, "No."

Ashley raised an eyebrow in his direction before turning toward Nyla, shrugging slowly.

"I saw it, Mason." Nyla's tone was soft and cautious, almost motherly, "I didn't think I could drag the cart with us. I'm sorry."

Abruptly, Mason raised his fists to the sky and fell forward onto the dirt road, screaming in frustration.

Ashley let her eyes drift quizzically between Nyla and Mason before asking calmly, "Is that blur and seasickness what it's like being Donathan—"

Ashley and Nyla suddenly realized what they'd forgotten and rushed to Donathan's crumpled form on the road. Rolling him over, they found a large knot on the front left side of his face. He was still unconscious. Nyla very gingerly tried to wake him with rousing tones and slight shakes of his shoulder until Ashley cocked a hand and slapped him full force.

Donathan shot up suddenly, rubbing his head and swearing.

Without hesitation, Ashley dragged Donathan's pack off his shoulder and fished through it to find a half-empty flask he had stashed within.

Donathan belted off a long swig. He grunted then let his eyes settle on the scene before him. The two girls crouched down over him with concern as Mason sobbed into the earth behind them.

Donathan rubbed one of his temples before holding up the empty flask in Ashley's direction and adding, "I'm going to need a lot more."

28.

Ridgemark
Fine Line Protectorate
Present Day

"WELL, I THINK IT'S an excellent location." Goblin sounded hurt.

Nym drew a deep breath and replied in a soothing tone, "It seems like a good place to bait them, but at this point, I think they'll fade off the main trail." Nym turned to admire a large empty warehouse.

Goblin threw on his charming tone. "There's not much to scavenge in here, but there are big, thick walls for the night. Towns are a ways apart, and I think this would be their choice for the best possible evening campout." Goblin looked over at Crooks before adding, "We could even leave out signs of running water here."

Crooks nodded and donned his furry bat head then began an old-school dance step called the Running Man.

Cynicism fell out of Nym's mouth. "What? Like...leave a sprinkler and hose running on the front lawn?"

Goblin gasped then muttered, "You are so ungrateful." He cleared his throat as Crooks started waving from across the room.

Goblin raised his voice in frustration while clenching a fist in Nym's direction. "The last three traps have worked, and—"

"Didn't work in Madrone," Nym interrupted.

Goblin stomped a foot and said, "Fine. Two! The last two traps have worked. Look, I"—Goblin motioned around himself as he stuttered—"I-I-I worked my ass off to find this location. I"—Goblin picked up a brick from a rubble pile on the ground—"I design most of these heavy-hitter ambushes, you know?"

Goblin shot a sinister stare at Nym from across the room. The knuckles of his hand holding the brick were solid white.

Nym eyeballed the brick, flexed her gauntlet-clad hand, and stepped across an imaginary line before adding with excitement, "What?"

Crooks was waving two hands at the far side of the room.

Goblin spun on his heel and threw the brick with a clatter into the cement wall next to them. "This is total bullshit, and you know it. One tiny iota of respect is all I ask for—"

Nym laughed. Goblin pointed an accusing finger and ranted on. At one point, he reached down and snatched a rock off the ground to throw it at Nym, who giggled and ducked out of the way. Goblin very rarely broke, but when he did, it was a Chernobyl-sized meltdown.

Crooks fished around in his fur suit until he pulled out a tiny white flag on a stick and ran between the two of them, waving it in one hand while jumping up and down forcefully.

Finally, both parties got the hint, and Nym crooned, "All right, all right. What, dahling?"

Crooks pointed at the large dollar sign painted on a rolltop door.

"Interesting," Nym added. "I suppose we should take a look, although this seems baity."

"You think?" Goblin said in a dull tone. "I am 'affluent' with sarcasm."

"Oh, look at you," Nym added while walking toward the roll-top door, "working on your vocabulary."

Goblin stepped up next to her nodding, "I found a dictionary in that last town." As Crooks pointed at a combination lock, Goblin continued, "Our fanfiction should be improving"—he smiled—"exponentially."

Nym golf clapped then pointed at the combination lock. Crooks walked back across the room to where Goblin had thrown the brick.

"Wait wait wait!" Goblin held both of his hands up then pointed at the lock. "I remember this from years ago."

He stooped down low to the base of the door and held the upside-down lock up an inch from the ground. "I can crack it."

Nym laughed and said, "You can crack it?"

"I swear I can," Goblin replied. "It's a simple tactic. First, you pull down," looking at the flipped-over lock, he corrected, "or in this case up and add just a little pressure to the lock then spin the wheel to the left...until..." The combination wheel clicked slightly, and Goblin said, "There! Seven!"

Crooks dragged off his furry head and set it down on the ground. He picked up the brick but looked intrigued by the whole exchange, calmly observing from across the room.

"So the first number is seven?" Nym asked.

Goblin shook his head. "No, the first number is seven plus five, so...eleven."

"Twelve," Nym said.

"Yeah, twelve." Goblin spun the combination several times around to the right. "So then we clear it out and put slight pressure the other way until it..." Goblin turned the combo again and spun it around to the same spot. Then he continued turning the lock's face around while tugging on it slightly. "So there's a little resistance in this direction on twenty-three, so the second number is twenty-three."

Crooks nodded with wide eyes in Goblin's direction, then, leaving his furry head behind, he sprinted across the room toward his friends.

Nym had leaned forward a bit and placed a hand under her chin. Her other hand draped across her midsection, resting under the elbow of her opposite arm. "So the numbers are twelve and twenty-three?"

"Right." Goblin was excited. "Now I pull this lock full force and spin it the other way and log all the numbers that are in between two digits where it halts." The lock's combo wheel had stopped spinning, and Goblin said, "Here it's stuck between eleven and thirteen. So that is twelve." Goblin loosened his grip on the lock and flexed his hand for another second before announcing, "Watch the master safecracker at work."

Nym giggled again as Crooks nodded excitedly in her direction.

Goblin just carried on. "The next part, it stopped not really between three numbers. So that doesn't count. Now, here it is between twenty-three and twenty-five, so that is twenty-four. After that, it's between thirty-three and thirty-five, so that's thirty-four." Goblin drew a deep breath then said, "The last place the lock halts is between thirty-eight and zero on the lock. So that is thirty-nine."

Still holding the lock, Goblin looked up at his friends and said, "Twelve, twenty-four, thirty-four, and thirty-nine. The only number that doesn't factor into those four digits is thirty-nine. So the combination is..." Goblin glanced down at the combo lock and spun the wheel with heightened energy, "Twelllve." The combination lock stopped at twelve and turned back in the other direction. "Spin past the number, then...twennnty-three." The dial stopped at twenty-three. Goblin added, "Then the last digit—"

Crooks smashed the lock with a brick, causing Goblin to yelp and jump back. Crooks continued hammering away at the lock until he'd broken the steel clasp holding the lock in place. After dragging the lock off the broken steel, he threw it across the room.

As Nym was hyperventilating from laughter, Goblin clutched his injured fist and ran down a list of curse words before adding, "I hope all your chocolate chips turn to raisins!"

Crooks looked up suddenly and shot Goblin a look of genuine disgust.

Nym pursed her lips and made a soothing tff tff sound in Goblin's direction. "I'm sure it would have worked."

Crooks rolled up the door. In the room in front of them dangled a long piece of rope with a stuffed animal hanging from it. The rope was fashioned into a noose. Crooks yelped in protest and charged into the room to try to undo the knot.

Sensing something was wrong, both Nym and Goblin rushed in after him urging him not to touch it. A second later, wet stuff rained down on them.

"What is this crap?" Goblin asked while smelling the white stuff covering one of his arms. "Wood glue?"

Crooks managed to get the stuffed animal, which turned out to be a dog, undone from the rope and was trying to wipe the glue out of the toy's matted fur.

"If this is a trap," Nym said loudly, hoping someone was within earshot, "it sucks."

A loud boom thundered from above them, and a flood of glitter dumped down with a whump. It was so sudden and thick that it knocked Crooks off his feet, sending a wave of plastic specks from the room into the attached warehouse. Nym coughed out a mouthful of glitter. Goblin wiped rainbow-colored bits from his eyelids while trying to reseat his feet on the two-foot-thick mountain of glitter that now covered the cement under them. Nym was still coughing as several paper airplanes drifted down, some colliding with the concrete walls then falling. One paper airplane, in particular, stabbed into the glitter at Goblin's feet with a tuft sound.

He picked it up, unfolded it, and told the coughing Nym, "It says, 'Fake vampires are fake.'" Goblin handed her the paper. "It's signed, 'Fuck you, love the Zombie Civil Rights Group.'"

Nym gagged before switching to spitting in an attempt to get the glitter out of her mouth.

Goblin looked down at his arms and said, "Tarred and glittered. How embarrassing."

Nym hacked and spat before saying, "Next runner that shows up from Falling Sands, don't eat them."

"Dear God, I have craft herpes in my nose." Goblin had a finger up one nostril. "Why? Wha' di' you have in mind?"

Nym was dark eyed and frozen, staring straight ahead. "We need to get word to the Protectorate that we need tech and men."

Still with a finger up his nose, Goblin asked, "Goin' after them in full force?"

Nym shook her head. "No. We're going after their friends."

Goblin bent over, blowing a snot rocket out of his nose then looked up to add, "About time."

29.

Natividad near Blue Sky Farming Enclave
Zombie Civil Rights Group
Present Day

"YOU THINK IT'S TIME?" Ashley asked.

The binoculars felt heavy in her hands, and the bodies strolling through the streets seemed pretty bunched together. They were ugly things with green-and-brown skin and strange scarring. Donathan reached out and took the binoculars from her.

Two weeks had passed since they'd encountered the FLP, and the reprieve was welcome. Deciding to stray from the Shytown Trail a bit seemed to work out, and they were doing odd hunter jobs in some of the quiet enclaves that formed around smaller abandoned cities. The problem with those locations was hordes would always move back in whenever they were cleared, so hunters had built a decent industry by helping those cities exterminate their problems. Also, zombie-harvesting enclaves would set up shop nearby to gather and resell some stock back to the science enclaves. The problem with that, of course, was that once the Protectorate caught wind of a harvester operation that they didn't have their hands in, they could show up and smash it down. Some of these enclaves seemed to be bustling with life. Perhaps the damage the ZCR had done to the Protectorate Army a few months back had been extensive enough that their reach became limited. One of the harvesters even offered them grand compensation if the ZCR could trap any of the undead. Mason didn't seem too keen on that, so they stuck to their usual hunt-and-kill jobs for the towns.

After a day of maneuvering into position on top of an abandoned auto dealership, they'd spied the current enclave's problem. Nyla called them the Sullen. She had explained that the reason the enclave needed them gone was that they were known to swarm on sound, and they weren't nocturnal like many of the other hordes. In fact, they never slept. Ever. They also had long scars down their arms where they would bite and consume their own blood to hold off starvation so that the horde could remain dormant en masse and wait for some unfortunate soul or unfortunate enclave to make too much noise near them, then they would attack.

"I guess the whole world is lucky their breed isn't more commonplace," Nyla joked. "Trade, farming, hunting, the world would be more stagnant than it already is. We'd never get a decent rest, either."

Ashley thought that, for all her previous life's obsession with tracking zombies, Nyla sure seemed anxious to help kill this breed. She and Mason had disappeared for most of the early morning hours, planting charges and setting up lures to try to bait them into specific places. Mason seemed like his old self again. The shock of losing so many art supplies had worn him out for a few hours until he realized his pack was still secure and overflowing with paint. He had repacked it without his canteen, though, and the gang had to track him down a plastic bottle to take its place for a while. Ashley wasn't sure Mason cared. If he could, he would drink ink.

"It's time." Donathan nodded in Mason and Nyla's direction near the edge of the building.

Nyla produced a panel of switches, and Mason, wide eyed, held up a hand to plead for control of the first one. Nyla nodded and gave him the mesh of wire and metal switches. Mason reached up and pulled down his hockey mask to reveal a fresh painting of the faces of tired people running a marathon. One was even splashing his face with water from a paper cup.

"Oh wait." Mason's muffled voice sounded surprised behind the mask before he raised it. "I almost forgot."

Setting the switches down, he sprinted across the roof and dragged a baby-blue sheet back toward them. It had been rolled up on the side he was gripping to conceal and pull the contents. Once he deemed the location fit, he unfurled the sheet, spread it out, set up a steel teapot on a Coleman campfire grill, and placed ceramic yellow teacups in four spots on the sheet.

"Huh," was all Ashley could muster.

Nyla skipped over and sat down on one side of the sheet, choosing a teacup and smiling.

"We found a store fully stocked with tea, running water, and even an ancient camping stove that still had propane." Mason sounded almost feverish. "I figured before I unveiled my latest piece, we should probably take time out to enjoy the day."

The stove hissed and popped to life as the kettle was set on top of it.

"Won't the kettle attract the horde from here?" Ashley asked.

"Probably not," Donathan answered while sitting cross-legged across from Nyla. "Even if it does, they'd still have to cross where we planted the biggest explosives. I think we're good."

Ashley watched Mason sit down between Donathan and Nyla while still fussing a bit with the tiny stove next to him, turning one of its dials up.

Gravel gritted around under Ashley's shoe as she stood up and stretched before looking at the deep-blue early-autumn sky, a few pearly-white cumulus clouds near the horizon. She let her eyes lower back down to her friends and their tea party. All of them stared at her as if anticipating her disdain.

Ashley let a smile stretch across her face before she echoed Donathan, "I think we're good." In an instant, she was kneeling down to grasp her yellow teacup, waiting for the water to boil.

———

The tea party had been lovely. Nyla discussed a science enclave that she knew, which might loan her some equipment. Donathan remarked that the tea was fantastic, but only after tipping his flask into it and lighting up a cigarette. Their own personal Mad Hatter, Mason, had pulled a small jar of pennies from one of his IBA vest pockets and woven patterns of round copper around his spot on the picnic sheet.

Ashley couldn't stop giggling and rambling on about how she missed those silly moments, and maybe something was to be said for keeping Mason well stocked in paint.

Mason lifted his head and nodded approvingly toward Ashley before adding, "Art is a statement. Art is an expression. Art is a feeling. But these days, it's mostly breathing when you've forgotten how."

A little tipsy, Donathan leaned forward and whispered in a voice of gratitude, "You know, when we found each other, Nyla included, it felt like we had finally crossed a threshold."

Everyone else was nodding.

"Like life was stirring in the world again. I mean... I know we could die at any moment, but quests for artifacts and people aside, it kind of feels like we're living again."

"I know what you mean," Ashley said. "I don't feel like I'm waiting for the other shoe to drop."

Smiling, Nyla motioned to the switches. "I think it's time."

Everyone stood up and stretched again before hunkering down behind the roof's edge as Mason pulled the series of switches in front of him.

Mason sat up a bit and waved a hand out toward the land ahead of them. "I feel I should explain this: We came across a shoe store, so this felt appropriate, but there's another theme here too. Throwing an object onto a power line is an act of defiance. Whether brought about through bullying or because you want to show off, leaving something on a power line is a statement of defiance, and that echoes true in our world. Basic things we needed and once loved are often just out of reach."

After a metallic click, a massive blast echoed off in the distance as objects began falling and draping over the power lines. The horde echoed the blast with a thunderous roar and charged up that street. From the ZCR's vantage point on the roof, they saw another blast between them and the horde. As the dust cleared, loud thuk thuk sounds echoed as shoes fell from the sky. Most had their laces tied together, and many wrapped their spinning forms around the power lines traipsing up the street. Most missed and fell harmlessly to the street or bounced off the buildings.

Nyla's excitement gushed out. "I figured out how to rig a garbage can so that it would throw the contents up instead of just incinerating them." Then her matter-of-factness showed through for a moment. "It's a pretty simple thing to do."

After another blast, shoes fell a bit closer from up the street. The horde was in full movement, loping up after the trail of raining and waving shoes adorned the power lines.

Mason stood up and stretched before adding, "Because people used to love and collect shoes so much before the world fell, I'm calling the piece, Sugar in the Gas Tank."

"Nice name," someone behind them remarked.

Everyone spun and froze. Mary Helen, the former general of the Protectorate Army, was standing in the middle of their tea set. Behind her, a large green Shat slammed down onto the roof with a crack. Dust and gravel scattered. Nyla lost her footing and fell backward over the edge of the roof with a scream.

"Nyla!" Donathan shouted, peering over the roof.

The giant armored spider rose on its spindly legs. It flexed a long front arm for an appendage, waving it in their direction. The creature clicked a hidden set of jaws tucked somewhere into its body. Mary Helen's usually pristine white-and-blue armor was dirty and stained. She held her chin low, dark circles under her eyes, which seemed to be screaming. Her gloves were missing, and her short-cropped hair was a mess of tangles.

The last time they had seen her, with Barbie's help, they had coaxed the large green Shat into stabbing and biting through a hole in the back of her head. It took control of her before everyone else fled and blew up Half Moon Bay.

"H-hey," Mason whispered, eyeballing his machine gun, still lying on the roof near the tea-party set. It had fallen over when the Shat leaped in. Mason edged forward.

Not even Donathan or Ashley seemed to move. The situation was new ground for everyone.

"Hey, Mary, you look…" Mason nodded some nervous encouragement. "All right. I mean…" He had managed to get within a foot of Mary Helen and slowly leaned around her, trying to get a glimpse of the back of her head. "I see that hole is healing over with some nice flesh. It looks…" Mason reached up and placed a hand on Mary Helen's shoulder. Her dark eyes were full of fire. "Not totally gross?" He slowly nudged her sideways until she was no longer standing on his already disheveled patterns of copper pennies, which he'd left on the picnic sheet.

Mary Helen let her face drift into a wide smile and narrowed her eyes as she grabbed Mason by one shoulder and tried to throw him over the edge of the roof. Instead, he slammed his side into the lip of the building and crumpled back into it, his mask clattering under him, one hand holding himself up as he gasped.

The Shat chirped and lunged at Mary Helen. She spun to face the creature, holding up a glowing blue hand. "You will fucking obey, Precious." The creature froze in place the second her hand rose.

Ashley signed to Donathan quickly, "The ring!" and pointed in her direction.

Furrowing her brow, Mary Helen held a sneer on her lips. The oversized green Shat behind her jolted and spasmed. At one point, it seemed to kneel forward on the roof as if struggling to hold up its own weight.

Ashley signed, "Why is the Shat fighting with her?"

Donathan signed, "Maybe they haven't bonded yet like Barbie and Beauty?"

Ashley pointed at Mason's machine gun then at Mary Helen's back.

Donathan signed back quickly, "We can't shoot her, remember? Her weird shield thing."

A large gasp came from Mary Helen as her hand stopped glowing blue. She spun back around to face the group. The green Shat stood up behind her and roared, its oversized arm angling in their direction. Its many legs stretched out from its form, looking sharp and dangerous.

"Do something!" Ashley signed with such force it resembled karate.

Donathan surged forward and wrapped his arms around Mary Helen's, pinning them down to her sides and looking down at her with wide eyes. "Holy shit. What am I doing?"

Mary Helen squeaked in frustration and struggled. The Shat waved its sword arm in their direction then pulled it back, spinning quickly in place before roaring in confusion.

Ashley cursed and then sprinted forward, tripping halfway. She scrambled back to her feet. Then she swung wide as Mary Helen sent a weak kick in her direction. It managed to knock Ashley down for a moment, but she leaped back up and jumped on top of them, trying to fight through the struggling forms and pull the ring off Mary's finger. Sometime during the struggle, Mason leaped on top of them. He was shouting that he had it but the ring was stuck. Mary Helen was screaming and cursing. They could still hear screams from the undead running up the street.

Suddenly, Mary Helen stopped struggling and looked shocked at Donathan. "Something is... Is he licking my finger? I am going to fucking kill you all!"

Everyone was struggling to hold Mary in place. Ashley's muscles ached. Donathan looked down into Mary Helen's eyes, which seemed filled with the fire of several splitting atoms. He drew a deep breath and placed his lips on hers, kissing Mary Helen deeply, letting his tongue connect with hers. Mary Helen shouted into his mouth, then squeaked, then gasped and kissed him back.

Ashley sat back, wide eyed, before pulling off them as they stopped struggling and settled into each other. "Are you kissing the queen of crazy town?" Ashley's shock turned into a whisper.

"I got it!" Mason shouted, jumping up and away from the kissing pair.

Donathan leaped to his feet and groaned, "Let's go." After grabbing Ashley by the cuff, he dragged her across the roof as Mason took hold of his machine gun and sprinted to the edge.

Mary Helen stood up quickly and ran a hand down the side of her head, attempting to straighten her hair. A starry look had glazed across her eyes before it turned into rage. She glanced down at her right hand before spinning to face the Shat, which was already swinging his sharp appendage across and into her. In the space of a sharp scream, Mary Helen was flung off the roof and out of sight.

The Shat unfolded its head and swung a bug-like face out from its abdomen, a long tentacle whipping in their direction and then up to the sky as it screamed at the three scattering friends. Gravel scattered audibly as the Shat leaped up off the roof in the direction of where it had flung Mary Helen.

Ashley's top lip was pulled up high, and she looked sideways toward Donathan. "Did she kiss you back?"

"Problems." Mason pointed toward the ground. "That horde is here!"

The Sullen were falling over each other, screaming and shifting below. The ground was covered with flexing undead as they clacked their jaws and clawed their way up the building.

"Fuck" was all Donathan could muster.

"Get down and fire off the last switch," Nyla shouted up to them from somewhere. "I moved the explosive closer."

Mason lunged down onto the metal detonator switches.

"What does she mean 'closer'?" Ashley asked as a wall of fire and flesh exploded up into the building, knocking her backward off her feet.

———

"So if you kissed her and she is infected by a Shat, does that mean you kissed a dead girl?" Ashley asked in a taunting tone.

"Shut up!" Donathan had had enough. "Shut up about it! It has been two days of this shit! When the building was collapsing around us and we were digging our way out of stone and dead flesh, I wasn't even thinking about the fact that night was falling. You know what I was thinking about?"

Mason joined in on the fun. "Mary Helen's wet smacker?"

Ashley's face lit up as she gave Mason a look of elation while trying not to hyperventilate. Donathan rubbed his hands across his temples before reaching down and pulling out a cigarette and his Zippo. A moment later, he dropped the lighter with a clatter on the tile floor.

"He dropped his lighter! It's true love!" Ashley squealed.

Nyla said, "I don't think this is very safe. We are way too loud for this time of night." She glanced around the darkened walls of the derelict hospital basement before adding, "We could wake the dead…and then Donathan would kiss it."

"You too?" Donathan shouted.

Ashley was rolling on the ground, laughing. Mason had dropped his mask and was propped up against the wall, trying to stand.

Ashley managed to calm the torrent of laughter for a moment to say, "Okay, maybe we should stop, I mean—"

"Over my dead body," Nyla interrupted.

Ashley, Mason, and Nyla all fell over at the same time, laughing. Donathan snatched up his lighter and strolled off to some darkened part of the hospital basement to hide. Ashley knew she had stomped his ego down pretty hard, and he'd probably be more quiet than usual over the next few days, but he'd had it coming.

Ashley was really enjoying tormenting Donathan. She didn't often get the best of him. He should have rolled with the punches better, and he definitely shouldn't have kissed Mary Helen.

30.

Salinas
Zombie Civil Rights Group
Present Day

"THEY HAD BEEN CAMPED just outside of Salinas, a short ways off the old 101 freeway, for over a week. That spot wasn't the best to stay in because a horde was in the area, which Nyla referred to as Gharoids and which Mason had been referring to as "The Gary-oids." They had leathery skin that flaked off, bug eyes, and a jawline so shrunken, compared to the top half of the skull, it looked comical. They were anything but comical, though. Each mouth was filled with long, sharp teeth jutting out at varying angles. They wouldn't scream or give warning of their presence until they were right on top of you, and when they did, the night would erupt with giant numbers of them. The last night had been a particularly hard one, with running between buildings in downtown Salinas, followed by hiding until the sun rose, before venturing back toward the 101 freeway. They were only hanging out there because it was the most obvious path to San Francisco that the traveling Knight's Moon festival would take. Nyla said that they could pass by sometime within the next two weeks and that, until Barbie was with them, they should avoid San Francisco.

They had found an old building next to a large oak in a field, which gave a decent view of the freeway. They cycled out in shifts, two awake, two asleep. The days were hot and long for autumn, and as tired though she was, Ashley couldn't rest anymore. So she had found her way out of the dark building and was standing, staring at the large oak tree on the hill, trying to come to grips with what she was seeing. Without thinking, Ashley found herself striding toward it, marveling at the fact that its branches were filled with open umbrellas, each with a yellow canopy fanned out to match the tree branches' angles. Eventually, she reached Nyla, who was standing at the thick base of the tree, looking up.

"I know I don't have to ask, but..." Ashley didn't even finish the sentence before Nyla pointed up the length of the tree.

Ashley stepped back and studied the tree some more until she found Mason's form far up the tree, his entire body extended and trembling with effort to hold himself in place, with his left arm curled around the tree trunk as his right arm attempted to balance an umbrella on a small branch. The task looked difficult, but Mason wasn't the sort to shy away from stuff like that.

Ashley's instincts took over. "Mason, for the love of God, get down before you break your neck."

Mason replied, "No."

"Do I have to go get Donathan?" Ashley asked in an annoyed tone.

Mason replied, "No." Then he dragged some twine out of a pocket, trying to lash an umbrella to the branch with one hand. He almost lost his grip on it but somehow managed to keep it from falling through the boughs. "Look...I only have, like, three more umbrellas."

"Get down." Ashley had had enough.

"No." Mason's tone was defiant as he glared down from the tree.

"Get down."

"No."

"Get down!"

"No."

Nyla shot a neutral look in Ashley's direction and let it trail up back toward Mason as the two kept shouting a tirade of "Get down!" and "No!" at each other.

"Get down, or I'm coming up there!" Ashley screamed.

Mason whispered down, "You couldn't climb this high even if someone threw you."

Ashley kicked the tree with a dull thwack. Mason lost the twine he was holding, and trying to snatch it out of the air, he lost his grip on the tree itself. A curse word and a snap of branches ripped through the day as he fell from the tall oak. Ashley panicked and ran under him to try to catch him, succeeding only in collapsing both of them in a heap.

More curse words ensued as Ashley tried to shove Mason off her.

As he scrambled to his feet, Ashley shouted, "Your stupid obsession keeps making the crappy world even more dangerous!"

Mason took offense and loosed a string of rage, pointing out how he would have never fallen if not for her. Eventually, the argument upgraded into a shoving match.

Nyla backed away slowly toward the building, where Donathan was standing out front, rubbing the sleep from his eyes.

"Should we try and stop this one?" Nyla asked Donathan in a curious tone.

Donathan cleared his throat and reached into one of his pockets to fish out a tiny flask, grunting in frustrated tones as he fumbled with the cap. A moment later he gasped from the cold whiskey and replied, "Best to just get out of the way. I think this one's been brewing for a while."

Nyla quickly stepped out of the way as Mason was sent careening toward where she was standing. When he finally came skidding to a halt, he scrambled to throw his pack off his shoulders and fish through it.

Ashley was halfway through a sentence when she ran back at him with an arm cocked up. "...tired of you risking your life over nothing. The whole world is fucked, and each day we're chasing you off cliffs—"

With a quick flourish, Mason produced a plastic bottle and sprayed globs of yellow into Ashley's face.

Ashley stumbled and halted while cursing. She tried to wipe the blobs from her face. The anger mixed with surprise turned her voice to a high-pitched scream. "Did you just throw paint in my face?"

Mason's eyebrows went up, and he looked down at the bottle in his left hand before replying, "No!"

Ashley looked at the yellow-covered palm of one of her hands before raising it slowly to sniff it and ask quietly, "What the hell? Is this mustard?"

"Hot mustard," Mason answered.

More screams of frustration erupted from Ashley as pain took hold of her and she tried furiously to rub the mustard off her face. Nyla eventually took pity on her and threw her a half-filled canteen. Ashley was sniffling from the spice, her face red as she dumped and wiped water furiously across her hands and face. Nothing seemed to help much. Her voice and sinuses sounded stuffed, but the pain had done the trick, and she'd managed to calm down enough to try to reason through the moment.

"Why?" She sniffled. "Why do you do this to us, Mason? Why don't you get it? We live in a broken world filled with half-living corpses! This is just colors and paint! Why are we always risking our lives over this? It is nothing."

Mason hissed audibly and looked as if Ashley had kicked his puppy suit, the suit of puppies that Mason had claimed might deter zombie attacks. "I don't know why you don't get it!" He scooped up the fallen umbrella, folded it back in on itself, and stepped back up to the oak tree. "Remember the urinal that was a trap. The piece that was inspired by Marcel Duchamp?"

"Yes, Dada?" Nyla chimed in as Ashley glared at her through swollen eyes for contributing.

"The Fountain," Mason wheezed as he scrambled up the tree's base and attempted to pull himself up one of the thick, low branches. "Duchamp took aesthetically neutral items and proved that they could be works of art."

"So fucking what?" Ashley shouted, still dumping water across her eyes. "So he made a sculpture out of a pisser."

"No, he didn't make the sculpture, he—" Mason drew breath as he leaped up to another branch and scrambled for a moment to hook his leg over it.

His mask fell off and clattered back to the ground, landing face up. Dull gray clouds spread across the mask, parted by a bright, sharp beam of light angling diagonally across it.

"He proved that we could find art in anything. It is considered to be the most influential piece of the twentieth century because it inspired everything after it. You'll never forget it. Try as hard as you can and resent it all you want—that piece will never leave your mind." Mason huffed and climbed higher. "It is solid in your memory. He put that there without even making the urinals himself." Mason paused to catch his breath and look down at his friend's wide eyes. "And none of you have even seen the actual pieces!"

Donathan let his eyes drift away from Mason and back down the tree. He mumbled, "This is too deep for me," before taking another pull from his flask.

"No, it's not." Mason sounded frustrated. "It's simple. It's the crack of a bat at a baseball game. It's the bullet leaving the chamber. It's Tupac and Biggie on a Sunday morning. Art can inspire, it can shock, it can break down barriers, it can even be a political statement and a weapon." He had unfolded the umbrella, settling on his spot on the tree. He produced some twine from a pocket and began the process of lashing the umbrella to the branch. His voice echoed out above the chirping of a flock of birds darting into the sky out of hidden places in the tree. "It isn't just form and color, but you're right." His voice rose in pitch. "We do live in a broken world filled with half-living corpses. That didn't change when the undead arrived! There were always people who floated through life, never appreciating the subtle blends of light. They didn't understand the dance that carried on around them. They never heard the music echoing into the heavens. They just hungered for themselves!" Mason finished lashing the final umbrella to the tree and balanced on the branch. One of his hands pressed hard against the main trunk of the tree. The other rose in victory as he stared down at his friends. "Yes! We can die at any minute. That has never changed! It is why we have to live for every moment! It is why I can't stop creating art, even in a dead world!"

Ashley, Donathan, and Nyla were all silent at the base of the tree looking up.

Ashley sighed deeply and raised a middle finger toward Mason. Donathan smiled and tucked his flask away then copied her pose, grinning up at his friend. Nyla followed their example. After a few seconds, they were all laughing.

———

Two weeks turned into a month, with still no sign of the Knight's Moon. Jae should have at least connected with the ZCR and reappeared to direct them on the proper path. Ashley thought Jae should have planned a rendezvous better. Nyla kept remarking that if she could get near another cache, maybe she could find more flares to signal Jae.

Donathan didn't want to move from Salinas, though. Most hordes didn't traipse through at night. Nyla said the absence of activity was odd. She had tracked the area for well over a year and knew their patterns shifted pretty well there. Still, the downtime was much needed by all of them. The problem was that when Ashley and Mason were stuck together somewhere, Ashley and Mason were bickering—brother-and-sister-in-the-new-world type bickering. If they had more ammo, one of them might have wound up dead by that point.

"There's no reason it should work. Zombies eat flesh. Puppies are made of flesh." Ashley loathed the puppy-suit argument, but they always wound up back at it, somehow.

Mason kicked a rock up the trail they'd been following, next to an old quarry they'd been rounding for about an hour, seeing if anything was there to scavenge. "It makes perfect sense when you think about it. Zombies used to be humans. They still have some remnant of emotion left in them."

Donathan coughed.

"See?" Ashley jeered. "Even Donathan doesn't agree with you."

"Don't drag me into the puppy-suit argument, Ash." Donathan stepped to the front of the trail and peered down into the quarry. "There is some old digging equipment down there."

Ashley continued her rant, rounding on Mason, standing in front of him, and jamming a finger into his chest. "After everything, how can you still think there's emotion left in those things?" Ashley hissed, "I've seen them eat babies."

Mason stamped a foot. "But we've seen them laugh."

Nyla stepped next to Donathan and peered down. "Is that a coil of rope next to the equipment? We can get a decent price for that at an enclave. There's something strange about that ground, though. There is also a train station nearby that I've been to before. It's pretty ransacked, though."

Ashley bapped Mason's mask off the top of his head.

Mason's jaw dropped as he shot an injured look at the mask in the dust before turning around to shove Ashley.

Ashley was laughing and trying to right her feet before tripping on a large rock embedded on the trail. She stumbled back while cursing.

Donathan and Nyla just watched the comical scene unfold as Ashley staggered back past them and fell over the lip of trail, tumbling down the hill into the quarry. She swore the whole way down.

"Well, who didn't see that coming?" Donathan asked as Nyla shrugged back at him.

Mason gathered up his mask and ran up next to them. Ashley had halted in the bottom of the quarry and was surveying her surroundings.

"Goodness!" Nyla remarked. Donathan and Mason peered down the quarry walls. "Is that mica?" Nyla realized she was asking the wrong people and shouted down to Ashley, "Is that mica?"

Ashley yelled back up, "I don't know what mica is!"

Nyla shouted in response, "Large sheets of crystal that break off flat like dinner plates."

Ashley said loudly, "Then it's mica! There's a lot of it. It's hard to stand here. Can we sell it?"

Nyla shouted back in a frustrated tone, "Don't move!"

Donathan cocked his head toward Nyla and raised an eyebrow. "What's going on?"

"Burrowers! They shouldn't be here." Nyla's eyes were wide with fear.

Mason whispered, "Like Burrowers burrowers? Teeth and all?"

Nyla nodded.

Large sheets of mica splintered and scraped.

"Something is happening!" Ashley screamed, reaching up over her shoulder to secure her aluminum baseball bat with her right hand. The ground shook and drifted downward. The sheets of mica warped around Ashley, dragging them with her in a sudden sea of shifting flat crystals. She started to lose her footing, still screaming obscenities.

Shifting her weight forward, she juggled the bat to her left hand, holding on to the bat's barrel and trying to press through the torrent of shuffling minerals threatening to engulf her. With a sudden jolt, the ground fell away out of sight into a dark hole that had appeared below her. Ashley hung in place for a moment as the dark cavern below issued forth a cry of rage. Her breath was shallow and quick as she glanced up past her hand, trying to figure out what had stopped her descent. Somehow, she was still holding tightly to the barrel of the bat. She found the grip of the bat wedged between two pieces of granite. Beforehand, the granite must have been buried by the mica. The knob of the bat held fast. The granite jutted out just above Ashley, from the edge of a new, almost-vertical, concave wall.

"Just don't move!" Donathan shouted from somewhere above.

As the shadows below her screeched again, Ashley raised her other hand to take hold of the barrel of the bat to attempt to pull herself up. She felt lightheaded, and a whisper of frustration slipped out, "Please...just don't—"

Another scream belted from below, and the granite let out a grinding sound as one of the rocks fell forward, away from the wall.

Ashley screamed as she fell into the darkness.

The darkness howled in the distance. Ashley fumbled around in her pockets until, finally, she produced her L-shaped flashlight. Some light was still beaming in from overhead, but it wasn't enough to make anything out. She toggled on the red light and took stock of her surroundings.

Tunnels were carved into the dirt and sand, the walls wavy and flowing with lattice patterns. As she aimed the flashlight, the light bounced and warped off the walls. The tunnels expanded and shifted to form odd angles. Something was walking toward her in the darkness. She stepped back and waved the flashlight behind her, following the tunnel away. Anything was better than that. She sprinted down the tunnel, light shining off the walls of polished dust and sand.

She had to be in a Burrower's den. No other answer was possible, really. Wanderers and scavengers would whisper about those things, but not too many had ever seen the inside of one and found their way out. She had to try, though. The tunnel branched in two directions. She sprinted left into the larger opening.

She shouted, "Donathan?"

Something screeched in reply, and Ashley skidded across the oddly polished ground into a nexus of tunnels. She sprinted back into a separate tunnel, that opening smaller.

She called out, a little more reserved, "Nyla?"

Shuffling and shifting was all she heard in the darkness. She ran the other way, back toward the nexus, and chose a tunnel across the path. That time, she halted after a few minutes, toggling off her light in the darkness and gasping to catch her breath. She could hear something moving.

She whispered, "Mason?"

A scream echoed through the tunnel, and she flicked on the flashlight. Only five feet in front of her stood a mass of quivering flesh. Some of its flesh flipped and rippled to form an elongated mouth of teeth, warped and inhuman. The rest of it looked stitched together by some fractal pattern across its skin. No eyes could be seen on it. It hissed and then screamed, more of its flesh flipping to widen the mouth and show long, sharp, pointed teeth in the darkness.

Ashley fell backward and kicked, her feet squeaking against the ground as she retreated away. Her hand reached behind her to unsheathe her bat. Her heart felt as if it was going to pound out of her chest.

The creature screamed again and lunged forward, then an explosion flashed, and flesh showered around the tunnel. Half of its head was missing as the Burrower smashed back into the tunnel wall.

Ashley stood up, confused, as the creature's form and flesh shifted around the tunnel wall, restitching itself together. A second mouth appeared on its back. It shifted its weight away from the wall and back toward Ashley. It edged forward again and exploded once more—another boom with a flash—and dead flesh splattered the walls. A third explosion followed, and what was left of the creature just collapsed in the tunnel. Screams echoed in the distance.

Donathan stepped out of the darkness into the red light, a tied rope forming an x around his chest, and he was holding a smoking shotgun defensively before him. "You okay?"

Ashley nodded, finally dragging her bat over her shoulder.

"We're officially out of shotgun rounds." Donathan nodded behind himself at the trail of rope. "C'mon."

They ran a bit down one tunnel to the nexus and back up another. Ashley honestly thought she'd run farther than that after falling. Finally, they found the rope angling up toward a tiny bit of sunlight shining down into the tunnel, with Mason and Nyla peering down at them.

Without words, Mason and Nyla tugged up the slack on the rope. The darkness screamed behind them, and another Burrower stepped out of the shadows. Its form had no visible mouth. Instead, every patch of flesh had been flipped, showing sharp teeth. One of the patches leaped off off its face toward Donathan. Ashley had stepped defensively between the creature and her friend. Rolling a shoulder, she swung her bat. A ping echoed down the hallway as the chunk of flesh zipped back past the creature and into the darkness. A slit split down the creature vertically, and a raspy voice screamed through it so forcefully that Ashley had to cover an ear with her free hand. Two more patches of flesh bounded off of it, and Donathan surged forward with a flash of speed as the shotgun clattered to the ground behind them and two cracks echoed from his nickel-plated pistols, now drawn. Flesh splattered the wall.

The creature shrieked, and all the patches lunged forward. More cracks rang out. Donathan yelped in pain. A few patches had made it past his shots. The patches were stabbing into his flesh, covering his form.

Ashley whispered, "No," and was suddenly aware of how far off Mason's scream was.

In an instant, Donathan was gone. The only thing left was a pulsing mass of flesh, no longer showing teeth. The severed rope fell from his form to the ground with a thump.

The creature's mouth reformed, and it screamed at Ashley with its ear-piercing shriek. Ashley backed away, dumbstruck from what she had just witnessed. The creature lumbered forward then pulsed with white. It shifted back three feet then unraveled. It fell off Donathan's form, pulsing and moving backward to where it had been standing moments before. Donathan stood looking down, gasping, sweat drenching his face, both hands white knuckled, with pistols aimed at the ground. He looked up at Ashley. The creature screamed again, turned bright white, then pulsed into dust, shifting apart as it fell and scattered across the tunnel.

Ashley's mouth was open wide, and she whispered, "Donathan, what was that?"

Donathan gasped, "No idea." He fished the rope off the ground and shoved it into Ashley's arms. "Climb now. Think later."

Ashley reached up high on the rope, wrapped one leg around it, pinning it between her feet, and shimmied up. A few minutes later, she was hoisted into Mason and Nyla's arms. Donathan lumbered up behind her. After that, they were scrambling up the angled quarry walls and toward the train station. When they breached the quarry, everyone swarmed on Donathan's sweaty form, hugging him and gushing with excitement that he was still alive.

Donathan was still gasping from the surge of adrenalin and said, "I have no idea why. I felt a lot of pain. The world panned out, and I could see the universe. Then the whole cosmos was shifting and pulsing around me. I felt something pop out of joint, and everything flooded back into place." He had finally gotten some of his breath back. "I don't know what it was."

"Fuck it. You're alive!" Ashley exclaimed.

Donathan groaned, "Yeah, but I'm getting real tired of stuff trying to smother me!"

For once, Mason's eyes didn't seem wild. They were just filled with tears. Nyla joined in on the cheers.

Eventually, Nyla regained her composure enough to remark, "The Burrowers didn't belong here. Something has changed."

They walked east, trying to put some distance between them and the Burrowers.

31.

Downtown Monterey
Zombie Civil Rights Group
Present Day

THEY'D MOVED DOWN the 101 and camped not far off it for a few long weeks, with still no sign of the Knight's Moon. Once, they had dipped into a town to spend the night and resupply. Not too many jobs were available right then. Things seemed disjointed. Some of the enclaves they encountered wanted nothing to do with them. That late in the year, most harvester enclaves were worried more about their coin than they were about clearing out hordes. Plus, rain had been falling on and off, and harvesters didn't tend to like chasing zombies in the rain. After the bad day with the Burrowers, Ashley couldn't complain much. She was just glad to be far away from them.

"You think it's them?" Ashley asked out loud.

They were following a tip from a random trader, that a gathering was heading to Cannery Row.

"They've never stopped here before," Nyla answered. "At least, not that I can remember."

The ZCR had topped a hill downtown and were in view of a large group of folks hustling around the old aquarium. Two large metal towers stood as tall as the aquarium, wire drifting off their forms, surrounding the pavilion below. A construction crane was busy at work. A sea of tents was camped around the base of the towers and blocking some of the ancient seaside buildings trailing away on both sides of the street.

"Yes!" Mason shouted while sprinting down the hill toward the festival.

"Probably attracting too much attention on their usual route," Donathan added.

As they edged out and around the street, they saw a throng of people waiting outside the front tents marking the entrance. Knowing the routine, the group of friends got in line.

A man with face paint and brightly colored clothing was shouting through an old-fashioned cone megaphone that everyone moving inside was to be blood tested. The crowd was full of excitement. Folks were juggling. Other people were yammering about when they had found the festival in the South Bay. Someone was complaining that they'd been camped two days during setup and no dancers or showmen were around to warm up the crowd. People were wearing bright colors and strange backpacks. Even Ashley started to feel excitement creeping in. The usual remnants of that world were browns and leather, but the second the traveling ravers showed up, everyone donned their colorful gear to spend one night away from the darkness, protected by the technology Nyla had perfected. At sundown, the Knight's Moon enclave would power up the fence line with an electrical current designed to keep the darkness out. Life was beginning to feel magical again.

Ashley glanced around at the crowd. "I've really got to get some—"

"Colorful clothes," Mason finished.

Ashley just smiled in his direction then gave him a nod. "We all should."

Nyla sighed, "I'm not a fan of being on this side of the crowd. These lines are long. Paul and Ginn must not be here yet. They'd at least be entertaining us with dancers and speeches while we wait."

They found their way to the front of the line, and each went into a separate tent. The dust in the tents there smelled sick and ancient, unlike the last time, when the tents had a little excitement and color. These seemed a bit more sterile, with just a box and a folding chair in the middle. The attendant had no face makeup but instead wore a red clown nose and orange wig.

"Please sit down." His gruff voice sounded excited, at least.

Ashley sat down in the cold chair and heard him rummaging through the box for a moment. A second later, she felt a sharp sting in her arm. "Hey, you didn't even wash me off first!"

The attendant cleared his throat and apologized. "Running low on time. The sun is going to set soon." Ashley was the first out on the other side of the tent. From there, she could smell chicken grilling in some of the vendor tents. People giggled in the crowd as they roamed past. A woman with blue hair and candy bracelets went by, waving at Ashley. Ashley returned her wave as Donathan and Mason arrived from their tents. Mason was missing his body armor and his machine gun. Donathan didn't have his pistols.

"They didn't take my bat?" Ashley said quizzically.

Donathan shrugged then stared at two men waving at them from across the crowd. Donathan returned their wave before the two guys strolled away.

"Was that Francis and Eddy?" Ashley asked.

Francis and Eddy had tried to rob them once before. They had seen Francis and Eddy again in Waterfalz's tent at one of the other festivals.

Donathan looked up and to the left before saying, "You know, I think it was," in a shocked tone.

Shouting erupted from the third tent, and Nyla stormed out. The attendant followed after her a ways then just waved a frustrated arm in her direction before stomping back inside his tent.

Nyla's spacey tone had been replaced by frustration at the commotion. "I didn't know him." Her weapon was gone as well.

Ashley remembered that the last time they'd run into Knight's Moon in Santa Clara, Paul ordered folks with jackhammers to remove the concrete from the roads and sidewalks. "I think you were right earlier. Paul and Ginn must not be here yet."

Mason was giggling and crouched down, his backpack splayed out across the ground and a paintbrush dabbing paint across his mask.

Ashley shrugged off an uneasy feeling. "I'm starving."

Donathan stared at a sign on a tent across the crowd. "I need a drink before sunset. Meet back here in twenty?"

"Fine." Nyla sounded defeated. "I'm going to go and try some of the regulars and see what's going on."

"Good plan. Go, team." Donathan's mind seemed elsewhere as he drifted away into the crowd.

———

They met again an hour later. The generators hummed to life as the sun dipped below the horizon. The wires forming a fence around the travelers' enclave powered up. Indigo at first, the wires changed to deep red as the current pulsed up to the tops of the cranes. Nyla started yelling, her voice shrill. Ashley couldn't quite make out what she was saying.

Donathan rushed forward defensively with his hands up, palms open and slowly flexing toward her. "Just calm down."

"Why are they red? They shouldn't be red!" Nyla sounded unusually frustrated.

Donathan shrugged. "Upgrades, maybe?"

Nyla gasped and stared wide eyed at Donathan. "No one can upgrade my tech but me. Someone has stolen this, and red does the opposite!"

"The opposite of destroying dead flesh and leaving living unharmed is..." Ashley's eyes widened more with every syllable.

Nyla nodded. Mason groaned and lowered his mask. The front of it showed a man with wild eyes holding a gun to his own head.

Donathan was studying the crowd. "Everyone looks pissed off too." He pulled out a cigarette, placed it between his lips, then lit it with his Zippo. "The vibe feels like the world is about to erupt."

That was true. People were shoving and shouting short and sharp words at each other. Many folks were sweating and glaring.

"Shit," Nyla said.

Everyone's eyes went wide. Nyla never cursed.

"That test wasn't a test. That's why it seemed strange to me. I didn't recognize the guy, and it was a syringe!"

"Yeah, inoculating people, right?" Ashley mouth was hanging open a bit, her eyebrows high. She looked down at her shoulder at the place of the pinprick.

"No." Nyla shook her head, sounding a bit spacey, like her normal self. "They inoculate against this by poking with a pin three times, using a dying version of the virus on the needle. They were injecting people—infecting people."

Mason lifted his mask, staring wide eyed. "Are we going to become zombies?"

"No, of course not," Nyla said as Mason's shoulders lowered a bit. "We've been inoculated. We won't turn. Probably about half of this crowd has been inoculated because they are all folks who try and follow the Knight's Moon on their tour." Nyla sighed. "We are just locked in with folks who are about to turn."

Donathan murmured through pursed lips, "And no weapons."

Ashley drew the bat off her back. "Well, almost none."

Just then, the bassy music drifted away, and the large view screen overlooking the stage lit up, "Well-y, well-y, well-y, well how is everyone doing tonight?"

The crowd cheered, some screamed, and Ashley's blood ran cold. She knew that voice.

Nym's face drifted across the screen. "I'm Nym, tonight's host for the Knight's Moon Festival at Monterey."

The crowd cheered, and a flat beat played in the background.

"On camera, we have Mr. Gobbles the Goblin, and of course, tonight's DJ—good old Crooksy!"

The camera shuffled as the cameraman sprinted across the stage. The camera then focused in on the full-fur-suited furry with a pair of headphones strapped up to one of the ears of a bat-faced head. On the other ear, an LA Dodgers baseball cap cocked sideways.

Ashley stomped her foot and said, "Really? The fucking Dodgers?"

The camera spun back around and focused on Nym. "What a wonderful night it's going to be, so let's all take a deep cleansing breath in and appreciate the fact that it's the apocalypse out there, but in here"—the camera zoomed in on her grinning face—"it's a party!

"That tickling sensation that's creeping up your spine... that rush of blood pumping through your ears so loud that you'll swear it's part of the beat?" Nym spun around on stage with her arms extended, looking toward the sky. "That's our doing!" She stopped suddenly and looked seriously at the camera. "That's our gift to you."

"I can make it." Donathan stomped out his cigarette and lowered his gaze at the crowd.

"No." Ashley followed his gaze. "No, you can't. What are we going to do once you start this fight?"

"Bring down those generators." Donathan pointed at the towers.

Nyla shook her head. "No, they stuck them on the towers and removed the scaffolding."

Donathan looked back at his friends. "Find a way." He turned toward the stage and cracked his knuckles. "You don't have a choice."

———

Nym was on stage, trying to get the crowd to chant, "P-A-R-T-Y," but the crowd had turned ugly, throwing things and screaming obscenities back, which seemed to entertain her more on camera. Donathan pulsed through the crowd and shifted down the lines of individuals then up, over, and onto the stage until his fist collided with Goblin's unsuspecting cheek. A moment later, the world surged back around him and the camera scattered into the crowd below the stage. Someone took the cue and retrieved it, aiming it back at the stage. On the large screen above, the camera focused on Donathan, who was standing there stone-faced, staring Nym down.

She looked genuinely shocked and said, "Where did—"

Donathan surged forward, knocking Nym to the ground. In a heartbeat, he yanked Crooks out of the DJ booth and sent the furry flying offstage. When the world halted, he noticed the crowd screaming in fright. Donathan grinned on camera. He hadn't even known he could throw people like that.

Nym was scrambling to her feet. Donathan heard a pop and a hiss. He surged back off the stage and around through the panicked crowd until he collided with Goblin. Donathan's shoulder checked him, causing Goblin to fly face-first out of sight. A guy could get used to fighting like that. The Uzi Goblin had been firing clattered somewhere into the crowd. Nym was shouting at Crooks for something and screaming about the ZCR being there. Whoever was aiming that camera from the audience hadn't missed a moment of it. Donathan surged back into the crowd where he'd left his friends. They were gone. A moment and a burst of speed later, he found them huddled together in an open canvas tent, facing one of the large metal tower girders.

"So what's the plan?" he asked.

"We..." Nyla just raised her palms in Ashley's direction while shrugging, wide eyed. "There's nothing. No cars in the fence line to smash into the tower. We don't know where our weapons are, and the crowd is turning."

The FLP had fled the stage. People in the crowd were screaming and shoving. The red neon fence line was pulsing here and there.

"I think people are running through the fence now and disintegrating." Mason sounded a bit panicked. "What do we do?"

Weapons were firing off in the crowd. Nym, Goblin, and Crooks were apparently taking no chances. People screamed and sprinted past the tent. Dark and ethereal roaring sounds and screeches erupted nearby.

Nyla whispered, "This is their zero-sum game. We are trapped."

Donathan tried to shut out everything: the crowd, the screams, the roars, and the gunfire. He just stared at the tower.

The screen on stage shifted. Someone was running across the stage with the camera. Whoever it was ducked into the DJ booth, and a loud slam echoed. A microphone bled feedback that seemed to shatter the fright.

After a moment of eerie calm, someone said, "It's always a beat that saves my life." That voice was so familiar. Nyla grinned and tensed up, cheering loudly and shaking her fists toward the stage.

The woman's voice continued, "And the beat just goes all night, yes."

The camera shifted away from the ground and focused on a grinning man, who said, "We heard someone was throwing a party in our honor, but we didn't get an invitation." Paul nodded into the camera.

A loud crack of gunfire erupted.

Paul looked around the DJ booth before grinning more widely. "So good of you all to make this room bulletproof!"

"Paul." Ginn sounded concerned.

"Ah, right." Paul continued, "Nyla and the ZCR, if you can hear us, we've got a bit of backup but left Barbie and Beauty with the Sages." The camera refocused on Ginn, who was placing a record on the platter. "You've got to take down the towers so our backup can get inside the fence line. If you are in the audience and follow us regularly, congratulations, you are now a member of the Knight's Moon, so fight like one."

Ginn cued up the music, and some heavy symphonic notes rolled in on the back of a decent beat.

"Find any weapon you can, and fight back against anyone who is turning! Help clear a path for the ZCR to the tower, and for God's sake"—the camera spun back around on a grinning Paul—"kick some imposter ass!"

"Paul, do you really think that's warming up the crowd?" Ginn lowered the volume of the music, causing the bass line to dip.

Paul frowned and said, "Too right." The camera swayed a bit as he struggled to hold it up with one hand and point his other hand toward the tower. "It's like dear old Mama used to say." The camera shifted around to aim up at one of the glowing red towers. "Tear this motherfucker down!"

The crowd cheered and surged in the other direction. People ripped the canvas tent apart around the ZCR and were turning its poles into weapons. Some held the cloth between each other as a makeshift trap as if they were in an ancient gladiator arena. In one sentence, Paul had galvanized the crowd to fight back. Mason, Ashley, and Nyla all cheered. Donathan was still studying the tower.

"Someone lowered them a ladder." Donathan pointed at the tower. "They're all up on it now."

Sure enough, Nym, Crooks, and Goblin were on the bottom platform of the tower, flipping off the crowd and looking quite smug from their position. Crooks held a rifle in one arm, the buttstock on his furry hip, the muzzle pointing toward the sky. Two folks, apparently loyal to the FLP, were making similar gestures from the top platform of the tower.

"We can do it." Donathan turned around to face his friends. "I can do it."

Ashley gave him a crazy-eyed stare, waiting for him to elaborate.

Donathan turned back to the tower. "I think I can throw someone up there with my speed."

"What?" Nyla cocked her head sideways at Donathan.

Donathan nodded toward the stage. "I threw that furry off-stage at an insane angle. I can throw someone. I'm just not sure I can aim them."

As Ashley stepped up shoulder to shoulder with him and stared up at the tower, Nyla asked, "Then what? You just throw us past it into the fence?"

Ashley turned around and held up a finger to her lips. "Wait, wait, wait, shush." She turned back around as Nyla and Mason lined up on her right. "I can hear it this time."

Someone in the crowd screeched, and folks were shouting commands in the distance. Nyla was straining to listen.

Ashley continued, "That thing that Waterfalz mentioned at the last festival. The thing Mason could hear. The beat."

Mason nodded excitedly.

Ashley went on. "There's a beat." She pointed to the tower. "It's up there. It's like I can hear it or see it. I don't know how to explain it. It's strange."

Nyla sounded frustrated. "The only beat I hear right now is coming from Ginn and Paul." She motioned toward the speakers. "It's 'Jedi Mind Tricks.' We need a better solution than 'Let's throw someone and—'"

"I can aim," Ashley interrupted, turning to face Donathan. "Your speed, my dexterity—I'll aim."

Nyla's eyes were filled with concern as she motioned up toward the tower. "It's still an impossible shot. You'd have to be extremely—"

"Lucky." Donathan and Ashley both finished her sentence.

Everyone was staring at Mason.

"Who to the what, now?" Mason hunched down, his eyes gigantic.

Ashley grabbed Mason by one shoulder and the back of his pants. She spun him around, almost knocking him off his feet until they were both facing the tower.

Mason waved his arms and shouted high-pitched screams. "No! No! No! Bad idea! I am not okay with this—"

Ashley looked over at Donathan and nodded. "Do it."

Donathan surged forward, grabbed Ashley by the arm, and flung her around and forward. Through the sudden burst of speed, Ashley managed to land three sure-footed steps then was twisted at the waist by Donathan, who was still holding her by the arm. A flash of the tower appeared through the blurring world. Ash, flexing her back and rolling her shoulder, let go of a screaming Mason. Her bat tumbled out of its sheath, clattering on the ground nearby. Pain jolted through her knees as she stood up. She had slid about ten feet. In the distance, she heard a thump, and she knew Mason had collided with the tower.

Gathering the bat and glancing at the tower, she sprinted back to Donathan and Nyla. "He made it?"

"He's up there near the generators"—Nyla pointed—"but I don't think he knows what to do."

Ashley watched Mason sprint toward a generator, chased by one of the FLP henchmen, a woman in a green tutu, white T-shirt and candy bracelets up to her elbows. Nym, Crooks, and Goblin were already climbing the long ladder up from the bottom platform. Crooks still had the rifle slung on his back.

"He is the lucky one." Nyla pointed up at the tower. "Just above that platform on that girder is a linchpin. If he pulls that pin, the top platform will topple forward. The whole thing should collapse in on itself."

Ashley took her eyes off the tower and squinted at Nyla. "But he'd die."

Donathan told her, "Remember? He's the lucky one!"

Mason was cornered on the far side of the platform opposite the generators. Some words were exchanged between him and the woman. He lowered his mask and dove sideways a second later, and the woman tripped and tumbled over the handrail, screaming as she fell.

Screams and shouts erupted from the crowd. More of the partygoers were turning. Nyla spun around and came face to face with a sweaty man pulling out clumps of his hair and shrieking. Donathan surged forward and sent the screaming man flying with a good punch. The crowd parted for a second then closed around Donathan, Nyla, and Ashley. At least the humans were organized enough to bring the fight to them.

Looking up, everyone could see Mason's luck wasn't holding. He had been pinned, his mask knocked free, and was being beaten in the face by another FLP henchman. Goblin, Crooks, and Nym were standing around him. Ashley couldn't hear the punches land over the music and the violence in the crowd, but every hammer fist brought down on Mason's face felt like lightning coursing through her. Punch after punch was causing forked tongues of rage to erupt. They cascaded through her until something snapped.

"Throw me," Ashley demanded.

"What?" Donathan sounded dumbfounded. "You're not the lucky one, Ash." He turned to face her and asked, "What's with your—"

"Just throw me, damn it." Ashley squared her shoulders. "I finally figured out what Waterfalz meant." Ashley jammed a thumb into her chest. "I'm the thread! If my power is dexterity, then I'll land on my feet." She drew the bat off her back, gripped it tightly in one hand, and turned back around, looking up toward the platform. All in one breath, she whispered, "Ready, steady, go."

The world lurched around her as she spun. She caught two feet on the ground and reached for another step, but the ground wasn't there. Everything slowed for a second as her feet trailed along, searching for somewhere to stand. She was ten feet up and could see the tops of partygoers' heads. The bat slipped out of her hand as she traveled higher. The aluminum mass floated ahead of her. She had to be fifty feet in the air. Her stomach shifted and threatened to make her nauseous. She stretched out, snagging the bat out of the air. Gripping it with both hands, she spun it in the air once and looked away from the ground toward the platform. Nym, Crooks, and Goblin were standing just ahead of her.

The platform was rushing toward her quickly, and she knew the collision was going to hurt. She choked up on the bat just as Crooks turned around. Ashley lowered her chin, leaned in with her shoulder, and followed through. A loud ping followed a bright flash of violet light. She tumbled forward into someone, then pain shot through her shoulder as she fell against the platform, smashing into the generator. Her ears rang, and she tried to shake sanity back into her head. She remembered the rage and stood back up, still gripping the bat while trying to catch her breath. Crooks and Goblin were gone. Nym and a dark-haired man with a sinister grin, ripped jeans, and a dirty Santa Cruz Skateboards shirt stood between her and Mason. Ashley couldn't see Mason's face, but she heard him groaning in pain and could see blood on some of the rubberized coatings on the platform. Everything was glowing bright red from the coils above. Red sparks showered down occasionally, and Ashley could feel the hair on her arms standing on end. She lowered her gaze toward Nym and the man.

The man lunged.

Before Ashley realized what she was doing, she connected a one-handed inside swing to his skull. Following through, she let her other hand grip the bat, shifting its form across. She smashed a second swing into his head in the other direction. Then she spun around down to one knee, letting her arm bring the bat back around. The bat smashed through the man's legs, sending him flying off the platform.

Nym's jaw hung open where she stood. She didn't look frightened, just stunned. "What the hell is wrong with your eyes?" she whispered.

Ashley just stood glaring at Nym, waiting for her move. Shouting echoed from below, over the loud buzz from the generator. Ashley stepped forward and flexed her arm holding the bat. Nym fell backward onto the platform, still wearing the same stunned look on her face.

Ashley pffted then walked over to Mason, who had a split lip and a busted eye. She picked up his hockey mask with her free hand, shoved it into his arms, and helped him stand up. Nym just sat a few feet away, staring. Ashley turned and walked toward the generator. In two steps, she rounded on the machinery and bent down to flip the switch. The generator wound down on that section as red light trailed out and away from the platform, disappearing down the coil. The music powered off, and people cheered as more shots rang out down below.

Ashley turned back around on the platform toward the defeated Nym. She motioned for Mason to follow her as she walked toward the ladder leading down.

"That's it, bitch?" Nym whispered. "But I ate your mom."

All at once, that fire exploded in Ashley. She dropped her bat, and grabbing Mason by one arm, she spun around toward the girder, ripping the lynchpin out in one full motion. A loud pop sounded overhead as the top beam fell forward onto the platform. Some of the coils above snapped off and fell. Other coils seemed to be straining under the sudden platform shift.

"No, no, no, nonono!" Nym scrambled to hold onto the rubber mesh but failed to get a foothold and slid backward down below. For a moment, Ashley forgot they were trailing after her and just relished the fear in Nym's eyes. Most of the guardrail ripped free when the pylon fell across it. Ashley managed to get hold of part of it with one hand, still gripping Mason's hand with her other. The tower creaked and dipped forward. Ashley hissed, feeling the full weight of Mason as her grip slipped. They were dangling off the quickly collapsing tower.

"OhmyGodohmyGod!" Mason dangled from her one arm and continued screaming, "OhmyGodohmyGod!"

Ashley grunted then shouted, "Mason, I need you to calm down and grab my hand with your other hand, then try to—"

Mason just got louder. "OhmyGodohmyGodohmyGod!"

Ashley winced and tried to stay calm. She could feel every drop of perspiration on her hand. She could feel her grip flexing. "Try to climb—"

Mason continued shrieking, "OhmyGodohmyGod!" While still screaming those three words, he deftly reached up her arm, looped a leg upside-down up onto her neck and then shoved himself awkwardly up, scrambling up her body until he was back on the slanted platform, perched on an outstretched bar of the handrail and pulling Ashley up onto it. He was still screaming, "OhmyGodohmyGodohmyGod!" in her face when she stood up.

"Shut up!" she shouted back at him, almost in tears, before managing a tight hug as they looked over the pavilion below. The tower jolted forward, and the bar tipped a few degrees downward.

"Ashley?" Mason sounded like a child. The night felt calm and still up there. The sound just carried with no ground to reverberate off of. "I'm so sorry for pushing you into that mica with those monsters."

She shushed him. "It's okay."

Mason continued in a high-pitched voice, "And I'm sorry I always argue with you about the puppy suit."

Ashley shushed him again and kept hugging him but held onto the handrail just behind him. She let her tone flood with comfort. "Mason, it's fine. It's fine."

Mason looked down, his voice strained. "It's really not."

Ashley felt her mother's voice flowing through her, "Shh, Mason, it's fine. It's going to be okay."

The tower lurched forward hard.

"Just hold on tight to the rail," she said.

Mason's eyes were wide and his breath short as the tower tilted a bit more forward. Through his busted lip, he said, "My mask fell."

The tower creaked as the beams below buckled.

He shouted, "I really miss my mask right now!"

Metal screeched behind them, and the tower spun from the coils trailing on the rear side. Strange metallic noises were grinding as the steel strained from the coils still mounted on the ground behind the tower. The wind rushed, metal grinding, and the tower's trajectory changed until it was falling forward into the Monterey Bay Aquarium roof. The force of them hitting the roof knocked the wind out of them, sending them skittering across the concrete. Mason lay gasping on his stomach, and Ashley was looking up at the stars, seeing whiteness creep in around her vision and feeling as though she was on the edge of passing out.

That fall had hurt, but they'd only fallen about twenty-five feet before the tower spun into the building.

Ashley could hear Mason gasping and, after a moment, dragged herself to her feet.

In another half hour, they were off the building. In the darkness, they'd had to find a way to get off the roof onto an awning below. Then they shimmied down from there with a couple more falls, but after having survived the first one, they felt up to the task. Mason kept yelling to Donathan and Nyla that they were banged up but okay.

Ashley was sure happy to see them both when she finally made footfall on solid ground again.

A crowd was still around them. The Knight's Moon enclave had made good on their promise and arrived in full force with weapons, lamps, torchlight, and glow sticks. Occasional rounds were popping off in the distance as the Knight's Moon held back the night. When Ashley and Mason limped up with Donathan and Nyla, loud cheers erupted from the crowd.

Moths flickered around the lamps and glow sticks in the parking lot. Ginn and Paul stepped into the center of them all, holding their arms wide with warm smiles. Folks cheered more loudly.

After a minute, when the crowd's volume died down, Paul said slyly, "It seems as though you all once again stole our limelight."

A few folks huddling in close chuckled.

"Paul, we're not exactly in a safe spot here," Ginn said, always the sane one.

Paul leaned back, staring at Ginn before adding, "Now, hang on a minute, a few of us just fell out of the sky."

"About that." Ashley sounded a bit somber, turning around to face the tower toppled across the roof. "Are the Fine Line Protectorate dead?"

As Ginn shook her head, Paul answered, "We saw two of them up there fall flat on their face." He lit up for a moment. "I mean, it was a sight to see! She left a dent in the ground and everything! Then just got up and trotted off." Paul shrugged. "They looked alive, but they aren't, right?"

Ashley answered, "Butchers or... They have different names, depending on which enclave you're closest to, but...high-functioning zombies. Strong when fed and can certainly take a hit. They still eat people."

Ginn kicked some dust and added in a small voice, "I knew the Protectorate had painted a bullseye on our back after the last run in, but this here..." She looked around at the recent desolation of Cannery Row. "This is dirty."

Donathan nodded. "They're infecting people, too, under the guise of your blood test."

Nyla chimed in, "Probably to kill your fans."

"I need to go find our stuff," Mason said under his breath to Donathan.

"No need," Paul replied in a confident voice before standing tall, raising his hands, and clapping to one side of his face.

Nothing happened.

Paul sighed, glancing from left to right, looking annoyed. He clapped again.

Only crickets chirped until someone in the crowd shattered the silence by coughing and sniffing.

"Really, people? That's the signal to bring their stuff forward." Paul's voice boomed with frustration.

Folks stepped up and dumped out Mason's mask, Ashley's bat, and their other weapons, which had been confiscated before the event, along with loads of ammunition.

"That ammo's not ours," Mason pointed out.

Ginn replied, "Compensation for a rough night."

They gathered up their stuff and made a large campfire. Ginn kept shooting Paul nervous glances, but Paul didn't seem too worried about the monsters in the night.

When they first started to build it and Donathan mentioned light discipline, Paul added, "We have plenty of guards against the monsters. Let them try."

Folks had been filtering by, re-establishing camp, shaking everyone's hands, and tending to Mason and Ashley's pain and cuts. Some wanted to know about the ZCR while others were asking about the fall from the tower. More than once, someone remarked while passing by that they were happy to finally be a part of the Knight's Moon. Ginn ran around establishing a guard rotation and urging those who weren't on guard to eat or get some shut-eye. She seemed like the mom to this clan of apocalyptic partygoers. She disappeared a short time later. The moon was high in the sky, and somewhere off in the distance, something howled and shrieked. Paul took Donathan aside to a quiet part of the clearing and, in a whisper, asked about the ring.

Donathan nodded. "Yeah, we've had it for a while. Do you want to see it?"

Paul shook his head. "No, no, I think it's better off with you all. I don't want that cursed thing."

Donathan shrugged. "What's the fuss over it?"

Paul harrumphed a moment as if wondering what he should say before asking, "Did you ever read Tolkien? The Lord of the Rings?"

Donathan replied, "I saw the movies when I was a kid."

Paul nodded. "Tolkien based the 'one true ring' after that thing. It's the original power ring, the ring of Solomon."

Donathan stood taller and asked, "Huh? So if I wear it, I'll turn invisible?"

Paul shook his head. "I don't think so. I heard Waterfalz talking about it one night when I believe she'd been dipping a little too deep into the sauce."

He chuckled as Donathan tried to imagine a drunk Waterfalz. The first time he'd seen her, she lectured him about drinking too much.

Paul continued, "For most folks, it controls the dead." Paul leaned in closer. "But to pure souls, it does other things. Apparently, that ring is the entire reason the world is the way it is now."

"So why not just break the damn thing?" Donathan asked.

Paul shook his head. "She said some of the other lore about the ring that Tolkien borrowed is true. You won't turn invisible, but it is supposed to be indestructible. Also, if you use it and you aren't undead or a Sage..." Paul grimaced in the moonlight. "Everything dark and sinister nearby will come running for it."

"Anything else?" Donathan's tone went up a bit on the last syllable.

"Not much," Paul shrugged and knocked the dust off his jeans. "Solomon was a mostly pure soul, so he did strange things with it, so I've heard. Some other weirdness about him throwing it in the ocean and him finding it later."

Donathan chuckled. "I must have missed that in Sunday school."

Paul half smiled while squaring his shoulders. "You still remember Sunday school?"

Donathan grinned then tried to look neutral before asking, "So what's Waterfalz want with it?"

Paul asked in a plain voice, "Is it her or us you don't trust?"

An uncomfortable silence passed, and Donathan finally just held his palms up in defeat before shrugging and adding, "This is the way of the world these days."

Paul nodded slowly. "I've heard she wants to take it away from our world. Maybe fix the balance. But"—he then held up his hands in defeat—"who knows, right?"

"Do you trust her?" Donathan asked.

Paul nodded. "She's not a Dark Sage."

Donathan lit up a cigarette and paused to take in a deep drag. "What's a Dark Sage?"

Paul's voice sounded a bit hoarse and forced in the darkness. "Try that ring on, and you're bound to find out."

32.

Downtown Monterey
Zombie Civil Rights Group
Present Day

DAWN BROKE JUST AFTER seven, and Mason awoke to take in the scene. Far more tents had been assembled in the night than he'd thought. Plenty of folks strolled around the perimeter, guarding. The camp spanned a ways up the streets both toward the ocean and angling toward downtown Monterey.

"Did you realize there were this many people here?" Ashley asked drowsily while standing up from a sleeping bag and rubbing her eyes.

Mason shook his head, and Paul answered while walking up, "Yes, I know. A sorry showing for us, but we only learned about the fake rave last week. We didn't have enough time to get our A-team here."

Mason beamed, and Ashley said, "Yes, yes. 'A-team.' I got it too."

Food smells wafted by, and Ashley and Mason hustled away from their camp, trying to find a tent vending meal. Donathan usually carried most of the coin, but Ashley always had an extra stash on her just in case.

To Mason's surprise, when they went to pay the woman serving apple hotcakes, she just told them, "We don't take money from the ZCR." She happily scooped them both a plateful and gave them glasses of milk too.

"Real milk?" Ashley stared down at the mug before looking back up at Mason with wide eyes.

Mason added, "I haven't tasted milk in years."

After downing both glasses, they each made a sour face and concluded it was probably goat milk, which made sense with a traveling enclave. When they turned around to walk away, a blur of dust arrived with Donathan standing in the middle of it.

"About time you woke up." Ashley grinned and walked Donathan back over to the vendor tent.

Mason went to go back to their campsite but noticed an odd hissing sound. The sound vanished. Clacking rang out and then more hissing.

I know this sound, Mason thought. It's— He took off sprinting through the camp, peering left and right until he found the culprits.

"Spray paint!" Mason pointed an accusing finger at two Knight's Moon members, a man and a woman wearing faded jeans and T-shirts. The woman had a purple do-rag tied back over her hair, and at their feet was a whole milk crate full of spray cans.

The man smiled and nodded at Mason. "Yeah, man!" His accent screamed of central-valley California. He held up a can, offering it to Mason. "You paint, brother?"

Something resembling a squeal crossed with a scream echoed from Mason, and he ran forward to hug the man before taking the can out of his hand and running to the wall. "Wait, no...this is blue. I need a block primer. Do you have white?"

The guy brought over the entire milk crate and set it at Mason's feet. "Knock yourself out!"

———

An hour passed. Ashley, Nyla, and Donathan had both edged past Mason painting on the wall. At one point, he sprinted back through camp to find a stepladder. When Ashley, Nyla, and Donathan had finally decided to check again on Mason's creation, they found a huge crowd had gathered. Folks who had initially been breaking down the camp to pack up and head out were all around. People were oohing and ahhing, and everyone seemed to be hanging on Mason's every move. To make matters worse, no one wanted to give up their space to let Ashley, Donathan, and Nyla walk through. It had taken them ten minutes just to get to the clearing right out front of the wall, but when they finally breached the crowd, they all froze midstep.

On an old brick wall of a corner building, catty-corner to Cannery Row, Mason had painted two large portraits. One was primarily done in purples and greens. It showed a stage that grew in perspective as the picture extended up to the second story of the wall. It had Ginn and Paul standing center stage, the crowd below them dancing and sweating, Barbie perched on the back of Beauty, off to the side and looking stoic. Great flowing feathery letters off to the side read "The Knight's Moon Enclave."

The other portrait showed Donathan standing with pistols drawn, one arm hanging to his side and the other gun pointing ahead, his eyes squinting down the iron sights. Ashley was standing next to him, looking up at something and holding her bat down at her side, her dark hair flowing slightly in the wind. Nyla was on the other side of him, looking to the side and aiming a shotgun while wearing a flowing white lab coat, with goggles on her head. Mason was crouched down next to Ashley's far side, showing a wide grin, holding his hockey mask with one hand

and painting it with a paintbrush held in his other. Block letters ran up vertically next to the scene, reading "The Zombie Civil Rights Brigade."

Folks in the crowd had been looking on, shouting encouragement and admiring the paintings. Mason was still gripping a paint can in one hand and staring intently at his work when Donathan walked up and clapped him on one shoulder, chuckling. "I don't really think we are the size of a brigade, you know?"

Mason turned around, looking dazed, and replied, "I don't really know what a brigade is."

———

They'd been bouncing on and off the road for two days, traveling up the Shytown Trail toward San Francisco. An older fellow and a young teen offered to give them a lift in their Volkswagen van. Their names were Dave and Sam, father and son. They droned on and on about how long they had been with the Knight's Moon and seemed interested in everything that happened that night. When Ashley had been launched up to the platform, Paul had gone back outside and gotten far enough from the stage to film what was going on. They were all legends now.

Dave seemed to have a dry sense of humor. Every time they passed a derelict building or a large toppled vehicle, he would joke about what manner of horde might be taking shelter inside it. Sam was a sandy-haired kid who just liked to look in his dad's direction and nod even when his father had made a joke and was expecting a laugh. They seemed like honest folks just trying to get by in the dark world.

In the midafternoon, he dropped everyone off in South City, San Francisco.

"You aren't coming with us to the docks like Paul planned?" Donathan asked.

Dave shook his head from the driver's side of the old VW. "No, that's not our rally point. We have to go set up staging area violet. SF is your rally point. We just wanted to see you off."

"Well, thank you for everything!" Ashley walked up to the van and leaned in the window to hug Dave and tousle Sam's hair. Mason ran around the other side of the car and shoved a piece of paper into Sam's hand.

Sam stared down at it with his jaw hanging open before looking up and smiling with tears in his eyes. Mason had drawn him and his dad at the beach. Sam hugged Mason through the window and thanked him. A moment later, the van's engine roared to life and putt-putted down the road.

The four friends turned and walked toward the city up the old 101 freeway. They chose a careful path around the broken-down vehicles and random trash, making doubly careful they didn't disturb any sleeping member of a horde. Dave's jokes had made the group a tad more paranoid than normal.

Half an hour passed before Mason asked, "Why do they issue different rally points?"

Browns and whites that had faded to grays spread densely across many of the caved-in or crumbling buildings stretched far out on both sides of the freeway. Most still stood, but they'd been derelict for decades, without many living taking shelter in them. The mass of abandoned buildings spread out ahead toward the horizon and stretching to the amber skyline.

Nyla grinned at the view of the city. "Since the enclave travels, it makes more sense to split it into different groups." She continued grinning but stepped up her walking pace. "That way, if one group is ambushed, the other will be okay. Plus, the enclave is too big. We don't want Falling Sands knowing our exact numbers. Plus, this way, most sites are prepared before the festivities roll through." Nyla's voice seemed an octave higher than normal, and she was taking longer steps. "It was a tradition that began when the Knight's Moon was formed, and it's probably why we do so well always being on the move."

Donathan added, "I bet it bothers the hell out of Falling Sands too. Makes you harder to track."

Nyla nodded. "You know they had a treaty?"

"What?" Ashley missed a step and stumbled a bit.

Mason pulled his backpack around and fumbled through it, pulling out a tube of paint and a paintbrush.

Nyla continued, "Yes, it wasn't like they were friends. Just at some point, Falling Sands had accepted they couldn't control us, so they had offered Paul and Ginn a peace treaty."

Ashley said matter-of-factly, "But I bet that all shattered the night they ambushed your event."

"Yeah, but none of that mattered." Nyla was actually skipping at that point. "No one ever trusts Falling Sands." Without missing a beat, she added, "Did you know San Francisco was the only place in the world you could make sourdough bread? It's the only place with this kind of atmosphere that can produce it!"

"I did not know that," Donathan said.

Nyla nodded excitedly. "And there was a bakery called Boudin that had a hundred-year-old living yeast that they kept using to produce the same kind of bread for the world."

"Wow, that's friggin' amazing." Donathan sounded genuinely interested in what she was saying.

Nyla skipped on. "And Mark Twain once said, 'The coldest winter I ever spent was a summer in San Francisco.'"

Donathan kicked a rock up the freeway and said, "Now, that one I'd heard before."

That back-and-forth banter continued until they were deep into the city. The sun was dipping low on the horizon when they finally decided to break off the freeway and search buildings for a safe shelter. They found an awful smell in one and assumed a horde might have taken up residence in it, so they quietly sneaked off until they found a run-down apartment building whose top floor seemed sturdy. Enough rubble was outside that they could drag it up the steps and barricade themselves in for the night. They even managed to find a room with no windows so they didn't have to exercise light discipline and could use lamps for a few hours into the darkness. Donathan unpacked a sewing kit and stitched up a rip in his undershirt while Mason picked through the rubble in the back of the room. Ashley and Nyla whispered quietly while sharing some bread they'd procured before leaving the camp in Monterey. All seemed right with the world.

33.

San Francisco
Zombie Civil Rights Group
Present Day

THE NIGHT WAS UNEVENTFUL. They heard some shuffling outside at one point in the evening, but whatever it was seemed to move on because the streets were quiet when dawn broke. They set foot in the street just after sunrise and followed Nyla's lead up the block.

"Where do we go from here?" Ashley asked.

Nyla chirped up. "Well, we need to move through Bernal Heights. Then through the mission district and head past the ballpark to the dock near the south of the Embarcadero."

Mason was trying to shift his machine gun around while he walked so he could paint his mask. He kept reseating the strap on his shoulder and then shifting the heavy bulk of the gun below his arm. "Seems easy enough since the streets are all quiet."

"Maybe," Nyla replied. "But we can't get near Union Square because it's usually filled with Rackhams. Nasty tumor-covered things that drip pus and paralyzing mist everywhere. They'll shriek and swarm if disturbed."

They turned and angled up a side street, following Nyla's lead.

"I'm pretty sure I've seen those before," said Donathan.

Ashley thought he sounded strangely remorseful when he said it.

Nyla sighed. "But that means we have to go directly past the ballpark to avoid that place, and that's where the Shat queen is nested most months out of the year."

"What?" Ashley yelled in surprise.

"No way!" Mason added with force.

Donathan just patted the pockets of his duster, looking for his smokes.

Nyla didn't lock gaze with anyone. "It's sort of safe since you have me with you and Barbie has marked me." Nyla kicked a rock up the road. "Shats tend to keep their word when someone is marked. Only..." Nyla drew in a deep breath.

"Well?" Ashley sounded annoyed.

Nyla turned to Ashley and squinted a bit while raising her shoulders defensively. "I've seen them still drag off friends of folks who were marked, from time to time."

"Screw this," Mason said and walked back the other way.

Everyone just stopped and watched him stomp off down the street and then trip over a hubcap and fall flat on his side.

They turned and kept walking.

After a minute, Donathan added, "He'll come running up as soon as he realizes we aren't with him. Don't worry. We'll be his courage."

Donathan was right. Mason rejoined them after about a mile, muttering to himself the whole time about everyone being insane. Ashley laughed about it, commenting on how rich hearing that from him was.

Around noon, they came upon the south gate of AT&T Park. It said in huge letters, "Home of the SF Giants." Various graffiti, probably left there since the fall of the world, were strewn across a brick wall next to a souvenir shop that looked as if fire had gutted it. Trolley tracks led up the street, and they could see the bay and all of the water at McCovey Cove.

When they were finally standing in front of the stadium, they had to stop and marvel at it through the bar fence. The gate's fence was split down the middle, no doubt where someone had driven a vehicle into it. Rocks and rubble were piled up on one side and closer to the stadium, and Donathan remarked that he was pretty sure he could see piles of white sun-bleached bones littered about the old ramps angling up to the stadium. Seeing from their lower angle was hard, but Nyla agreed they were probably bones.

Ashley seemed lost for a moment, standing before the stadium, staring up with wide eyes. "I remember it, you know?" She walked up close to the fence. "My dad took me through this gate right here." She was smiling up at the stadium as she said, "Right before everything went sour." She looked back at her friends with a broad smile. "I remember being up on his shoulders looking down as we went into the stadium to watch the Giants." Ashley stepped closer to the fence and placed a hand on the green bar. "Then afterward, we went to a place up the street that made these cream puffs," her voice trailed off at the end. She took another breath and added, "It was a magical day."

Mason remarked, "It kind of makes me wish we had a working digital camera."

Everyone nodded in agreement. They turned and walked farther up the street, following the trolley tracks.

"So why exactly do the Knight's Moon use this as a rallying point?" Donathan asked.

"Well, they have a working cruise ship that they used to launch from the north docks so everyone could avoid all this," Nyla answered as Donathan nodded, "but that was when they had a strong working truce with Falling Sands." She stopped to look up a moment at a building across the street then continued walking. "A few years back, they began to suspect that truce was on shaky ground, so they moved it to here. If it's dangerous for us and we've been marked, then it's super dangerous for big groups of troops trying to wander through here. Ergo, safe from the evil living soldiers in the Protectorate Army. Only the marked or the living dead can roam through here unassaulted."

Ashley added, "Shats don't eat dead flesh, right?"

Nyla beamed. "That's exactl—"

"We prefer 'Spiderlings.'" The voice rang out from across the street.

Everyone froze except Nyla, who just turned around slowly.

A small woman with ragged hair was wearing a pair of ratty, torn khakis and a tie-dyed T-shirt. Behind her was a large yellow Shat. The creature's carapace had darker highlights growing along ridges leading up to its bulbous body, held aloft by its eight spindly legs. Slowly, its head folded back, showing a mouth full of fangs and a giant tentacle stretching out from it. It appeared ready to hiss and roar, but it just remained silent and threatening. The tentacle stretched out and came to rest on the woman's shoulder.

She turned with soft eyes and shushed it before adding, "It's okay, Attraction."

Nyla just held out an upright arm, showing her wrist in the woman's direction. After a few moments, the Spiderling drew its tentacle back into itself as the woman strolled across the street to stand before Nyla. When the woman halted, she was just a foot in front of Nyla, giving her a stare that could cut glass. She finally leaned in and sniffed Nyla's wrist before standing back up and straightening her shirt.

When she was satisfied, she added, with venom in her voice, "That damn pink runt has stolen more meals than I care to admit."

A moment later, she let her gaze turn to Ashley, Donathan, and Mason, studying them.

"Wait a minute," her voice sounded alluring. "Even from here, I can sense they aren't marked."

Nyla stepped directly in front of the woman's gaze and shook her head. The woman sidestepped Nyla and started walking toward them. The Shat shifted its weight forward as if waiting to pounce.

The woman's hand reached up and patted Ashley on one shoulder before tracing down across her neck and Ashley's other shoulder. Still stepping along, the woman let her hand reach out to Donathan, trailing across the front of his duster until she stopped cold in front of Mason. The woman stared. Mason looked over at Ashley and Donathan then back to the woman, reached up, and pulled down his mask slowly to reveal a green one-up mushroom from the game Super Mario Brothers.

"Don't do that." The woman sounded as though she was scolding a child, and she reached out to raise his mask, catching his gaze. "Don't hide that face." She reached up and caressed his cheek, looking a bit lost in his eyes. "Pretty face."

Mason shifted from one foot to another but managed to hold mostly still with her hand on his face. His cheeks turned bright red. The woman reached down and squished his lips with her hand and mimicked talking while she spoke. "We prefer 'Spiderlings.' 'Shat' sounds too much like 'shit.'"

"So what's your name?" Ashley asked.

The second Ashley's last syllable fell, the woman spun on her heels and slid past Donathan to shove Ashley to the ground, hissing. The Spiderling across the street thunked its heavy legs in anger as it edged closer.

Ashley instinctively had her hand on the hilt of her bat peeking over her shoulder.

The woman, fingers outstretched, faced Ashley and bared her teeth. Even her eyes appeared sharp somehow. "Unmarked girl speaking freely to me, have you lost your mind?"

Mason was visibly trembling.

After a few moments, Nyla edged into the woman's line of sight with her hands held up defensively. "She's sorry."

Still facing Ashley, the woman pointed a finger at Mason and said, "Make him ask my name."

The city was silent save for the wind thundering in off the waves.

Mason finally stuttered, "W-what's your n-n-name, ma'am?"

In an instant, the woman's stance changed. She seemed to remember she was human and looked soft and inviting as she stood tall again, strolling back past Donathan and waving him out of her way before stopping in front of Mason. "And polite too? Very well." She leaned in uncomfortably close to Mason and whispered, "I'm Jenna."

Mason froze.

After a moment, she reached up and placed her hands on his lips, mimicking talk again, and said, "Nice to meet you, Jenna."

Another uncomfortable moment passed, and Jenna stepped back before looking in Ashley's direction and laughing hysterically. The Spiderling behind them seemed to relax too. After catching her breath, she added, "I was never going to hurt you, girl." She grinned. "I overheard you talking about the Giants." She nodded. "I loved them once too."

Ashley stood up and mumbled, "Thank God."

Jenna instantly hissed and turned sharp again.

More silence passed for what seemed like an eternity until she turned back to Mason and said plainly, "Needs a mark."

"What?" Mason whispered, looking at Donathan nervously.

Nyla walked up, grabbed Mason's arm, and held his wrist under Jenna's nose. Jenna sniffed and, after a moment, licked slowly up his wrist to his elbow.

The Shat roared to life with an ear-piercing shriek. The ground rumbled.

"You should all go." Jenna's voice was suddenly full of fire. "Now!" she shouted before sprinting across the street and leaping onto the yellow Spiderling's back.

The ground rumbled more, and a large purple object extended up out of AT&T Park. It resembled a hill at first then became vertical and stretched up and up. Flocks of birds took off from it. It halted when its form reached the clouds. Smaller things stalked across it. The Spiderling and Jenna launched up onto the side of the ballpark and then leaped up the stadium wall and onto the purple mass, skittering up out of sight.

"The fuck is that?" Ashley didn't even try to hide her fear.

Nyla sounded very dull in replying, "The Shat queen is awake."

"Don't you mean Spiderling?" Donathan replied.

Nyla just shrugged and began walking up the street again.

Mason was still holding his wrist out ahead of him, and he ran up to Nyla, asking, "They mark you by licking you?" his voice oozing with disgust.

Nyla shook her head. "Not usually. Barbie just breathes on it."

Mason lowered his arm, angling his head in Nyla's direction and asked, "So then what the hell was that?"

Nyla just continued walking. "I think she marked you for herself." She kept trotting. "Like for breeding."

Mason stopped dead in his tracks. "Wait, what?"

Donathan and Ashley both burst out laughing.

Nyla kept walking. "Yeah, she liked you."

"I thought she was going to eat me!" Mason said defensively.

Nyla continued, "Well, I mean she still might. I've heard that's not uncommon after the act."

"We are never coming back here." Mason stomped one of his feet before jogging to catch up to his friends.

Nyla just kept walking and shook her head. "She can probably still find you wherever you go with that kind of mark."

Neither Ashley nor Donathan had stopped laughing.

Tears were streaming down Ashley's cheeks. Between laughs, Ashley said, "You're screwed!" followed by high-pitched laughter then, "Maybe literally!"

Even Nyla started laughing.

"She's lying, right? Nyla, you're kidding, right?" Mason looked like he was going to cry.

Nyla just replied, "Nah," and kept walking towards the Embarcadero.

———

The sun was high in the sky when they came upon the docks. The Knight's Moon cruise ship had been created from an old Princess Cruise Lines ship. The dock and street nearby were abustle with activity—folks carrying crates, loading cargo onto pallets, and using what looked like a gas-powered winch-and-pully system to lift supplies by crane up and over the side of the ship. Somehow, the hull of the ship looked bright, white, and untarnished. Even the chrome handrails gleamed in the sunlight. For a moment, they seemed to have escaped the fallen world and settled back into peace.

About halfway up the dock, they came upon Jae crouched in front of a series of crates, checking their contents and marking them on a clipboard.

Donathan couldn't help himself. "Princess Jae and an old Princess Cruise Liner."

She turned around and grinned mischievously the second she heard his voice. "You made it."

Ashley nodded and ran over to hug her. "Almost in one piece."

Jae laughed. "I heard." She tousled Mason's hair before drawing Nyla and Donathan in for a hug. "You four are the talk of the town, it seems."

"Did you run into any trouble on your jaunt back up here?" Donathan asked.

Jae nodded. "A bit. Patrols of the Protectorate Army are heavy in Sunnyvale, Santa Clara, and San Jose right now. They'd been making it hard for folks to get up here."

Mason raised an eyebrow curiously and added, "But we made it through there just fine."

Jae gave him a dry look with a half smile before adding in a plain voice, "You're welcome." She looked back to the crates. "Now, if you wouldn't mind heading down the street and helping drag cargo boxes to the docks, we don't have our wired fence system up in San Fran, and we'd like to be launched by sundown."

———

Most of the boxes were stored in small dockside warehouses, but some had also been stored in residences nearby. Thankfully, some folks had dollies and carts to drag them along, so the group walked about as far as they could up one of the streets and went to work helping to clear out one of the last houses of crates. Apparently, it contained mostly supplies for the Knight's Moon events, tech, and some medical supplies. Nyla said they always packed food first, so the ship was probably bursting with items already.

The work was hard, but it seemed to make the day go quickly. That afternoon was strange in San Francisco. Gusts of wind were whipping off the water and into the city streets with a sound that resembled linen left out on a clothesline during a heavy wind. Folks often arrived, loading carts, then thanked the ZCR before moving back down the streets. Then Ashley, Mason, Donathan, and Nyla would all climb back up into the house and drag more boxes from the rooms, down the stairs, and into the sunlight. Often, someone would recognize them and chatter about the night of the fight or the morning after. Other folks who weren't there would get enthusiastic and share all they'd heard about the event in Monterey then start a tirade of questions.

"The whole thing feels a bit surreal," Ashley observed as she and Donathan were setting down a heavy box by the sidewalk. "We're sort of famous now. Is this what Nyla, Paul, and Ginn always feel like around here?"

Nyla said in a spacey tone, "No." She huffed, shoving a box down onto the sidewalk. "I feel way cooler than most."

Ashley gasped. "So many jokes today, Nyla." She smiled. "You really are one of us now."

Nyla asked over her shoulder as she was walking back up the stairs, "I wasn't before?"

The sky was turning amber, and the sun was low by the time they loaded the last box onto the sidewalk.

"Where's Mason?" Ashley asked while wiping sweat from her brow.

Nyla sounded a bit winded. "He went up the street to search a few houses for art supplies. I tried to tell him we have some on the boat, but he had that look in his eye."

Donathan chuckled. "We'll go find him." He nodded to Nyla. "You head back to the boat and let Jae know we're done back here. Make sure there's nothing else to do."

Nyla nodded and wandered down the sidewalk toward the dock. Ashley and Donathan stepped out into the middle of the street to search for their friend.

Donathan's usually neutral face was somehow grinning again. Ashley almost pointed it out but decided that would ruin the moment.

They found Mason around the corner, standing in the middle of an intersection staring up the street.

Driving up the road at a snail's pace was a pickup truck, but what was strange about it was the top and the back were covered by a dingy white canvas sheet. The canvas covered the windshield almost entirely, flaring as the truck drove, so the driver didn't seem able to see where they were going.

"That's...odd," Donathan said.

Ashley asked, "What happens if there is debris in the road in front of them while they do it."

Mason shrugged. "Should we go?"

"Well," Ashley was still staring at the truck, "Nyla did say only the marked or the undead can get through there, so it has got to be one of the Knight's Moon."

The vehicle edged closer and picked up speed.

"Wait." Ashley shot Donathan a concerned look. "The Fine Line Protectorate count as undead, right?"

The canvas flew off, and Nym and Goblin both grinned from the cab of the truck. Crooks was wearing his furry bat head behind the wheel. As the truck continued forward, the rest of the canvas peeled off the back, revealing a power coil. Green energy popped and fizzed between the coil and the bed of the truck.

A generator surged to life on one of the rooftops, causing Mason to jump almost a foot in height. Half a second later, white fluff above them flurried down toward the ground.

"Is this tiny bubbles—" Ashley held out a hand, curiously catching one of the pieces of fluff.

Mason finished her sentence. "Fake snow."

"Screw this," Donathan said and stepped forward.

Ashley yanked back on one of his shoulders. "Don't." She cautioned him with stern eyes. "Green light." She was motioning toward a bubble. "Remember what happened last time with the water drops?"

"Let's just run, then," Donathan answered.

All three friends turned to sprint down the street and stopped dead in their tracks. Mary Helen and the green Spiderling stood between them and the docks. Donathan drew a pistol, but Ashley shook her head.

The FLP's vehicle came to a halt about fifty feet behind them, and Nym was already shouting while exiting, "I was hoping you'd shoot. We took bets on it—"

"Stop toying with them!" Mary Helen shouted from ahead of the three.

Mason spun the other direction and then back, confused as to whom to keep his back toward. Eventually, he settled on facing Mary Helen and the Shat. Donathan turned and continued facing Mary Helen next to him. Ashley lined up on their back, facing the FLP.

"They're dangerous!" Mary Helen shouted.

Nym turned to Goblin and in a plain voice said, "God, I am

so sick of—" Then she shouted over them at Mary Helen, "Who is running this ambush?"

An uncomfortable silence passed, and Nym cocked her head to one side, looking back at Crooks before sighing and turning back to the ZCR. "You will drop your weapons."

Donathan shrugged and threw down his pistols. Mason's jaw dropped.

Donathan whispered, "We can't use them anyways."

Mason dragged the machine gun sling off his shoulder and set it down. Ashley left her bat holstered. Mason also dragged the camouflaged Kevlar vest off and threw that down on the ground with an unusually loud thump. Ashley looked at him curiously.

"What?" Mason raised his arms and shrugged. "I'm hot." His clothes hung damp from sweat on his skinny form.

Donathan shouted, "So our weapons don't work? You still can't shoot us while that thing is on."

Goblin stepped out ahead of Nym, shaking his finger and sounding annoyed, "Oh no no no." Jamming a finger in the direction of the coil, he added, "We shut that thing off, and you're gone in an instant"—his tone turned snide as he stared at Donathan—"Barry Allen."

Nym and Crooks both turned in his direction. Nym had an eyebrow upturned and was looking up and away before turning toward Goblin then back up the street. She gazed past the trio toward Mary Helen, who squinted and lowered her head a second before shrugging back.

"Barry Allen." Goblin sounded defensive. "The Flash?"

Mason yelled, "I got it!"

"Of course you did," Ashley said.

While waving a finger between his friends, Goblin added in a low voice, "You people need culture."

"So what, then?" Donathan shouted. "If we can't shoot and you can't shoot..."

Nym sounded annoyed. "You surrender."

"That's not going to work for us!" Donathan shouted back.

More silence passed. The Shat hissed a bit and stepped forward.

"What happens if we punch them with that green light going?" Ashley whispered.

The Fine Line Protectorate ran toward them. Mary Helen and the Shat also dipped into a low run. The Shat leaped forward, high into the air, its silhouette blocking out the sun. Mason reached up to grab his mask, panicked, and threw the mask forward off his head. It flowed freely through the fake snow. The mask hit the bottom of the Shat and slammed hard into the pavement. The green Spiderling roared and was flung into the sky, out of sight.

Donathan shouted, "Throw things! Go!"

Ashley reached down and grabbed a handful of pebbles, Mason scrambled a few feet forward to grab his mask off the pavement then reached into his pack to pull out a paintbrush and paint.

"Not now, Mason," Ashley said through clenched teeth.

"I have an idea," Mason replied.

A rock whizzed between the two friends and they realized that the Fine Line Protectorate had caught on. Donathan scrambled for the nearby yard and came away with a white picket fencepost. He threw it at Mary Helen who ducked out of the way. Donathan dove to the ground to pick up a rock before being beaned by a pebble and sent crashing into a house.

"Dodgeball time," Nym announced with a roar.

Ashley threw a handful of pebbles in her direction. With a loud crack, Nym skidded out of sight past the truck.

"Nice dodge, bitch." Ashley grinned wickedly and leaned down, pulling up a flattened rock. Crooks reached up to hold his furry head and sprinted at Mason and Ashley. Mason quickly squirted paint from a bottle onto his brush and flung the paint in an arc towards Crooks. The paint splashed onto Crooks, who bounced backward into the pavement, skimmed into a streetlight, and ripped it in half before sliding to a halt. He stood up without his fur head on, rubbing a hand across his forehead and wavering slightly.

"Oh God, yes!" Ashley shouted.

Mason swung around to face Mary Helen, who was still twenty feet back. He held up his paintbrush, making her freeze. "I will do it too." He waved the brush before himself like a sword.

The green Shat appeared on a roof nearby and leaped down. Mason couldn't see it because of the direction he was facing.

"Mason, look out!" Ashley shouted as the Shat's form descended quickly.

Mason was still turning about, and Ashley felt as if time slowed down, but then she realized the Shat was just hanging in the air, floating as fake snow flowed past. It roared and kicked its legs violently as it glowed a deep azure blue.

"What the f—" Ashley held the last syllable.

Mason finally looked up and fell to the ground, covering his head. The Shat was still hanging in the air. Mary Helen was still, stopped with an eyebrow arched and her mouth hanging open. Nym ran back up the street to join her friends and slowed her jog to a halt, looking confused at the floating Shat.

Mason uncovered his face, still lying facedown on the ground and peering ahead toward the house. Donathan was holding a hand aloft, which was glowing the same deep blue.

"It's D!" Mason shouted. "He's doing it!"

"My ring!" Mary Helen shouted and ran toward Donathan.

Mason snapped up and flung paint at the Shat. Once again, it flew back across the sky and out of sight again. Donathan aimed his hand at Mary Helen, who froze in place and glowed blue. She struggled and swore, but her arms and legs were limp like a rag doll's. Ashley stared at Mary Helen. Mason's eyes locked on Donathan.

Behind Donathan, three vicious-looking teddy bears with bloody mouths crawled out of the window of a house. One of the bears fell to the ground, and one of the others helped it stand back up. One waved an angry fist in Donathan's direction, and all three ran off down the side yard of the house, disappearing from view.

Mason rubbed his eyes and shouted, "Evil teddy bears!" at the top of his lungs.

Donathan dropped his gaze from Mary Helen to look at Mason with confusion. Mary Helen was already running at him. Nym had been closing the gap too.

"Kill the generator, and just shoot them!" Nym shouted.

Goblin was sprinting toward the back of the truck. Donathan took off the ring and threw it over Nym and Mary Helen toward Mason.

Mason looked up and held his hand out. The ring of Solomon flipped in the air, sunlight glistening off its golden surface. It edged closer to Mason's hand. Time seemed to slow down again. Goblin shut off the generator, and the green light faded right as Ashley reached out and snatched the ring from the air.

"Stop doing that Lord of the Rings shit," she yelled at Mason. "Get the weapons." She spun on her heels with the ring on her finger to face Goblin, who was racking back an AK-47. "How does this damn thing—"

Ashley held up her hand, and the ring pulsed blue that flowed over her hand just as Goblin froze and lowered his rifle to his side. Donathan surged past her and flung Mary Helen, sending her soaring away. He zipped back in the other direction to shoulder-check Nym out of sight. The green Shat landed with an explosive thump in the middle of the street, and Ashley spun from her place in the yard to face the Shat. The creature was engulfed by blue and began struggling.

"Go away!" Ashley shouted at it, and it ran off down the street.

Ashley looked at Donathan in confusion while mouthing the words "holy crap." She turned back to face Goblin just in time to see him firing the AK-47.

Donathan surged forward to grab her then zipped across the street behind a wall. Mason had run the other way and was hiding in the side yard where he had seen the evil teddy bears run off. Bullets continued whizzing down the street. Ashley and Donathan could see Mason from where they were.

"I don't think I can get through the line of fire!" Donathan shouted at Ashley over the gunshots.

A second gun erupted. Nym had apparently found her weapon. Rounds popped and hissed at the walls in front of them.

Ashley took off the ring, jumped up and down waving to Mason until she was sure she had his attention, then she threw it across the street. It pinged off the wooden fence in the side yard. Mason grabbed it off the ground and waved before putting it on. Rounds were still ripping up the edge of the house in front of them, and the gunfire was getting closer. Mason stepped out from behind the house and aimed a hand at the FLP members rushing up toward Donathan and Ashley. Strange azure patterns gathered in the street, then a large white monster warped in, a small person wearing a fur-clad hood riding on its back. The yeti punched Nym, sending her flying out of sight, and then turned its gaze toward Goblin and Crooks. Both looked at each other and sprinted away. The yeti lumbered after them.

"What the hell was that?" Ashley asked, dumbfounded.

"I think it was Nunu from League of Legends," Mason sounded just as surprised as she was. Mary Helen came running up the street from where Donathan had flung her.

Ashley pointed and shouted, "Do it again!"

Mason aimed the ring at her, and the ground rumbled and shook. A second later, the sidewalk parted, and a large metal machine swung into view. It unfolded itself around her into a wide dome, extending high above. A metal shape with an elongated face and a yellow eye slid into view just above Mary's small form. She froze, looking up at it. Its eye whirred, and the metal form spun on its center axis, twirling down at an angle to aim at her.

"Hello, and welcome to the Aperture Science Enrichment Cente—hang on. This isn't the enrichment center." The machine whirred and spun around, looking out at the street before settling its gaze back on Mary Helen and whirring in close.

Mary Helen stomped a foot then reached a hand out, jamming a finger onto the machine's elongated form. A loud popping and cracking could be heard as the metal casing began to rip. A fracture appeared in the machine's face, and it whirred around Mary Helen then back up to the cascading fissures of metal trailing down its form and up to the dome.

The machine spun around, its cybernetic eye lighting up red before saying in a furious voice, "I'm still alive, bit—"

The dome above shifted and folded in on itself before collapsing forward. Mary turned to run ahead, but the dome fell forward on her.

"We should go, like, now." Donathan jolted backward, grabbing all their weapons. Then he slowed next to his friends, who were sprinting up the street. He had already replaced his pistols in his holster but managed to shuffle over most of Mason's gear as they scrambled over the crumpled dome and kept running.

"Was that-?" Ashley sounded amazed.

"I'm not really thinking these through, you know?" Mason had managed to sling his weapon and was running up the street still holding his body armor and mask in one hand and the paint bottle in the other. His brush was tucked into his back pocket.

They cleared the street and turned toward the dock. Folks were already running up the gangplank.

Donathan shouted, "We have to go now!" while sprinting.

When they arrived at the docks, all three scrambled up the gangplank in the setting sun, gasping that they needed to leave immediately.

Princess Jae nodded. "We kind of figured that when we saw a Shat go flying by a few times and the ground started shaking. These days, you folks are California's earthquake weather. We would have sent help, but it all happened so fast. Anyways, we are trying to fire up the engines now." The last syllables she spoke hung visibly in the air, surrounded by strange red symbols warping and shifting about.

"What the?" Ashley asked. Her jaw hung open. "Mason, did you do that? Why is that happening?"

Mason looked down at his ring then up at the words, which were fading from view. Yelping, he removed the ring and threw it across the boat toward the ocean.

Donathan tried to zip to the far side of the boat to catch it, but the ring slipped between his fingers. Staring at the hunk of metal plunking into the ocean he shouted, "Why would you do that?"

Mason held up his hands, shrugging, blank faced. "I panicked!"

Ashley waved a fist at Mason. "That's not a good kind of panic, you know?"

"There's a good kind of panic?" Nyla asked, joining her friends at the side of the boat.

Jae turned around and said, "Shush!" The word didn't hang in the air that time, but her voice sounded as if it was filled with static. She gazed off the boat a moment then yelled toward the aft of the boat, "How long until the engine is ready to go?"

Someone yelled back, "Still a few minutes. We are having a power issue."

She looked down at her arms. Strange red, floating characters were gathering around her hands and shifting up her elbows until they formed regal-looking red sleeves that resembled crushed velvet and flared cuffs. A collar began to form around her.

"Has anyone seen Waterfalz recently?" she shouted. The words hung in the air in a bold, sharp-edged font.

Mason studied the letters then whispered something about needing a camera.

Most of the boat yelled back to Jae, "No!" and one person shouted out late, "Haven't seen her in weeks!"

The characters floating off of Jae glowed then took on a deeper red hue. They converged around her neck, and a collar began to appear.

Ashley whispered to Nyla, "What's happening?"

As Donathan and Mason edged into a small semicircle with them, Nyla whispered back, "Sages can power up when they like, but if one is powered up and another is near, it triggers their powers as well. Waterfalz disappears often, and we're never sure where, but she doesn't tend to power up without warning Jae, so—"

Donathan asked, "There's another Sage around? So what? Isn't that a good thing?"

Princess Jae answered in a plain voice and the words appeared, floating in large letters behind her, "No. It could be a Dark Sage."

"That's probably bad," Mason added before reaching up to lower his mask, revealing a painting of small boy standing on the edge of a cliff and staring down at the drop.

Donathan swore then remembered, "Paul warned me that the ring would attract dark stuff."

"Ashley!" Jae's words were sharp and clear in the air. "Ashley?" Jae grabbed Ashley's face forcefully and stared deep into her eyes before turning Ashley's head back the other way, peering from a different angle. "When did you start ascending?"

Ashley shook free of Jae's grasp, "I... What?"

Pointing at Ashley's face, Donathan announced, "Your eyes are purple again."

"Shit," Jae cursed and then shoved past them, walking down the gangplank onto the dock. "You can't even be in this kind of situation right now." As she walked, the shifting red characters flowed out behind her, knitting together a flowing cape that became longer and longer with each step. It seemed to float a few inches above the ground no matter where she moved.

"You're becoming a Sage!" Nyla said.

Ashley glanced over to find Nyla just inches from her face, staring at her eyes.

"It looks almost like purple lightning."

"So I'm going to become like that, with all those weird floating letters?" Ashley asked while pointing at Jae.

Nyla shook her head. "Remember, Jae's powers are perpetually glitched. She glitches reality itself. I actually call it glitchkinesis. Every Sage has different powers." Nyla looked as if she was studying Ashley's face. "Waterfalz's powers are more nature tuned. But when they supercharge near other Sages, you get some effects like these."

The deck of the boat rocked a bit, and a loud rapping noise reverberated in the air. Ducking low and crawling out from a door leading to the cruise ship's mezzanine were Barbie and Beauty. Barbie waved at the ZCR then, without a word, quickly vaulted up onto the back of Beauty, who leaped off the ship with a jolt and landed next to Princess Jae, who had a long crown with sharp red points extending from her head. Barbie slid off Beauty to stand next to Jae. Barbie smiled and curtseyed before drawing two sharp knives from her belt behind her back. She then turned to face out toward the city, searching the cityscape and waiting.

"Barbie must have sensed it too. She's not a Sage, but Spiderlings are pretty in tune with the world." Nyla was grinning. She seemed to love being in information mode.

"Well, let's go help them." Ashley was already walking for the gangplank when Nyla grabbed her shoulder.

"You can't," Nyla warned. "If it's a Dark Sage and he sees you, he'll try to steal your ascension. He'll want your power. He'll probably kill you too!"

Donathan was rummaging through his pack. He pulled out a pair of wide, single-frame sunglasses and placed them on Ashley's face. "These look dorky as hell, but they'll hide your eyes." He turned back to Nyla. "Stay with the ship." Then he motioned to Ashley and Mason. "Let's roll."

"That's not a good idea," Nyla cautioned.

Donathan nodded. "I know." As they trotted down the gangplank, he shouted over his shoulder, "I'm full of them!"

When they set foot back on the dock, Jae argued until Ashley looked up at her in her glitch princess outfit and thumbed her nose in her direction. Jae gave up and turned back toward the city. When Ashley spun back around, Barbie was grinning widely in her direction.

"Should we put our headphones on for this fight?" Mason asked.

Donathan shook his head. "We need to be listening for them. Plus, we don't really know what we're up against right now. Let's just set up behind those leftover pallets over there."

They stacked and shifted the pallets as best they could to hide their profiles and stage a decent defense. Mason set his machine gun across the top, and Ashley and Donathan crouched next to him, Donathan with his pistols drawn and Ashley with her bat still holstered, eyeballing the city. The problem was that, if bullets started flying, that wood wouldn't block many shots for too long. If the attackers were undead, though, they might do all right.

"It's near," Jae said. "With any luck, they'll get the boat started and we can avoid whatever this is."

The sun was almost below the horizon, and the whole city held a deep amber glow. Bats screeched and flew out from behind a building. A moment later, another cloud of bats screeched and darted out of an alleyway before dashing in other directions overhead. The Spiderling Beauty stretched and edged in closer to Barbie. Jae sniffed. The wind whipped deep off the water.

A raspy voice echoed from the city and into the streets. It had a nails-on-a-chalkboard quality. "Sage, Sage, come out to play and bring the ring, oh what do you say?"

Mason was wide eyed. "It sounds like Gozer the Gozerian. Gozer the Destructor."

Donathan whispered, "What?"

Ashley pulled the sunglasses down just enough to give him an eyeful of violet and ask, "Do you not know Ghostbusters?"

The sinister voice rang out again, "Give me the ring, Sage, and I'll only kill you."

Jae stepped forward a few feet, and the cloak trailed behind. She flicked her right hand out in front of her, and a crimson sword extended with a wide handguard. Some of the characters changed and left a trail of silver filigree down the blade. The sword left a trail of red characters as she moved.

A second later she shouted, "Come take it!" Her words hung in the air as a menacing scribbled font that looked ready to light the world on fire.

The darkening alleyways on the left screeched, and a horde of creatures came scrambling out. Their noses were long and sharp, their arms pulled tight into their sides, every step loping longer and faster.

"Ravens!" Donathan called out.

The Ravens fell into a quick sprint, and Mason took aim with his machine gun, firing off two bursts and taking out the front line. Ear-piercing shrieks came out from an alley on the far side of the docks.

"Cacophony! Three of them! One o'clock!" Donathan pointed a knife hand in their direction.

Cacophony were dangerous because of their paralyzing screams. Mason climbed up onto the pallets and swung the gun a bit so he could get a target and avoid hitting the Spiderling with its big gait. He opened fire on the three undead. A moment later, they were just rotten flesh collapsed on the ground. The rest of the Ravens were getting dangerously close. Donathan readied his pistols, but Mason just jumped forward again off the pallets and fell prone with the machine gun, firing more rounds into the Ravens and dropping what remained. He shouted something and pulled his pack off his back, throwing it next to himself. Donathan sprinted around the pallet and fished out another belt of ammunition from Mason's pack. Mason snapped the links and threw the extended belt off to one side.

When Donathan ran back around the pallet and grinned at Ashley, she grinned back, remarking, "Our gunner's gotten better."

Donathan nodded then shouted, "I think you leveled up, Mason!"

Skinny creatures that Donathan didn't recognize came screaming out of another alleyway, only to be mowed down by more machine-gun fire. A fat, bulbous zombie waddled out from an alley and headed for the dock.

Barbie impatiently said, "Ours!"

The Spiderling leaped forward and bashed the zombie sideways, sending it flying out of sight. Beauty skittered back to Barbie's side. Piles of undead flesh littered the alleyways and cement leading up to the dock. A deep azure light lit up in the center of some of that flesh, and a robed figure arose from it. Symbols lined the edges of a hood and trailed down the front of the robe. The figure's long sleeves had characters similar to Jae's around the edges. When the figure stopped rising, he stepped forward, and a scythe appeared in one of its hands. The hilt planted firmly on the ground, and the blade was long and wide, extending out quite a few feet in front of him.

The figure cackled then pulled the hood off his head. A bald man with some long scars crossing his face stood before them all.

The cackling turned into a snarl, and the man clacked his jaw once before eyeballing Princess Jae with a wide, menacing grin and narrowed eyes, saying, "I'm Razorwrist. I don't believe we've had the pleasure."

"You won't!" Donathan shouted as he fired both his pistols and Mason went heavy with his trigger finger, sending a wall of lead in Razorwrist's direction.

With lightning reflexes, Razorwrist pulled the blade of the large scythe over to one side, and white-hot ricochets flashed off of it. He didn't take his eyes off Jae.

After the rounds stopped impacting, Razorwrist held the scythe out ahead of himself and flicked it forward. The blade snapped up into what resembled a long spear with a sword on the end. He spun on a heel and slashed it through the air in the direction of the ZCR. A bright flash of azure light appeared, sending the group and pallets crashing backward onto the dock. Barbie jumped up onto Beauty, and a second later the Spiderling lunged forward. Just before they landed on Razorwrist, he sprinted back and out of the way. Beauty hit the ground hard, sending the piles of dead flesh scattering.

The spry man sprinted and halted, eyeballing the Spiderling. "Dirty thing," Razorwrist spat. "Unclean. Not quite dead but never quite natural."

Beauty lunged again, and Razorwrist's form split into hundreds of bats. They flew apart then rose together, looped backward, and flew forward full speed toward Barbie and Beauty. Razorwrist solidified back into form a second later, with a foot extended, straight into Barbie's face. In a sudden explosion of force, she was launched backward to crash into the hull of the ship before sliding down into the bay. Beauty shrieked and leaped back to the edge of the dock. She vanished out of sight into the water.

Razorwrist simply landed on the ground and threw off his robe, revealing a clean glowing azure tuxedo. The robe vanished once it hit the ground.

"Time to punch the clock." he flicked the scythe again, and the blade clicked back to its original shape. He darted forward and swung it deftly in Jae's direction. She swatted it away with her sword in one fast motion. She leaped over Razorwrist, swinging down when she was midarc overhead. He sidestepped the chop and swung a wide arc in the direction she was going to land. Before the scythe connected, the characters around her warped, and her form shattered into—

"Butterflies?" Ashley asked. She stared in the direction of the Sage fight while helping Donathan and Mason drag off the pallets and stand up.

"Is she dead?" Mason sounded panicked, glancing from where Jae was back to his friends.

"Hardly," Nyla shouted down, "and they're moths!" She waved them in. "C'mon! The boat's running."

Ashley and Mason looked at Donathan.

He nodded. "We're outclassed here."

"I lost your sunglasses anyways." Ashley rubbed the side of her face.

Mason pointed out, "Plus, we told ourselves we should run."

They sprinted up the gangplank as they heard sharp metal sounds mixed with strange energy pulsing. Jae was still in the fight.

A crew member patted Donathan on the back as he reached the top. Most of the crew on the boat was out, crowding around the boat's edge and watching everything play out. The rest were standing in a circle around the dripping-wet pink Spiderling. Barbie had been dragged back onto the boat, and people were shouting various first-aid comments. She seemed to be in grim shape.

The trio rushed back over to the edge of the boat, and a few folks graciously stepped aside.

Jae had her sword held aloft and was heaving as she pressed back Razorwrist's scythe while he stood just in front of her. Jae's strange glitch characters floated around her, and Razorwrist was surrounded by a glowing azure light. Both colors mingled but were at odds with settling in one place. Razor seemed to be looking past Jae at Ashley.

"Your eyes." His voice hissed out the last syllable. He shrieked, "Ascension!" and threw the scythe aside to sprint toward the boat.

Jae took two steps after him, shifted into moths, and dashed forward through the air. Razorwrist lunged from the dock, high into the air toward Ashley, who fell back onto the boat's deck. Razorwrist's head was right there, hanging in the air over her. Weathered and stitched flesh spread across his face. His jet-black eyes were narrowed slits, his teeth jutted out, angled and yellow. He just held there in the air, struggling, as Ashley scrambled back, kicking and flailing her feet to get away.

Jae fell off the guardrail she was standing on, dragging Razorwrist back toward the edge.

"No!" Razorwrist shouted, clawing at the air between Ashley and himself before disappearing off the side of the boat.

"Go!" Jae shouted as she fell.

The ship lurched forward. Bats flashed up into the sky, but whenever they looped down towards the boat, large red moths would send their cloud scattering.

When the boat was a fair distance from the harbor, Razorwrist appeared back on the shoreline, shouting, "Run all you want, novice. I'll find you and that ring!" He cackled before screaming, "This world is already mine!"

Jae's small form appeared next to him and, in a flash of red, took a swipe at him with her sword. Azure flashed back, and their tiny forms darted away, fighting.

"Don't worry about Jae." Paul had sneaked up behind Donathan and Ashley, who were standing by the railing. "She'll be fine. She's good at the Sage thing."

Nyla was standing near the railing and nodding in agreement. Paul walked over toward Barbie to check on her. Nyla leaned back against the boat's railing. Paul passed Mason and patted him on the shoulder. Mason dragged the machine-gun strap off and set the weapon down on the ship's deck. Nyla smiled at him.

The ship was far enough down the shoreline that much of the city had cleared, giving way to trees. In the growing twilight, a large form lumbered out of the trees and sprinted with furious speed, trying to match the ship's pace. Donathan pointed at the shape.

Ashley turned and squinted then said, "Green." She coughed and asked, "Is that Mary Helen on her Shat?"

A shot rang out. Everyone jumped at the sound of the heavy crack. Mason had red across his face. Nyla's grin turned to wonder. She looked down and saw a red spot on the right side of her abdomen. She dabbed it and looked up at Mason, holding two red fingertips up in his direction.

She asked calmly, "Are you painting again?"

Mason's mouth was open in confusion. He shook his head. Nyla looked down and saw the red spreading over her white top. She pressed her hand tight onto it and fell forward. Donathan caught her and helped ease her to the ground while cradling her in his arms.

For the first time in a long time, Donathan looked truly frightened. "Help!" he screamed at the top of his lungs.

Several people sprinted over from Barbie's side. They called for more kits.

Ashley just blinked, her jaw hanging open. Mason started crying. Donathan stared down at Nyla, trying to hide panic as folks ripped away the bottom part of her shirt and examined the wound. Paul ran up and saw Nyla there, and his eyes went wide. He placed his palms on his temples with fingertips laced up into his hair. He didn't seem as though he could find words.

"Hang on," Donathan begged.

Nyla whispered, "Everything is turning gray."

Donathan reassured her, "You're going to be okay. Just fight." He took a breath and steadied his voice. "It's what we always do."

"I get it now," Nyla whispered then winced before continuing, "It was you three. I remember. It's always been you three."

Nyla shut her eyes.

34.

Off the Coast of California
Zombie Civil Rights Group
Present Day

"WELL, SHE'S ALIVE." Ginn did little to mask the fear in her voice. Her T-shirt and jeans were smeared with blood from helping carry Nyla belowdecks. "I don't know for how long.".

Ashley, Donathan, and Mason were standing on the main deck. The only deck higher was the one perched above the mezzanine, which had a large cylindrical object strapped to it with thick red coiled wires stretching out from it, and it left a trail of steam as the ship chugged along.

Folks seemed to be in a good mood regardless of the tragedy they had just witnessed. People rushed back and forth, helping out, and some were decorating. Apparently, the ship did this jaunt down to San Diego every year to drop off the enclave to begin its run back up the coast. Falling Sands controlled all the waterways and entrances in and out of

California. Donathan seemed to remember Nyla mentioning that this would be the first year without that treaty in place. The voyage could be dangerous.

"So, can't your medics do anything?" Donathan asked.

Ginn shook her head. "Their skills are mostly basic first aid." She shrugged. "One is a midwife even, but the only person who was well versed in medicine and surgery is the same person who supplied us with all our science."

"Nyla." Ashley sighed while looking out at the ocean.

"What about a medical enclave?" Mason asked.

"Know of any without ties to Falling Sands?" Ginn asked. "We used to have decent medical support back at Half Moon Bay when it was a science enclave, but the Protectorate gutted all of that a decade ago."

"If only Nyla wasn't hurt." Mason sighed. "She'd know what to do." He settled down on the ground and pulled out all his paints from his backpack to redesign his mask.

Paul appeared from belowdecks, holding a microphone. A few folks cheered and gathered around. Someone hastily set up a stand with turntables and ran a few cords. Minutes later, large speakers were dragged out from the mezzanine door entrance and mounted nearby.

Barbie limped up with a crutch under one arm. Beauty was still belowdecks.

"How are you feeling?" Ashley asked.

Barbie held up her crutch and lifted her hurt leg, smiling. "I'll live. Thankfully, Beauty walks for both of us."

The boat's lights kicked on. Overhead lights, inside lights, and even old strings of white Christmas lights winding through the railing going around the ship lit up. Ginn waved to someone, who dragged over deck chairs and a lounger. Ashley, Ginn, and Donathan sat in a semicircle of chairs. Barbie lay down on a lounger, and Mason just continued sitting cross-legged and painting his mask while staring intensely at it.

"How do you power and fuel all of this?" Donathan asked Ginn.

Ginn smiled. "Well, not everyone knows that the Shytown Trail still has power running up it, leading to Falling Sands. The Protectorate makes sure that it is up and running for them. but God help you if you leech off their power without permission."

Ginn giggled. "But we're always on the move, and we know the trail better than anyone else, so we have some good spots where we take full advantage of the fat cats."

Donathan nodded.

Ginn continued, "The fuel, on the other hand, has been trickier." She took on a somber tone. "I'm sure you know the Protectorate has their dirty slave trade that they use to man the oil refinery in Martinez. They've also got most of Stockton and Sacramento for their science enclaves and tech, and they live in comfort. Then there are their various oil and mining projects back there, leading up to the Sierra Nevada." She clenched her teeth and leaned forward. "But the rest of us? If your enclave can't pay their protection fee, you get caught breaking their laws, or they just don't like you, they'll put you in chains, and you'll work their territory for life."

"Yeah, that..." Donathan just trailed off and nodded.

Ginn understood and nodded back. "Those rotten sons of bitches."

"Are we all ready for the night's festivities?" At the microphone, Paul sounded galvanized.

"Festivities?" Ashley asked.

Ginn nodded. "This is our time for a private party down to San Diego. Our booze cruise." She sighed. "Regardless of what happened, Paul still has to make an appearance."

Many folks had been cheering since Paul first spoke. The DJ had scratched out a few beats. Some glow sticks had appeared in the crowd, but none of the folks were very dressed up. Donathan guessed they had enough of doing it year-round for show. Some Knight's Moon denizens breezed past and brought Barbie a drink in a large glass with sliced fruit on its edges.

Donathan eyeballed the drink, and Barbie waved a hand then motioned in his direction. Two people appeared with trays full of drinks. One gave a drink to Donathan, and the other brought two more to Ginn and Ashley. Mason waved them off when they tried to give him one. He couldn't seem to drag his eyes away from his work.

Donathan was still awestruck at the drink and looked curiously in Ginn's direction. She was sipping at hers through a pink straw.

After a moment, she pulled off, swallowed, and said, "What? Work hard, play harder when you can." She waved a hand about herself and laughed. "The world's gone to hell, after all."

Donathan nodded in agreement and went to work on his drink. Ashley took a sip, coughed, and set it down on the deck. Barbie just continued to grin and sip the drink, staring at the crowd gathering around Paul.

Paul climbed onto the higher deck housing the strange apparatus and looked down at the boat. He motioned for the music to lower.

"It's been a rough year, has it not?" Paul asked while looking down at the crowd as if surveying his fiefdom.

The crowd murmured in agreement.

"It's been harder to gather, and coin seems a little harder to come by, but that," he strolled to the other side of the deck, still looking down and smiling, "that doesn't slow us down one bit."

The crowd cheered.

"Our cold war with the Protectorate has gone hot."

The crowd booed.

Paul grinned. "Oh well." He reached up with his free hand and dusted off his other shoulder. "Some of us don't mind the heat. Am I right?"

The crowd laughed with him.

He stopped laughing suddenly and turned from where he was standing, gazing out at the shoreline. As the crowd grew quiet, he brought the microphone slowly up to his lips. "And the darkness.

Well, we've all seen it. It's become meaner. It waits for most of us, hissing and spitting, drooling for the marrow in our bones."

He turned to face the audience, and a wicked grin spread across his face. In a thick tone, he asked, "Do you know what I say to that? I say—"

"By order of the Protectorate Army of Falling Sands, I order this vessel to stand down and prepare to be boarded." The voice carried by megaphone across the water.

Everyone turned at the same time and rushed over to the guardrail. An old maritime destroyer sat in the water about a thousand yards off their side.

Ginn giggled. "Oh damn." She set down her drink and rushed over to the guardrail.

Ashley and Donathan did the same. Even Mason put down his mask and scrambled to his feet.

Ginn took one look at the destroyer and waved across the boat. Other folks waved back and ran off.

"Can I finish?" Paul said into the mic, sounding irritated.

The person with the megaphone responded in a gruff voice, "Negative. Cease and desist all activities, and prepare to be boar—"

"Can I finish?" Paul interrupted with a higher-pitched voice.

Someone waved up to Paul.

"Negative. Cease an—"

"Can I finish?"

"Negat—"

"Can I finish?"

"No!"

Paul grinned wickedly. He stood up and pointed an unyielding finger at the boat. "From the Knight's Moon with love." He followed that by shouting, "Fire the N.O.I.C.!"

The coils wrapped around the large sideways pylon on the top deck lit up bright orange as the arm itself swung around, aiming at the destroyer. A moment later, a loud noise hummed then whumped. The cruise liner rocked sideways as folks shouted while darting across the deck. A loud crack echoed in from off the ocean. Drinks fell over, spilled, and clanked across the cruise-liner deck. White-hot metal showered down into the sea as the destroyer began to sink.

Paul got on the mic. "Enjoy the swim to shore, boys. Hope the night doesn't devour the rest of you." He grinned as the crowd cheered. "Remind the Judge that, since the treaty was broken, we no longer have to play by his rules."

Donathan turned to Ginn and asked, "What's an N.O.I.C.?"

Ginn thanked someone who was breezing past and replied, "The No Orbit Ion Cannon. Nyla named it." She grinned. "It's not actually an ion cannon, but it is quite vicious. It has to remain cool, which is why it stays on the boat. The bottom of it reaches through the hull and is suspended in the Pacific." Ginn thanked someone else walking past and waved at another person. "We've only tested it once, and apparently we only have a few more shots left with it." Ginn chuckled. "It took Nyla an entire month to make it."

Mason returned to painting his mask.

Donathan nodded. "If only we had two of her."

Mason jumped up, eyes wide. His body seemed frozen in place, but his eyes shifted from left to right and back again before staring far off.

Ginn nodded. "I know. She's really the secret weapon here. The Mad Scient—"

Mason waved frantic hands, stomping his feet. "Everybody, shut up a second!"

Everyone stared in confusion at Mason while suffering the awkward silence.

Someone started speaking a few feet away from them, and Mason again shouted, "Shut up!"

Mason's eyes still looked far off, and he was holding a hand in the air, finger ticking off an imaginary line as if stepping something through.

Someone else said something across the deck, and half the boat shushed him.

Mason held up two hands defensively. "Just…" He waved his arms while his eyes glanced up and away. "I need just…" He reached down and grabbed his mask, trembling, then dragged a few bottles of paint over to his feet. He dabbed a paintbrush in the white and smeared away the work he'd recently completed on his mask.

"Don't anybody…" He said curtly, "I need to think and paint."

People crowded around in silence. Gulls cawed in the distance. Everyone on deck shuffled in as close as they could. Paint slushed across layers of paint on the hard plastic mask. Even with all the folks around, Donathan noted the night still felt a bit chilly on the Pacific.

After a few minutes, Mason held up his mask triumphantly. "I did it!"

The whole boat cheered.

Ashley looked at the mask and cocked an eyebrow. She shouted over the cheering, "But what is it?"

"Nyla's eyes!" Mason shouted excitedly. "Take us all to Half Moon Bay!"

"Mason, just calm down and explain this." Donathan sounded frustrated, his hands outstretched cautiously toward his friend.

Mason pointed to his mask and shrugged. "What's confusing? I saw Nyla's eyes in Half Moon Bay. Let's go get her."

Donathan asked slowly, "Like… you had a vision?"

Mason's jaw dropped. "No, I didn't have a vision! I'm not crazy. You were there too!"

Ashley put a palm on her face. "We're on the boat Ma—"

Ginn chimed in, "Let me try." She stepped in front of Mason and placed a hand on his shoulder then said in a soothing voice, "Hon, slow down and explain what you saw and when."

Mason sighed and raised one hand in front of himself, the other still clutching his mask. "The last time we were in Half

Moon Bay, we were in Nyla's secret lab." He asked Ginn, "Do you know it?"

Ginn nodded.

Mason continued, "Okay, so there's this machine there. I peeked under the cover."

Ginn nodded. "I know of it. Nyla's dad built it."

"Well, we have to open it." Mason sounded adamant. "Nyla is in there!"

She grinned for a second and nodded across the deck to Paul. A maritime bell rang out somewhere.

Ginn then donned a sour face and asked, "Are you sure? I mean, Nyla is below deck, barely clinging to life."

"No!" Mason stomped a foot and pointed away from the boat, out at the water. "Nyla is also there in Half Moon Bay!"

Ashley coughed and mumbled, "Half Moon Bay is the other way."

Mason adjusted the direction he was pointing and repeated, "Nyla is also there in Half Moon Bay!"

Ginn shrugged but then smiled slightly.

Mason clenched his fists. "Look, I saw her eyes staring back at me from the machine!" He shut his eyes and lifted his head up toward the sky. "I know it's crazy. She walked up next to me, saying her dad called that machine his insurance policy or something, but," Mason opened his eyes and gave his friends the most determined look he'd ever mustered, "I know what I saw! I can't forget things like that! She is also in that machine!"

Everyone stared at Mason in silence for a moment before Donathan said in a firm tone, "This is where we trust Mason. Get us to Half Moon Bay, now."

35.

Half Moon Bay
Zombie Civil Rights Group
Present Day

THE SHIP DROPPED ANCHOR on the far side of Half Moon Bay. Paul and Ginn exchanged a few words before they brought an unconscious Nyla out on a stretcher and loaded her into a white lifeboat. Ashley, Mason, and Donathan climbed into the boat and paddled toward shore. The moon reflected off the water of Half Moon Bay, and the night held an eerie calm. The undead avoided the place, but no one seemed to know why. The living avoided it too because the Protectorate had made an example of the science enclave that had taken up residence there a decade before. The place had been off limits ever since, unless you were Princess Jae and Nyla and had a secret lab hidden there.

Before the Protectorate ripped down the science enclave, Nyla's dad had built a secret lab in a cave hidden around the cliff's edge. You had to know of the cave and, even then, had to know the secret code to get inside. Various contraptions were hidden there, but more importantly, that was where they had the zombie inoculation synthesized to be distributed.

The lifeboat edged close enough to shore that Donathan jumped out and dragged the vessel toward the beach. The Pacific was its usual freezing self, but Donathan never showed it bothered him. When they hit landfall, everyone else jumped out to help drag the boat farther up onto the shore. They caught their breath then heard a giant splash in the ocean. A large object stretched out of it, and Beauty waded to shore with Barbie on its back. She pointed at Nyla and waved a beckoning hand. After a few minutes, Nyla's litter was carefully loaded onto the Spiderling, who walked up the beach. The sand made a pat pat noise under everyone's feet. They had to wade through foot-deep water around the cliff's edge until they made it inside the cave. The secret entrance looked no longer secret as the door had been blasted partially open. Seawater dripped down the ladder, flooding into the lab. Barbie agreed to watch Nyla and wait for them while they explored inside.

Cold seawater stung Ashley's hands as she gripped the metal rungs, climbing the ladder into the darkness. Donathan led the way, having already turned on his red L-shaped flashlight and clipped it onto his collar. The water there was waist deep.

Ashley pulled her flashlight out and held it aloft in one hand while she unsheathed her bat with the other. Mason fell off the ladder and was submerged in the water for a second before popping up, coughing and sputtering. They waded up the dark hallway for what seemed like an eternity. When they made it into the lab, the higher area seemed relatively dry. It was flooded but only about ankle deep.

"They must have drains down there," Ashley said while trudging through the water.

They climbed around the metal scaffolding and went down the ladder into the lab. Sand and water were everywhere, but most of the equipment looked intact in the front, at least. The very back of the lab was a wreck where part of the cliff had caved in on some of the terminals. In the middle of the room, half covered by a canvas tarp, stood the apparatus. Mason pulled the tarp off a large metallic pod with some coils coming out of the back and large cords of wire stretching up to the ceiling.

"I'm really not sure if those wires were there last time or if they fell in after the explosions," Mason said. He ran around to the front of the pod and pressed his face against the glass. "I can't see her eyes," Mason's voice was a bit muffled against the pod, "but I think I know what to do. We need to turn this thing on."

Ashley tried not to sound defeated. "Even if you know where a power outlet is, it's probably not safe to—"

"Just climb onto something," Mason warned.

Ashley and Donathan went back to the front of the lab and climbed onto the desk with terminals that they'd seen Nyla messing with when they had been there before.

Mason still stood in the water and said, "Remember what Waterfalz said? Throw copper! I've got a whole pocketful of pennies." He jiggled his wet pants to prove it but mostly just made a sloshing sound. After a moment, he produced a handful of copper pennies. "I don't know how shiny these are, but..." He sent a whole handful of pennies plinking off the top of the machine.

Nothing happened.

Mason shrugged and ran around the machine, throwing pennies off the front door. They pinged and crescendoed off the door before thunking into the water. He ran back around, shrugging, then threw another handful of pennies into the air, sending them splashing down into the water. His shoulders slumped forward. Even in the darkness, with the red light casting strange shadows on the water and his face, Ashley could make out Mason's frown and eyebrows hanging low.

After a minute, he looked up, clearly crying. "I did what she said I—"

All at once, the lab powered up. The fluorescent lights lit like the sun. A computer terminal flickered on, and an enormous amount of popping echoed through the lab. Ashley screamed, and Mason fell face-first into the water, twitching.

———

A beat echoed in first. It flowed in like a heartbeat, gentle but somehow full of fury. A moment later, a break kicked in. It was sharp, a perfect snare that carried a wise melody in with it. Trumpets hung strong in the air, which was ruled by sounds.

Mason counted to four and opened his eyes, whispering, "Heavenly hip-hop."

Ivory carvings lined the walls. They looked less like letters and more like hieroglyphics. Mason took a step, and the ground lit up. Bars of light appeared on the walls at about ankle height, and he followed their path out of the tunnel into a bright, focused light. When his eyes adjusted, he stood in a garden filled with lush green hills, ivory benches, and walkways. Golden pillars led into the sky with large green vines stretching up and around them. The vines converged in some places and reached overhead to other pillars but never seemed to block out the light shining in from all around. People were lounging everywhere, some talking, some eating fruits, some kissing.

"Am I dead?" Mason asked, turning in circles to stare at all the folks. He could hear various discussions, but none seemed to stand out. The heavenly hip-hop still hung strong in the air.

Just as he stopped spinning, someone behind him said, "Kinda."

He turned around and found a strong, round-faced, muscular man with a shaved head standing in a white dress shirt, black bow tie, white slacks, and shiny white shoes.

"Hi?" Mason said apprehensively.

The man grinned and stepped forward, hugging Mason tightly.

Somehow, Mason felt enough trust to hug him back. After a minute, the man pulled away, smiling down at Mason with big blue eyes, saying, "You know there's no word for old friends who have just met?"

Mason cocked an eyebrow.

The man apologized, stepping back and shaking his hand forcefully. "I'm Chris Mason." Chris grinned at Mason then, with a thick Alabama accent, said, "I believe your daddy named you after me."

Chris waved Mason forward and turned toward a path. As they walked, Mason planted himself next to Chris. No words were exchanged as the park folded into a road. The horizon looked to be around sunset. The change of scenery was so sudden Mason wasn't quite sure what had happened. The sides of the road were edged with lime-green foliage growing up around the borders of gray blacktop. A single split yellow line was centered in the road and drove straight into the horizon. Mason let his eyes drift from the horizon up into a crimson that bled into violet and indigo crisscrossing the sky. Only a few white fluffy clouds could be seen in the distance.

Chris waved a hand, and a cherry-red 1934 Ford Coupe appeared. He reached into his pocket and pulled out a set of keys then, grinning at Mason, said, "You ride shotgun."

The interior of the car was a deep auburn finish with leather seats. It was a few degrees warmer but not uncomfortable, although a bit of humidity hovered in the air.

Chris fired up the car and aimed it down the road. He drove straight up the double yellow lines, not bothering to steer on the right side.

"What is this place?" Mason asked.

"As far as I can figure," Chris looked over, grinning widely, "it's my own personal heaven." He turned back to the road and flexed his hands on the wheel. "It appears when I need it."

"So heaven's real?" Mason asked.

"Yup." Chris nodded. "It's here, and most folks have bits and pieces of it. They'll call it paradise or all the answers of the universe revealed or heaven, only not everyone down there ever has the full story." Chris shrugged. "Just bits and pieces."

"You like summer rain?" Chris cocked an eyebrow in Mason's direction.

Mason shrugged.

Chris turned his attention back to the road. Large drops of rain began to hit the windshield, and the road fell into a slight shadow as they drove. The rain picked up a bit until a steady pitter-patter rang out over the sound of the engine. Mason rolled down the window and held his hand out to catch some of the warm drops.

Mason was still staring out the window up at the sky when he asked, "What's a typical day like for you up here?"

Chris slowed down the car a little and looked at Mason, who met his gaze. Chris exclaimed, "It's great! I get to go to the range and shoot every day, and I never have to clean a single weapon!" Chris chuckled hard, and Mason couldn't help but giggle too.

"I wonder what my heaven will be like," Mason added with a smile.

Chris frowned and looked back at the road. In a serious tone, he said, "Listen, kid, I love having you here, but it's not really your time. We just needed to have words." When Mason sighed, Chris continued, "We see most things up here, but we never get to play the game anymore. We just watch."

As if to emphasize his point, the sky lit up with a view of Ashley and Donathan shouting at Mason's limp body in the lab, shaking him, trying to wake him up. His friends seemed frantic, shouting and screaming. The sky returned to its normal stormy hue after a moment.

Chris raised an eyebrow and glanced at Mason. "I'm sure I don't need to tell you the whole world is out of whack. The balance has been disturbed by that sum-bitch that calls himself the Judge."

Mason nodded.

"Using that ring, he's removed most natural death from the equation. Most folks that die don't wind up here, and none of you down there are very happy either." Chris jammed on the gas pedal as the road began to wind a bit. He cut a corner sharply, but the car clung to the road even in the rain. "You all have to put it right." He put emphasis on the last word. "You need to get that ring back and rip down the walls of the Judge's city."

He jammed his foot down harder on the accelerator, and the rain pounded the windshield. The view outside became nothing more than wavy shapes through the torrent. Lightning cracked the sky.

"Only then will the world start to heal." Chris slammed on the brakes and turned off the car. "If you fail, well then..." He just lowered his hands, shaking his head. Opening his door, Chris motioned for Mason to do the same. "This is our stop."

The second he set foot outside the car, the rain ceased, and the stormy night suddenly became a sunny day. Mason's jaw fell open. He was back in the park, where people seemed to be crowding around something off in the distance.

As they edged closer to the group, Mason recognized a face. "Nyla!"

She didn't respond. Her eyes were shut tight, and her arms were chained up above her to a tree branch. Folks were talking to her, trying to help her. Some were even floating off the ground, taking turns flying through her, trying to grab hold of something and drag her off the tree. After a minute, Nyla began screaming.

"She'll scream for hours before she takes a break," Chris added.

Mason didn't even try to hide his fear. "What's wrong with her? Is she dead?"

Chris shook his head. "Almost. Her life is in the balance, but she's just enough in your world still that we can't help her."

Mason nodded and chose his path carefully through the crowd. Folks seemed to notice he was different and stepped back, clearing a path as he approached. Everyone grew silent except for Nyla's shrill scream. Mason strode up and wrapped his arms around her. The chains shattered and faded away as her body went limp.

"Shh." Mason held her close. "I've got you now." A second later, his foot slipped, and they both fell forward through the ground. They were falling fast.

Nyla looked as though she had passed out. Mason held her close, looking around at the sky whizzing around them. Some of the folks were matching their fall with determined looks on their faces. One woman nodded in Mason and Nyla's direction before smiling. She then leaned back and immediately disappeared up and out of view. A second later, another did the same, then another, until Mason noticed the last person matching his descent was Chris, who grinned warmly and waved before arching his back and disappearing out of sight.

The air rushed around Mason and Nyla, its sound like the sky screaming. Mason tilted his head forward to see where he was falling and immediately recognized the top-down view of Northern California except a giant mass of black pulsing veins was lying across it. They covered all of Sacramento, Stockton, and part of the Sierra Nevadas. The threads converged on Vallejo, now known as Falling Sands.

Chris's voice echoed over the rush of wind. "Now, don't forget what I told you!"

The black veins ignited with red and orange flames, which trailed up to Falling Sands, and in an instant, the city burned to a crisp. The sound of rushing wind froze, and Mason and Nyla just hung still in the air for a moment as the cinders of Falling Sands split into ash and scattered apart on an invisible wind. Chris's voice sounded warm and Southern. "Your pops is proud of you! So am I!"

Everything drifted from view as Mason opened his eyes.

———

"Mason!" Ashley shook him gently.

Mason was suddenly very conscious of bone-chilling wet cloth pressed against his skin. His legs stung sharply, drenched in the ocean water from the lab floor.

The whole world warped and shook around him for a moment. Mason focused on Ashley's eyes and said, "The watch is broken, the ticker stopped, and the rabbit ain't here ...cause the rabbit got... clocked," before shoving Ashley aside and rolling over to throw up.

He huffed, heaved, and gasped for a few moments until the world felt a bit more stable. Then, looking around the room, he asked, "What happened?"

"You about died is what happened," Donathan's tone was dry and seemed a bit overwhelmed. "After tonight, I don't think my heart could have taken that."

Ashley helped Mason stand in the water. "The whole lab powered up and shocked the shit out of you for like..." She blinked away tears and hugged Mason tightly. "Too long. Then all at once, something popped in the back of the lab, and the lights went off in that half. The water was no longer electrified, so we could get to you." She wiped away more tears from her cheeks. "It was another ten minutes until you opened your eyes."

"Is Nyla here?" Mason asked. "I saw heaven, I think."

Donathan just shook his head with an eyebrow raised quizzically.

Ashley added, "This half of the lab still has power, but the pod never opened. It—"

A large fizzing noise like the pop of a can of soda jolted through the lab. All three of them jumped. Some of the ground water was draining away. At the rear of the pod, two doors opened.

They ran around to the other side of the pod, but it was too dark to see into. The darkness inside it looked unnatural, almost like ink hanging in the air. Finally, a face wearing glasses with a familiar set of eyes poked through. A moment later, a tall man with dirty blond hair, wearing glasses and a lab coat stepped out. He coughed a bit then stood up, straightening his lab coat and spinning around the room, taking in the view.

He cleared his voice before announcing, "Well the lab's seen better days." He turned and looked down at Mason, Donathan, and Ashley before adjusting his glasses and asking, "Who might you be?"

"It was your eyes!" Mason exclaimed. "You have Nyla's eyes!"

The man nodded. "I should hope so, genetics and all. She's my daughter."

Donathan stepped up and squared his shoulders. "Well, I..." He took a deep breath. "She's almost dead, sir."

"What?" he shouted. "What do you mean almost?" The man stumbled a bit and reached up to grab the edge of the pod. "Does she need medical help?"

Ashley nodded.

The man's eyebrows shot up, and he stood taller. "Then for God's sake, bring her here!"

Ashley was already running for the tunnel when Donathan surged past her at breakneck speed. A few moments later, they carried in an unconscious Nyla on the aid-and-litter stretcher.

"I don't think there's any decent medical equipment in the lab here," Donathan added.

"Of course not!" the man added and waved them over. "This lab looks like a bomb went off in it."

"Over it, actually," Mason replied, still standing frozen in the same spot where he'd been when the man appeared.

The man waved again near the pod and stepped into it. "This way!"

Mason stepped up with his friends and helped them angle the stretcher ahead, and all four of them stepped into the inky blackness together.

The gentle hum of computers and mainframes hung in the air on the other side. Mason stepped through last and rubbed his eyes in disbelief, then looked back toward the dark pod.

"It's the lab?" Mason asked in a confused voice, spinning in a circle and admiring all the blinking lights and computer terminals lining the walkway.

"It's never looked this good," Ashley added. Her mouth hung open a bit, her eyebrows both raised.

Donathan's nose wrinkled, and both his hands rose in confusion. "Why would you build two labs? I mean, at least this one is in better shape than the other one."

"No, it's not." The man stepped over to a computer terminal and punched a few buttons. With a whoosh, the door to the pod slid shut.

He then motioned to Nyla's stretcher. Mason and Donathan rushed to the handles and followed the man through the tunnel. They neared the end, and the man turned around, looking down at Nyla's wound. Then he placed a hand on her cheek and sighed. Another minute later, he nodded, carefully lifted the unconscious Nyla off the stretcher, slung her across his shoulders in a fireman's carry, and began the slow process of maneuvering up the ladder at the end of the tunnel. Donathan went up after them. Mason hoisted the stretcher. Ashley followed, trailing behind. The sound of crashing waves grew in intensity when they made it back out of the tunnel and onto the sand. Day had broken.

"How is it morning?" Ashley asked. "It was just the middle of the night!"

The man lowered Nyla slowly to the stretcher before nodding to Mason and Donathan. They picked up the ends of the litter, and everyone maneuvered around the cliffside while trying to keep out of the surf.

The man chimed in, "Back in the lab, I meant it: It's not two labs."

"Time travel," Mason said in a voice filled with awe. His sandy hair rippled a bit in the morning wind as they trotted along. "We went into the future when Half Moon Bay was rebuilt."

The man chuckled. "For you, this is the past. By my calculations, that time tunnel is actuated to roughly an eleven- or twelve-year span."

"The past?" Donathan asked as they came around the corner.

The sight was so beautiful that they all stopped for a second to take it in.

Half Moon Bay was bright. The ocean was cobalt blue, and jade trees and thriving sagebrush adorned the hillside. Beach grass was combing the edges of the cliffs. The houses lining the beach were all intact. No rubble was visible save for the occasional cliff rock near the brink of the sand—no torn-up roads.

"There aren't even scorch marks," Ashley added.

The man stopped and turned back around to face them. "I told you—my present, your past!" He spun back around on his heels and fell into a trot up the sand.

They needed a minute to realize life was all around them. People were peering down from the beach houses. Folks were throwing nets into the sea. A few people peeled off from fishing to sprint up the sand toward Nyla's dad.

Words were exchanged, and one person fell into a dead sprint up the beach toward the main enclave off in the distance. Two others ran over and, without words, took the litter carrying Nyla from Mason and Donathan then jogged ahead with it. Nyla's dad turned around and waved for them to follow. He continued walking past the folks fishing.

The trio jogged a few feet to catch up to him. Donathan tried to ask the man something, but he just shook his head and kept walking. Eventually, they reached the entrance to the science enclave. It resembled a small sports arena. Triangular panels, with edges that curved and jutted out, formed a steel ball-shaped mesh around it. The front panel had a terminal with a numeric keyboard mounted under it. The man paused to enter a code, and a large set of doors, invisible at first, folded out from the enclave. They were triangular and matched the outside mesh. Stepping inside, the group were greeted by beaming white lights and stale air filled with humming and activity. People were all around, talking about various subjects. Someone nodded to Nyla's dad.

"Let me know her vitals before they prep for surgery." He looked sternly in the direction of Donathan, Ashley, and Mason before he looked back and continued, "Gunshot wound, it looks like."

The other scientist in a lab coat nodded and sprinted off down a hallway. Up above, folks were holding clipboards and standing on catwalks, peering into various cages. White hospital colors and sterile smells filled the place.

Nyla's father crossed his arms and managed to look menacingly at the trio before continuing, "I guess you're her friends?"

Donathan nodded and stepped forward apprehensively. "Sir, we—"

"Save it," the man said with a hand in the air. "And my name is Charles. Doctor Charles Faulkner." He adjusted his glasses and turned to walk down the hallway as everyone followed him. "I trust my daughter's judgment. I just can't figure out how you opened the tunnel from that side."

Mason said, "I threw copper, and then the electricity kicked on, and I went to heaven and met my dad's friend, who told me how to save the world."

Charles stopped midstep and turned around slowly, his jaw hanging open. He stared for half a minute at Mason before turning back around slowly and continuing his walk.

Ashley squinted out of one eye and mouthed the word "why?" to Mason. He just shrugged and followed behind his friends.

The tunnel gave way to a massive room filled with shouting and activity. Up above them, a part of the round dome could be seen. Below were folks rushing to and fro in lab coats. Some were standing around in a garden filled with crops and an artificial track-lighting system. Others were sitting at tables, poring over documents. Some were trotting along scaffolding that lined the walls while still others were peering into microscopes and taking notes. Many tables with lab equipment sat everywhere. The sound of hydraulics fizzed and hissed before a man sitting on a big pair of metallic legs with hinge joints going the opposite direction of human knees said, "Excuse me." Ashley stepped out of the way, and he punched a few buttons on a keyboard and moved a joystick then continued on his path forward. Other folks were standing out front of several menacing oversized machine gun turrets, in heavy discussion. The crowd churned and moved. More strange devices and experiments were everywhere.

"Goodness!" Ashley didn't realize she was shouting. "I knew this science enclave was huge, but I never imagined!"

A few folks turned away from their work to laugh, and Charles said, "Actually this is small. The underground part is much larger."

People rushed past Donathan, Ashley, and Mason, so the ZCR squeezed in closer to Charles.

Donathan nodded in response to Charles and without thinking added, "Yeah, Nyla said it was a sight to see before Falling Sands destroyed it."

Everyone froze. The sounds of hydraulics, voices, and all activity faded away in an instant. Eventually, someone coughed.

A scientist closest to Charles turned to him and said, "Destroyed it? I goddamned told you they'd never honor those treaties!"

A red-faced scientist rounded on Charles with ferocity in his eyes. "We just informed them that we have almost synthesized an inoculation! We're probably a year out from saving the world!"

Another woman scientist stepped through the crowd, shouting at Charles, "That's exactly what we get for getting in bed with slavers!"

More folks were yelling and shoving. Charles had his hands up defensively and shouted, "What else were we supposed to do? They have the largest standing army."

The male scientist closest to Charles, a bald, skinny man who looked to be in his fifties, motioned to the machine guns and the strange mechanized legs and said, "Well, if they want a fight, we will give them a helluva fight!"

A few folks shouted their agreement, and Charles raised his hands higher, shouting, "Enough!" Everyone grew quiet.

Charles turned to Donathan and, with wide eyes overflowing with frustration, asked, "When?" His voice sounded strained. "When do they attack us?"

Donathan's face turned red and he raised his palms defensively.

Ashley stepped up. "Nyla said about twelve years ago."

Charles sighed. "So...any day."

The crowd erupted again in rage.

Charles barked commands across the room, telling folks to prepare their sectors for attacks. People sprinted off out of sight, and even more folks pushed through. The giant enclave resembled an angry beehive complete with a human swarm. Charles waved the three friends forward.

They crossed the room and went up another static hallway until they were standing outside a glass window. The laboratory inside was filled with shiny silver cages. Several lab-coat-clad scientists were distracted inside. Two were taking notes furiously on clipboards while one looked attentively at a small creature held in two hands. The creature was dark, with a shiny body and several legs. Above the room's front window, in a wide font, was written Spiderling Human Aggregation Telesthesia Experiment."

Charles banged on the window, and everyone snapped their attention toward the glass except the Spiderling, which just hunched lower in the scientist's palms. "I'm sorry." His tone was clinical. "I'm afraid you're going to have to burn the lot." He shrugged to the scientists on the other side. "We don't have time to tackle this experiment any longer." A female scientist stepped up to the glass to bark protests back at Charles.

Donathan stared up at the sign. "Spiderling Human An—S H A T. Shat." He pointed but looked back in Ashley's direction, confused. Then he reached across and tapped Charles on the shoulder, saying, "Set 'em free."

"Pardon?" Charles looked frustrated. "We can't set these creatures free. They're dangerous, and we don't know—"

"Yeah," Donathan nodded and agreed. "They're terribly dangerous but also necessary. Set 'em free."

Charles protested, "We don't even know if they'll live long. They haven't their own digest—"

"Doc," Donathan interrupted, stepping closer and placing a hand on Charles's shoulder. "You've got to let these things live. We need one eventually."

Charles sighed then nodded to the scientists on the other side of the glass. He turned and walked farther up the hallway. The female scientist who had been arguing with Charles mouthed the words "thank you" to Donathan.

The cement hallway angled down and away. The tunnel grew dark, and Charles announced, "Lights track on me."

LED light strips lit up at the edge of the wall near the footpath. The ZCR trailed him in silence. Eventually, they passed a few more labs empty of equipment and people. The tunnel gave way to a huge bay filled with more of the strange power suits alongside turrets and pallets of ammunition. Several folks were crowding in a group in the center of the room. Donathan, Ashley, Mason, and Charles walked up midconversation.

"I still feel that the best action is to stage an ambush on both sides of the point where Highway One enters into our town. If they want hell, we bring it to them." A man in a lab coat was looking toward two spots on a large map unfolded on the floor.

A balding man in a blue suit with red letters reading Security spoke up. "Are you kidding? First of all, you can't stage an ambush on two sides on equal ground! You'll have cross fire. Secondly, we have enough technology inside and outside this enclave that we can decimate them remotely without ever having to be here!"

A few folks chimed in with their agreement.

"Let's leave and let the autoturrets do their job."

"And do what?" Charles added his two cents. "You think people aren't going to notice this technology somewhere else?"

The crowd had gone quiet.

Charles motioned toward Donathan, Mason, and Ashley. "Plus, we already have word from the future that they destroy us!"

The man wearing the security outfit tutted his disapproval. Everyone else just looked frustrated and lost in thought.

"Hang on." Ashley raised an eyebrow in confusion. She glanced from Charles back to her friends. "Back on the boat, Ginn said she was originally from Half Moon Bay."

"Ginn? As in Ginnifer, spelled G i n n?" The man wearing the security uniform was wide eyed.

Ashley looked up a moment while shrugging. "I think so?" Then leaning forward a little, she asked, "Do you know her?"

The man's jaw dropped. A smile crept across his lips. "She's my daughter."

Donathan shook his head. "That doesn't make any sense though, Ash. Remember the only real scientist traveling with the Knight's Moon is Nyla." Donathan's shoulders slumped a bit, and he turned toward the crowd of scientists. "Look, I think you guys die."

Everyone started arguing and shouting all at once. Curse words erupted as the crowd grew loud once more. Mason had taken off his mask and spun it around. He was staring at the painting of the eyes in the darkness.

"Excuse me?" Mason said meekly.

Everyone continued shouting.

Mason held up his mask, repeating himself. Ashley, noticing her friend's cues, put two fingers up to her mouth, and belted out an ear-piercing whistle until everyone grew silent. She nodded to Mason.

"I don't think anyone has to die. Remember the machine?" Mason added, pointing at his mask.

Charles stared for a moment at the mask. "Goodness. I think he's right." Charles sounded relieved. "We set this place up to fight automatically, and we can all go through the time tunnel and come out in the future."

A woman gasped and added, "We can even bring most of our equipment there!"

The man in the security uniform added, "We can set the enclave to explode so they have no idea what any of this is!"

"That doesn't work either." Donathan shook his head. A second later, he swore loudly then added, "I've got it. Half." Donathan pointed toward the ground. "Half of you have to stay here and create the Knight's Moon Entertainment enclave."

"Entertainment?" someone muttered.

Some folks cocked their heads sideways. One woman even shot Donathan what looked like a mix of both a sneer and disgust.

"What?" Charles's jaw had dropped, and he was rubbing one of his temples, staring at Donathan.

"In our..." Donathan took a deep breath before trying to explain. "In your future, the Knight's Moon is an entertainment enclave that travels around and keeps people safe for a night of partying, away from the undead."

"Why the hell would we do that?" Charles asked incredulously.

Ashley stepped up. "Eventually, when the inoculation is synthesized, it lets you secretly build an army of followers while distributing the vaccine to keep people from becoming zombies."

Mason continued, "Because Falling Sands would never let you distribute that vaccine."

Donathan nodded. "They want the world in turmoil because they profit off of it, and they rule here, safe behind their enclave walls and their army."

Charles's mouth still hung open, and he asked, "It's not actually a vaccine. It's an inoculation, but you know of it?"

Ashley nodded. "Nyla helps synthesize and distribute it."

Charles stood tall, squaring his shoulders. He stuck his chest out a bit, straightening his lab coat. "My Nyla does molecular biology, biochemistry, and microbiology?"

Donathan nodded and added, "But she's always complaining that she doesn't know enough plain chemistry."

A man with gray hair above his temples stepped out of the crowd and added, "I mean, it kind of makes sense. Keeping the undead away is certainly within our ability at this point."

"Because of the blue-light electricity you all developed that destroys dead flesh?" Mason asked.

The whole crowd drew a breath.

Stunned, Charles asked, "What? What blue electricity that destroys dead flesh?"

The man with the gray hair shook his head. "We've only been experimenting with certain sound frequencies that keep the undead away." He cleared his throat. "In fact, we've hidden solar-powered versions of this tech all around Half Moon Bay."

Donathan looked up and away for a moment, then it was his turn to stand tall, squaring his shoulders. He mumbled, "Nyla must have developed all of that without any influences."

Charles grinned at Donathan.

Donathan stared him straight in the eyes and said, "Ny is..." He seemed to be searching for a definition but settled on saying, "Special. She can mimic skills, absorb knowledge, and borrow talents. You raising her here means she's absorbed everything around here. She's the only scientist you need to leave behind. Leave whatever might help her replicate your vaccine results or build these electrical experiments."

"We will do one better." Charles grinned. "Since we know this electrical technology works, we will try to begin researching it with her immediately and give her a leg up."

Donathan nodded then turned to the man in the security uniform. "Leave Nyla." He opened his mouth a bit, staring off above most of the scientists' heads. "Leave young Nyla here along with anyone else who isn't a scientist." He looked back at the security guard. "When Falling Sands arrives, make sure they have a path out of Half Moon Bay to safety." He pointed down. "Make the attack from Falling Sands look like it succeeded, for Nyla, and leave the automatic defenses of the enclave to fight to cover your escape." Donathan waved a hand at the scientists. "But the rest of you, pack up and come with us to the present...or future?" Shrugging off the confusion, he stepped forward and squared his shoulders. "Where you already have an army waiting, which you've kind of built...?"

"Oh." After Ashley gave Donathan a determined grin, she nodded and added, "And Princess Jae has to go with Nyla!"

"Okay, who the hell is Princess Jae?" Charles asked.

Ashley looked as if she had said too much. "I guess some of you meet her later."

36.

Half Moon Bay
Zombie Civil Rights Group
Twelve Years Earlier / Present Day

THEY STAYED AT THE ENCLAVE and rested for just over a week. Nyla's surgery went well, and she was recovering nicely. The trio visited her in her room a few times. All four of them laughed over the situation. The scientists had begun shifting equipment out of the enclave. Charles had even spoken with the older Nyla, getting the details on what was about to transpire.

During that week, they hid the equipment transition from Nyla's younger counterpart. Charles was making sure to put the youngster around as many working scientists as possible over the week. Ashley, Mason, and Donathan all managed to avoid Nyla's younger counterpart until one moment in the enclave's cantina, where they crossed paths fetching food. Adolescent Nyla was wearing a small lab coat, jeans, a purple

T-shirt, and smaller framed glasses, but that was unmistakably her. She walked past the trio and paused to ask Mason about his mask. Without thinking, Mason took it off his head to show her a painting of a time-traveling DeLorean with blue and cyan electricity surging off it. Little Nyla remarked that she remembered that movie and thanked Mason before walking on. Ashley excitedly commented on how she was so cute. Donathan shook his head, annoyed, and reminded them that stuff like that could change everything.

———

Just before midnight on the eighth night, they stepped out of the enclave. Charles met them in the street. Together, they walked up to the beach, the sand making tuft-tuft sounds as they moved. Bright light from flashlights, lamps, and various campfires greeted them. People were crowding around everywhere, hugging and saying goodbye. Some folks were crying, and even more people were laughing and joking about the situation.

As they walked down the beach, Mason caught sight of someone next to one of the campfires. He tapped the shoulders of Ashley and Donathan before pointing and exclaiming, "Look!" After a few moments of them hunting for what they were looking for amongst the faces huddled around the campfire, Mason said, "The little boy!" He was pointing at a boy with green pants, a white sleeveless T-shirt, and a blue rag tied across his head. "Isn't that Paul?"

Ashley gasped and ran up to hug him.

Both Donathan and Mason shouted, "Don't!"

Everyone froze, including young Paul, who was staring at the trio. Ashley was still hunched over with her arms out. She backed away slowly before straightening up and falling into a sprint until she was behind Charles, Mason and Donathan trailing up after her.

Donathan whispered, "So—"

"Yeah, I know," Ashley said curtly. "We don't want to mess up the timeline." Her tone turned to frustration. "He was just so cute! Little Paul!"

"I think it's fine," Mason added sheepishly. "I mean, we already lived it. Nothing's changed."

Charles maneuvered up the beach through the crowds until he was standing next to a hospital gurney in the sand. They rounded the gurney to find a grinning Nyla staring back at them. She adjusted her glasses then held her arms out for hugs. Everyone rushed forth and chimed in all at once, happy to see their friend.

A woman's voice sprang up beside them, emitting from a small blond woman. "Alwight, give her some space." She was wearing a purple turtleneck sweater and blue jeans.

"Mom!" Nyla announced. "These are my friends!"

The woman nodded and then signed, "Yes, but your friends need to remember you just got out of surgery a few days ago."

Ashley signed back, "Sorry, ma'am." She slowly finger spelled "ma'am."

Donathan nodded.

Mason just stared.

"You know sign?" The woman asked out loud in a surprised tone.

Donathan nodded and signed, "Yes. Mason taught us. It helps with being silent around the undead."

The woman asked, "Wait...Mason?"

Mason still stared, unmoving in the dim light. Finally, he asked, "Mom?" Then he dashed forward to hug the woman tightly.

She stepped back and held his face with her hands before screaming, "It is you!" She pulled him tightly to her chest, hugging and crying.

Ashley cocked an eyebrow, angling a look toward Donathan, who was rubbing his head. "I don't understand," she said.

The two couldn't stop hugging, both of them sobbing loudly. After a minute, Mason peeled back and said, "I thought you were dead! I saw them drag you off!"

The woman shook her head. "No, I..." She was still crying, but her voice carried through the sobs. "I looked evewywhere! I thought you were dead! I heard about your father!"

They huddled in, hugging tightly again.

"Still confused," Ashley added, and Donathan nodded.

The woman apologized and wiped tears from her eyes before extending a hand toward Ashley. "I'm Megan. I'm Mason's mom." She shook Ashley's hand and then reached two hands toward Donathan who took them both. "I thought he was dead! But I still kept looking. Eventually, Charles found me malnouwished and dying." She looked as if she was gathering her thoughts. "Then he took me in here and nursed me back to health. I fell in love with him and had Nyla."

Donathan took a hand back and pointed to an ear. "So your accent is because—"

She nodded and signed while speaking at the same time. "I'm deaf. It's how Mason knows sign." She pointed at Nyla. "It's how Nyla knows sign."

Charles had been silent through the whole exchange. He cleared his throat once but still looked as if he was unsure of what to say.

Mason pointed at Nyla and then looked at his mom. "So she's my..." His words trailed off before he asked, "Wait, what is she?"

Charles finally found his voice. "That would mean she's your half sister." He looked from Nyla back to Mason then said in a confused mumble, "I...I thought it was just a coincidence that you were named Mason like my wife's first child." Sounding a bit more sure, he continued, "I had no idea."

Megan rushed over to Nyla and threatened to smother her with hugs and kisses. Through the whole exchange, she said, "You found your brother! How lucky! My lucky daughter!"

Nyla struggled and finally managed to push her mom back enough to add, pointing at Mason, "No, Mom, he's the lucky one."

Late into the night, folks finally fell in line behind them. A second column lined up in the darkness, some folks holding torches and flashlights while waving goodbye.

Charles waved the trio forward. "Our scientists are opening the tunnel's gateway as we speak." They trotted around the cliff's edge through the surf. "You'll lead the way through, of course, with a few of our scientists who will secure the exit. Then we'll bring a few other folks and the brunt of our equipment through."

They centered on the open security hatch and climbed down into the lit tunnel, following the hum of computers and mainframes.

"Now, although an equal amount of time has passed, remember that it's always off by about twelve hours, so you should be exiting midafternoon." Charles turned around and walked backward at a decent pace into the lab, cautioning them, "Don't be shocked this time."

The lab was a flourish of activity. Scientists in lab coats with yellow gloves and goggles were sprinting back and forth. A few other researchers were tapping away at terminals.

Donathan gazed around the lab and asked, "So the tunnel is always twelve years off?"

As Charles shook his head, one of the scientists on the catwalk above chimed in. "It is now." He barely looked up from his clipboard. "When we first assembled the thing, we only had control of one end of the time tunnel. It was held in place by us, but we weren't sure where the other end was."

Charles nodded up at his colleague before turning to the trio. "Our end of the tunnel wasn't even a tunnel. We had a massive gate in the center of downtown Half Moon Bay." He shook his head and looked down at the ground. "Some poor soul actually drove through it." He looked at Donathan incredulously. "He started cursing at us then spun his vehicle around and drove back through the time anomaly."

"Where did he go?" Ashley asked.

Charles shrugged. "We have no idea!" He sighed and continued, "The other end wasn't held down like the two ends of this lab. It was spinning through points of time and cycling through space from anywhere within a three-hundred-mile range. It could very well have taken him from sometime in the past or thrown him into sometime and somewhere in the future, or vice versa. Who knows?"

Charles looked at another scientist. The scientist nodded and punched a few buttons on his keyboard while pointing his other hand toward the large pod in the center of the room. The doors whizzed and swung open, leaving trails of white vapor in their wake. Mason, Ashley, and Donathan stepped up toward the pod. Donathan paused to thank Charles before stepping through the pod. Ashley waved to everyone and went through the inky portal next.

Mason turned to Charles and asked with wide eyes, "So are you my stepdad?"

Charles coughed, blindsided by the question, and just whispered, "I...I don't know," before motioning toward the pod. Mason looked into the darkness then followed his friends through the contraption. After a flash of light, they were all standing back in the old rundown lab. The smell of stale seawater hung in the air.

A scientist stepped through behind them, cursing, then stuck his head back into the dark pod, yelling something through time. After a moment, he pulled his head out of the darkness and said, "It's okay. We can fix most of this, I'm sure."

Mason waved Ashley and Donathan over while pointing at a glowing monitor on the far side of the room. It held an image of Nyla, Mason, Donathan, and Ashley staring upward in the dark rubble of an old hotel room.

"Is that where we saw ourselves?" Ashley asked.

Mason nodded at her then stepped up to the monitor, draping his hands on it and peering at it with his face close to the screen.

Donathan grinned at Ash. "Well, we know how this conversation goes."

———

A few more scientists had stepped through, remarking about the lab being in disarray, but none had noticed the trio signing to the monitor in the back. When the exchange was finished, Ashley, Donathan, and Mason made their way in the darkness down the tunnel, up the ladder, and out the broken hatch.

As they were picking their path around the cliff in the surf, Mason said, "There's just one thing that doesn't make sense. Wouldn't they have all known—"

All three froze in place, standing in the surf and facing the main beach. Lined up on the beach in the same spot where the trio had left them was the second column of folks. People were throwing streamers and confetti. They all cheered at the ZCR. Someone unrolled a banner that read Welcome Home! Farther down the surf, near the old burnt-out enclave, the Knight's Moon cruise ship was anchored.

"Holy shit!" Ashley said as they all sprinted up the beach.

Music erupted from somewhere, and folks broke into dance. More confetti scattered and flew into the air as people encircled the trio, laughing and cheering. Eventually, Ginn and Paul stepped out of the crowd. Paul had a devilish grin on his face. The crowd hushed a bit, but people kept throwing confetti and occasionally clapping the members of the ZCR on the back.

"We just left you a week ago!" Mason said.

Ginn nodded and replied through a grin, "We know."

Paul added, "Time travel is funny like that."

"So you knew the whole time?" Ashley asked while spinning around, still trying to accept what she was seeing.

"Well," Paul stepped forward, with his arms raised skyward

while shrugging his shoulders, "we suspected it was you after that first fight against the Protectorate Army." He lowered his arms and grinned. "But we knew it was you when you showed up with Nyla at the rally point in Santa Clara." Paul shot a sly smile towards Ginn. "But keeping it from you took some serious effort on our part."

"So what was that whole song and dance on the boat?" Donathan asked.

"Well," Paul sounded a little hurt, "we knew you'd get there just fine." He grinned and waved toward the crowd. "You can't blame the actors for acting."

The crowd parted, and more cheering erupted. Folks were trickling around the cliffside and coming into view of the beach. Nyla limped around the corner, holding her stomach with one hand and leaning on her mother for leverage with her other. The crowd's cheering intensified. She waved to the ovation, and people sprinted out of the crowd to help her.

The crowd had stopped paying attention to Ginn and Paul, and everyone was shouting and doing their own thing. Folks that had said goodbye, crying in the dark twelve years before, were saying hello and hugging while remarking how funny it was to see each other in different states of aging.

Donathan maneuvered among the throng of folks and shouted over the crowd, "So what happens now?"

As Ginn laughed, Paul shouted back, "Now we go get Oakland and bring the fight to Falling Sands."

"Say that again." The Judge had just woken up in his oversized desk chair and was abnormally red faced, even for him.

The Coadjutant drew a deep breath and steadied himself before repeating, "Most of our forces in the South Bay were attacked by the Jae woman, and after she had pushed through, they were outright ambushed by a lot of undead hordes working in unison. Then that mass of creatures was last seen heading into San Francisco."

"Hordes of undead working together?" the Judge asked.

The Coadjutant just nodded.

Groaning slightly, the Judge shifted forward in his chair and wrenched open a drawer on his desk. After dragging out a bottle of dark liquid, he set it down on his desk with a thump. A moment later, he produced two glasses and, in a strange show of humanity, motioned for the Coadjutant to take the seat across from him before pouring the alcohol into both glasses and continuing.

After both men had taken sips of the foul-smelling liquid from their snifters, he asked, "How many undead grouped together?"

The Coadjutant shrugged. "Spotty reports, but apparently thousands."

The Judge took another long sip. Some of the liquid dribbled out of his lips before he wiped his mouth and added, "Even with the ring, that's not possible." He sneered, his wide cheeks unable to hide the disgust in his gaze for the bald man. "There's far too many."

The Judge let his eyes trail around the room to his paintings of meadows and trees, lining the walls of the office. After a long silence, he asked, "Any news from my general?"

The Coadjutant set down his glass. "We get bits and pieces about Mary Helen. Mostly that she refuses to come in and she's always seen with that creature." He brought the glass back up to his lips and added, "Maybe she's gone feral," before taking a long swallow.

"And the Fine Line Protectorate's ambush with all those troops and tech we sent down South?" The Judge's patience was wearing thin.

The Coadjutant reached across the table and took the liberty of pouring himself another glass of liquor. Raising the glass, the bald man took a deep sniff before saying, "Their ambush was ambushed by the Knight's Moon." He sounded a bit unfazed. Then he took a large gulp and gasped a bit, not bothering to look up. "Most of our troops on loan to them were slaughtered or scattered. Then we had one of our destroyers blasted out of the water by some kind of laser cannon the Knight's Moon had mounted to their ship." The bald man just stared at the glass blankly. "So we've lost positive control of our waterways now too."

The Judge shoved the bottle of alcohol and his glass across the desk, sending both to shatter on the floor. "So no good news?"

The Coadjutant hadn't even flinched. He just shook his head. "There's even paintings springing up in various places, showing the Knight's Moon and the Zombie Civil Rights Brigade in heroic poses. They're calling themselves a brigade now... So their numbers must have grown."

The Judge sat back, rubbing his temples and sighing with frustration. "Ghost or no ghost, I've got to get up and handle this."

The Coadjutant slugged back what was left of the alcohol before asking, "Ghost?"

The Judge shook his head. Straining, he stood up out of his chair. Stretching and groaning, he walked toward the hallway. The bald man stood up, following his lead. The Judge passed the kitchen and popped in momentarily to grab an armful of apples before heading farther down the hallway and passing the banquet hall, the war room, and various offices and quarters until he was standing near the front entrance to the main building. The Judge barked at the guards to unseal the door.

Night had fallen outside, and the rain was a steady downpour. Fall had finally decided to arrive in California. The smell of fresh rain filled the air, and the Judge stepped outside the building, surveying the cement walls and dusty roads of the inner sanctum of Falling Sands. He let his eyes trail up the road leading to the main gate then back down the same road in the opposite direction, toward the bridge in Benecia. The bridge led to the rest of their enclave, which encroached on Stockton and Sacramento and led up through the Sierra Nevadas toward Truckee—the peaceful enclave where the only undead ever allowed in were boxed, chained, and shipped through to science enclaves for coin, where power, gas, and oil were abundant for everyone in his favor, thanks to his advances. It was all his kingdom.

The Coadjutant cleared his voice and added, "In all my years here, I've never seen you set foot outside the main building, Judge."

The Judge nodded and dropped most of the apples to the ground. Holding one shiny red apple, he spun around in the rain, peering up and down the street. Slowly, he raised the apple to his lips and took a bite. Chewing apprehensively and wide eyed, he turned back around once more before taking another bite.

After a minute, he held the half-eaten apple up toward the Coadjutant. "Look, man! No ghosts!" The Judge laughed maniacally and then took another bite before presenting the apple again. "Not a ghost in sight!"

The Coadjutant pursed his lips tightly, one eyebrow raised. "Uhh, yes." He shook his head. "I don't believe I've ever seen a ghost here."

The Judge threw down the core of the apple then picked another off the ground, rubbed it on his rain-soaked shirt, and took a large bite from it. Through a mouthful of fruit, he asked, "Do we still have all those scientists from Lockheed-Martin and the Berkeley Science Labs held in Sacramento?"

The Coadjutant sniffed a bit. "Well, some of the older fellows passed, but we have most of them."

The Judge nodded, staring up the street. "What about that Zuckerberg fellow? The tech futurist?"

"He's still around." The Coadjutant cleared his throat. "Although he's never been happy about being held here."

The Judge took another bite of an apple before throwing it up the street. "Dust them all off. If the dead are amassing and the people are getting testy, we need new defenses and tech."

"How do you propose we make angry scientists we've kept prisoner for decades develop new tech for us?" the Coadjutant asked.

The Judge shrugged. "Gunpoint?" He kicked an apple up the street. "We need new weapons."

———

"What do you think?" Goblin asked aloud while handing the binoculars over to Crooks.

The fur-suited man had his bat head on and held the binoculars up to his face even though Goblin knew he had zero chance of seeing through them.

Nym stared off the cliff's edge of Half Moon Bay down at the celebration on the beach below them. She sucked on her teeth for a minute, making strange noises. Goblin knew that behavior. She wasn't happy.

Finally, drawing a deep breath, Nym said in a high-pitched voice while waving a hand down toward the beach, "They have a fucking army now. Can you believe it?"

Crooks set the binoculars down on the cliff and lifted his costume head off, shaking his head at Nym.

Goblin turned to Nym. "We don't really have a choice, do we?"

Nym shrugged. "I mean, we're off the leash. We could just raise hell up and down the Shytown."

Both Goblin and Crooks grinned widely.

Goblin nodded a bit. "I like that plan, but"—reason had crept into his tone—"eventually, we have to go back." He nodded down toward the beach before reiterating what Nym said. "They have an army now."

"Fine," Nym said, "but we still need to nerf the fast one."

Goblin raised an eyebrow. "Do you have a plan for it?"

Nym chuckled and stepped forward, placing her hands on her friend's shoulders. "No." She giggled. "But I have a Goblin."

———

Mary Helen was perched on the back of Precious, staring up at the large purple form rising from the old Giants stadium.

"This is where you..." She paused to correct herself before patting Precious on the back. "Where we are from?"

The green Spiderling shifted forward instinctively.

"Hang on." Mary Helen's voice had caution in it. "I'm still trying to ready myself for this." She let her gaze trail from the stadium's base up the almost-vertical, oversized legs leading up to the monstrous violet carapace in the cloud bank above. "Fine. I do this for you, but afterward, you take me to Falling Sands." The Spiderling chirped a bit before crouching low and, with a sharp jolt of force, leaping high into the air toward the stadium.

———

"Rotten woman," Razorwrist spat through clenched teeth. He had spent two days gathering up most of his upper torso. What working muscles he had held were twitching at awful angles. Bits and pieces of him had crawled across dirt and rocks. Pain had screamed through him the whole time.

Most of his army had scattered during the process. The mental control required to move bits of himself back together hadn't allowed enough concentration to keep the hordes in place. Even his favorite, Tom Zombie, had left him days before.

He could sense his legs down a cliff near the beach, so late last night, he had tumbled over and scattered once again, having to shift and remold himself. Currently, he was just five feet from a leg, dragging his own torso with his arms and shoving his head ahead of himself. The process was quite tedious.

Razorwrist growled, "She'll pay for this... They'll all pay for this!" That blue flame burning within him was screaming for violence. Once he was back together, there would be no stopping him. First, he would find the lady approaching ascension and steal her power. That was without question. His hunger for more power was never sated. Then he'd amass an army and just trample over every bit of life the world had left. No more playing cat and mouse with Sages—he'd just crush life wherever he found it.

An arm rolled his head forward, and he was treated to the disorienting view of sand, sky, sand again, then the cliffside. A piece of sand had managed to worm its way into his left eye.

"Why can't I sense my neck?" Razor didn't bother to hide his frustration.

If he couldn't find his neck, he was going to have to carry his head around until he found a healthy enough neck to steal. Everything about the situation was bothersome.

Eventually, he maneuvered up to the leg, took hold of it, and placed it at the base of his torso. Tendons stretched into it, taking hold. He felt nerve endings reconnect, and the leg tingled painfully, the ultimate in pins and needles, as the nerves reknitted themselves together, transmitting new electrical signals as control surged back. Finally, he could crawl one-legged toward the last limb.

Forcefully throwing his head ahead of himself toward the other leg, he said, "I'm going to reap every bit of life from this world..." He stopped a moment then rolled over onto his back, his disembodied head ahead of himself laughing up at the sky, before announcing, "Even if it kills me!"

ZOMBIE CIVIL RIGHTS SERIES

GOODBYE FROM THE EDGE OF NEVER
DEEP CUTS FROM THE EDGE OF NEVER

AVAILABLE FROM AMAZON.COM
FOR UPDATES FROM THE AUTHOR, VISIT STEVEMIX.COM

www.ingramcontent.com/pod-product-compliance
Lightning Source LLC
Chambersburg PA
CBHW071142100726
47908CB00002B/228